TELL NO TALES

PIRATES OF THE SOUTHERN SEAS

BY SAM MAGGS AND
KENDRA WELLS

AMULET BOOKS
NEW YORK

HUGE THANKS TO KENDRA, FOR THEIR PARTNERSHIP; BLAIR, FOR ALL HIS LOVE; MY PARENTS, FOR THEIR UNENDING SUPPORT; LUCIDITY EDITORIAL, FOR THEIR SENSITIVITY READ; MARIA VICENTE AND CHARLOTTE GREENBAUM, FOR BELIEVING IN US AND IN THE BOOK; AND TO LITTLE EEVEE, FOR THE CUTENESS
— SAM MAGGS

TO MY COMICS PEERS WHO INSPIRED AND EMPOWERED ME, TO ALL THE D&D SHOWS AND PODCASTS THAT KEPT ME COMPANY WHILE I WORKED, TO MY THERAPIST FOR EVERYTHING, AND TO MY FRIENDS, MY FAMILY, AND PAT FOR EVERYTHING ELSE
— KENDRA WELLS

Library of Congress Control Number 2019950077

Hardcover ISBN 978-1-4197-3966-8
Paperback ISBN 978-1-4197-3980-4

Text copyright © 2021 Sam Maggs
Illustrations copyright © 2021 Kendra Wells
Book design by Megan Kelchner

Printed and bound in China
10 9 8 7 6 5 4 3 2 1

Amulet Books are available at special discounts when purchased in quantity for premiums and promotions as well as fundraising or educational use. Special editions can also be created to specification. For details, contact specialsales@abramsbooks.com or the address below.

Amulet Books® is a registered trademark of Harry N. Abrams, Inc.

ABRAMS The Art of Books
195 Broadway, New York, NY 10007
abramsbooks.com

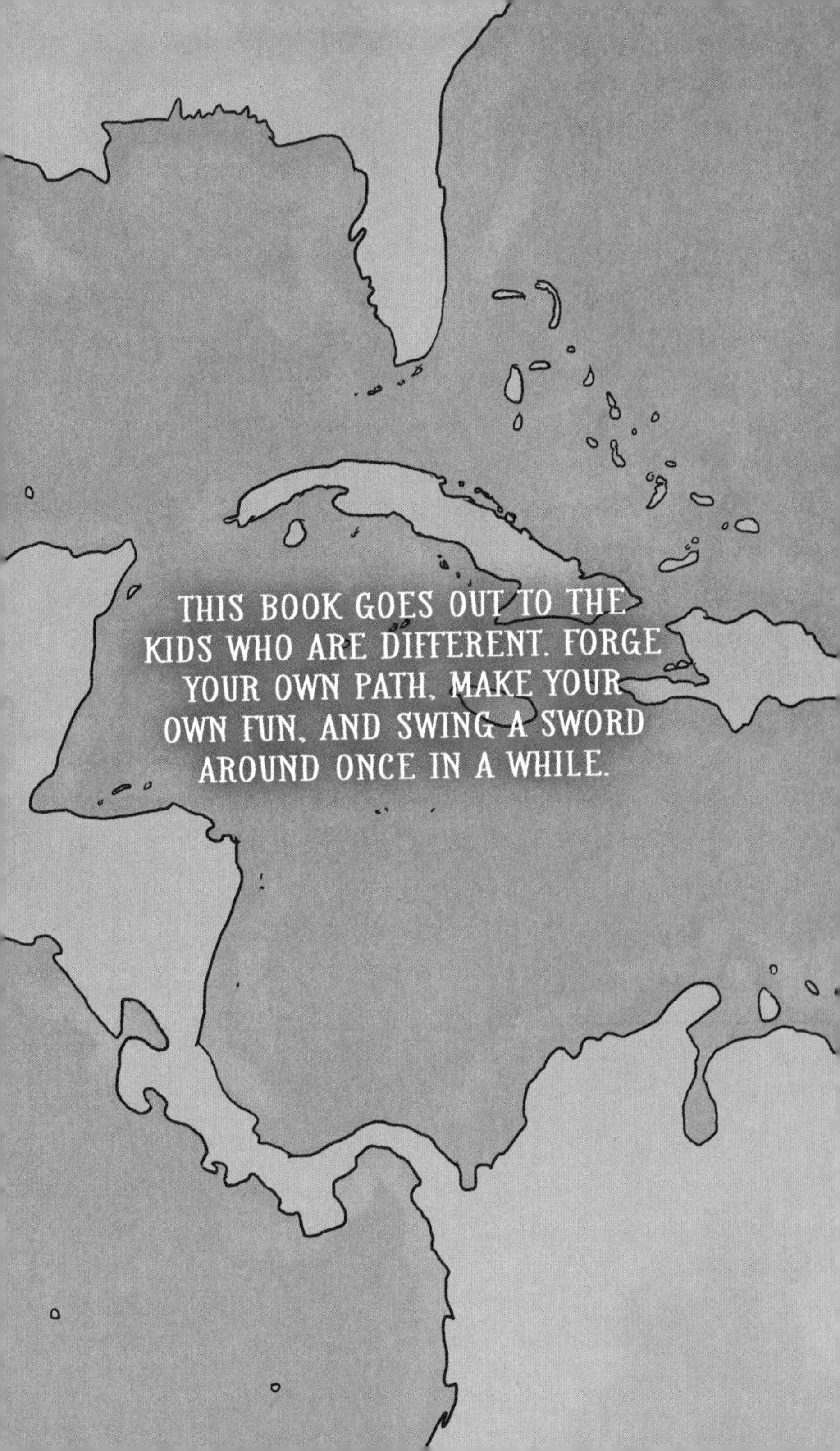

THIS BOOK GOES OUT TO THE KIDS WHO ARE DIFFERENT. FORGE YOUR OWN PATH, MAKE YOUR OWN FUN, AND SWING A SWORD AROUND ONCE IN A WHILE.

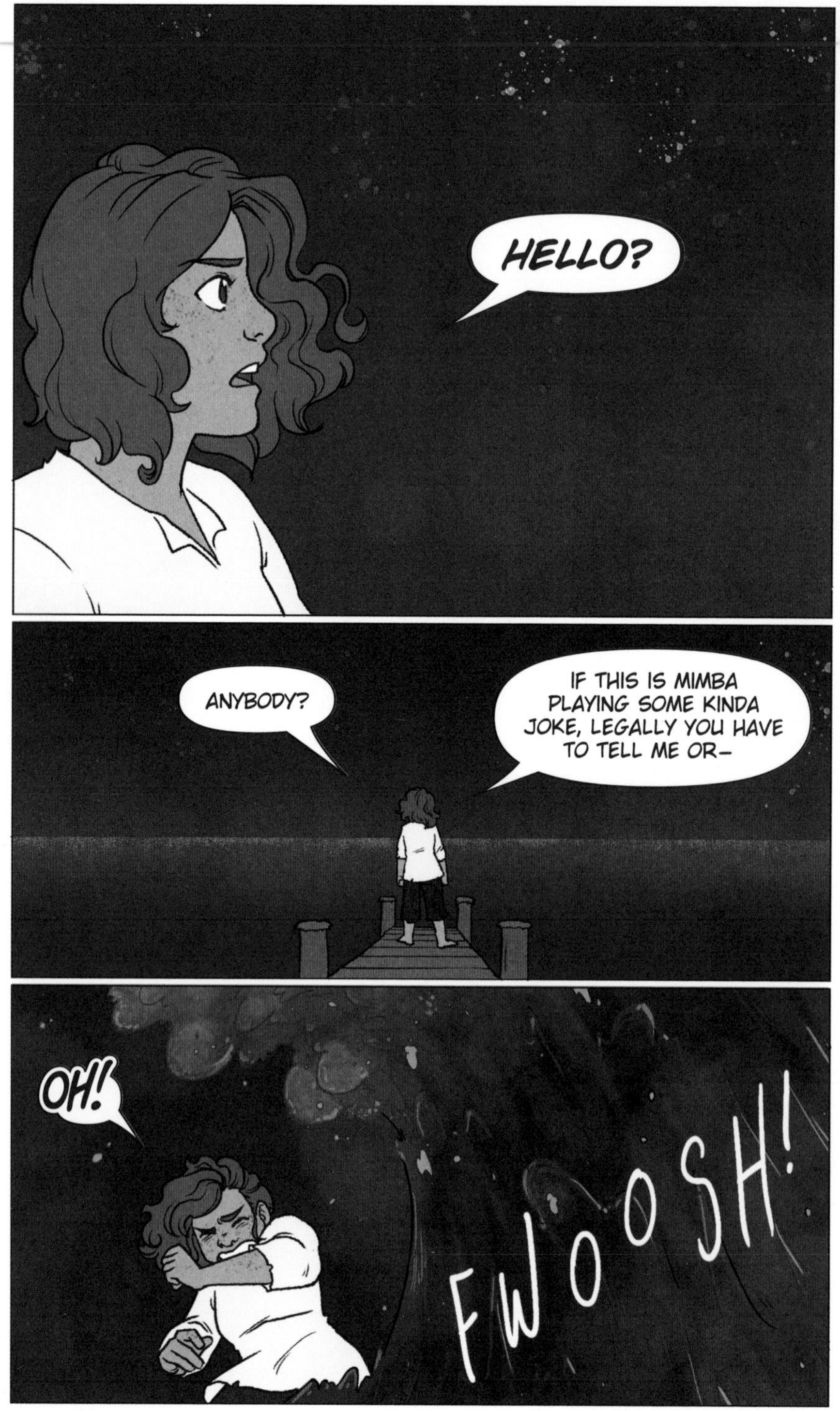
HELLO?
ANYBODY?
IF THIS IS MIMBA PLAYING SOME KINDA JOKE, LEGALLY YOU HAVE TO TELL ME OR—
OH!
FWOOSH!

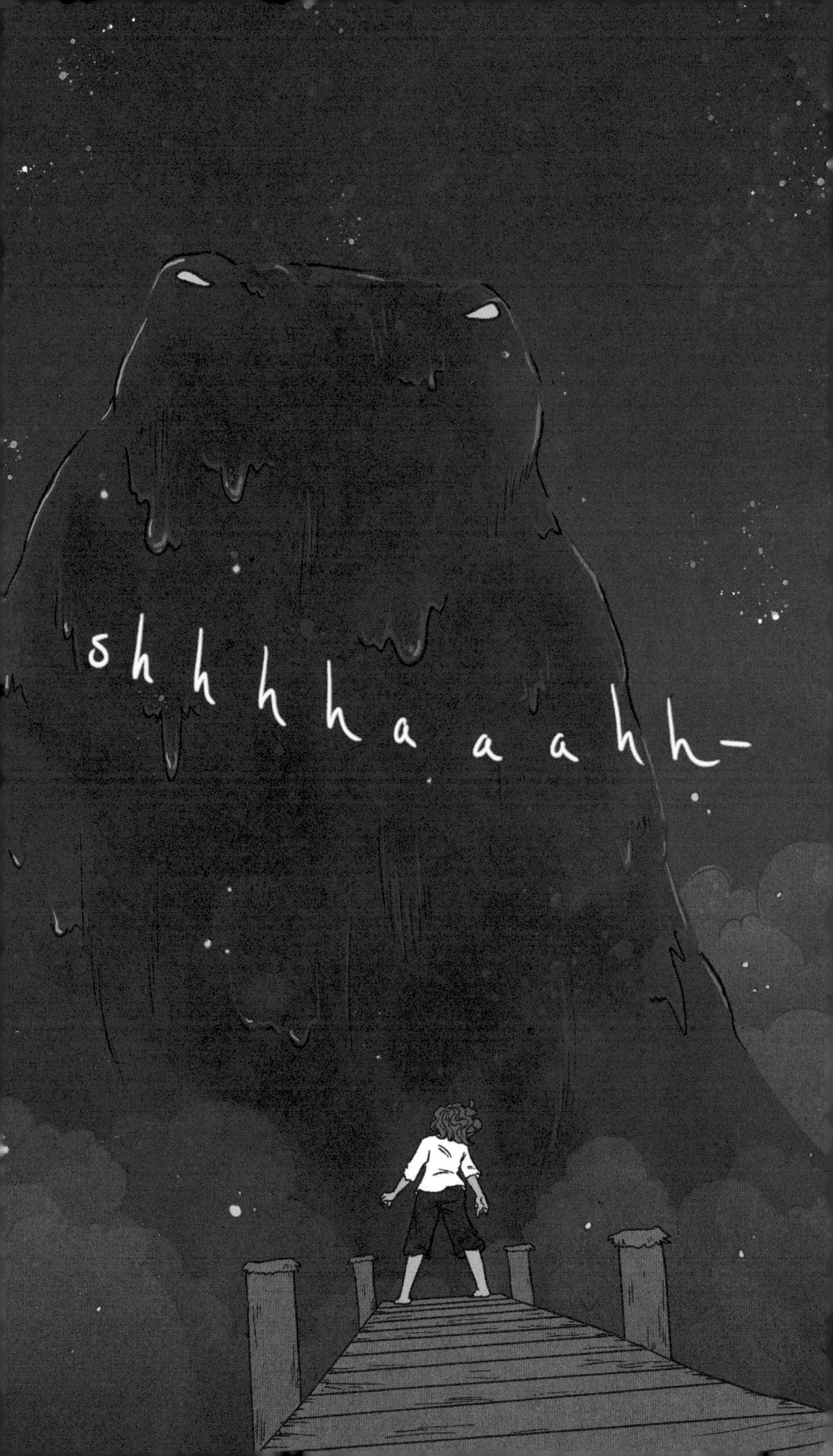
shhhhaaahh-

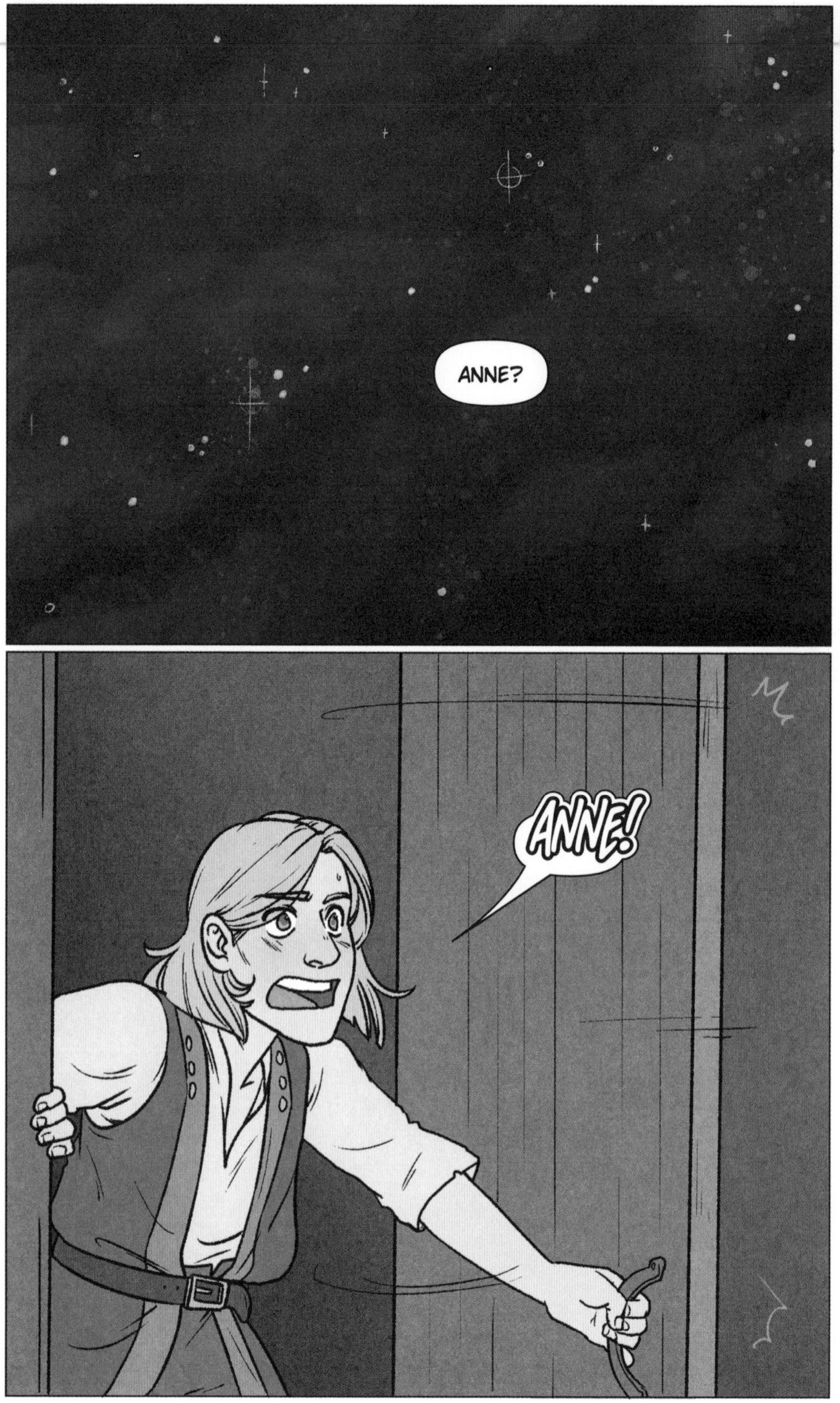
ANNE?
ANNE!

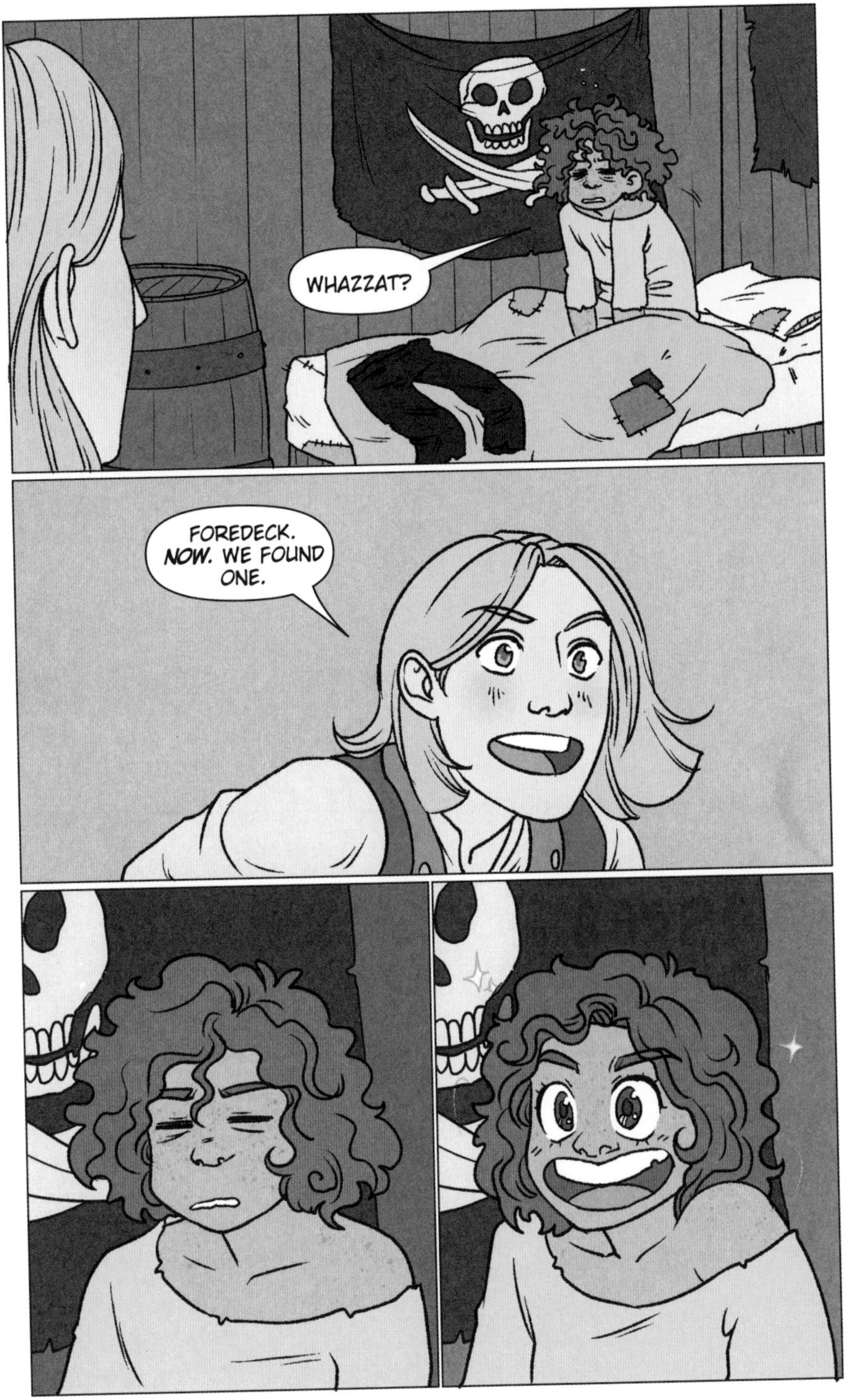
WHAZZAT?
FOREDECK. NOW. WE FOUND ONE.

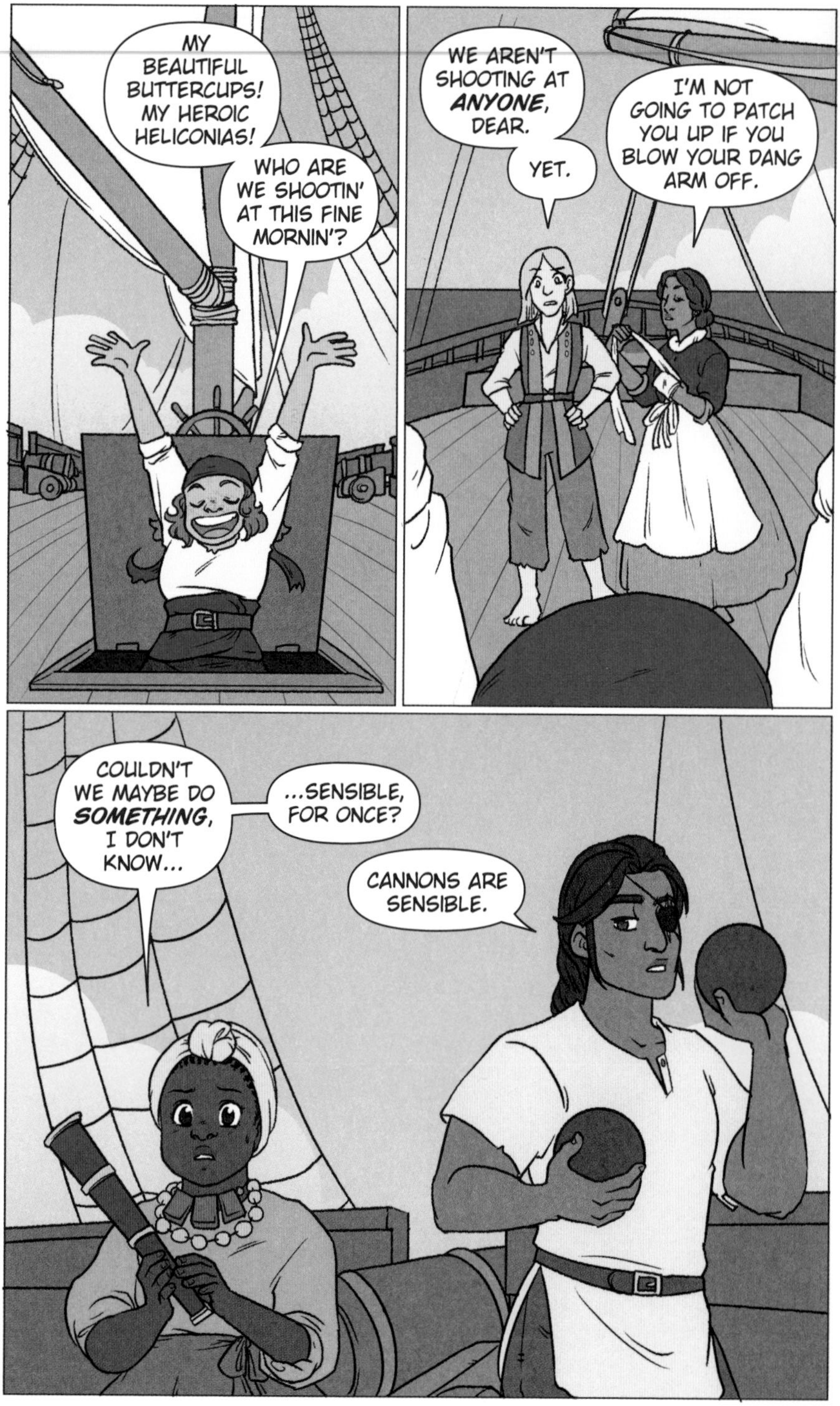

MY BEAUTIFUL BUTTERCUPS! MY HEROIC HELICONIAS!
WHO ARE WE SHOOTIN' AT THIS FINE MORNIN'?
WE AREN'T SHOOTING AT ***ANYONE***, DEAR.
YET.
I'M NOT GOING TO PATCH YOU UP IF YOU BLOW YOUR DANG ARM OFF.
COULDN'T WE MAYBE DO ***SOMETHING***, I DON'T KNOW...
...SENSIBLE, FOR ONCE?
CANNONS ARE SENSIBLE.

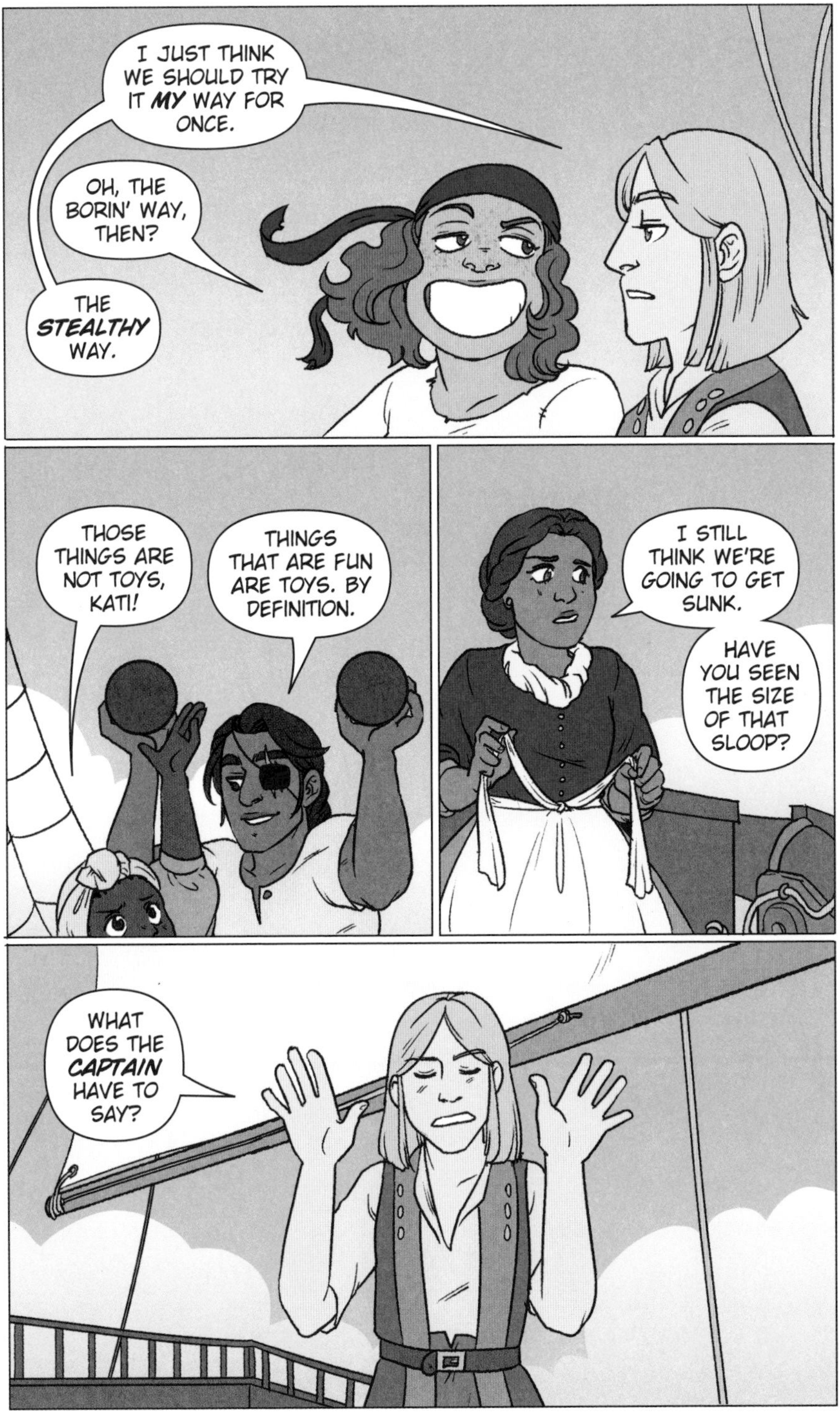
I JUST THINK WE SHOULD TRY IT **MY** WAY FOR ONCE.
THE **STEALTHY** WAY.
OH, THE BORIN' WAY, THEN?
THOSE THINGS ARE NOT TOYS, KATI!
THINGS THAT ARE FUN ARE TOYS. BY DEFINITION.
I STILL THINK WE'RE GOING TO GET SUNK.
HAVE YOU SEEN THE SIZE OF THAT SLOOP?
WHAT DOES THE **CAPTAIN** HAVE TO SAY?

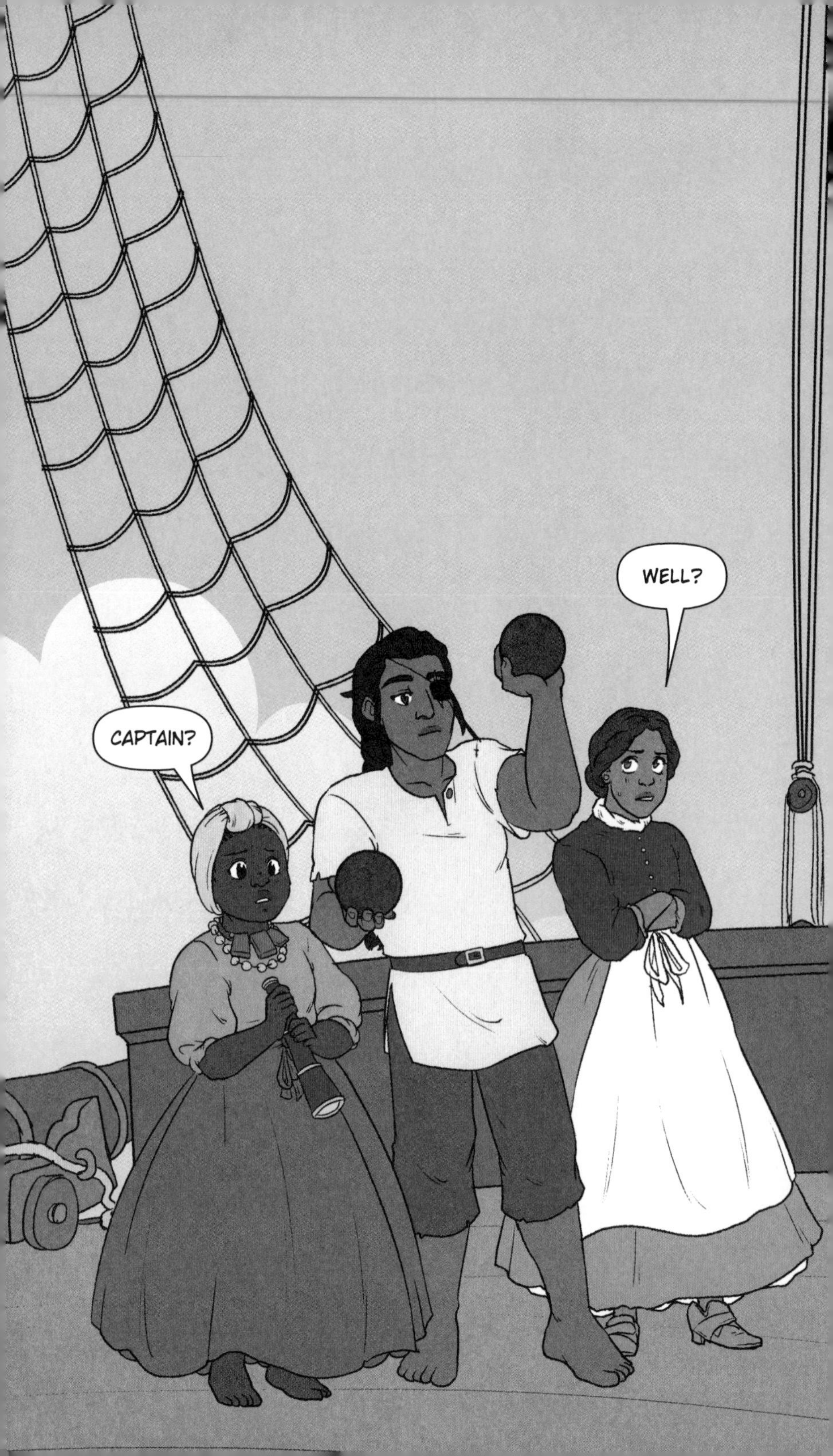
CAPTAIN?
WELL?

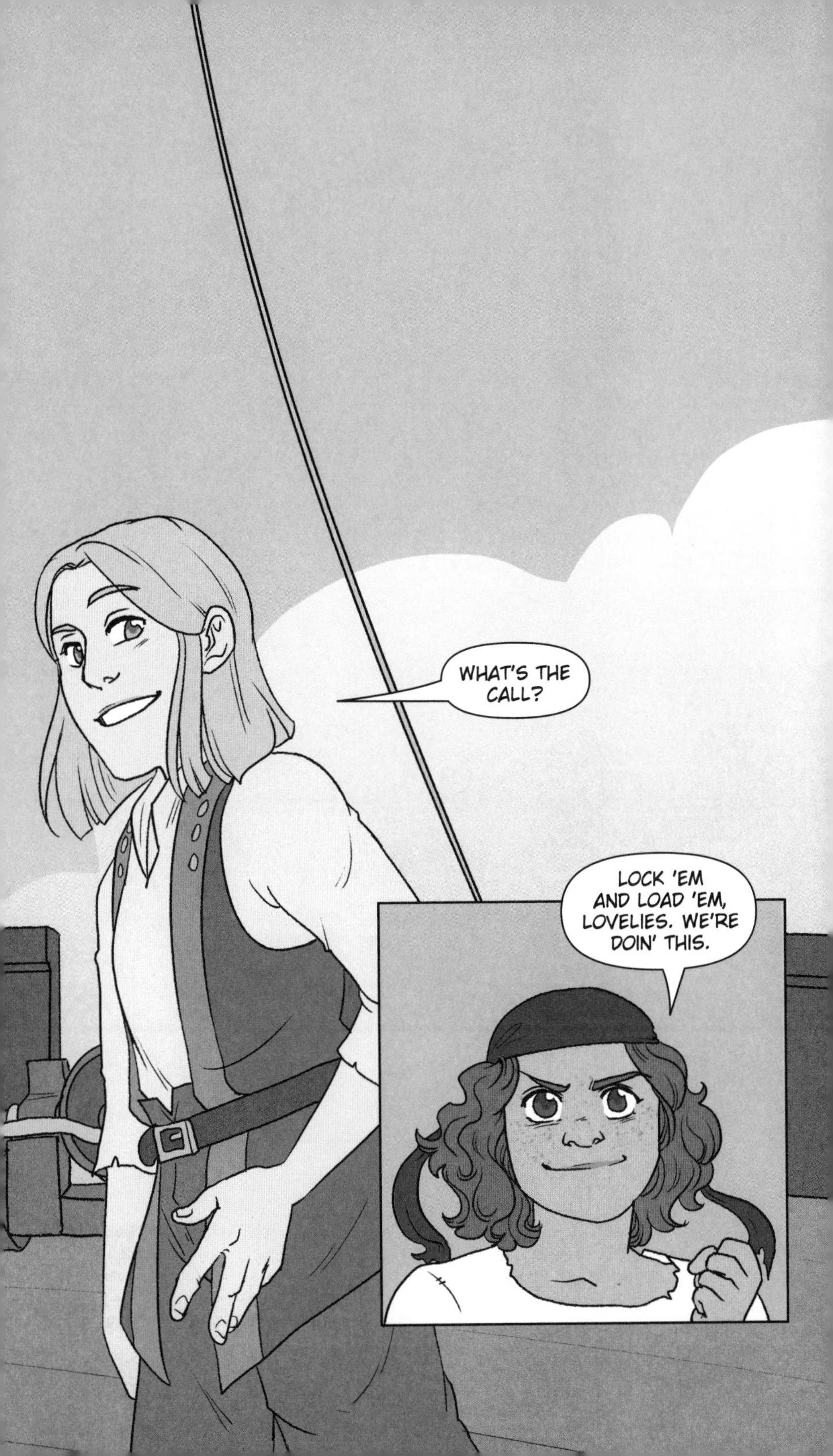
WHAT'S THE CALL?
LOCK 'EM AND LOAD 'EM, LOVELIES. WE'RE DOIN' THIS.

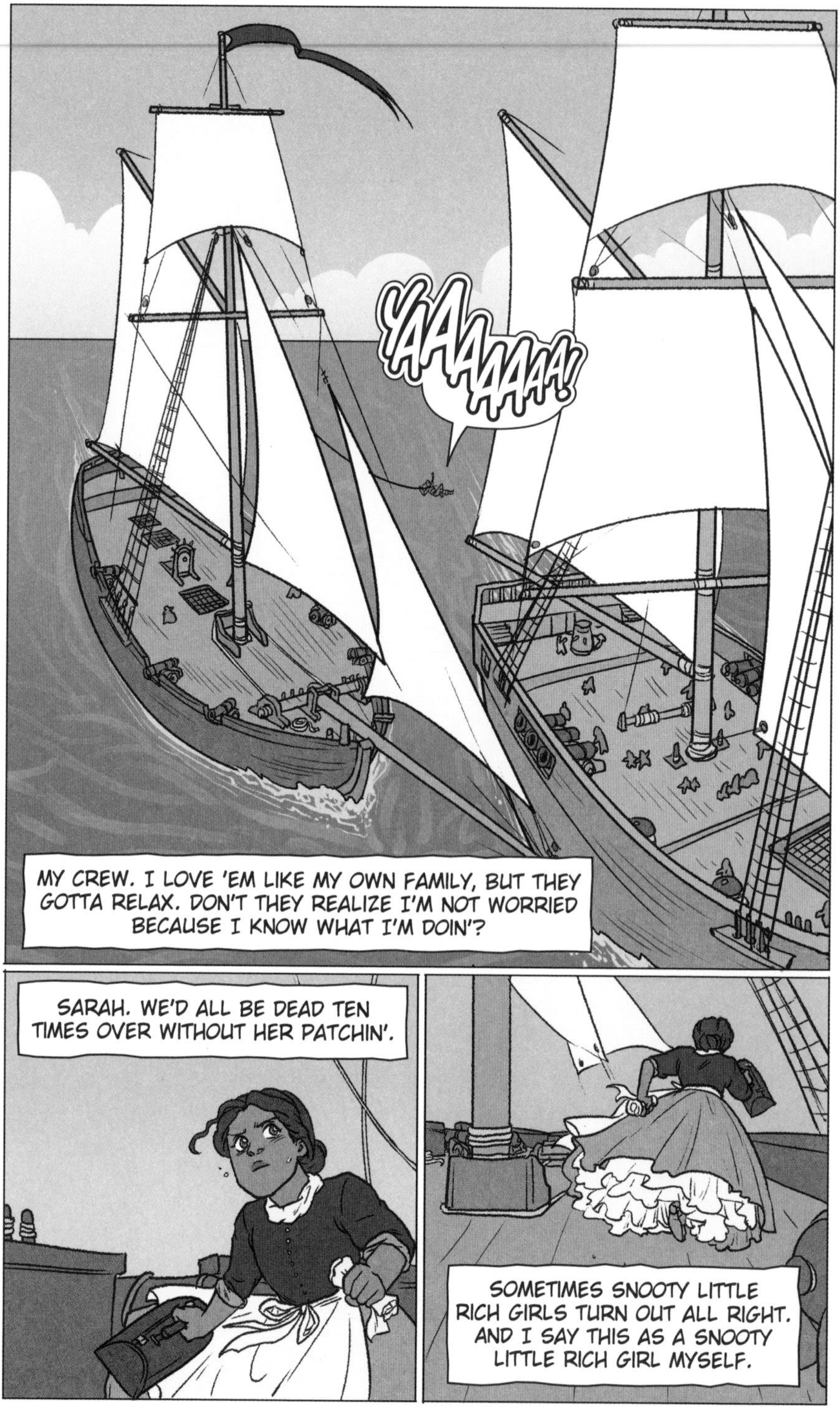
YAAAAAAA!
MY CREW. I LOVE 'EM LIKE MY OWN FAMILY, BUT THEY GOTTA RELAX. DON'T THEY REALIZE I'M NOT WORRIED BECAUSE I KNOW WHAT I'M DOIN'?
SARAH. WE'D ALL BE DEAD TEN TIMES OVER WITHOUT HER PATCHIN'.
SOMETIMES SNOOTY LITTLE RICH GIRLS TURN OUT ALL RIGHT. AND I SAY THIS AS A SNOOTY LITTLE RICH GIRL MYSELF.

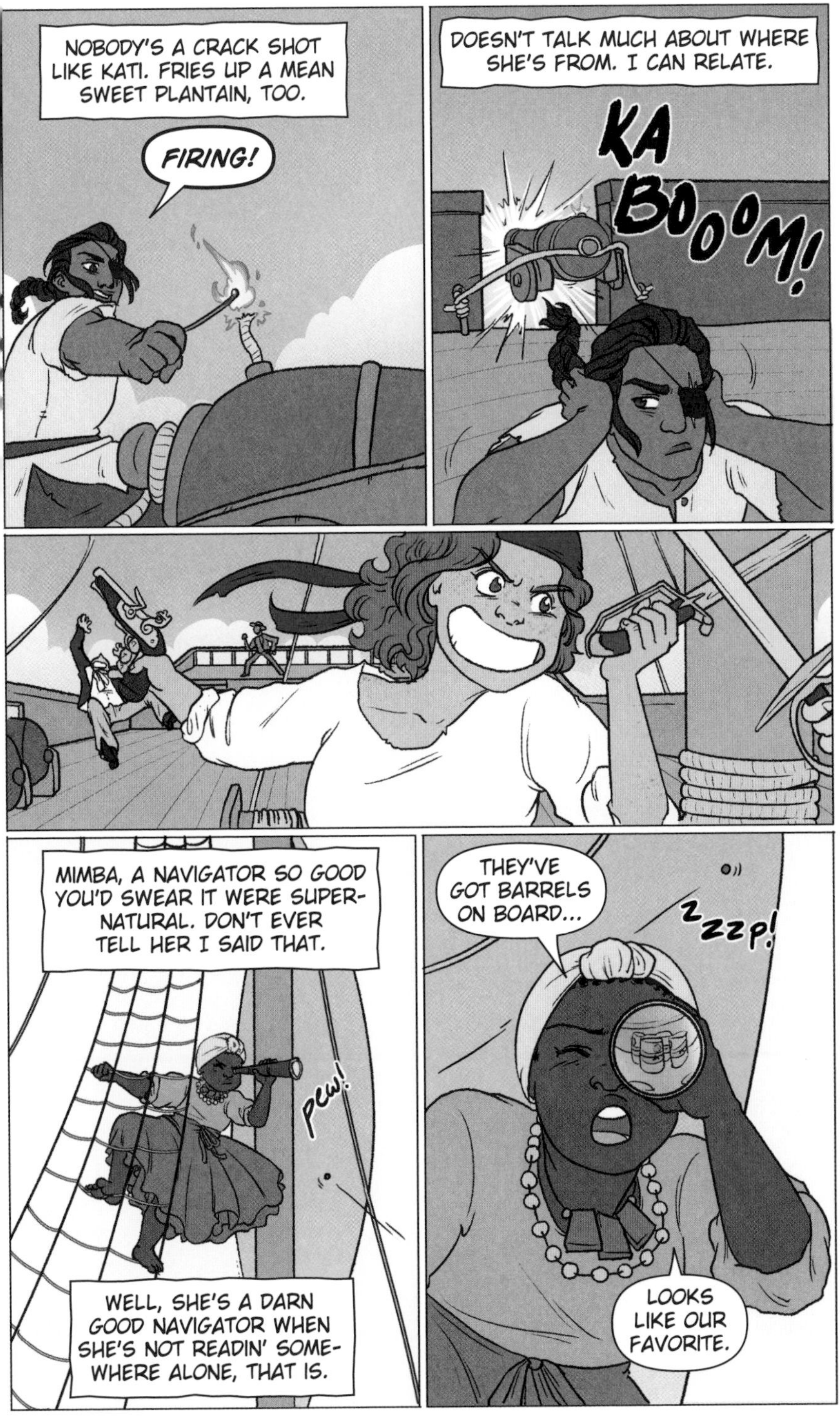

NOBODY'S A CRACK SHOT LIKE KATI. FRIES UP A MEAN SWEET PLANTAIN, TOO.
FIRING!
DOESN'T TALK MUCH ABOUT WHERE SHE'S FROM. I CAN RELATE.
KA BOOOOM!
MIMBA, A NAVIGATOR SO GOOD YOU'D SWEAR IT WERE SUPER-NATURAL. DON'T EVER TELL HER I SAID THAT.
PEW!
WELL, SHE'S A DARN GOOD NAVIGATOR WHEN SHE'S NOT READIN' SOME-WHERE ALONE, THAT IS.
THEY'VE GOT BARRELS ON BOARD...
ZZZP!
LOOKS LIKE OUR FAVORITE.

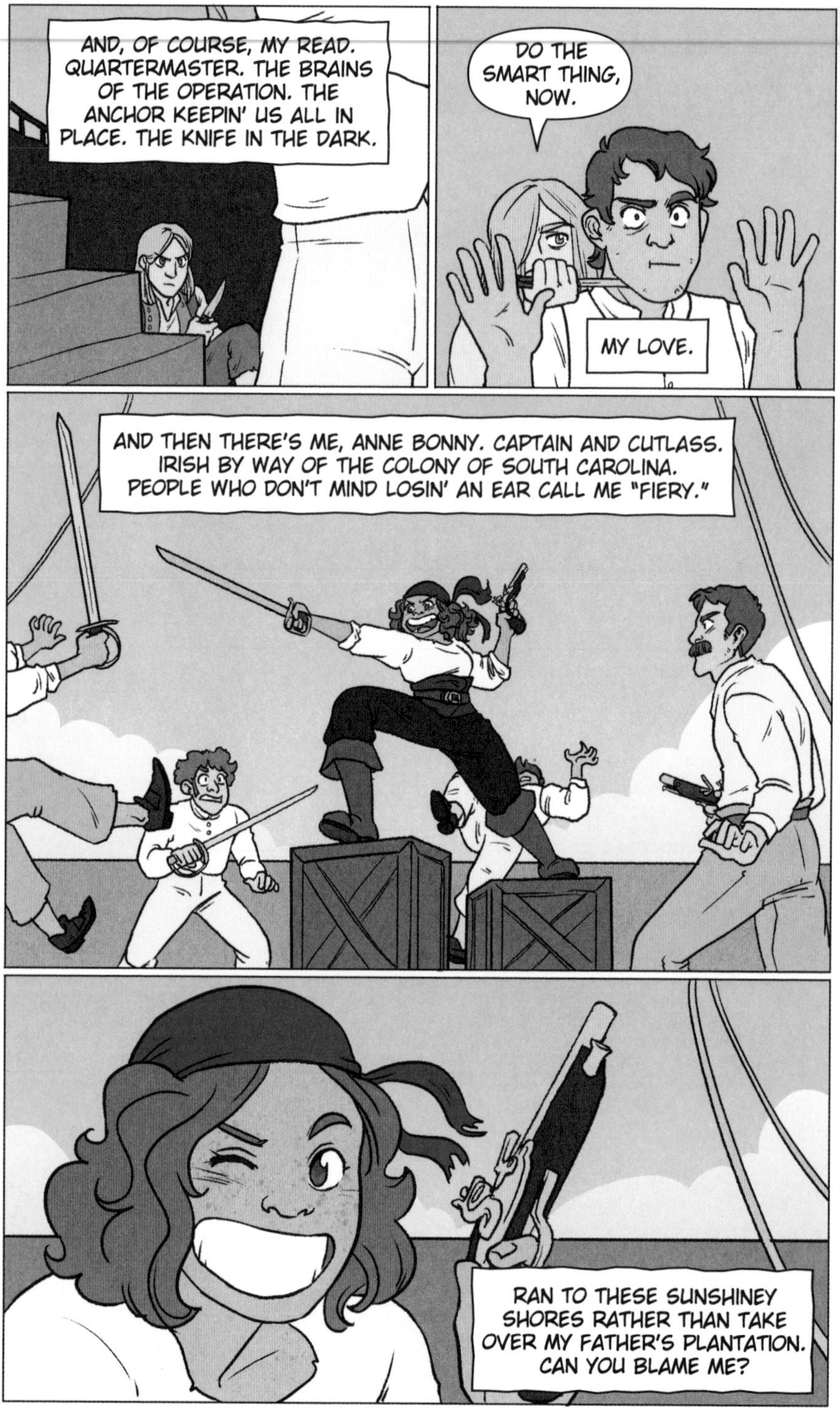
AND, OF COURSE, MY READ. QUARTERMASTER. THE BRAINS OF THE OPERATION. THE ANCHOR KEEPIN' US ALL IN PLACE. THE KNIFE IN THE DARK.
DO THE SMART THING, NOW.
MY LOVE.
AND THEN THERE'S ME, ANNE BONNY. CAPTAIN AND CUTLASS. IRISH BY WAY OF THE COLONY OF SOUTH CAROLINA. PEOPLE WHO DON'T MIND LOSIN' AN EAR CALL ME "FIERY."
RAN TO THESE SUNSHINEY SHORES RATHER THAN TAKE OVER MY FATHER'S PLANTATION. CAN YOU BLAME ME?

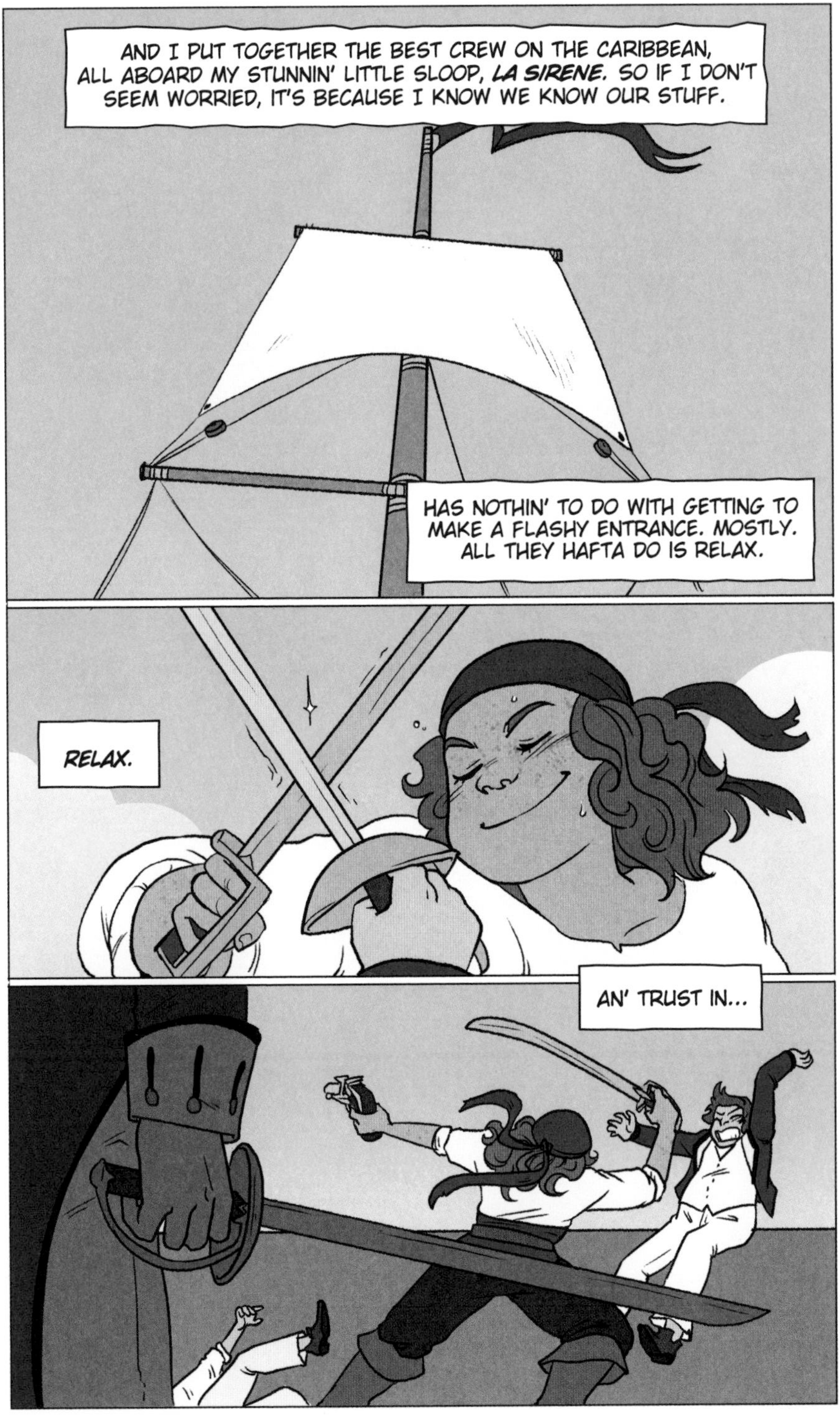
AND I PUT TOGETHER THE BEST CREW ON THE CARIBBEAN, ALL ABOARD MY STUNNIN' LITTLE SLOOP, *LA SIRENE.* SO IF I DON'T SEEM WORRIED, IT'S BECAUSE I KNOW WE KNOW OUR STUFF.
HAS NOTHIN' TO DO WITH GETTING TO MAKE A FLASHY ENTRANCE. MOSTLY. ALL THEY HAFTA DO IS RELAX.
RELAX.
AN' TRUST IN...

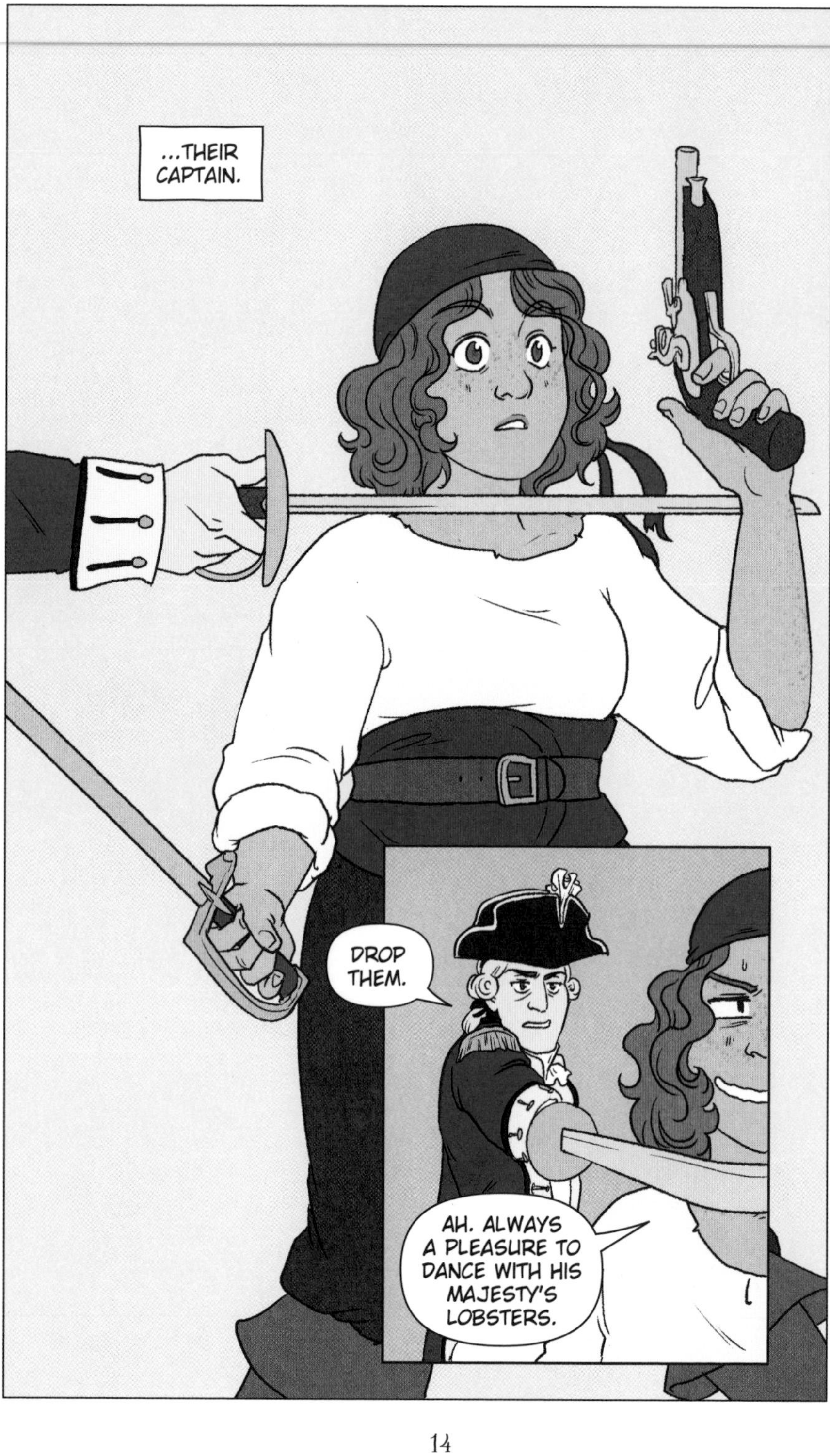
...THEIR CAPTAIN.
DROP THEM.
AH. ALWAYS A PLEASURE TO DANCE WITH HIS MAJESTY'S LOBSTERS.

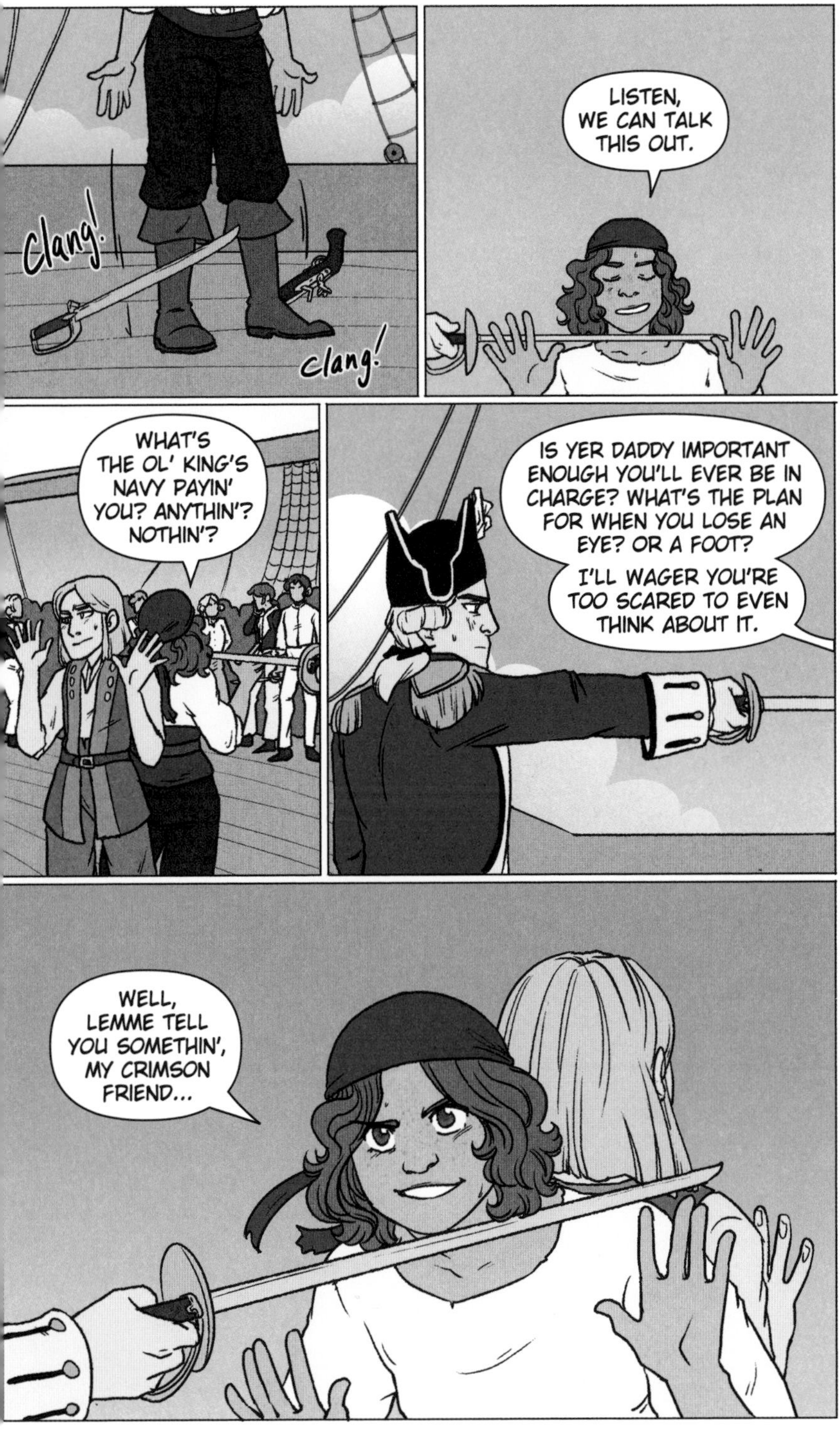
Clang!
Clang!
LISTEN, WE CAN TALK THIS OUT.
WHAT'S THE OL' KING'S NAVY PAYIN' YOU? ANYTHIN'? NOTHIN'?
IS YER DADDY IMPORTANT ENOUGH YOU'LL EVER BE IN CHARGE? WHAT'S THE PLAN FOR WHEN YOU LOSE AN EYE? OR A FOOT?
I'LL WAGER YOU'RE TOO SCARED TO EVEN THINK ABOUT IT.
WELL, LEMME TELL YOU SOMETHIN', MY CRIMSON FRIEND...

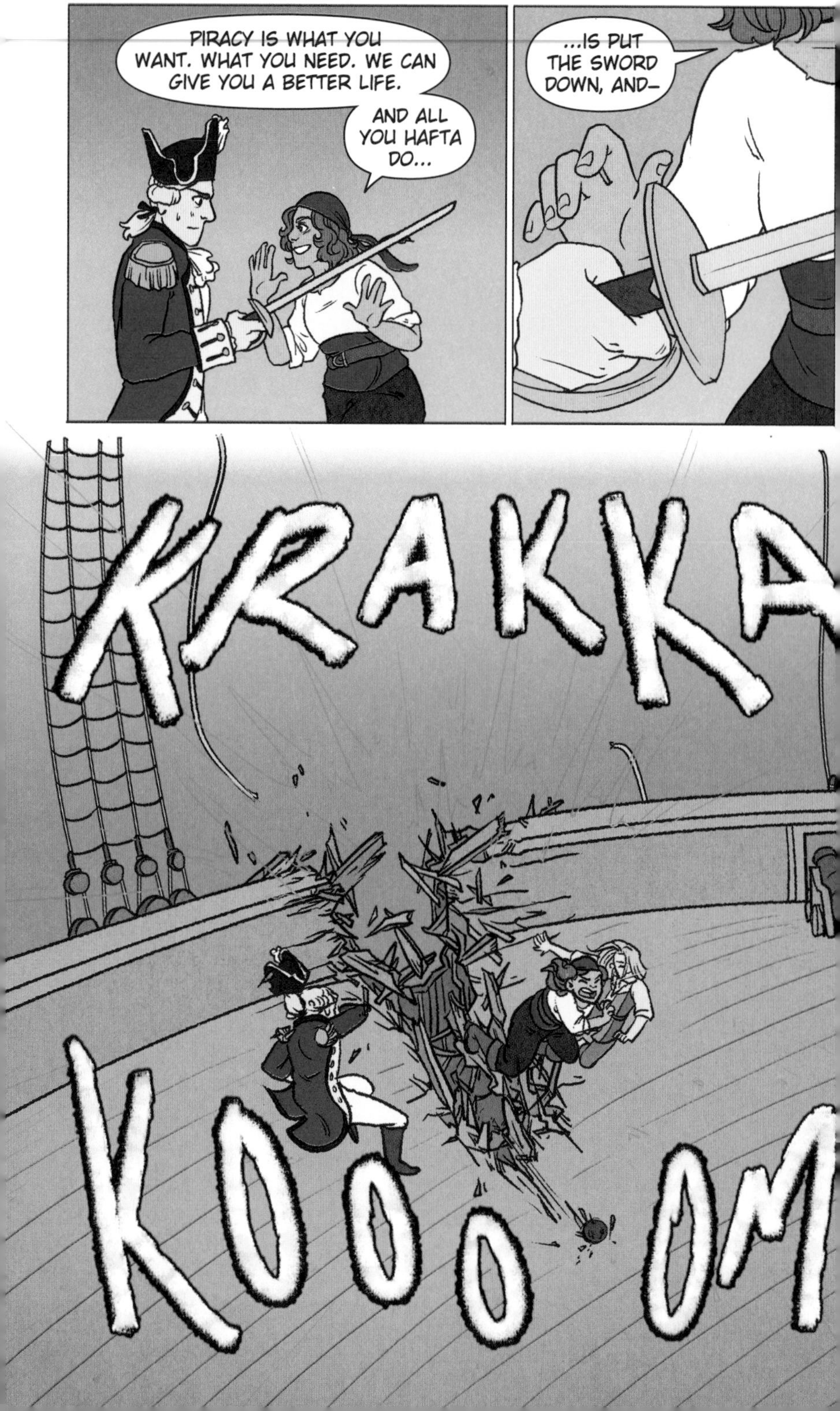
PIRACY IS WHAT YOU WANT. WHAT YOU NEED. WE CAN GIVE YOU A BETTER LIFE.
AND ALL YOU HAFTA DO...
...IS PUT THE SWORD DOWN, AND—
KRAKKA
KOOOOM

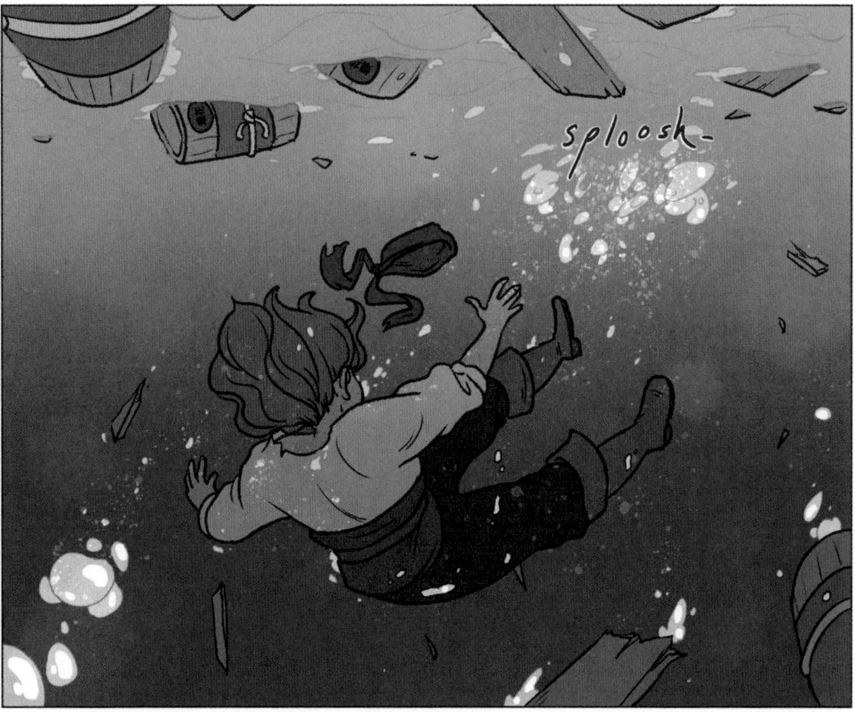
sploosh-

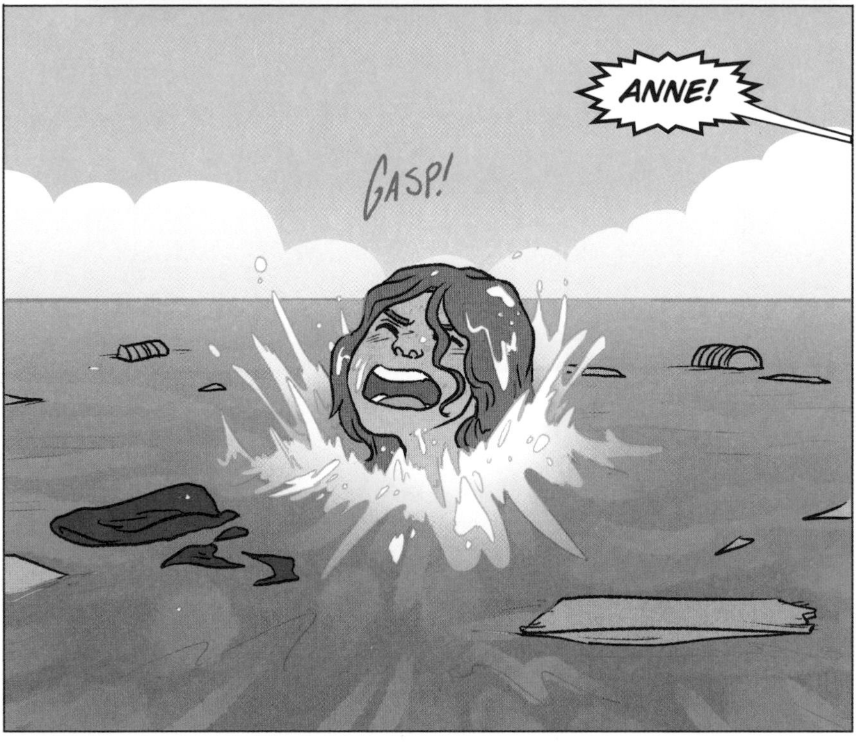
ANNE!
GASP!

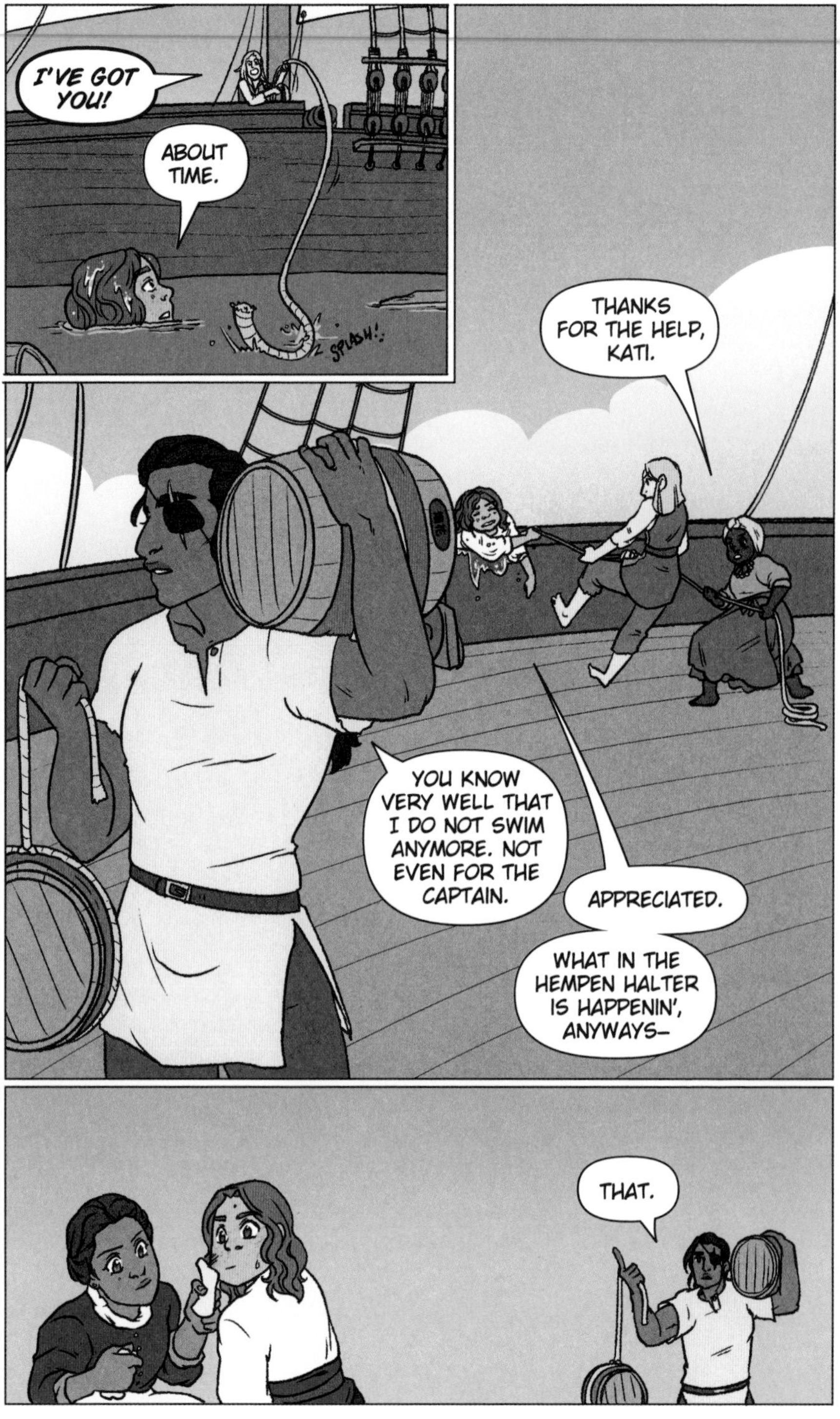
I'VE GOT YOU!
ABOUT TIME.
SPLASH!
THANKS FOR THE HELP, KATI.
YOU KNOW VERY WELL THAT I DO NOT SWIM ANYMORE. NOT EVEN FOR THE CAPTAIN.
APPRECIATED.
WHAT IN THE HEMPEN HALTER IS HAPPENIN', ANYWAYS–
THAT.

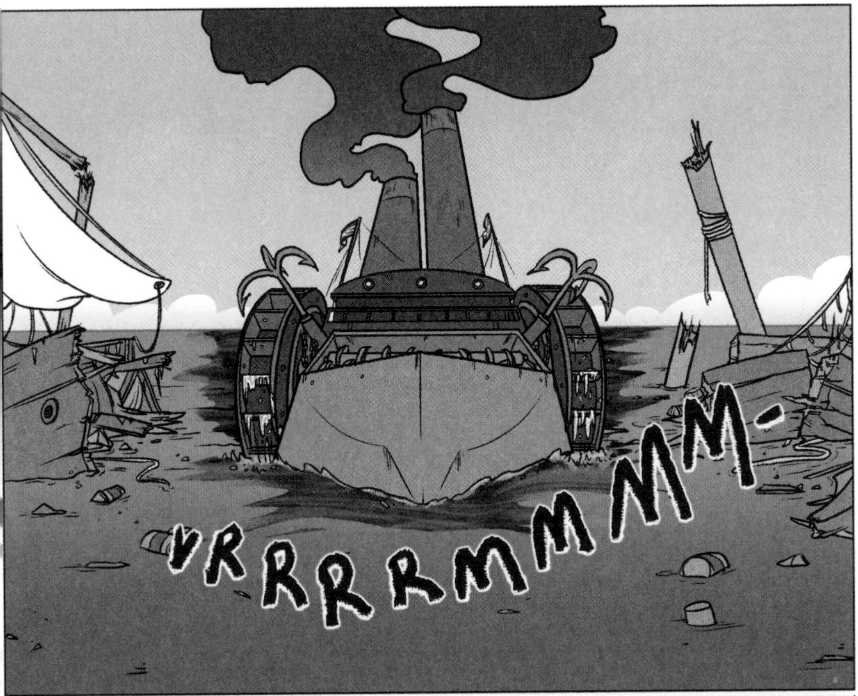
VRRRRMMMMM-

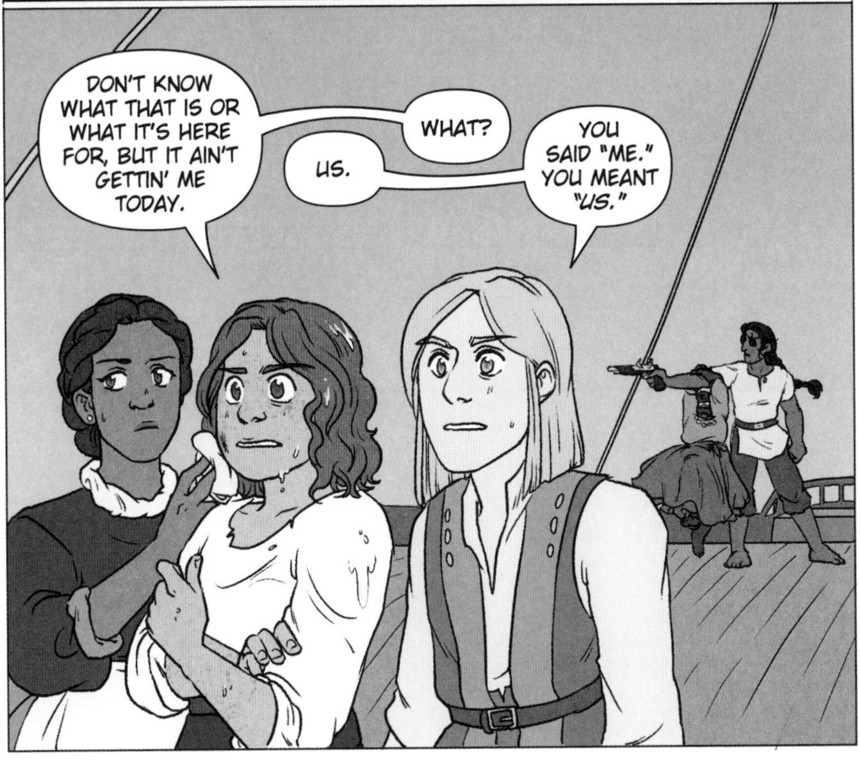
DON'T KNOW WHAT THAT IS OR WHAT IT'S HERE FOR, BUT IT AIN'T GETTIN' ME TODAY.
WHAT?
YOU SAID "ME." YOU MEANT "US."
US.

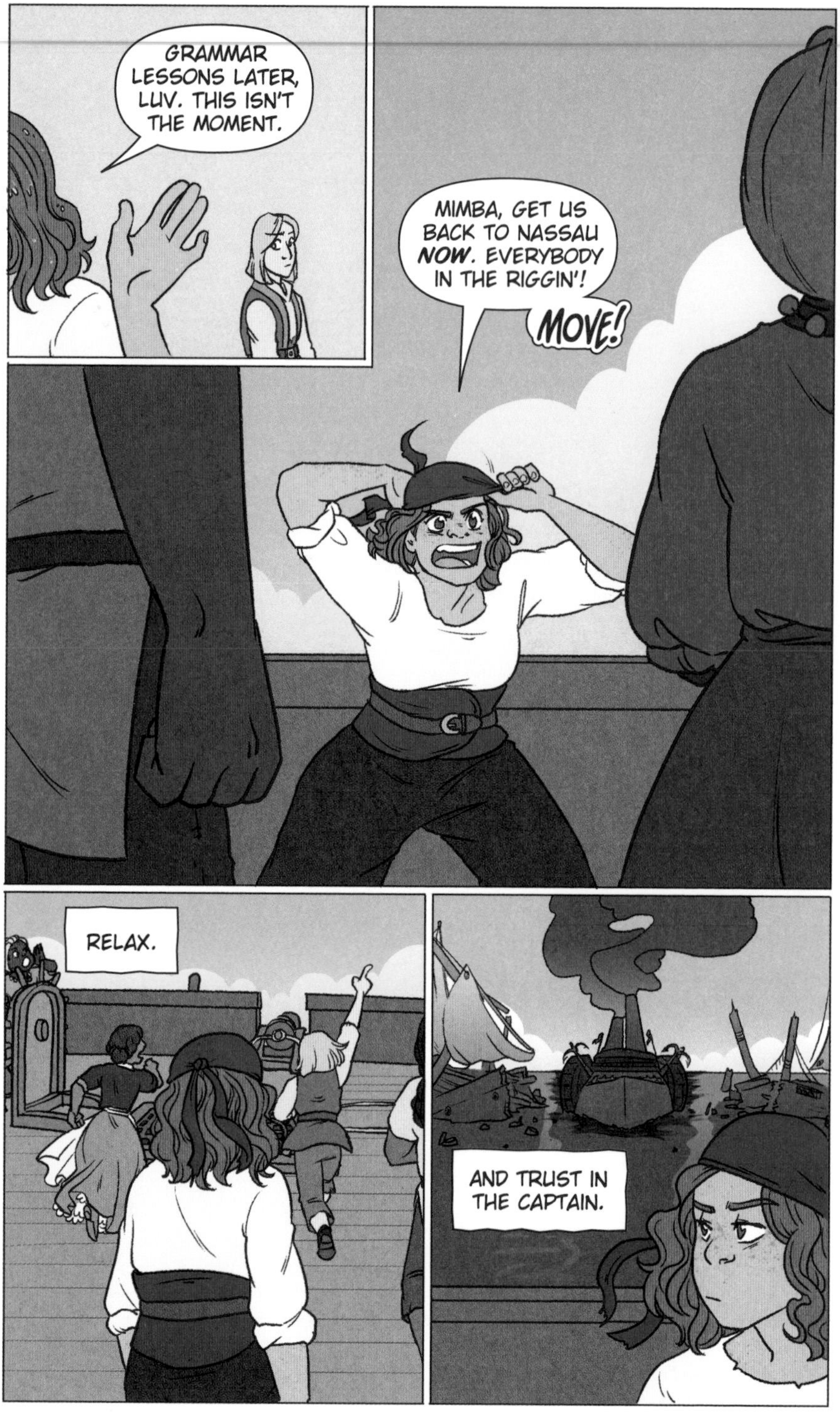
GRAMMAR LESSONS LATER, LUV. THIS ISN'T THE MOMENT.
MIMBA, GET US BACK TO NASSAU **NOW**. EVERYBODY IN THE RIGGIN'!
MOVE!
RELAX.
AND TRUST IN THE CAPTAIN.

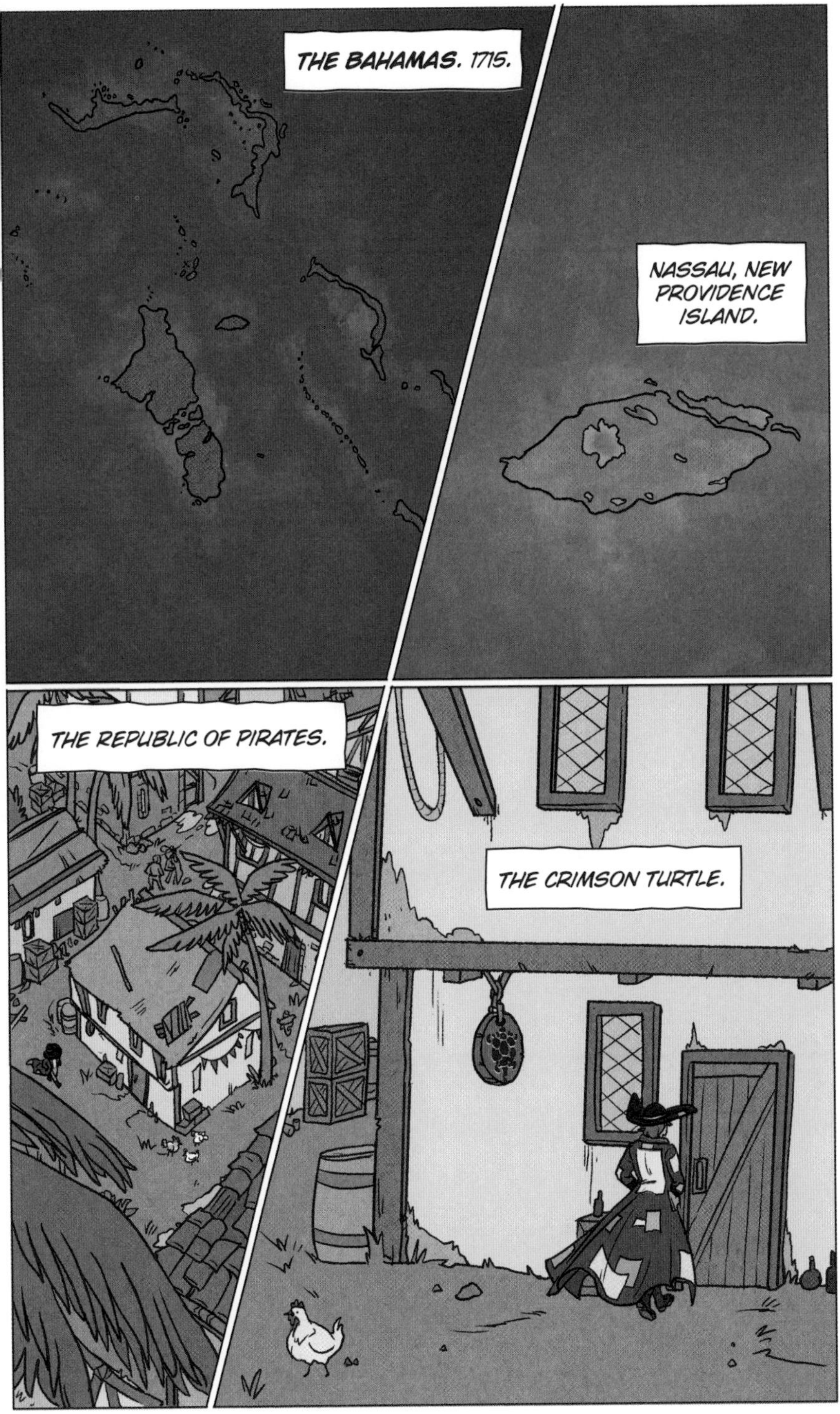
THE BAHAMAS. 1715.
NASSAU, NEW PROVIDENCE ISLAND.
THE REPUBLIC OF PIRATES.
THE CRIMSON TURTLE.

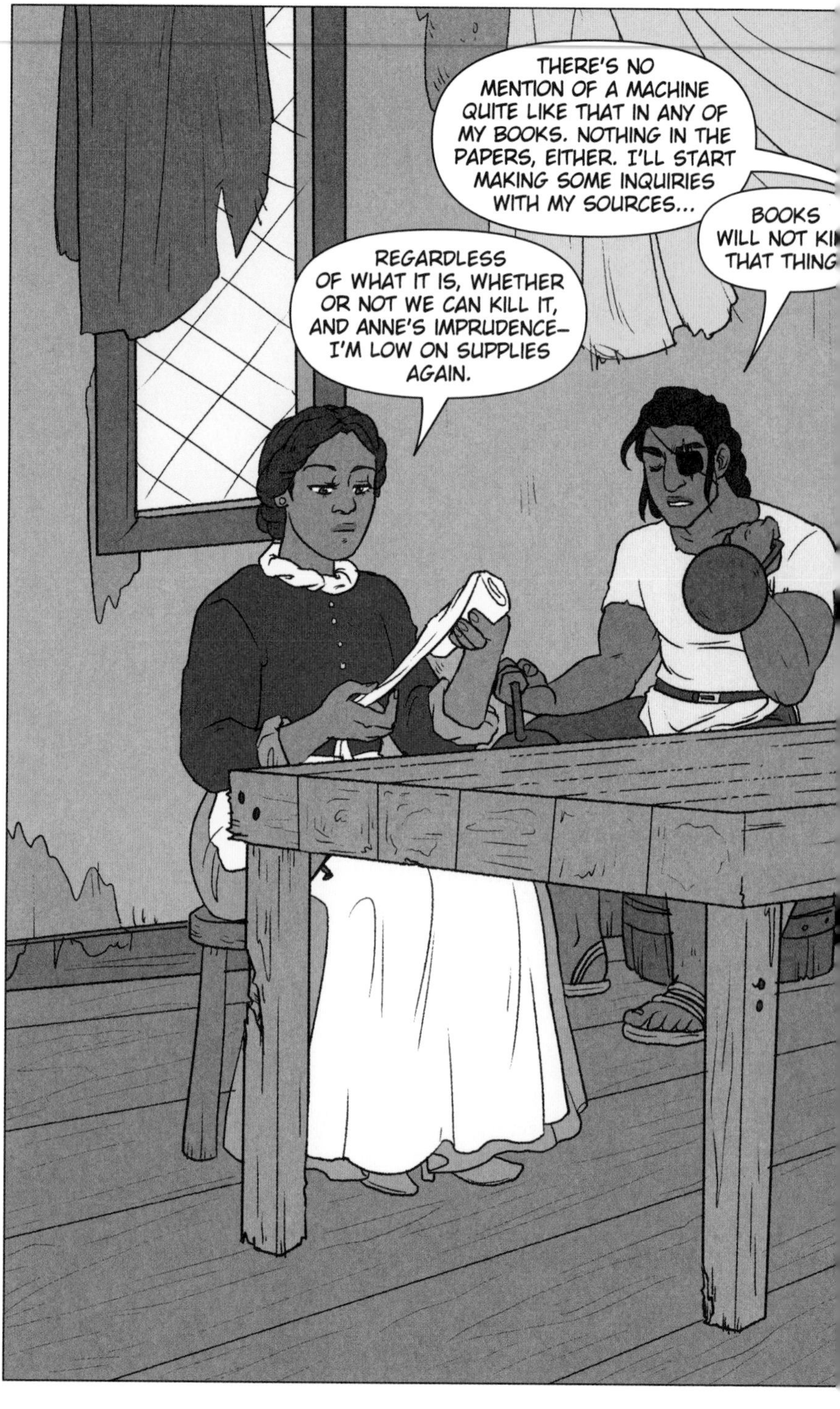
THERE'S NO MENTION OF A MACHINE QUITE LIKE THAT IN ANY OF MY BOOKS. NOTHING IN THE PAPERS, EITHER. I'LL START MAKING SOME INQUIRIES WITH MY SOURCES...
BOOKS WILL NOT KI THAT THING
REGARDLESS OF WHAT IT IS, WHETHER OR NOT WE CAN KILL IT, AND ANNE'S IMPRUDENCE— I'M LOW ON SUPPLIES AGAIN.

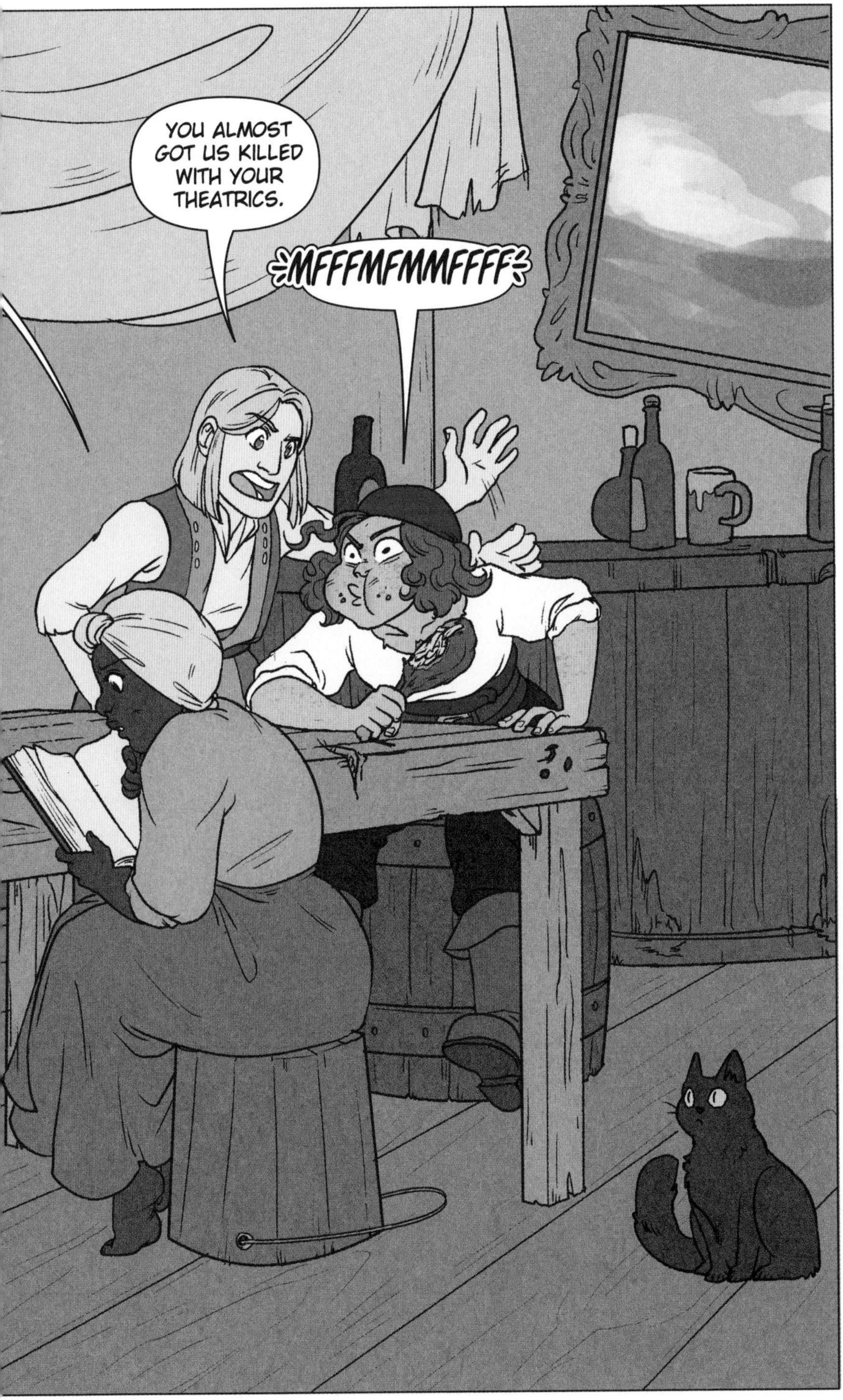
YOU ALMOST GOT US KILLED WITH YOUR THEATRICS.
MFFFMFMMFFFF

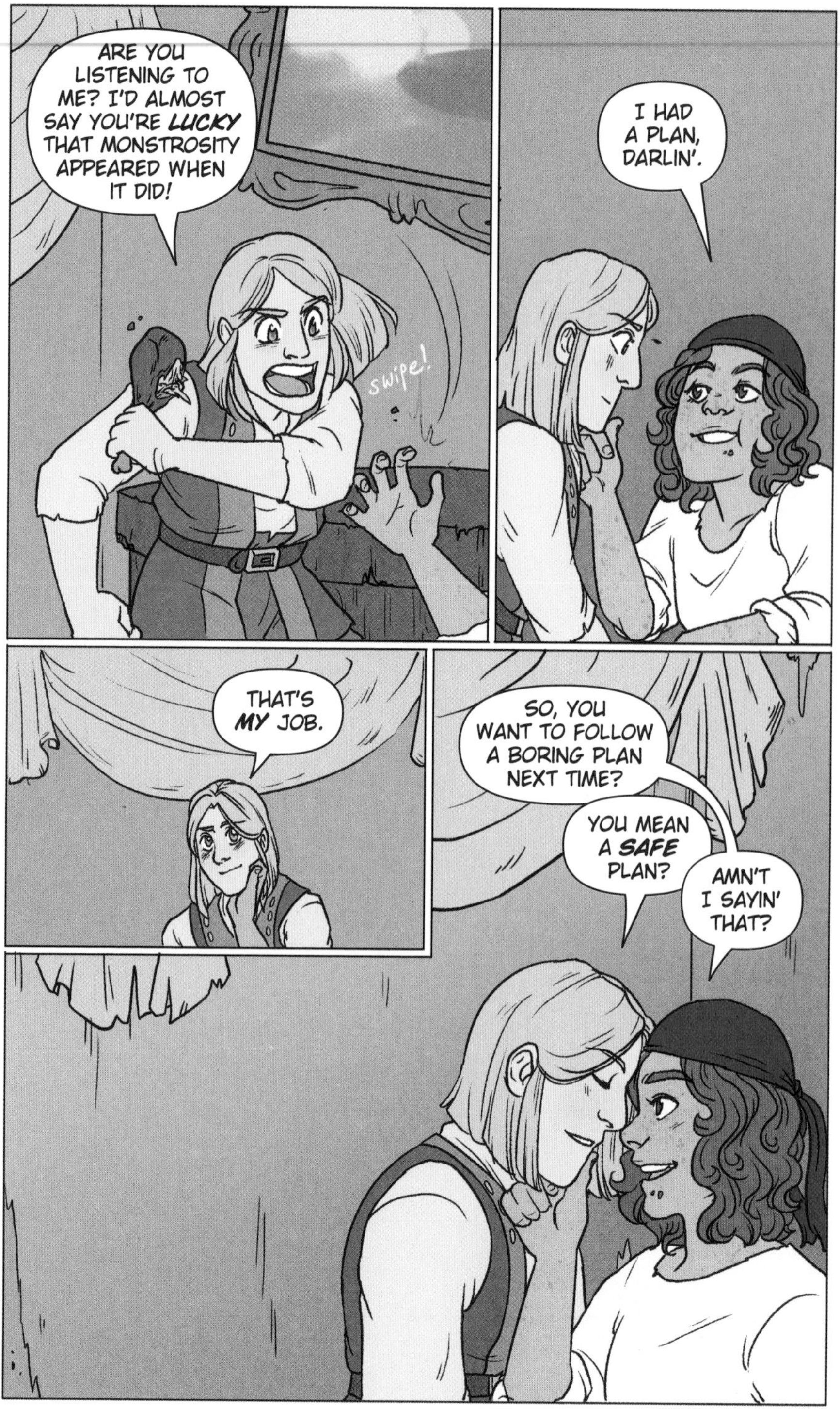
ARE YOU LISTENING TO ME? I'D ALMOST SAY YOU'RE **LUCKY** THAT MONSTROSITY APPEARED WHEN IT DID!
swipe!
I HAD A PLAN, DARLIN'.
THAT'S **MY** JOB.
SO, YOU WANT TO FOLLOW A BORING PLAN NEXT TIME?
YOU MEAN A **SAFE** PLAN?
AMN'T I SAYIN' THAT?

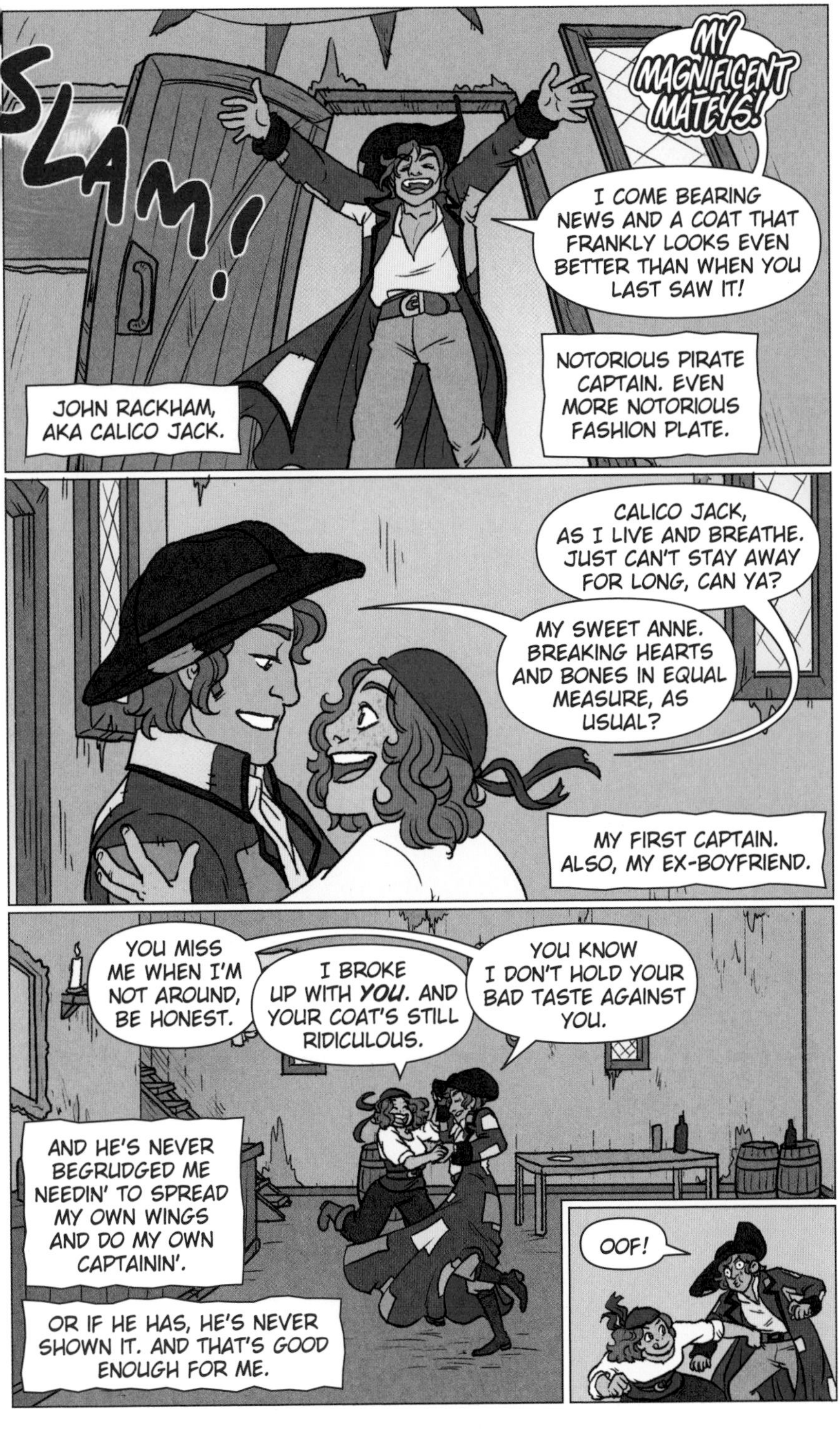
SLAM!
MY MAGNIFICENT MATEYS!
I COME BEARING NEWS AND A COAT THAT FRANKLY LOOKS EVEN BETTER THAN WHEN YOU LAST SAW IT!
JOHN RACKHAM, AKA CALICO JACK.
NOTORIOUS PIRATE CAPTAIN. EVEN MORE NOTORIOUS FASHION PLATE.
CALICO JACK, AS I LIVE AND BREATHE. JUST CAN'T STAY AWAY FOR LONG, CAN YA?
MY SWEET ANNE. BREAKING HEARTS AND BONES IN EQUAL MEASURE, AS USUAL?
MY FIRST CAPTAIN. ALSO, MY EX-BOYFRIEND.
YOU MISS ME WHEN I'M NOT AROUND, BE HONEST.
I BROKE UP WITH ***YOU***. AND YOUR COAT'S STILL RIDICULOUS.
YOU KNOW I DON'T HOLD YOUR BAD TASTE AGAINST YOU.
AND HE'S NEVER BEGRUDGED ME NEEDIN' TO SPREAD MY OWN WINGS AND DO MY OWN CAPTAININ'.
OR IF HE HAS, HE'S NEVER SHOWN IT. AND THAT'S GOOD ENOUGH FOR ME.
OOF!

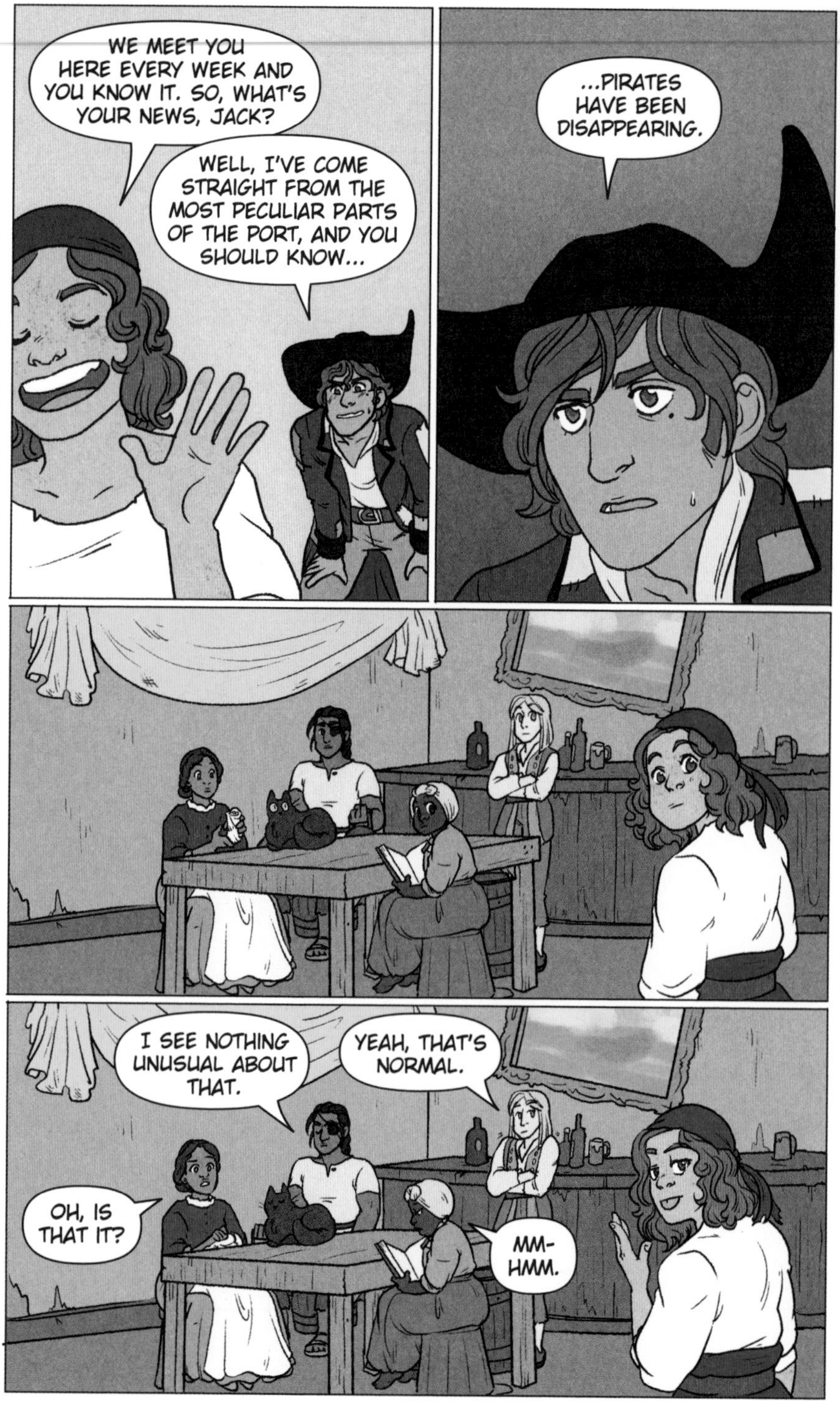

WE MEET YOU HERE EVERY WEEK AND YOU KNOW IT. SO, WHAT'S YOUR NEWS, JACK?
WELL, I'VE COME STRAIGHT FROM THE MOST PECULIAR PARTS OF THE PORT, AND YOU SHOULD KNOW...
...PIRATES HAVE BEEN DISAPPEARING.
I SEE NOTHING UNUSUAL ABOUT THAT.
YEAH, THAT'S NORMAL.
OH, IS THAT IT?
MM-HMM.

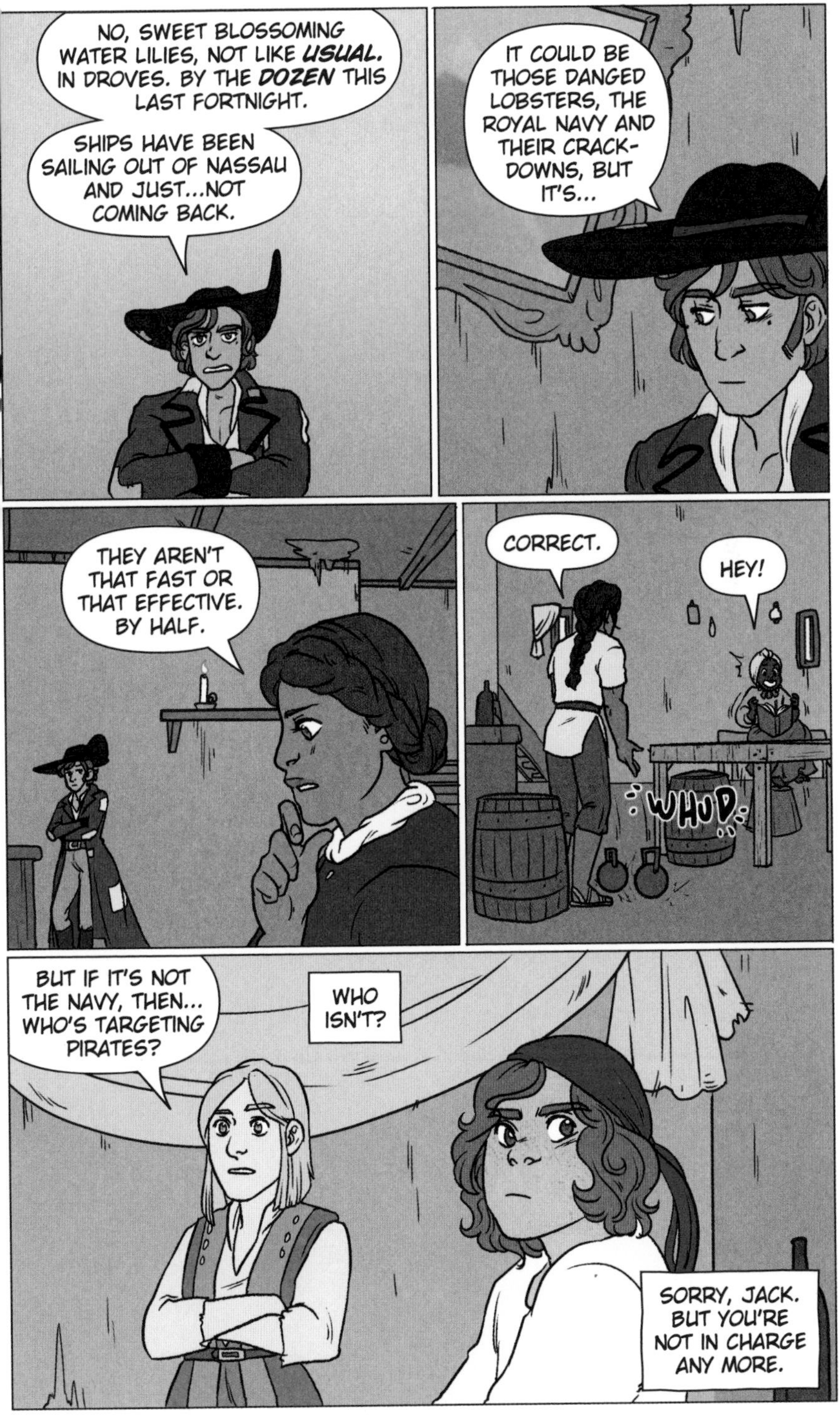

NO, SWEET BLOSSOMING WATER LILIES, NOT LIKE *USUAL.* IN DROVES. BY THE *DOZEN* THIS LAST FORTNIGHT.
SHIPS HAVE BEEN SAILING OUT OF NASSAU AND JUST...NOT COMING BACK.
IT COULD BE THOSE DANGED LOBSTERS, THE ROYAL NAVY AND THEIR CRACK-DOWNS, BUT IT'S...
THEY AREN'T THAT FAST OR THAT EFFECTIVE. BY HALF.
CORRECT.
HEY!
WHUD
BUT IF IT'S NOT THE NAVY, THEN... WHO'S TARGETING PIRATES?
WHO ISN'T?
SORRY, JACK. BUT YOU'RE NOT IN CHARGE ANY MORE.

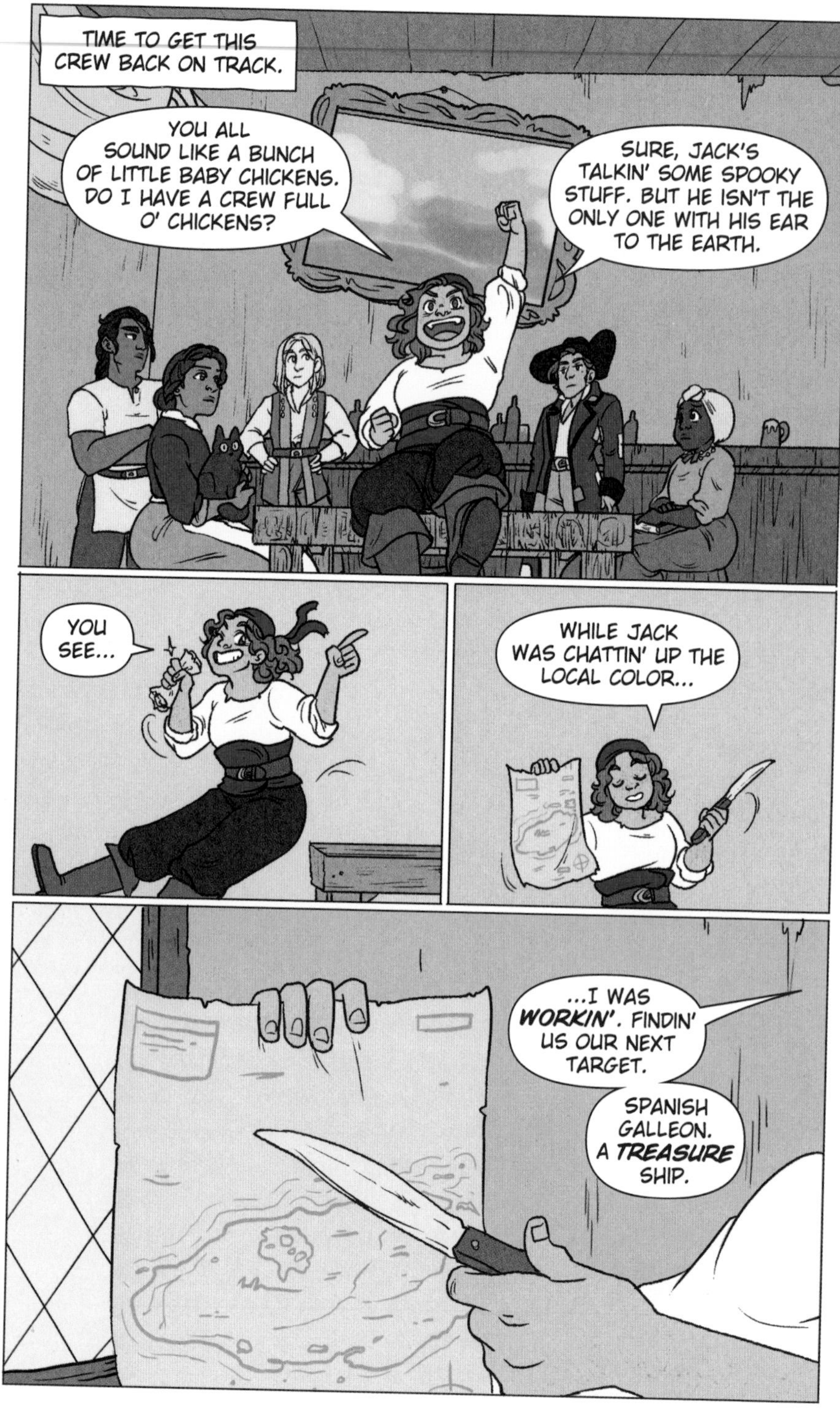
TIME TO GET THIS CREW BACK ON TRACK.
YOU ALL SOUND LIKE A BUNCH OF LITTLE BABY CHICKENS. DO I HAVE A CREW FULL O' CHICKENS?
SURE, JACK'S TALKIN' SOME SPOOKY STUFF. BUT HE ISN'T THE ONLY ONE WITH HIS EAR TO THE EARTH.
YOU SEE...
WHILE JACK WAS CHATTIN' UP THE LOCAL COLOR...
...I WAS **WORKIN'**. FINDIN' US OUR NEXT TARGET.
SPANISH GALLEON. A **TREASURE** SHIP.

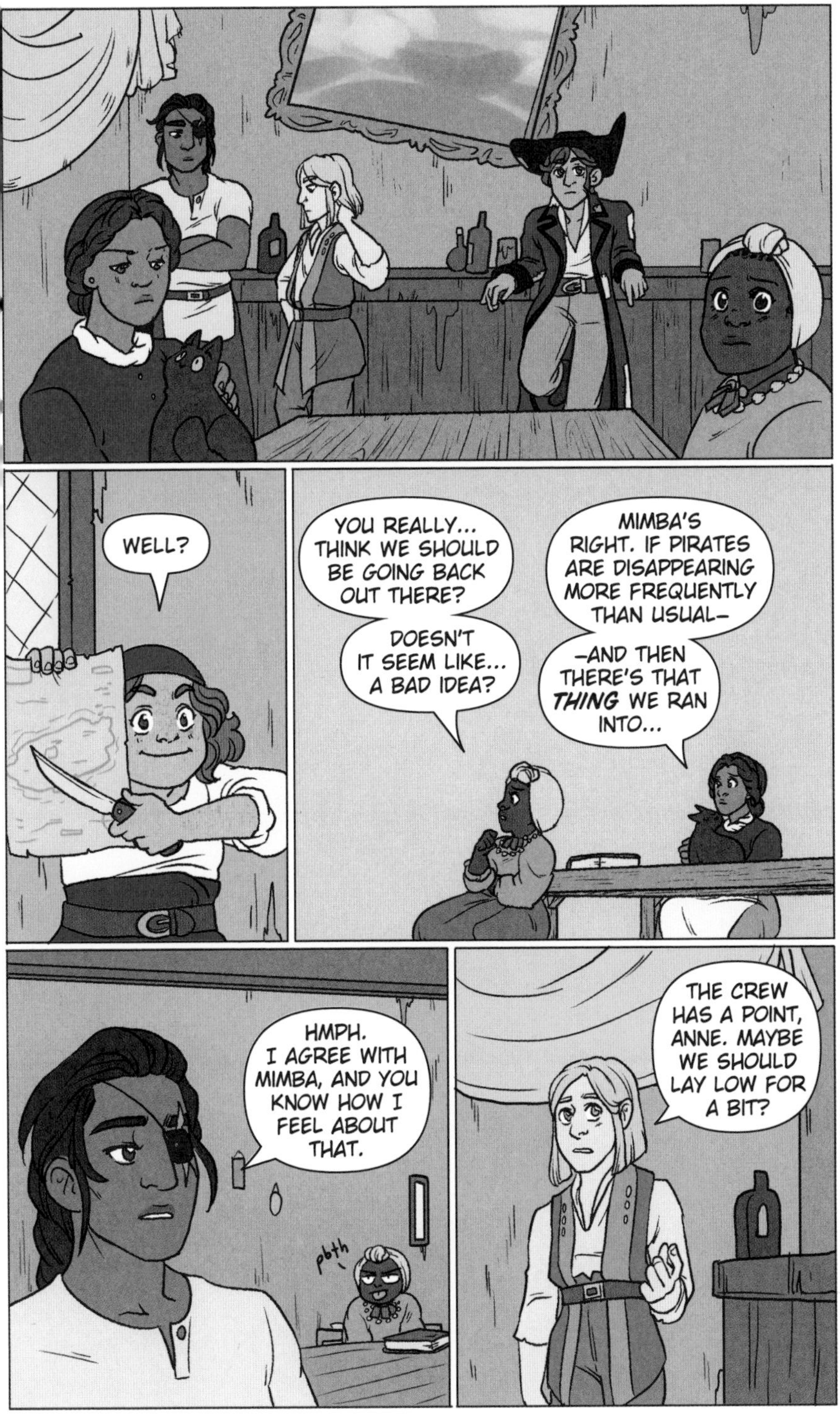
WELL?
YOU REALLY... THINK WE SHOULD BE GOING BACK OUT THERE?
DOESN'T IT SEEM LIKE... A BAD IDEA?
MIMBA'S RIGHT. IF PIRATES ARE DISAPPEARING MORE FREQUENTLY THAN USUAL–
–AND THEN THERE'S THAT *THING* WE RAN INTO...
HMPH. I AGREE WITH MIMBA, AND YOU KNOW HOW I FEEL ABOUT THAT.
pbth
THE CREW HAS A POINT, ANNE. MAYBE WE SHOULD LAY LOW FOR A BIT?

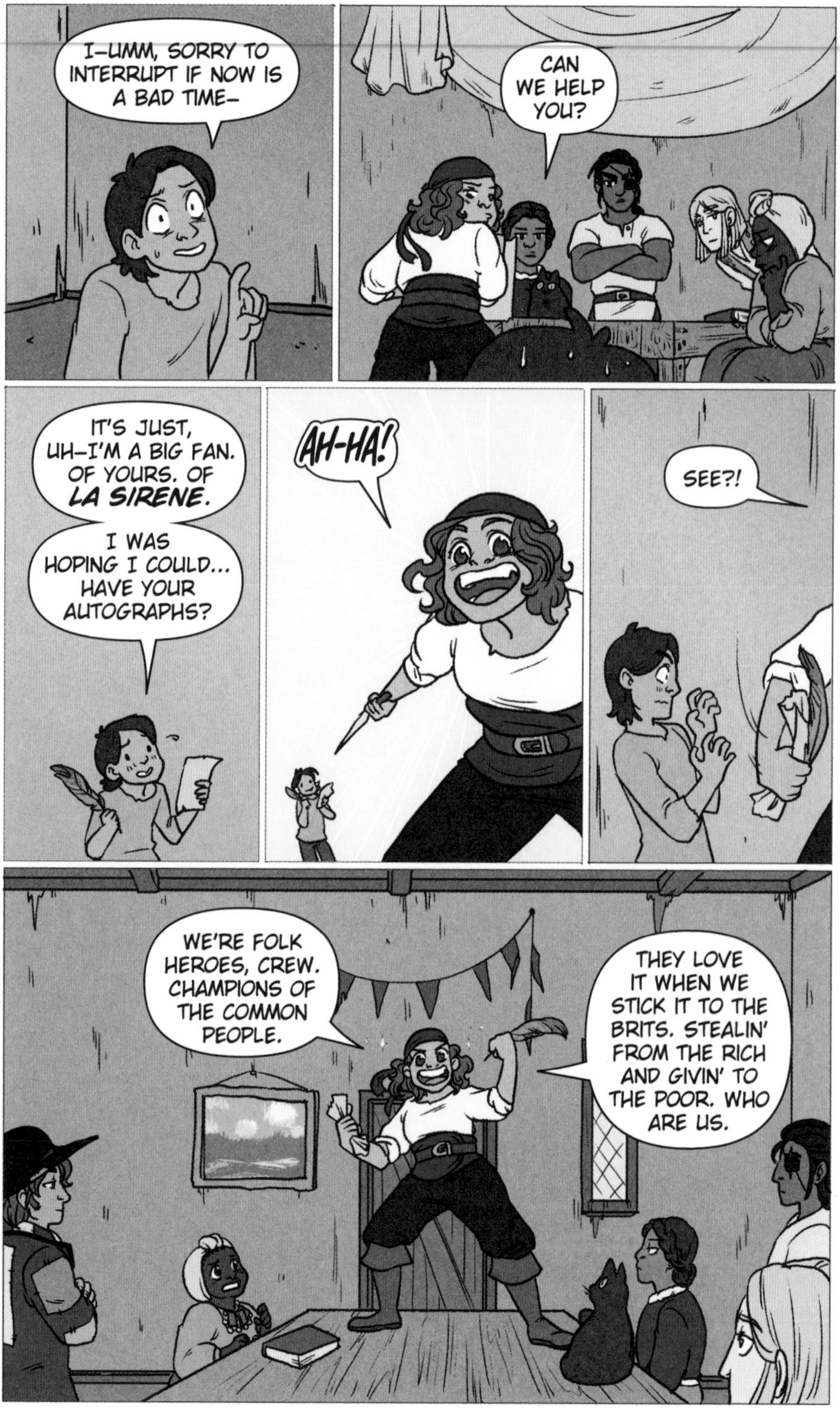
I–UMM, SORRY TO INTERRUPT IF NOW IS A BAD TIME–
CAN WE HELP YOU?
IT'S JUST, UH–I'M A BIG FAN. OF YOURS. OF *LA SIRENE*.
I WAS HOPING I COULD... HAVE YOUR AUTOGRAPHS?
AH-HA!
SEE?!
WE'RE FOLK HEROES, CREW. CHAMPIONS OF THE COMMON PEOPLE.
THEY LOVE IT WHEN WE STICK IT TO THE BRITS. STEALIN' FROM THE RICH AND GIVIN' TO THE POOR. WHO ARE US.

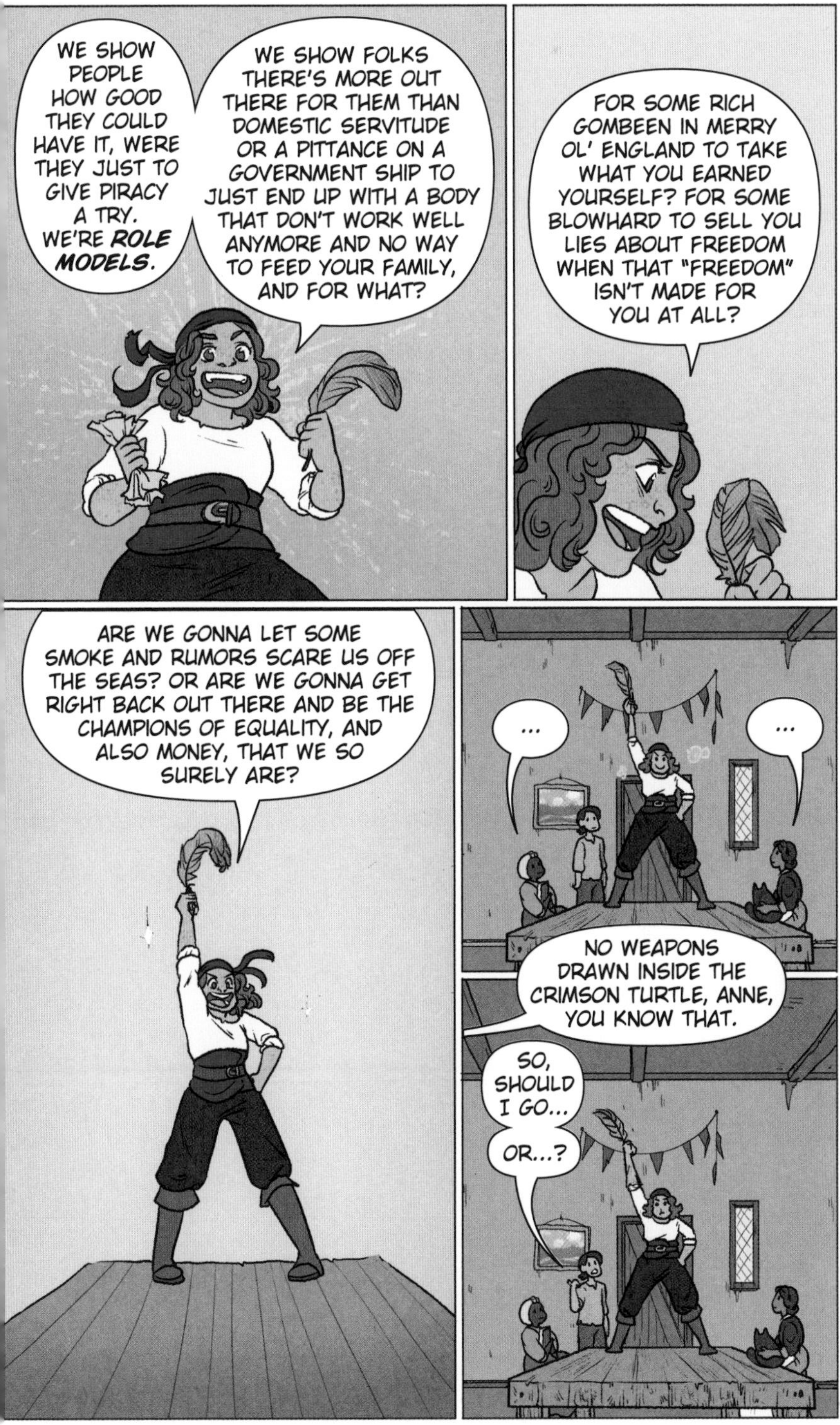
WE SHOW PEOPLE HOW GOOD THEY COULD HAVE IT, WERE THEY JUST TO GIVE PIRACY A TRY. WE'RE ROLE MODELS.
WE SHOW FOLKS THERE'S MORE OUT THERE FOR THEM THAN DOMESTIC SERVITUDE OR A PITTANCE ON A GOVERNMENT SHIP TO JUST END UP WITH A BODY THAT DON'T WORK WELL ANYMORE AND NO WAY TO FEED YOUR FAMILY, AND FOR WHAT?
FOR SOME RICH GOMBEEN IN MERRY OL' ENGLAND TO TAKE WHAT YOU EARNED YOURSELF? FOR SOME BLOWHARD TO SELL YOU LIES ABOUT FREEDOM WHEN THAT "FREEDOM" ISN'T MADE FOR YOU AT ALL?
ARE WE GONNA LET SOME SMOKE AND RUMORS SCARE US OFF THE SEAS? OR ARE WE GONNA GET RIGHT BACK OUT THERE AND BE THE CHAMPIONS OF EQUALITY, AND ALSO MONEY, THAT WE SO SURELY ARE?
...
...
NO WEAPONS DRAWN INSIDE THE CRIMSON TURTLE, ANNE, YOU KNOW THAT.
SO, SHOULD I GO...
OR...?

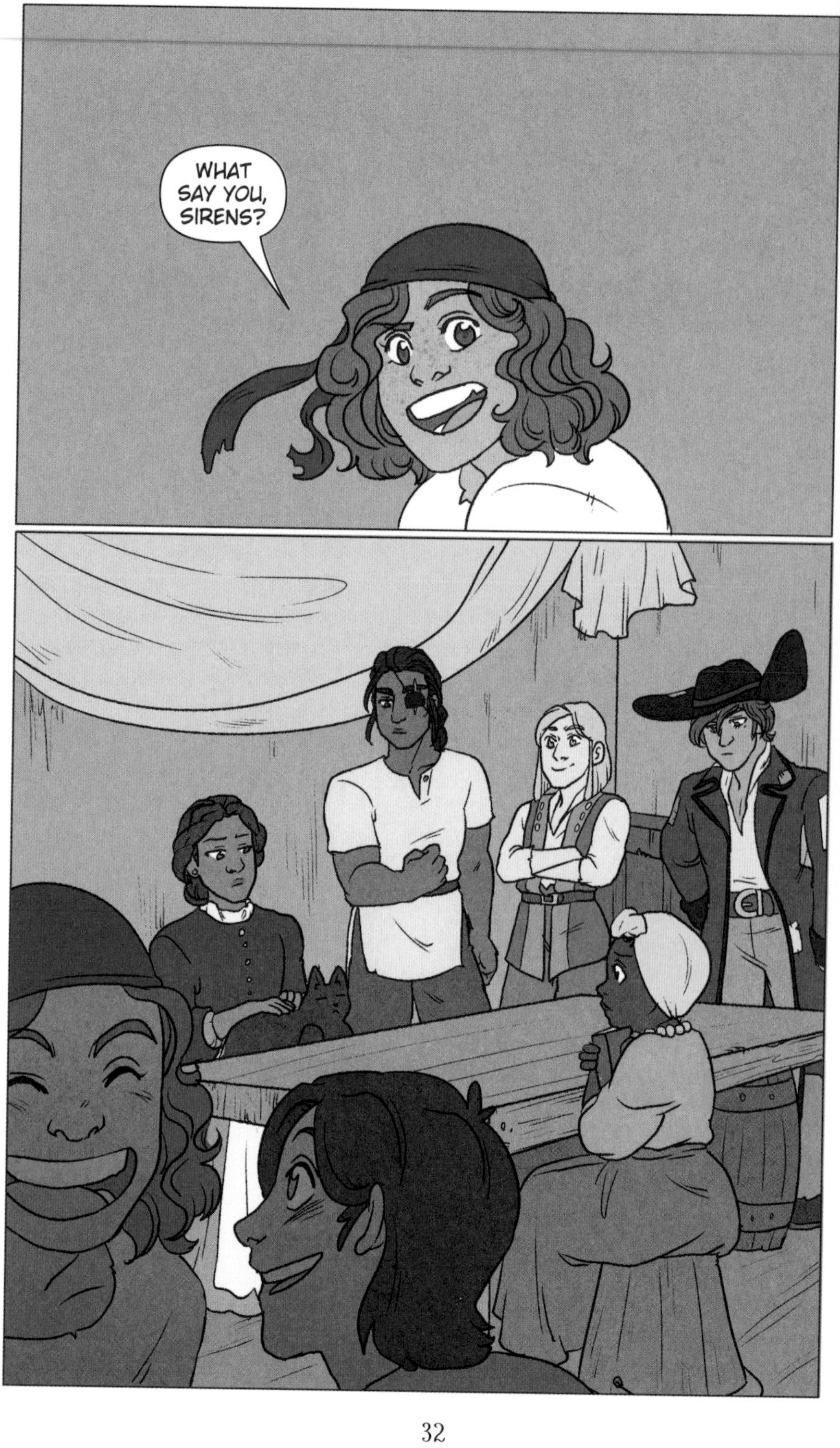
WHAT SAY YOU, SIRENS?

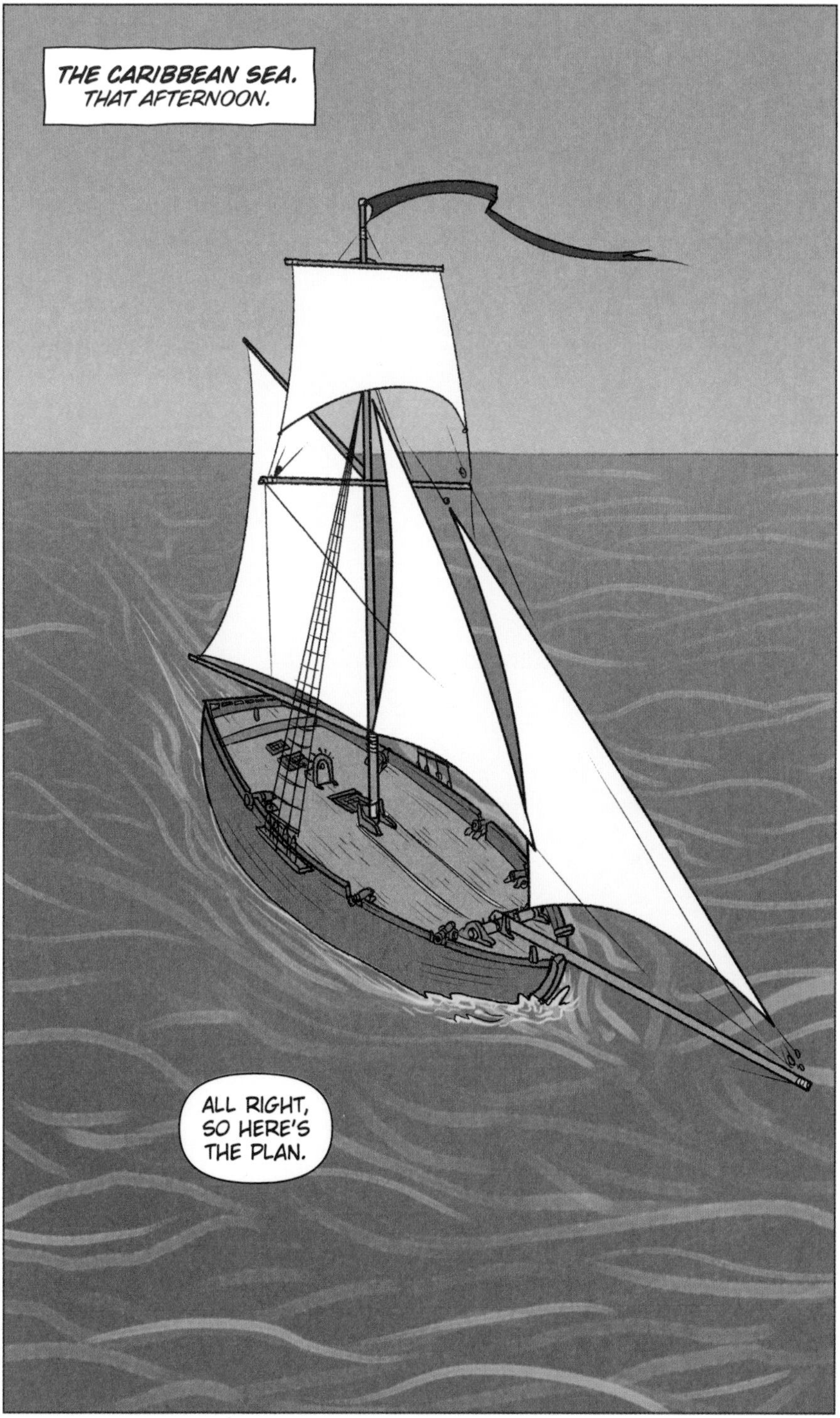
THE CARIBBEAN SEA.
THAT AFTERNOON.
ALL RIGHT, SO HERE'S THE PLAN.

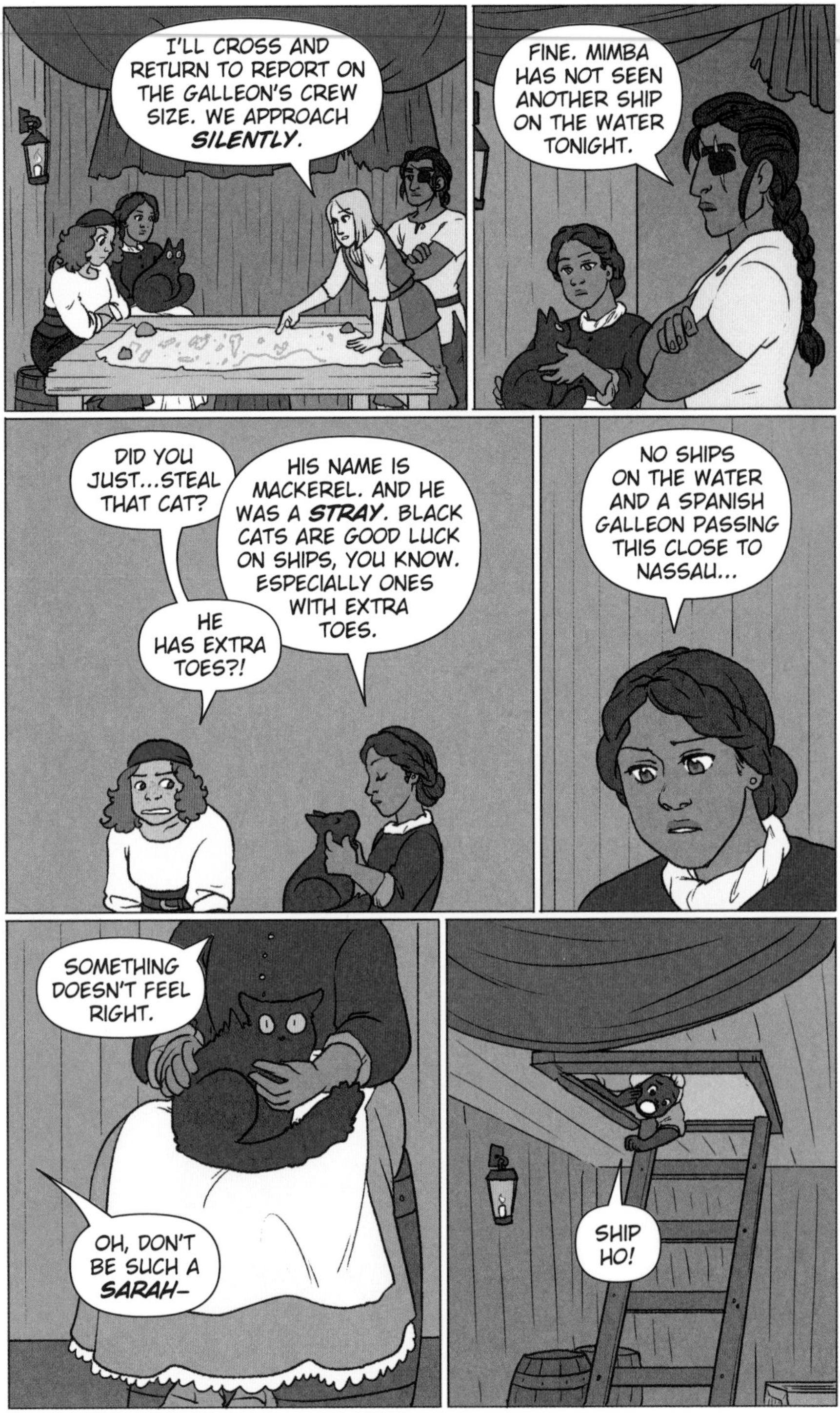
I'LL CROSS AND RETURN TO REPORT ON THE GALLEON'S CREW SIZE. WE APPROACH *SILENTLY*.
FINE. MIMBA HAS NOT SEEN ANOTHER SHIP ON THE WATER TONIGHT.
DID YOU JUST...STEAL THAT CAT?
HIS NAME IS MACKEREL. AND HE WAS A *STRAY*. BLACK CATS ARE GOOD LUCK ON SHIPS, YOU KNOW. ESPECIALLY ONES WITH EXTRA TOES.
HE HAS EXTRA TOES?!
NO SHIPS ON THE WATER AND A SPANISH GALLEON PASSING THIS CLOSE TO NASSAU...
SOMETHING DOESN'T FEEL RIGHT.
OH, DON'T BE SUCH A *SARAH*–
SHIP HO!

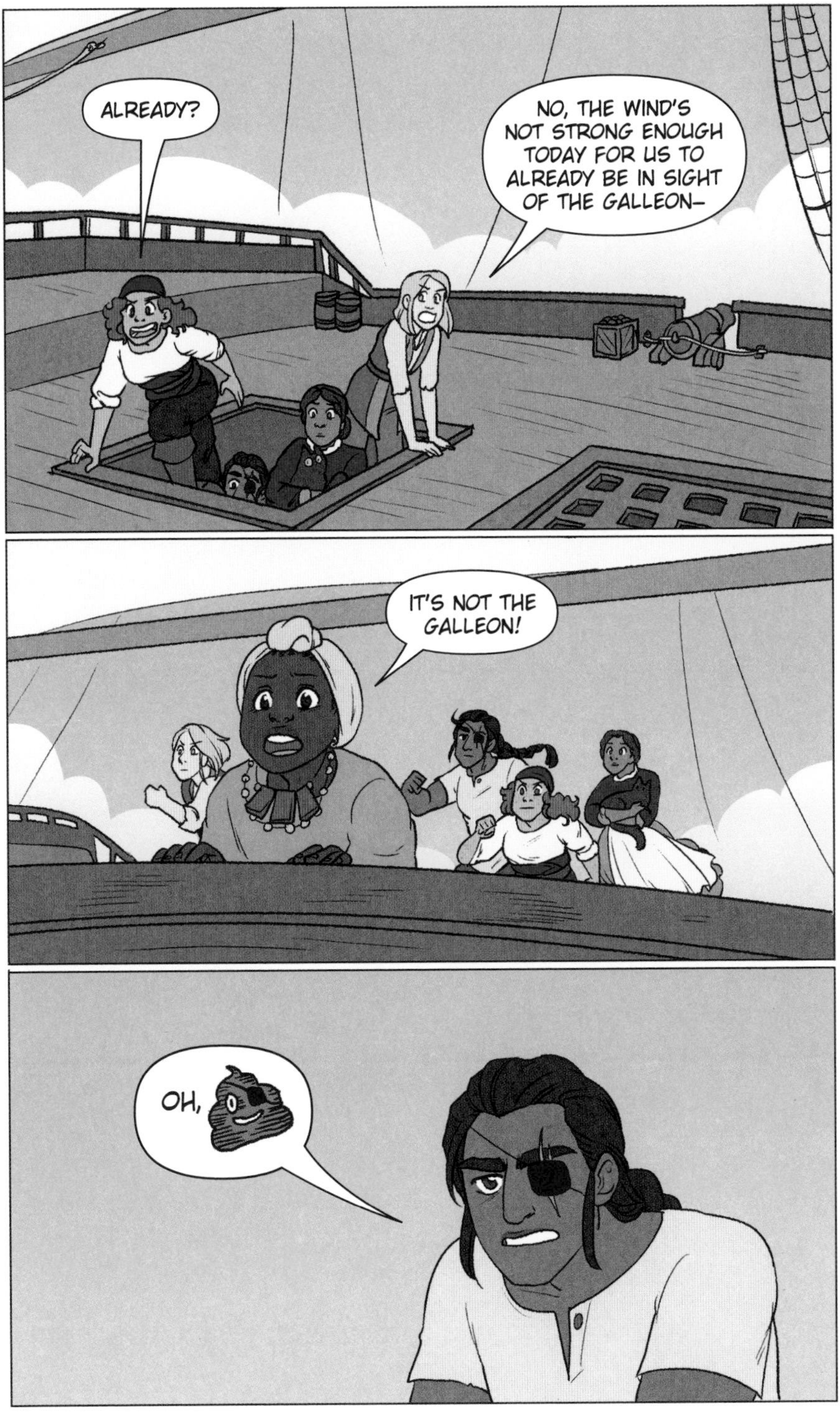
ALREADY?
NO, THE WIND'S NOT STRONG ENOUGH TODAY FOR US TO ALREADY BE IN SIGHT OF THE GALLEON—
IT'S NOT THE GALLEON!
OH,

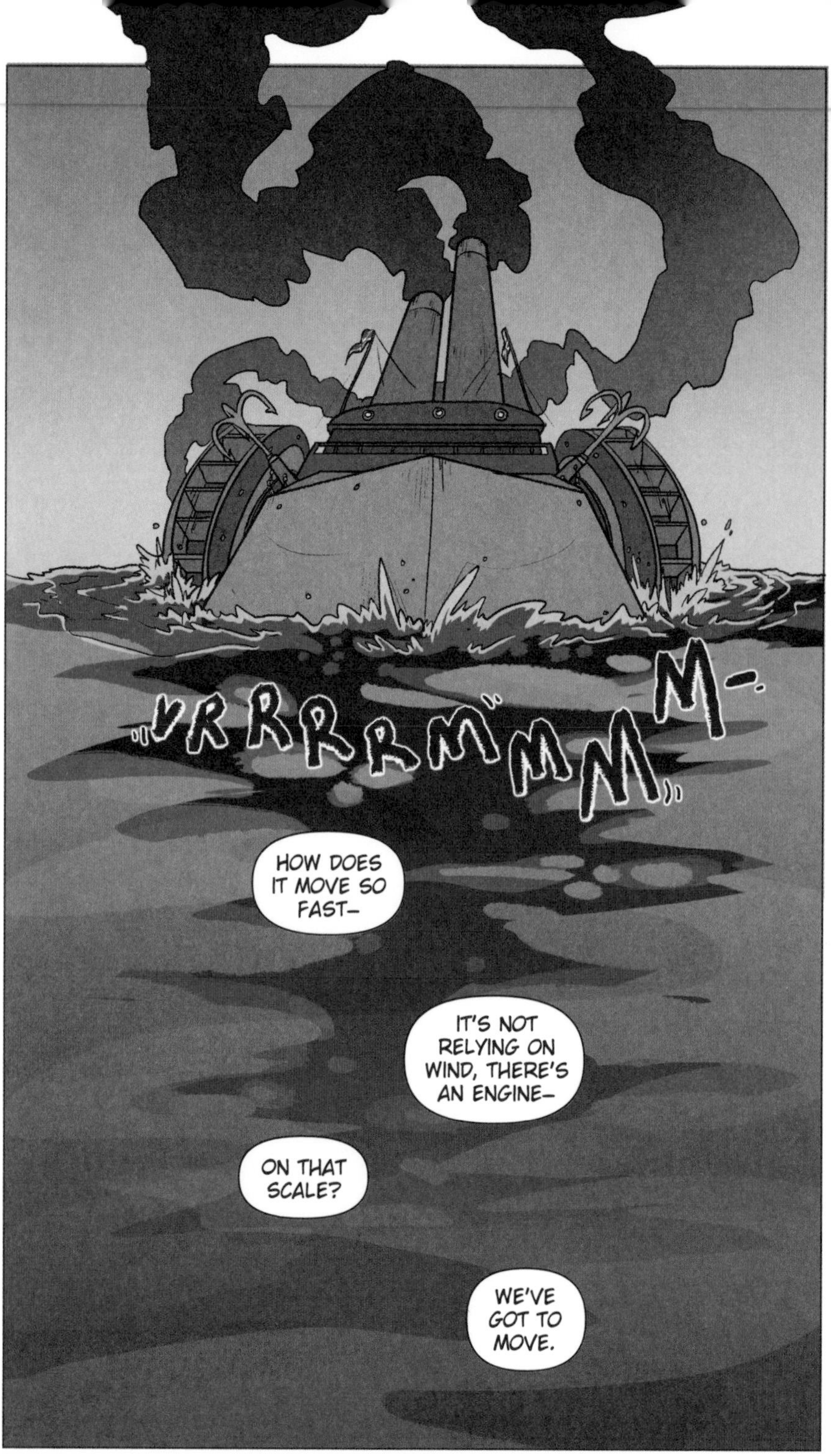
VRRRRMMMMM-
HOW DOES IT MOVE SO FAST-
IT'S NOT RELYING ON WIND, THERE'S AN ENGINE-
ON THAT SCALE?
WE'VE GOT TO MOVE.

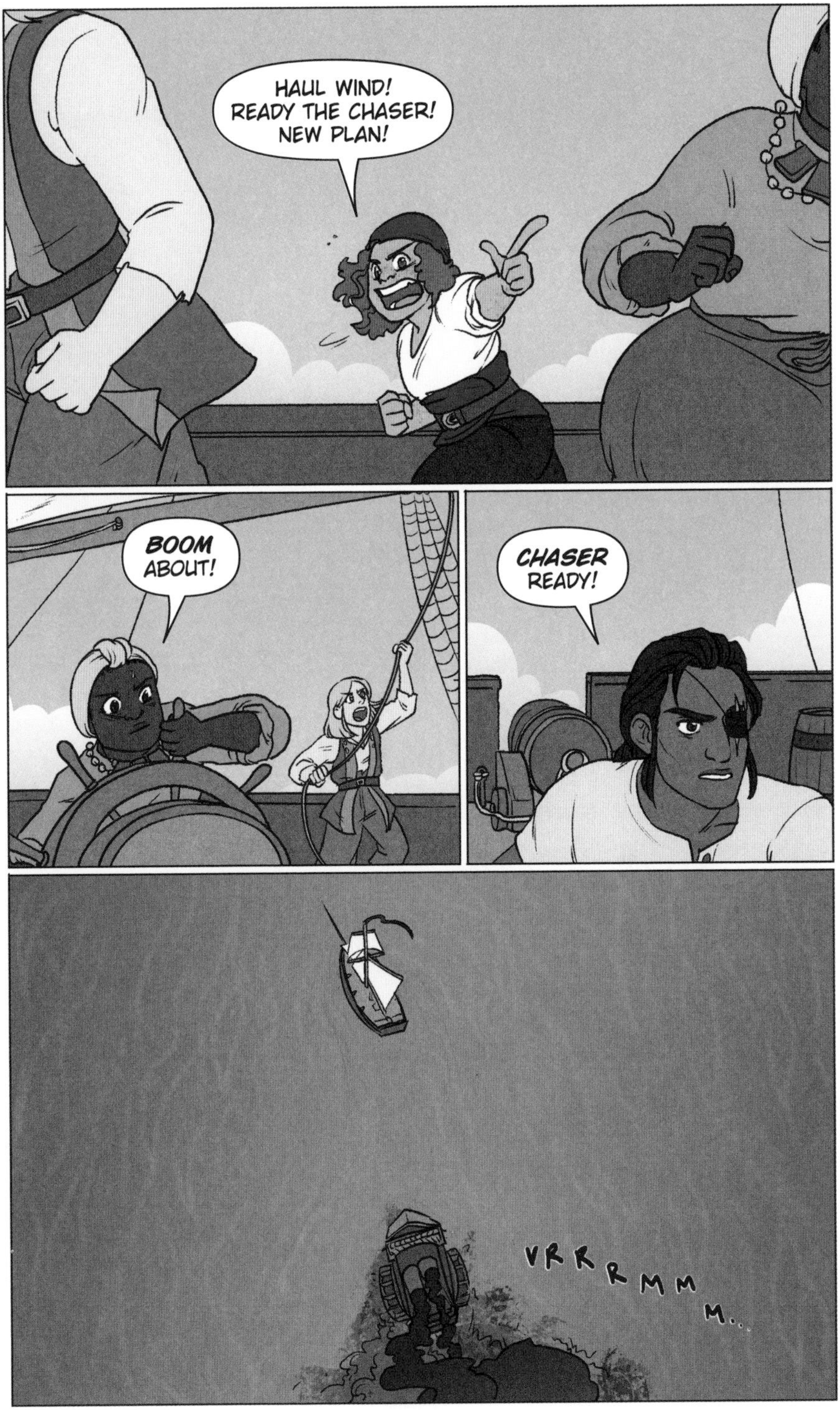
HAUL WIND!
READY THE CHASER!
NEW PLAN!
BOOM ABOUT!
CHASER READY!
VRRRRMMMM...

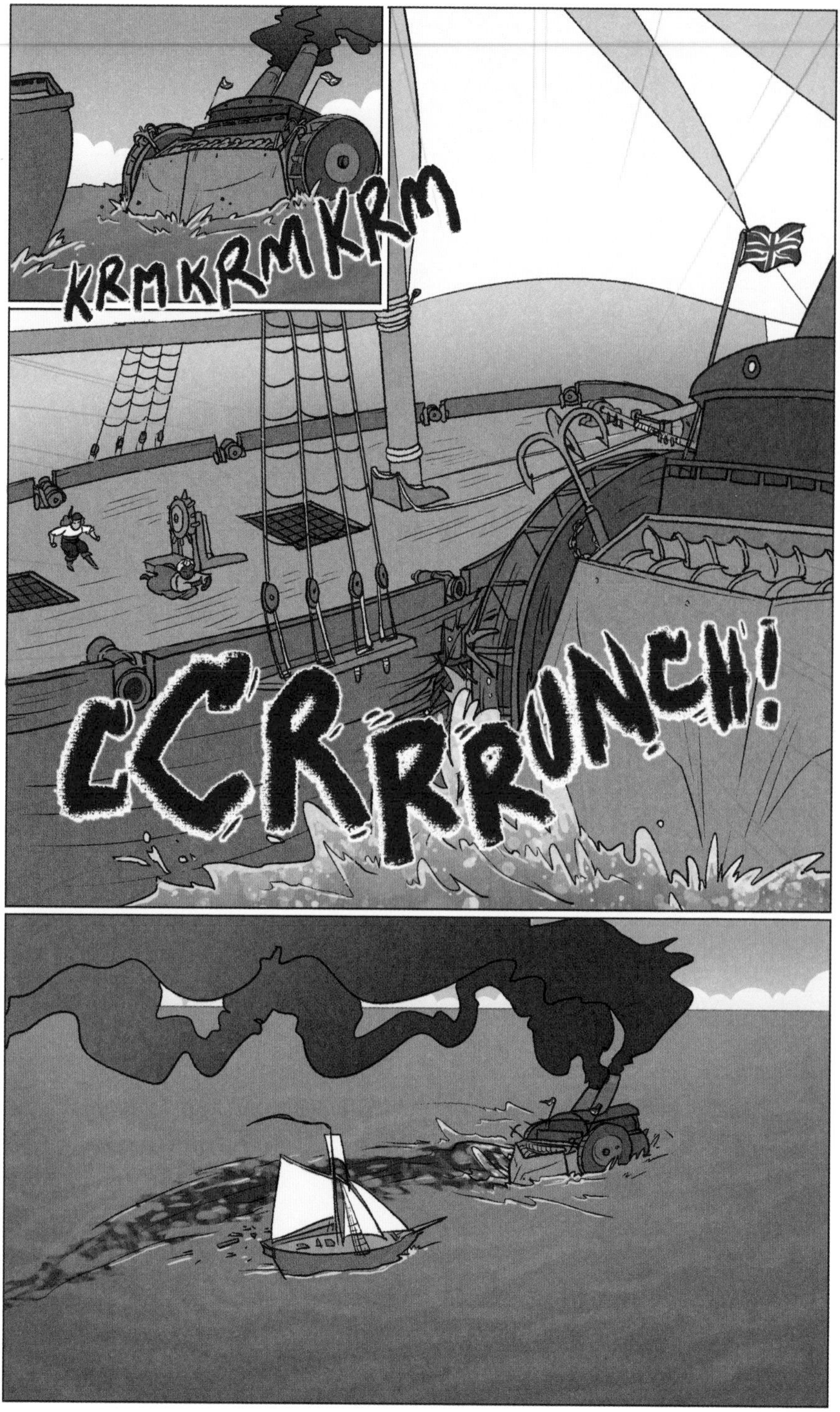
KRMKRMKRM
CCRRRRUNCH!

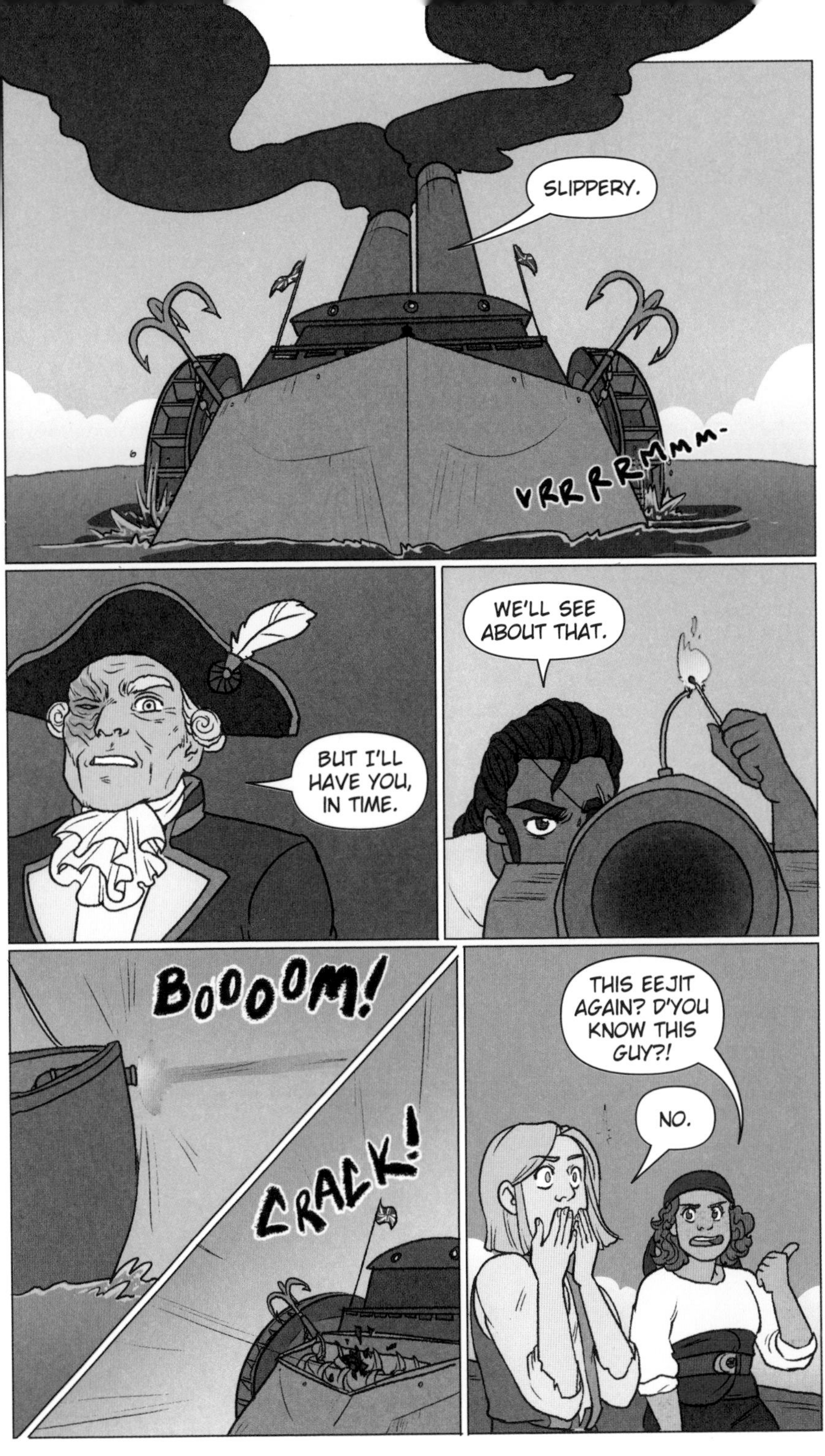
SLIPPERY.
VRRRRMMM-
BUT I'LL HAVE YOU, IN TIME.
WE'LL SEE ABOUT THAT.
BOOOOM!
CRACK!
THIS EEJIT AGAIN? D'YOU KNOW THIS GUY?!
NO.

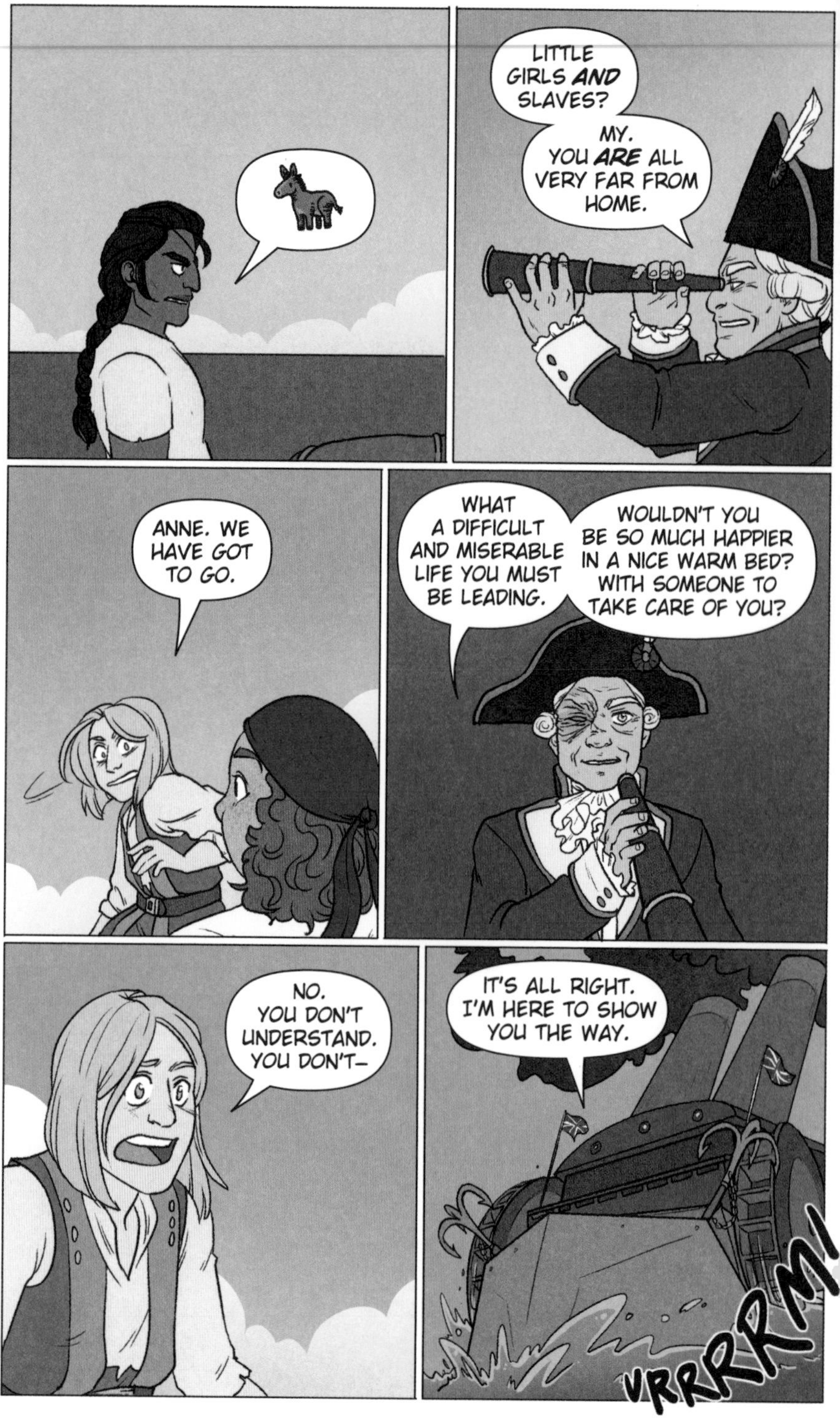
LITTLE GIRLS AND SLAVES?
MY. YOU ARE ALL VERY FAR FROM HOME.
ANNE. WE HAVE GOT TO GO.
WHAT A DIFFICULT AND MISERABLE LIFE YOU MUST BE LEADING.
WOULDN'T YOU BE SO MUCH HAPPIER IN A NICE WARM BED? WITH SOMEONE TO TAKE CARE OF YOU?
NO. YOU DON'T UNDERSTAND. YOU DON'T–
IT'S ALL RIGHT. I'M HERE TO SHOW YOU THE WAY.
VRRRRM!

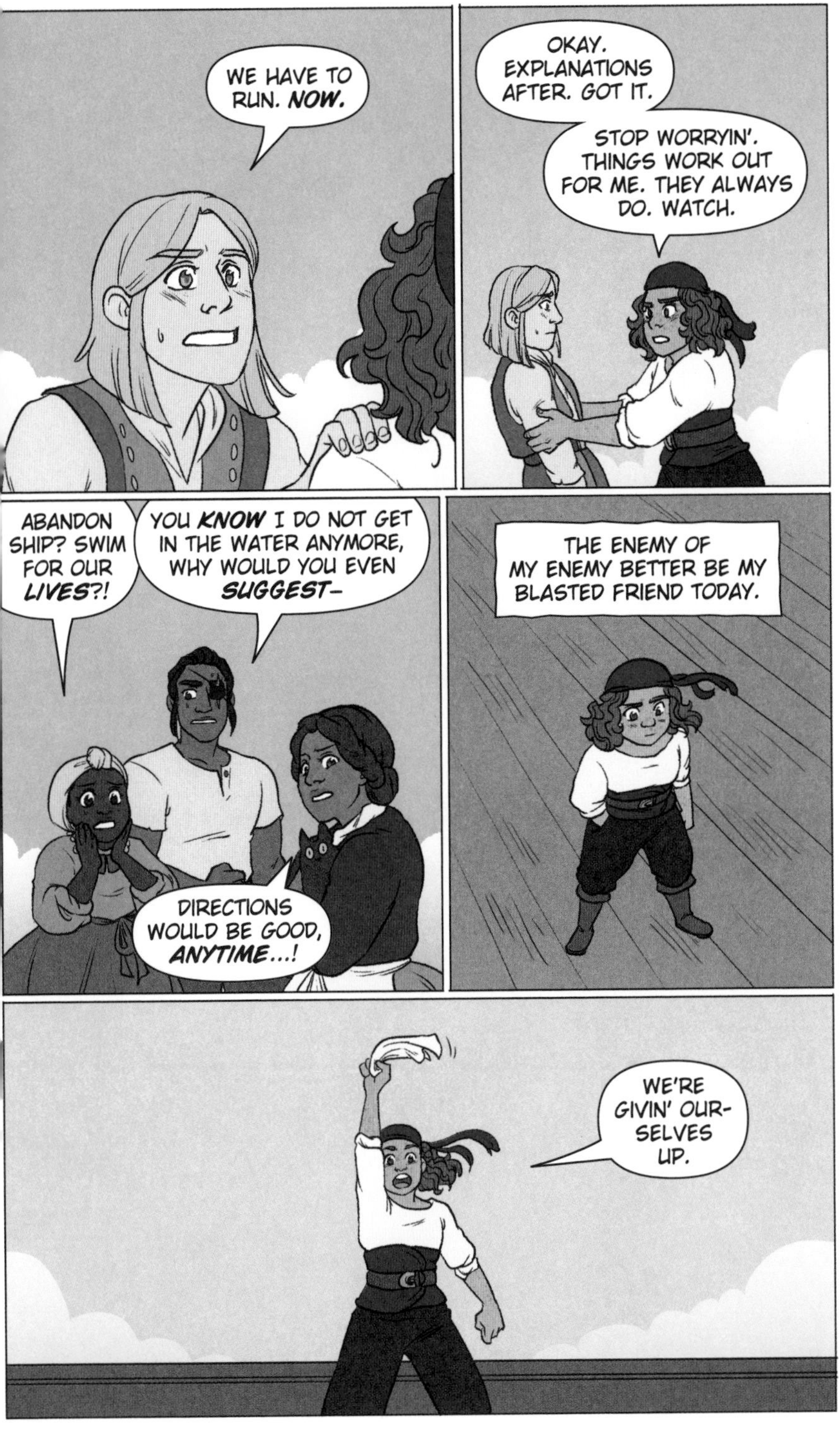
WE HAVE TO RUN. NOW.
OKAY. EXPLANATIONS AFTER. GOT IT.
STOP WORRYIN'. THINGS WORK OUT FOR ME. THEY ALWAYS DO. WATCH.
ABANDON SHIP? SWIM FOR OUR LIVES?!
YOU KNOW I DO NOT GET IN THE WATER ANYMORE, WHY WOULD YOU EVEN SUGGEST–
DIRECTIONS WOULD BE GOOD, ANYTIME...!
THE ENEMY OF MY ENEMY BETTER BE MY BLASTED FRIEND TODAY.
WE'RE GIVIN' OURSELVES UP.

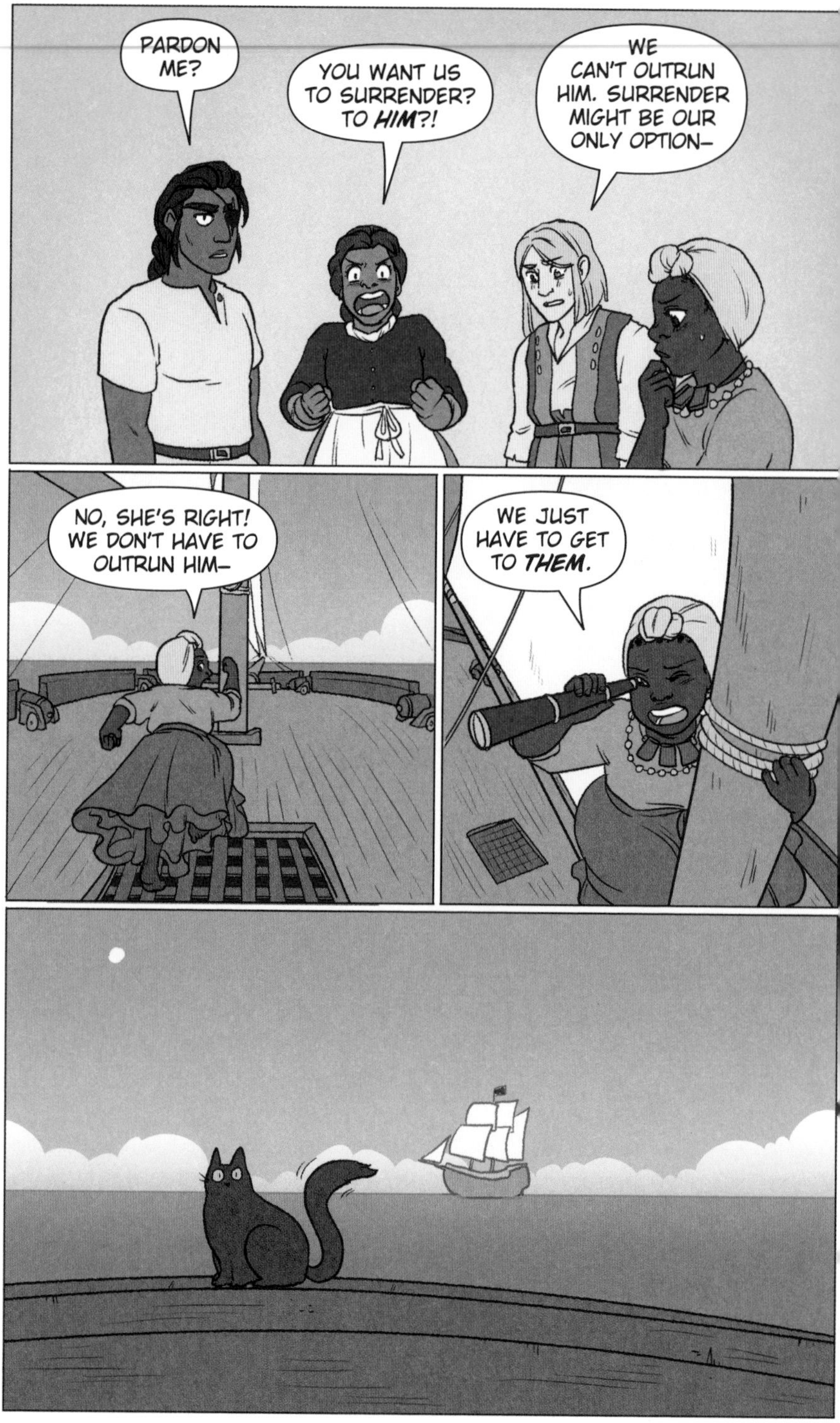
PARDON ME?
YOU WANT US TO SURRENDER? TO *HIM*?!
WE CAN'T OUTRUN HIM. SURRENDER MIGHT BE OUR ONLY OPTION–
NO, SHE'S RIGHT! WE DON'T HAVE TO OUTRUN HIM–
WE JUST HAVE TO GET TO *THEM*.

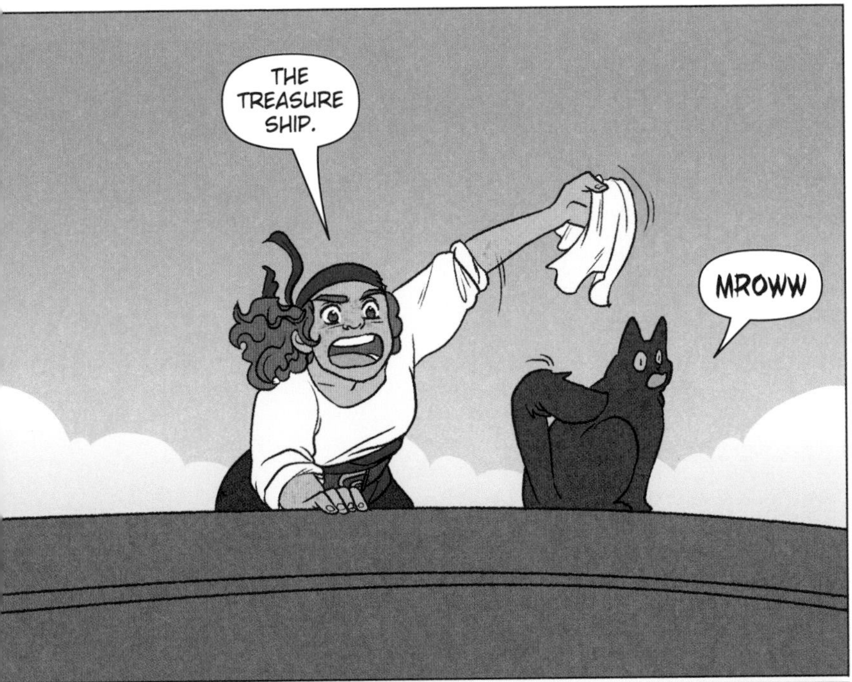
THE TREASURE SHIP.
MROWW

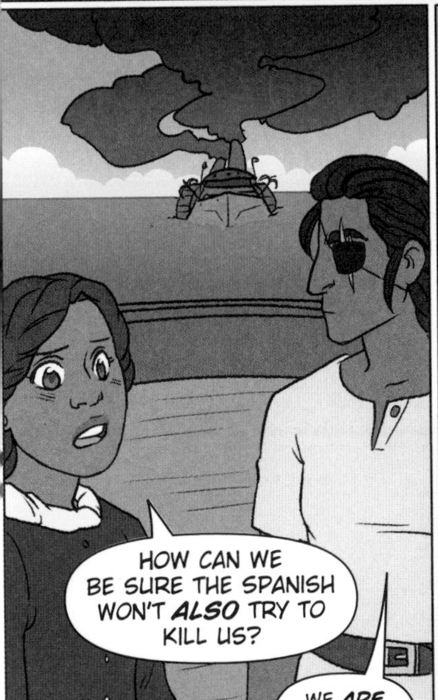
HOW CAN WE BE SURE THE SPANISH WON'T ***ALSO*** TRY TO KILL US?
WE ***ARE*** PIRATES, AFTER ALL.

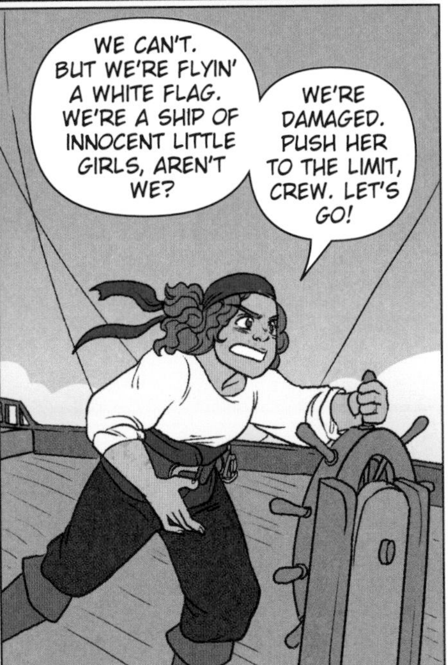
WE CAN'T. BUT WE'RE FLYIN' A WHITE FLAG. WE'RE A SHIP OF INNOCENT LITTLE GIRLS, AREN'T WE?
WE'RE DAMAGED. PUSH HER TO THE LIMIT, CREW. LET'S GO!

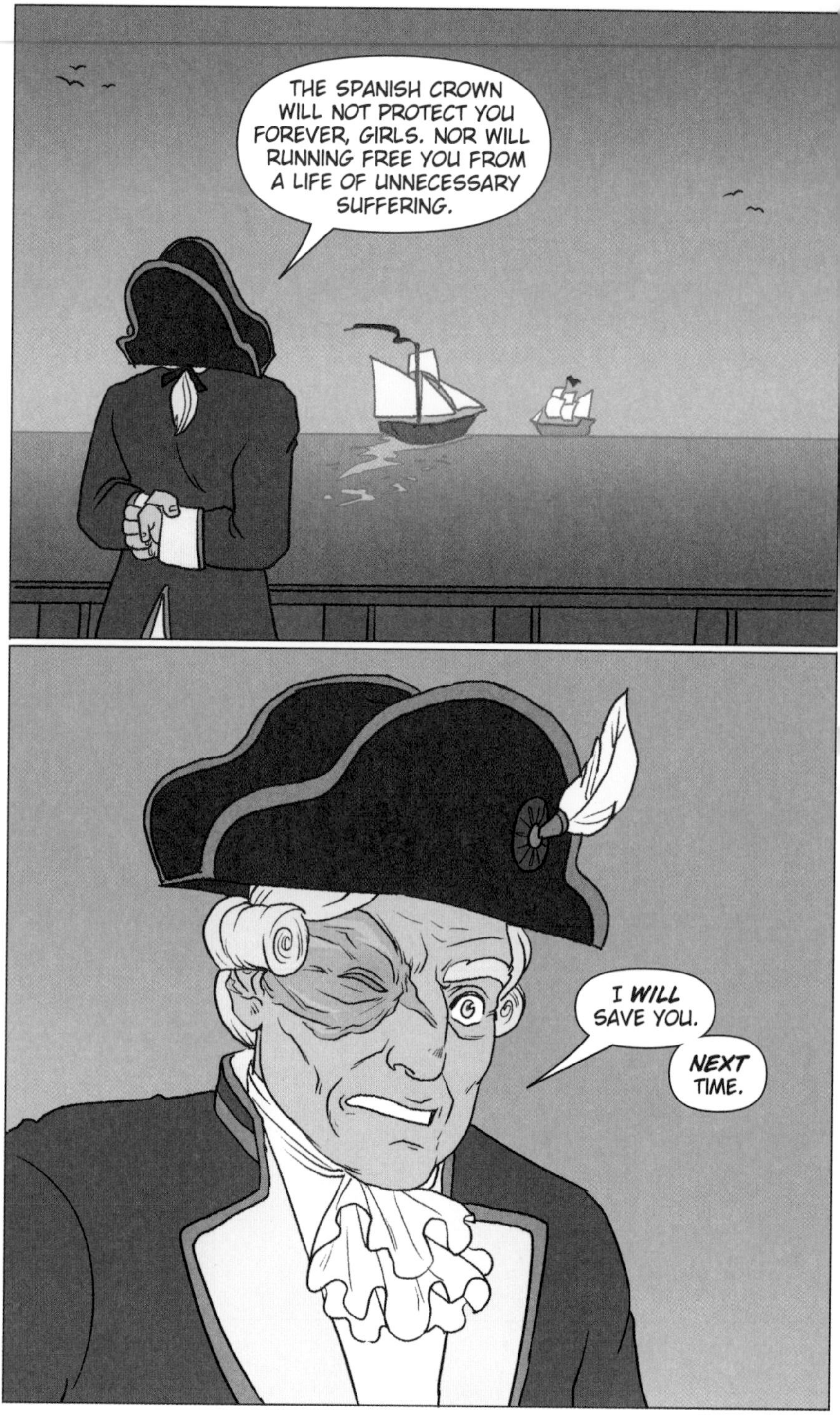
THE SPANISH CROWN WILL NOT PROTECT YOU FOREVER, GIRLS. NOR WILL RUNNING FREE YOU FROM A LIFE OF UNNECESSARY SUFFERING.
I *WILL* SAVE YOU.
NEXT TIME.

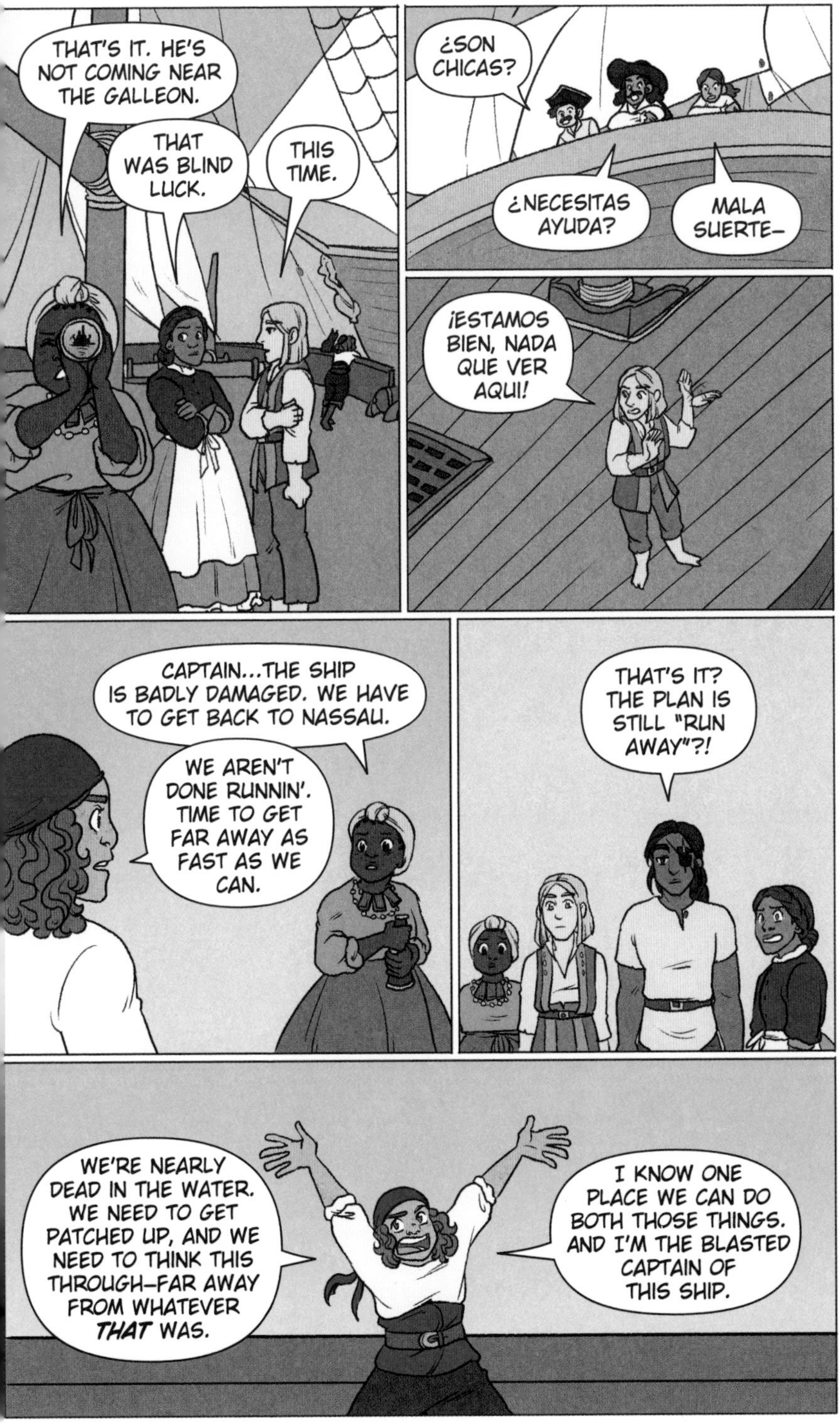
THAT'S IT. HE'S NOT COMING NEAR THE GALLEON.
THAT WAS BLIND LUCK.
THIS TIME.
¿SON CHICAS?
¿NECESITAS AYUDA?
MALA SUERTE–
¡ESTAMOS BIEN, NADA QUE VER AQUI!
CAPTAIN...THE SHIP IS BADLY DAMAGED. WE HAVE TO GET BACK TO NASSAU.
WE AREN'T DONE RUNNIN'. TIME TO GET FAR AWAY AS FAST AS WE CAN.
THAT'S IT? THE PLAN IS STILL "RUN AWAY"?!
WE'RE NEARLY DEAD IN THE WATER. WE NEED TO GET PATCHED UP, AND WE NEED TO THINK THIS THROUGH–FAR AWAY FROM WHATEVER *THAT* WAS.
I KNOW ONE PLACE WE CAN DO BOTH THOSE THINGS. AND I'M THE BLASTED CAPTAIN OF THIS SHIP.

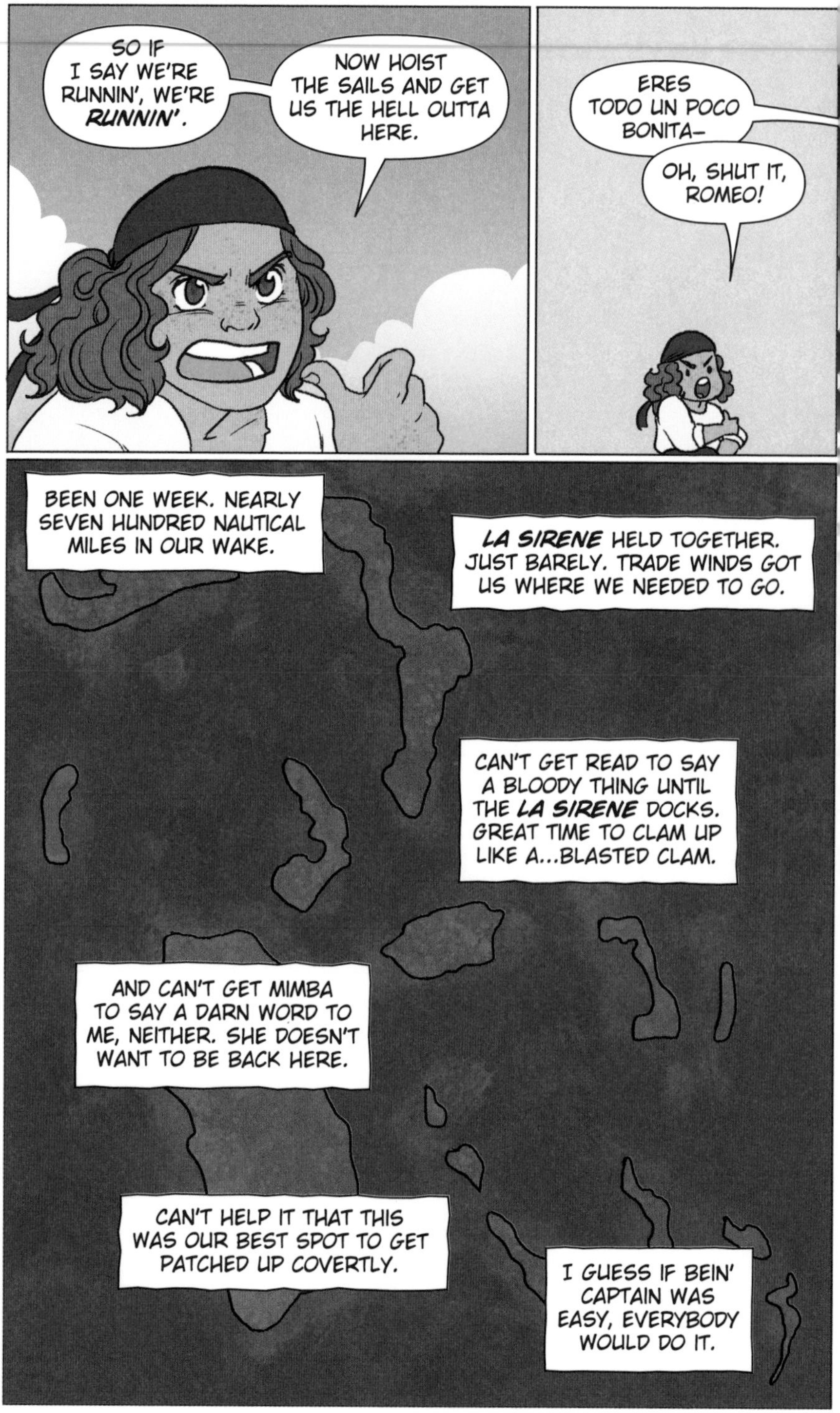
SO IF I SAY WE'RE RUNNIN', WE'RE *RUNNIN'*.
NOW HOIST THE SAILS AND GET US THE HELL OUTTA HERE.
ERES TODO UN POCO BONITA–
OH, SHUT IT, ROMEO!
BEEN ONE WEEK. NEARLY SEVEN HUNDRED NAUTICAL MILES IN OUR WAKE.
LA SIRENE HELD TOGETHER. JUST BARELY. TRADE WINDS GOT US WHERE WE NEEDED TO GO.
CAN'T GET READ TO SAY A BLOODY THING UNTIL THE *LA SIRENE* DOCKS. GREAT TIME TO CLAM UP LIKE A...BLASTED CLAM.
AND CAN'T GET MIMBA TO SAY A DARN WORD TO ME, NEITHER. SHE DOESN'T WANT TO BE BACK HERE.
CAN'T HELP IT THAT THIS WAS OUR BEST SPOT TO GET PATCHED UP COVERTLY.
I GUESS IF BEIN' CAPTAIN WAS EASY, EVERYBODY WOULD DO IT.

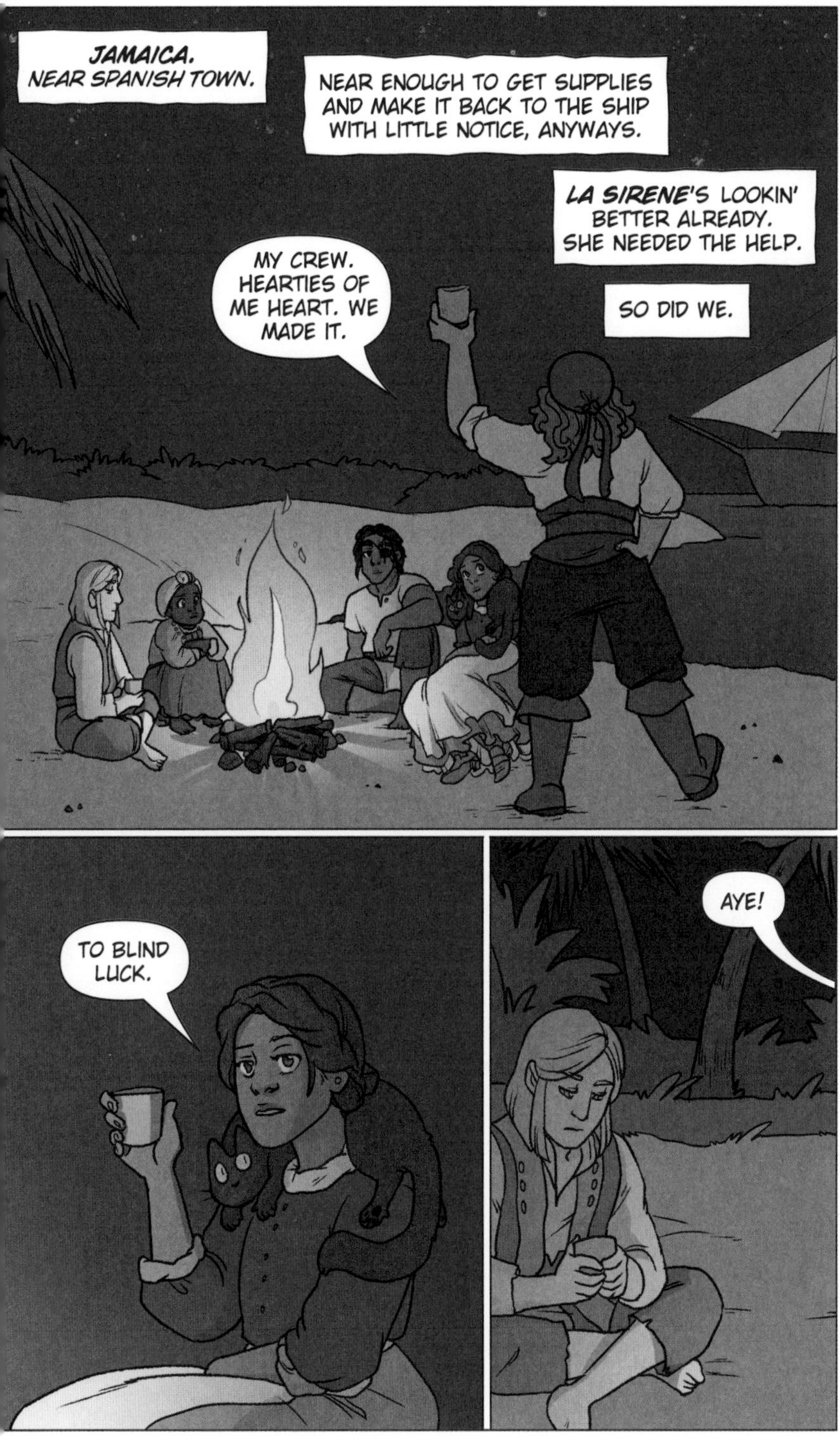
JAMAICA. NEAR SPANISH TOWN.
NEAR ENOUGH TO GET SUPPLIES AND MAKE IT BACK TO THE SHIP WITH LITTLE NOTICE, ANYWAYS.
MY CREW. HEARTIES OF ME HEART. WE MADE IT.
LA SIRENE'S LOOKIN' BETTER ALREADY. SHE NEEDED THE HELP.
SO DID WE.
TO BLIND LUCK.
AYE!

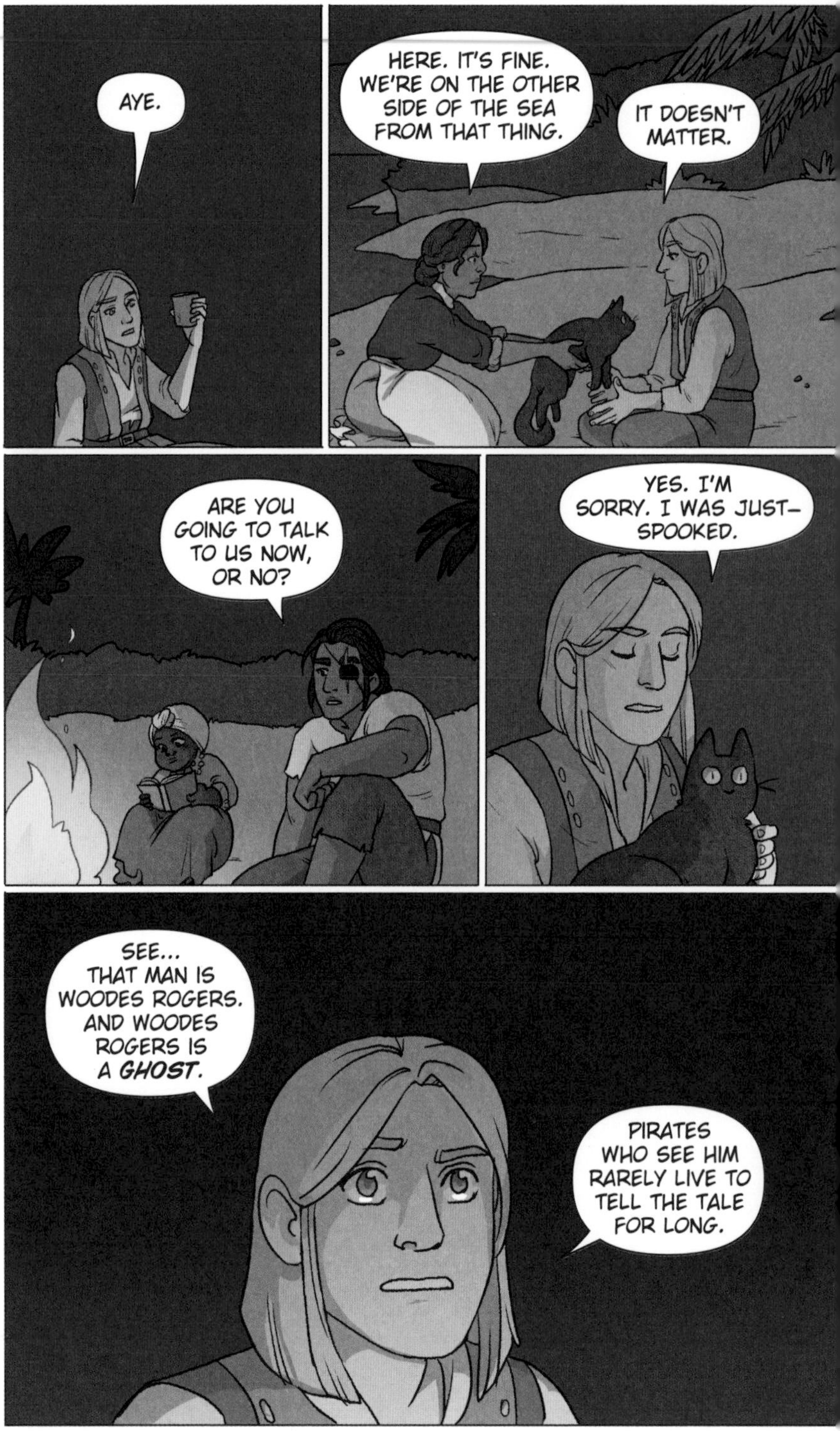
AYE.
HERE. IT'S FINE. WE'RE ON THE OTHER SIDE OF THE SEA FROM THAT THING.
IT DOESN'T MATTER.
ARE YOU GOING TO TALK TO US NOW, OR NO?
YES. I'M SORRY. I WAS JUST— SPOOKED.
SEE... THAT MAN IS WOODES ROGERS. AND WOODES ROGERS IS A ***GHOST***.
PIRATES WHO SEE HIM RARELY LIVE TO TELL THE TALE FOR LONG.

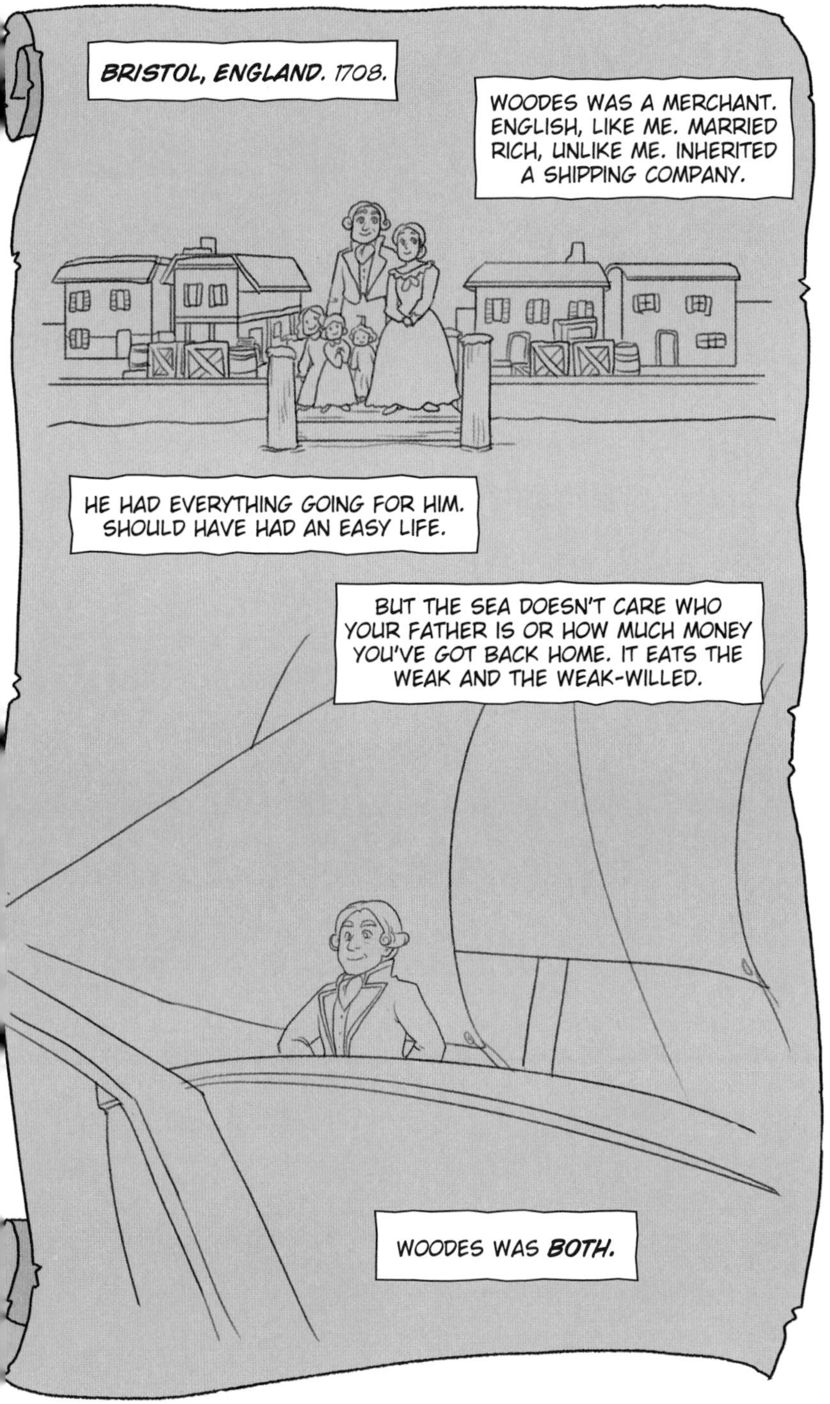
BRISTOL, ENGLAND. 1708.
WOODES WAS A MERCHANT. ENGLISH, LIKE ME. MARRIED RICH, UNLIKE ME. INHERITED A SHIPPING COMPANY.
HE HAD EVERYTHING GOING FOR HIM. SHOULD HAVE HAD AN EASY LIFE.
BUT THE SEA DOESN'T CARE WHO YOUR FATHER IS OR HOW MUCH MONEY YOU'VE GOT BACK HOME. IT EATS THE WEAK AND THE WEAK-WILLED.
WOODES WAS BOTH.

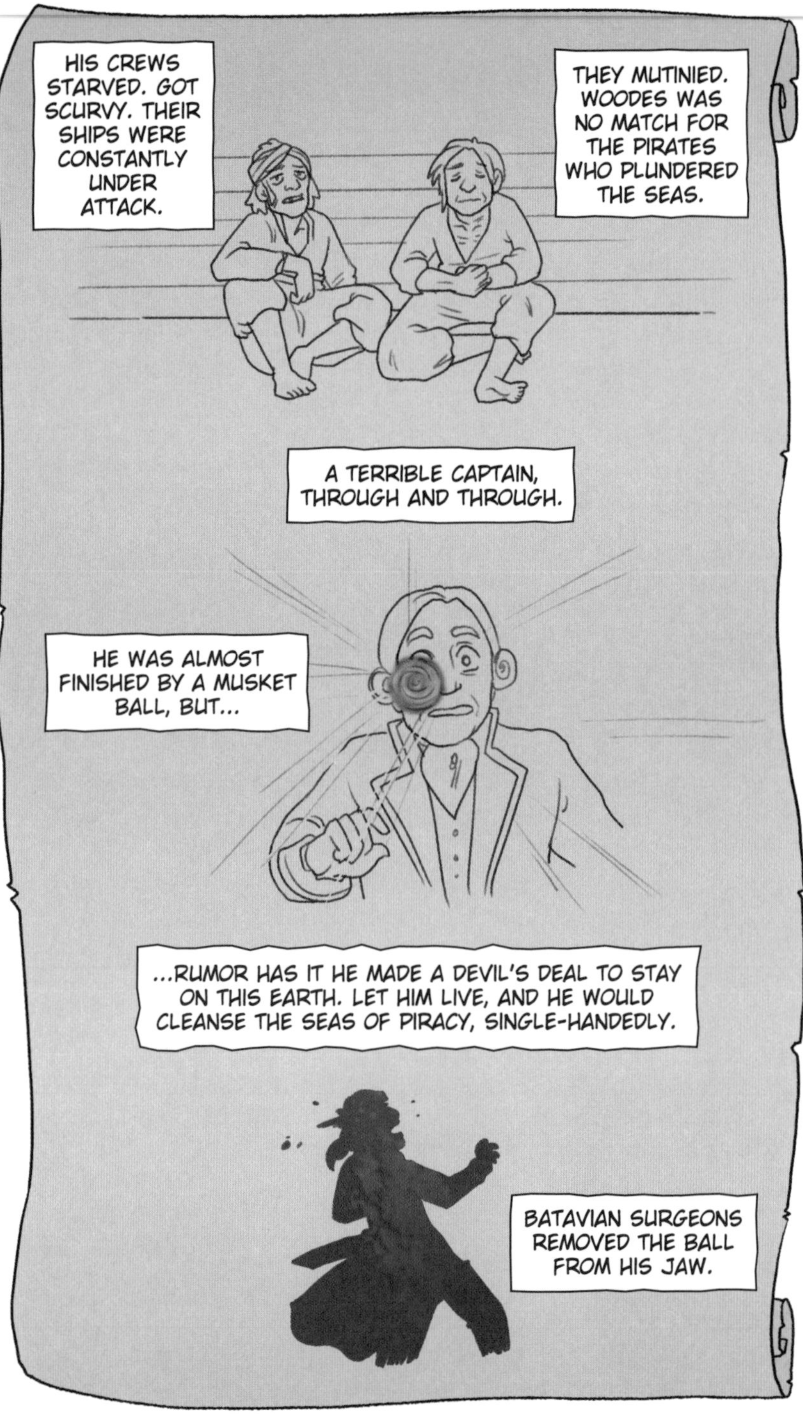
HIS CREWS STARVED. GOT SCURVY. THEIR SHIPS WERE CONSTANTLY UNDER ATTACK.
THEY MUTINIED. WOODES WAS NO MATCH FOR THE PIRATES WHO PLUNDERED THE SEAS.
A TERRIBLE CAPTAIN, THROUGH AND THROUGH.
HE WAS ALMOST FINISHED BY A MUSKET BALL, BUT...
...RUMOR HAS IT HE MADE A DEVIL'S DEAL TO STAY ON THIS EARTH. LET HIM LIVE, AND HE WOULD CLEANSE THE SEAS OF PIRACY, SINGLE-HANDEDLY.
BATAVIAN SURGEONS REMOVED THE BALL FROM HIS JAW.

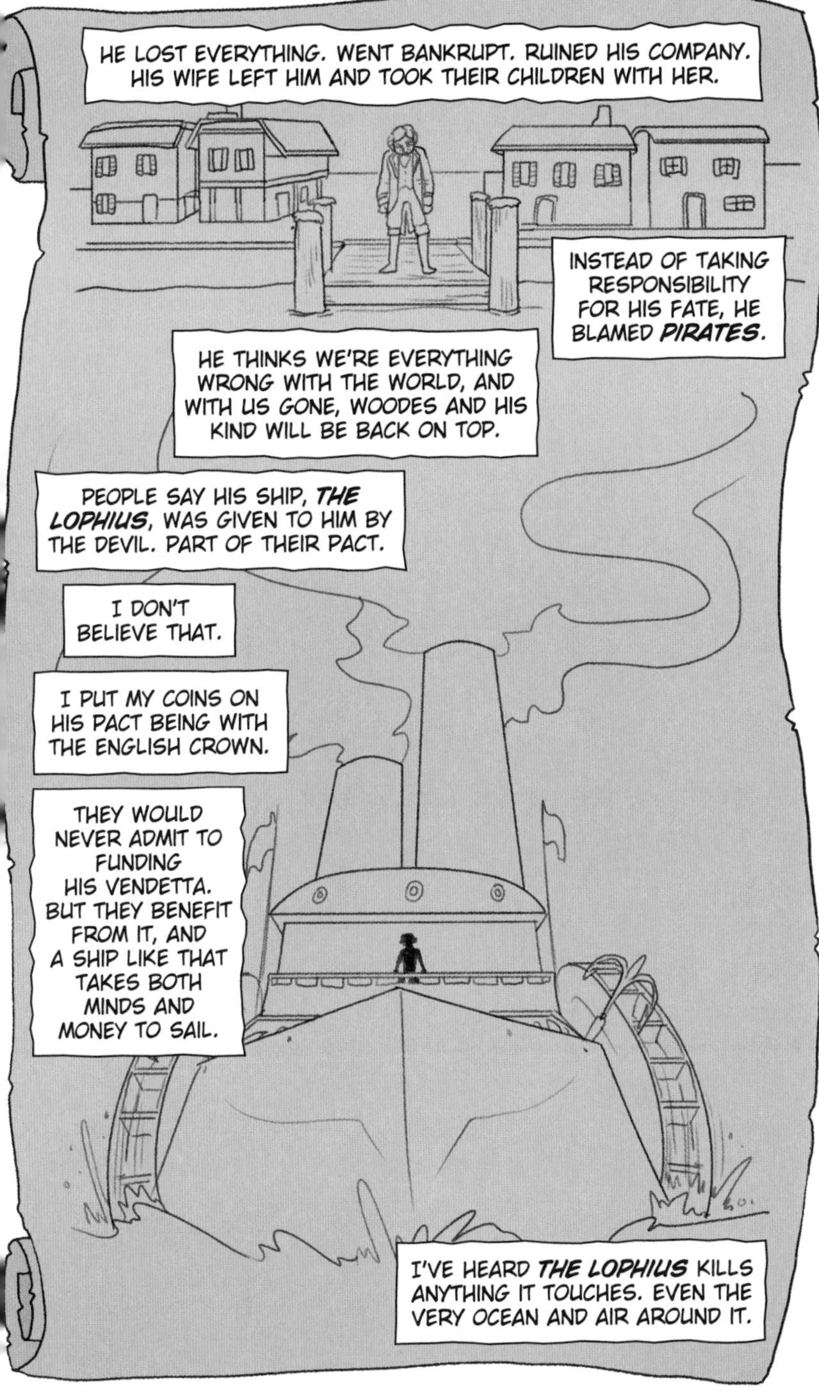
HE LOST EVERYTHING. WENT BANKRUPT. RUINED HIS COMPANY. HIS WIFE LEFT HIM AND TOOK THEIR CHILDREN WITH HER.
INSTEAD OF TAKING RESPONSIBILITY FOR HIS FATE, HE BLAMED ***PIRATES***.
HE THINKS WE'RE EVERYTHING WRONG WITH THE WORLD, AND WITH US GONE, WOODES AND HIS KIND WILL BE BACK ON TOP.
PEOPLE SAY HIS SHIP, ***THE LOPHIUS***, WAS GIVEN TO HIM BY THE DEVIL. PART OF THEIR PACT.
I DON'T BELIEVE THAT.
I PUT MY COINS ON HIS PACT BEING WITH THE ENGLISH CROWN.
THEY WOULD NEVER ADMIT TO FUNDING HIS VENDETTA. BUT THEY BENEFIT FROM IT, AND A SHIP LIKE THAT TAKES BOTH MINDS AND MONEY TO SAIL.
I'VE HEARD ***THE LOPHIUS*** KILLS ANYTHING IT TOUCHES. EVEN THE VERY OCEAN AND AIR AROUND IT.

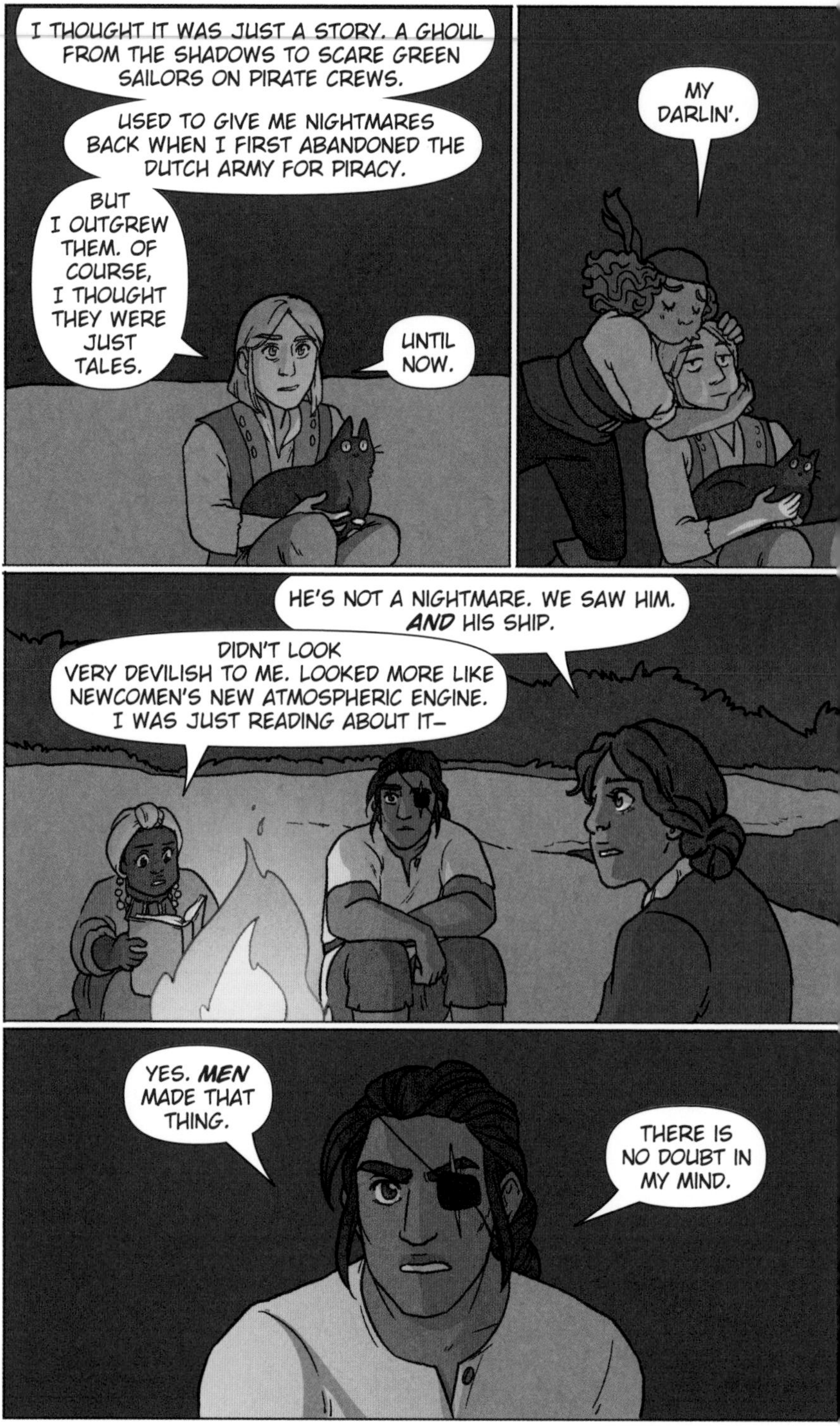
I THOUGHT IT WAS JUST A STORY. A GHOUL FROM THE SHADOWS TO SCARE GREEN SAILORS ON PIRATE CREWS.
USED TO GIVE ME NIGHTMARES BACK WHEN I FIRST ABANDONED THE DUTCH ARMY FOR PIRACY.
BUT I OUTGREW THEM. OF COURSE, I THOUGHT THEY WERE JUST TALES.
UNTIL NOW.
MY DARLIN'.
HE'S NOT A NIGHTMARE. WE SAW HIM. **AND** HIS SHIP.
DIDN'T LOOK VERY DEVILISH TO ME. LOOKED MORE LIKE NEWCOMEN'S NEW ATMOSPHERIC ENGINE. I WAS JUST READING ABOUT IT–
YES. **MEN** MADE THAT THING.
THERE IS NO DOUBT IN MY MIND.

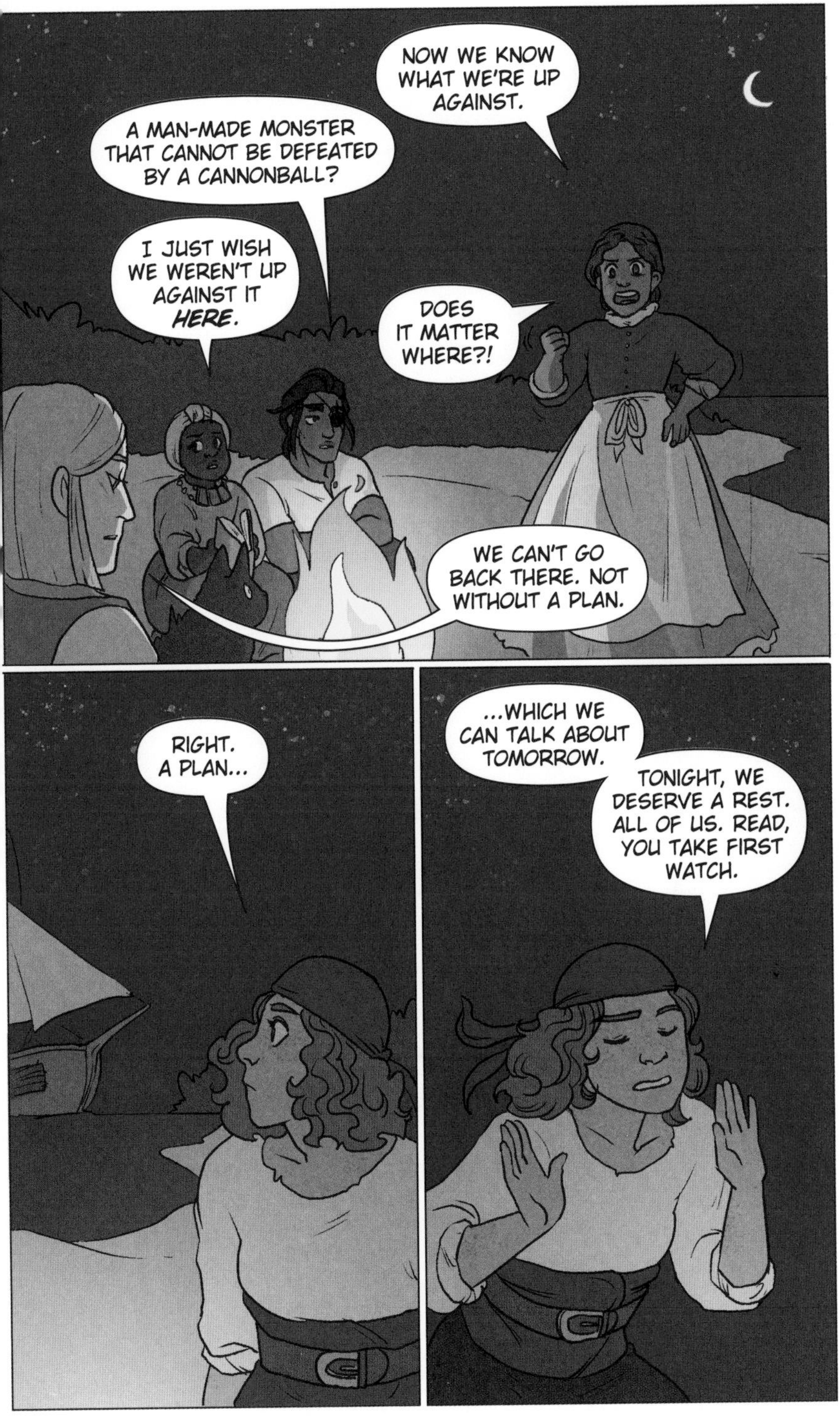
A MAN-MADE MONSTER THAT CANNOT BE DEFEATED BY A CANNONBALL?
NOW WE KNOW WHAT WE'RE UP AGAINST.
I JUST WISH WE WEREN'T UP AGAINST IT *HERE*.
DOES IT MATTER WHERE?!
WE CAN'T GO BACK THERE. NOT WITHOUT A PLAN.
RIGHT. A PLAN...
...WHICH WE CAN TALK ABOUT TOMORROW.
TONIGHT, WE DESERVE A REST. ALL OF US. READ, YOU TAKE FIRST WATCH.

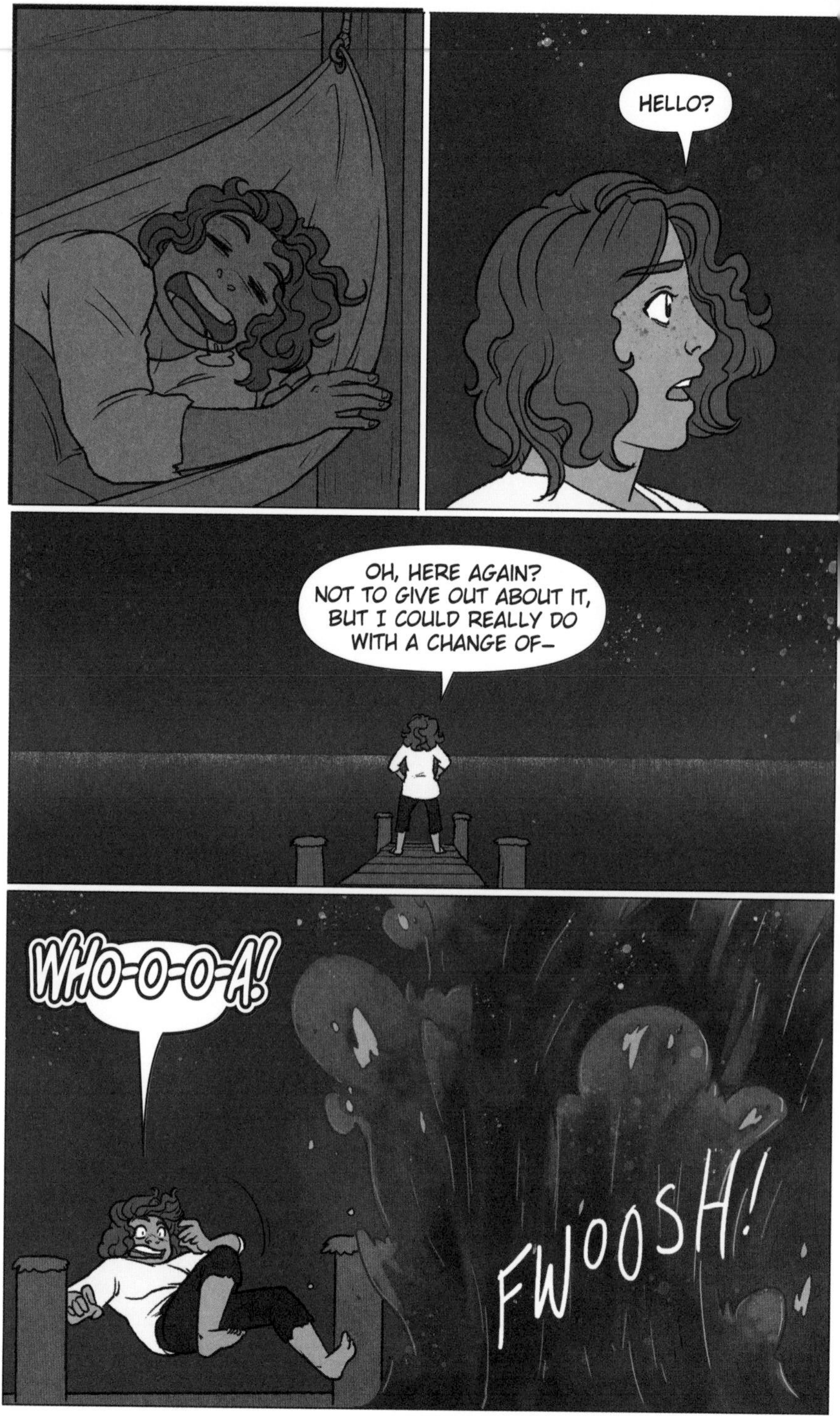
HELLO?
OH, HERE AGAIN? NOT TO GIVE OUT ABOUT IT, BUT I COULD REALLY DO WITH A CHANGE OF–
WHO-O-O-A!
FWOOSH!

shhaaahhh-

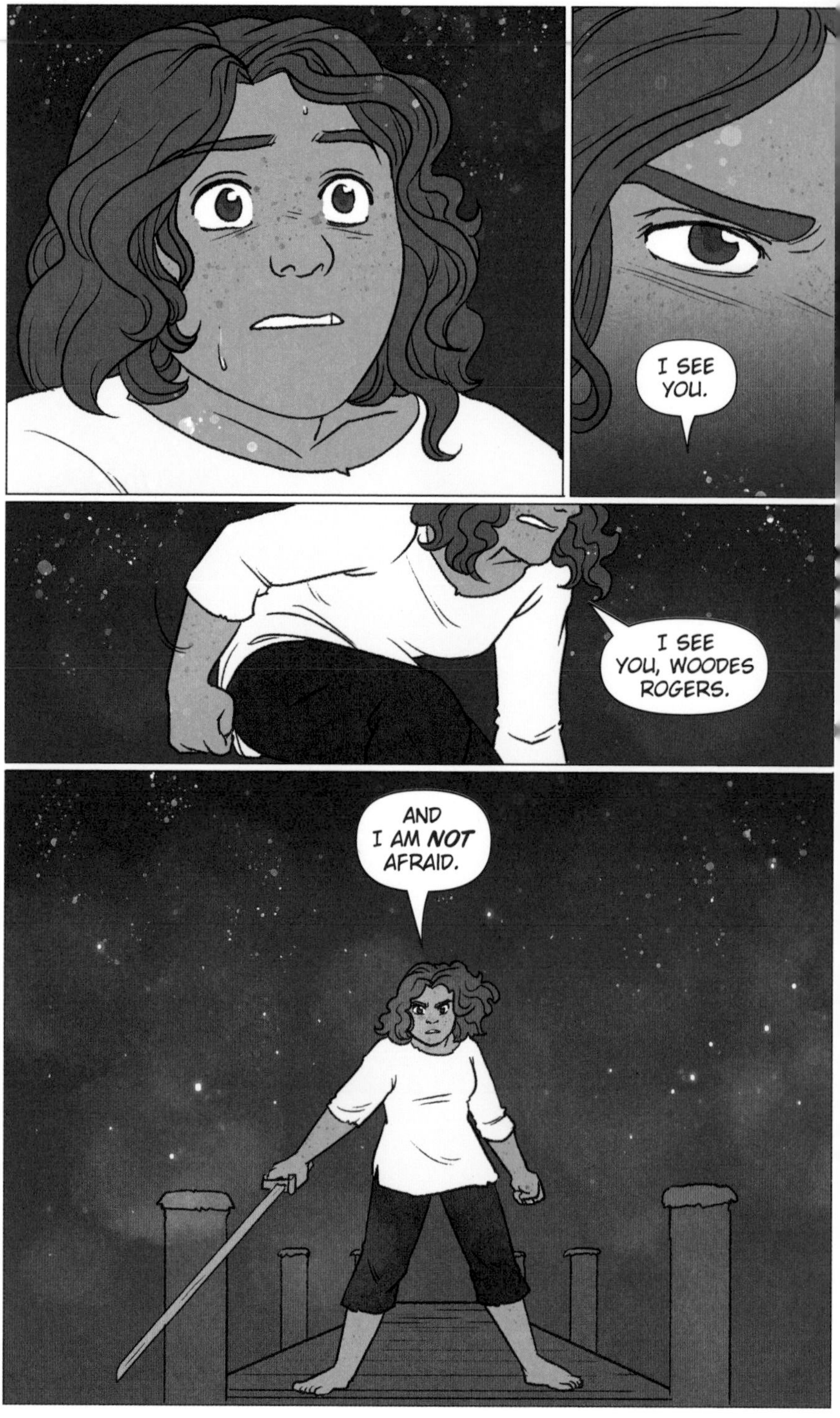
I SEE YOU.
I SEE YOU, WOODES ROGERS.
AND I AM *NOT* AFRAID.

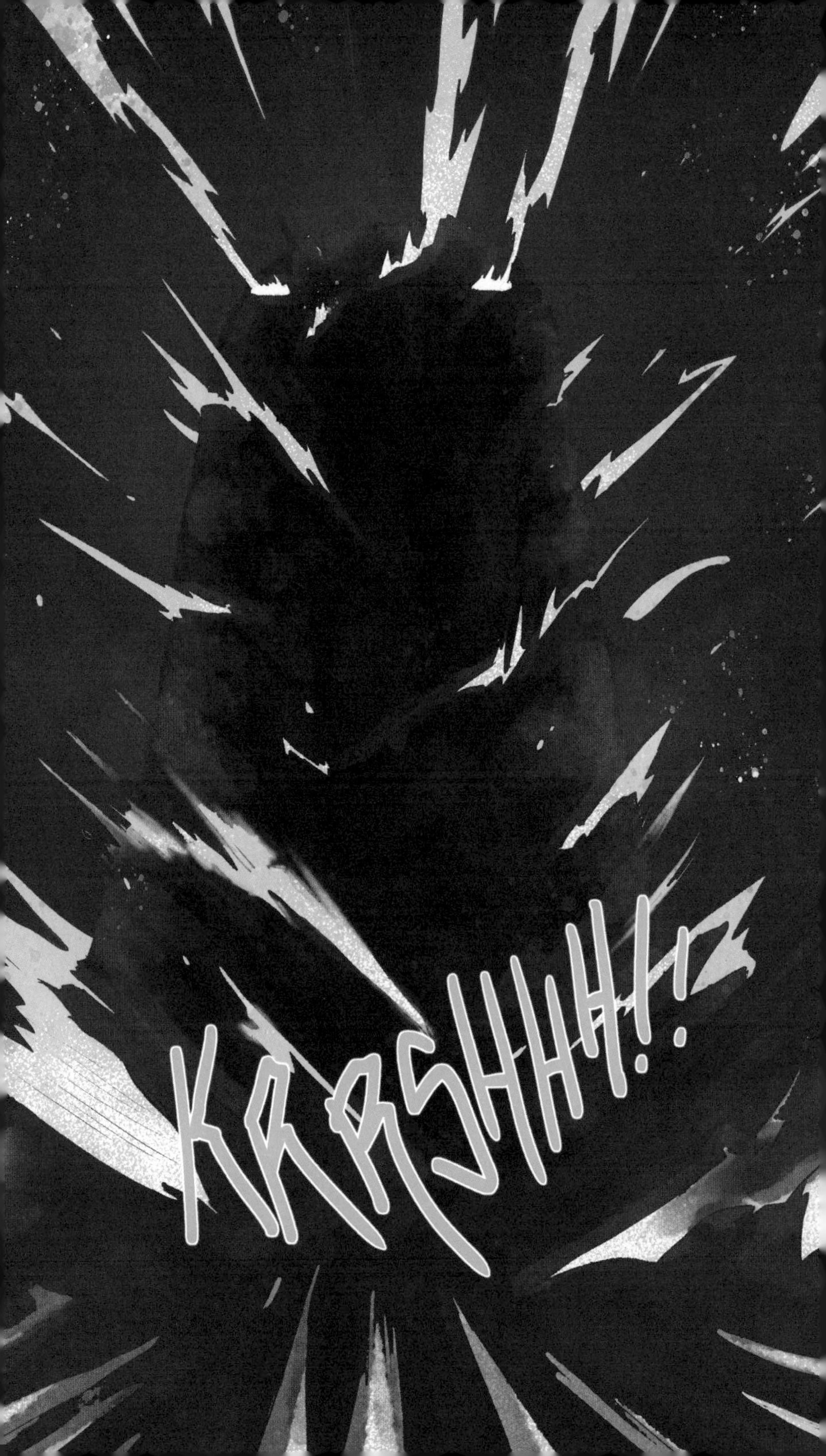
KRRSHHH!!

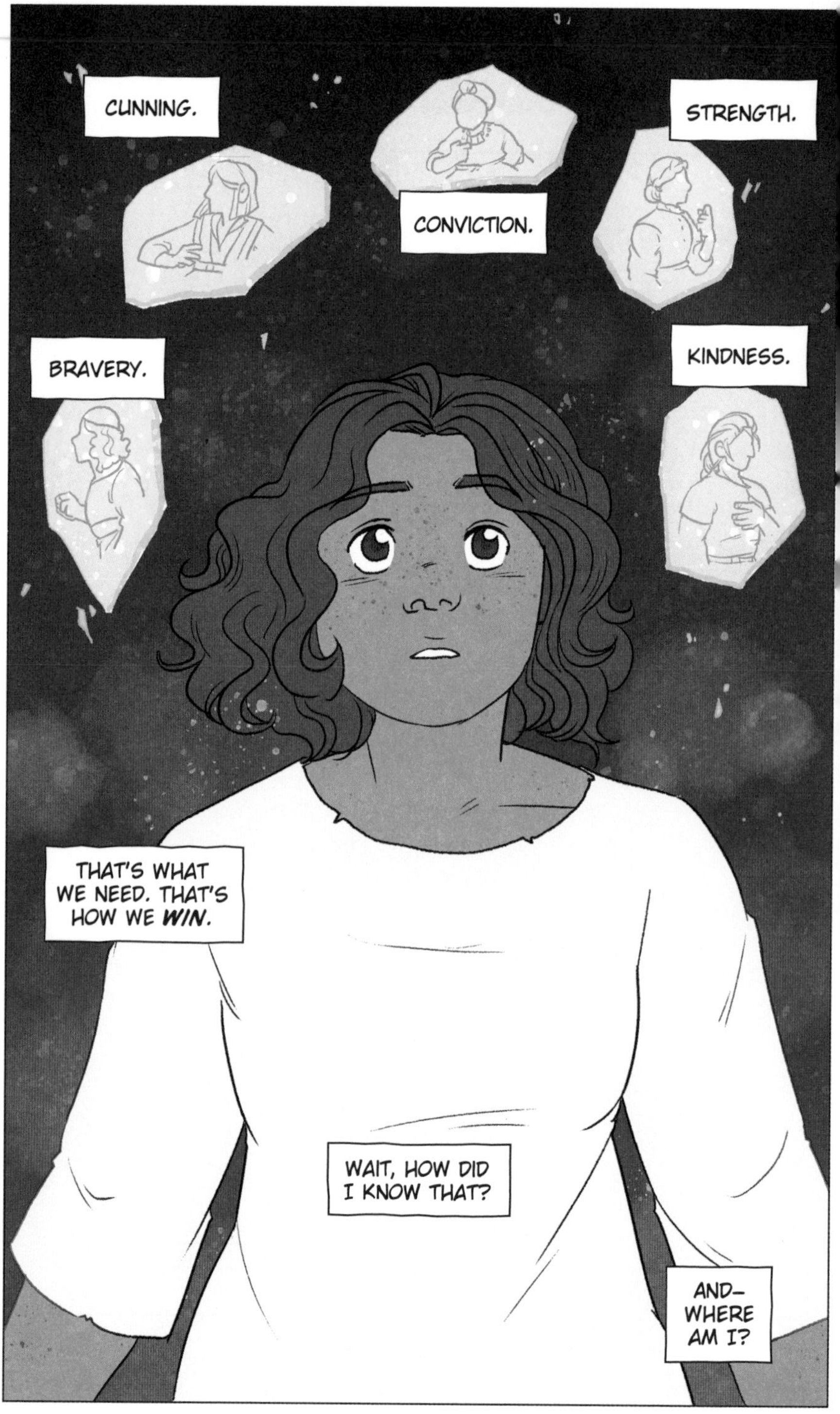
CUNNING.
CONVICTION.
STRENGTH.
BRAVERY.
KINDNESS.
THAT'S WHAT WE NEED. THAT'S HOW WE WIN.
WAIT, HOW DID I KNOW THAT?
AND— WHERE AM I?

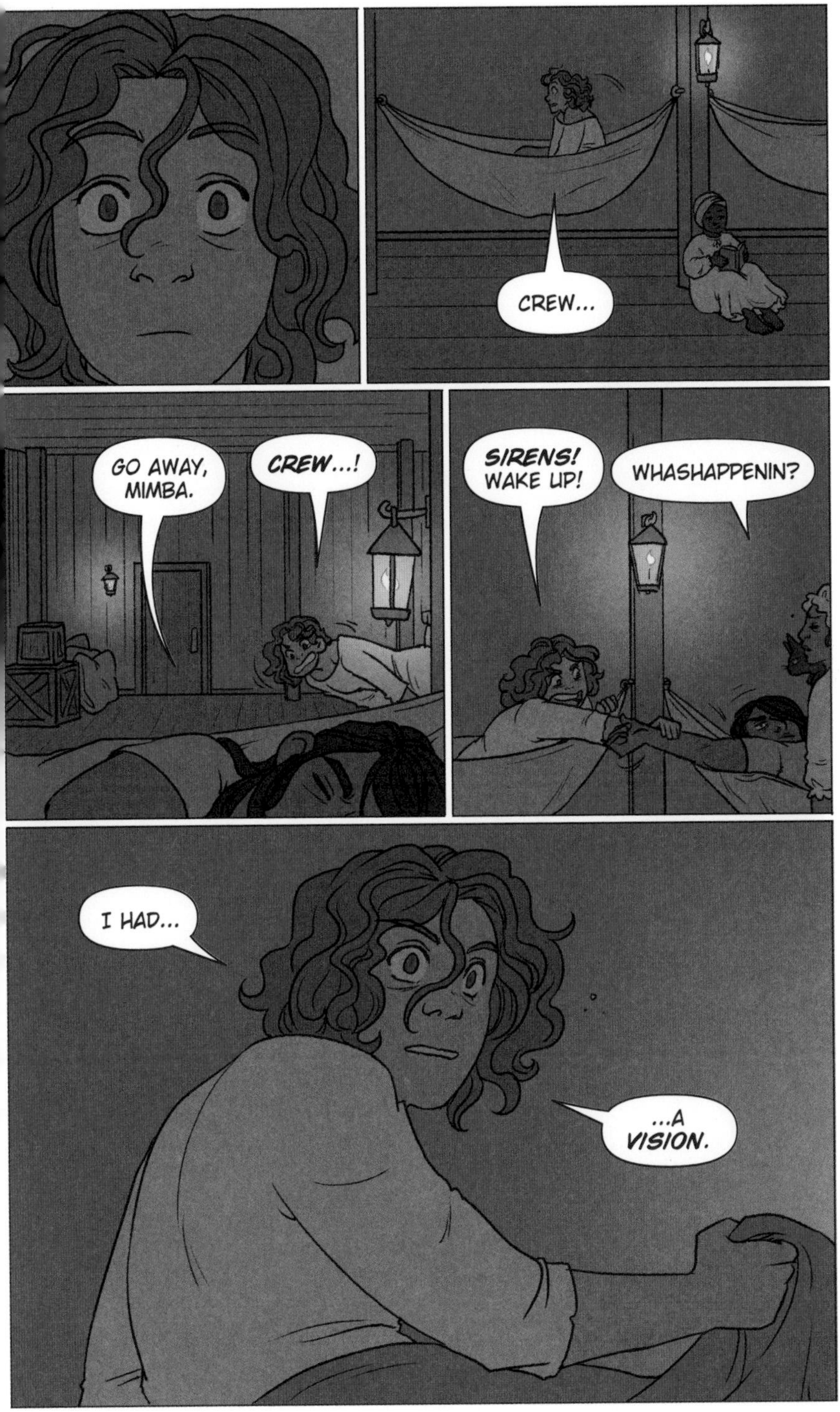
CREW...
GO AWAY, MIMBA.
CREW...!
SIRENS! WAKE UP!
WHASHAPPENIN?
I HAD...
...A VISION.

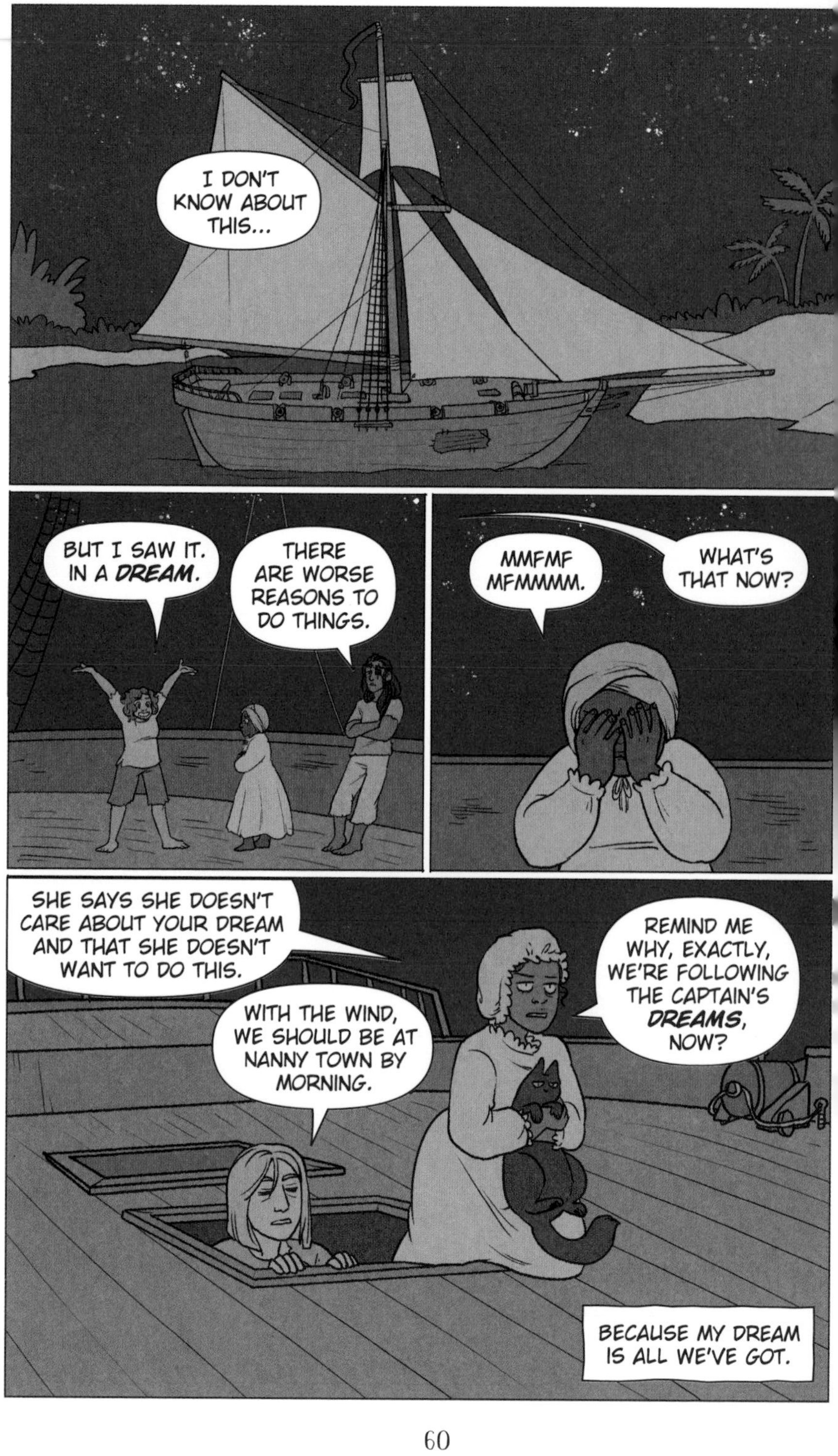
I DON'T KNOW ABOUT THIS...
BUT I SAW IT. IN A **DREAM**.
THERE ARE WORSE REASONS TO DO THINGS.
MMFMF MFMMMM.
WHAT'S THAT NOW?
SHE SAYS SHE DOESN'T CARE ABOUT YOUR DREAM AND THAT SHE DOESN'T WANT TO DO THIS.
WITH THE WIND, WE SHOULD BE AT NANNY TOWN BY MORNING.
REMIND ME WHY, EXACTLY, WE'RE FOLLOWING THE CAPTAIN'S **DREAMS**, NOW?
BECAUSE MY DREAM IS ALL WE'VE GOT.

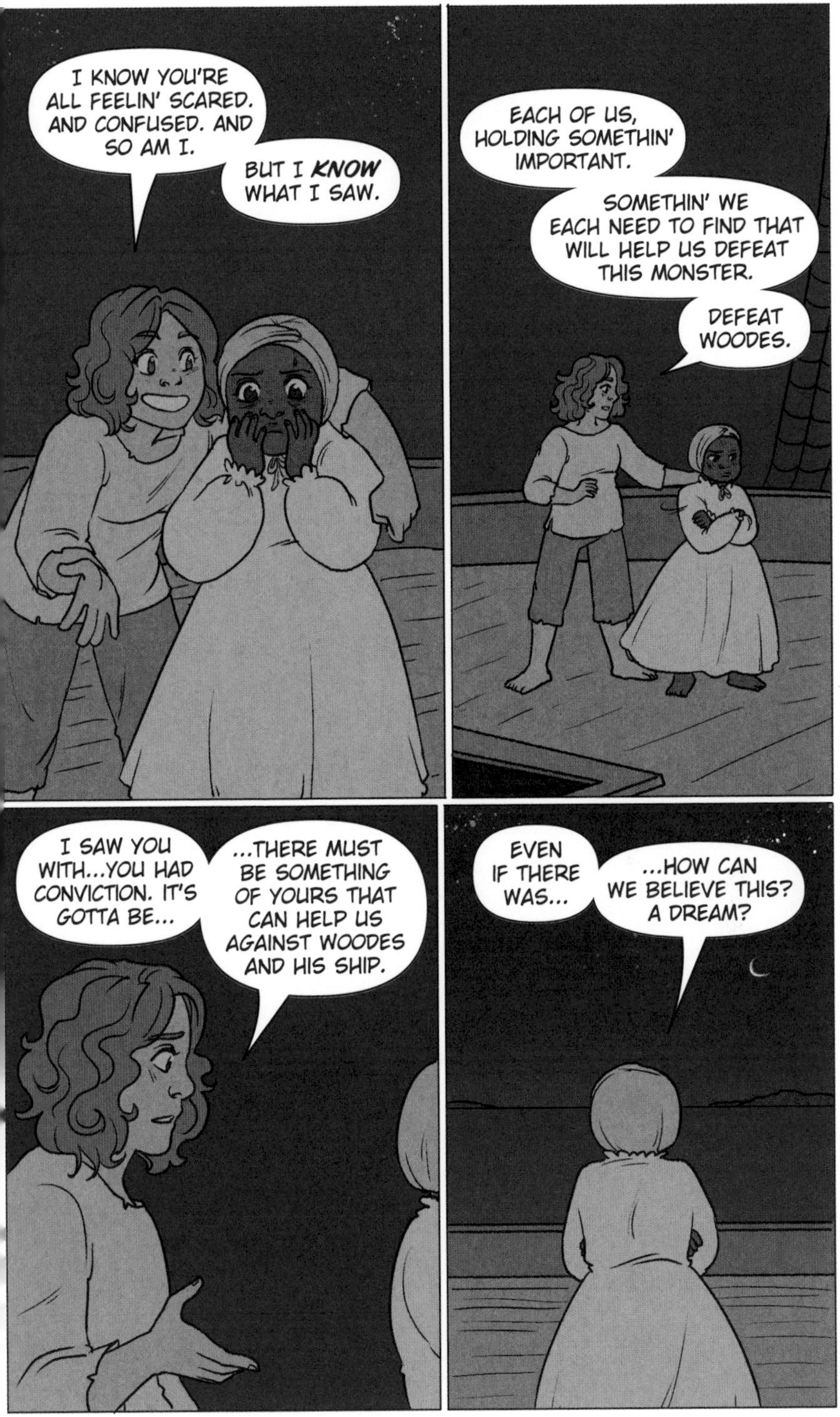
I KNOW YOU'RE ALL FEELIN' SCARED. AND CONFUSED. AND SO AM I.
BUT I ***KNOW*** WHAT I SAW.
EACH OF US, HOLDING SOMETHIN' IMPORTANT.
SOMETHIN' WE EACH NEED TO FIND THAT WILL HELP US DEFEAT THIS MONSTER.
DEFEAT WOODES.
I SAW YOU WITH...YOU HAD CONVICTION. IT'S GOTTA BE...
...THERE MUST BE SOMETHING OF YOURS THAT CAN HELP US AGAINST WOODES AND HIS SHIP.
EVEN IF THERE WAS...
...HOW CAN WE BELIEVE THIS? A DREAM?

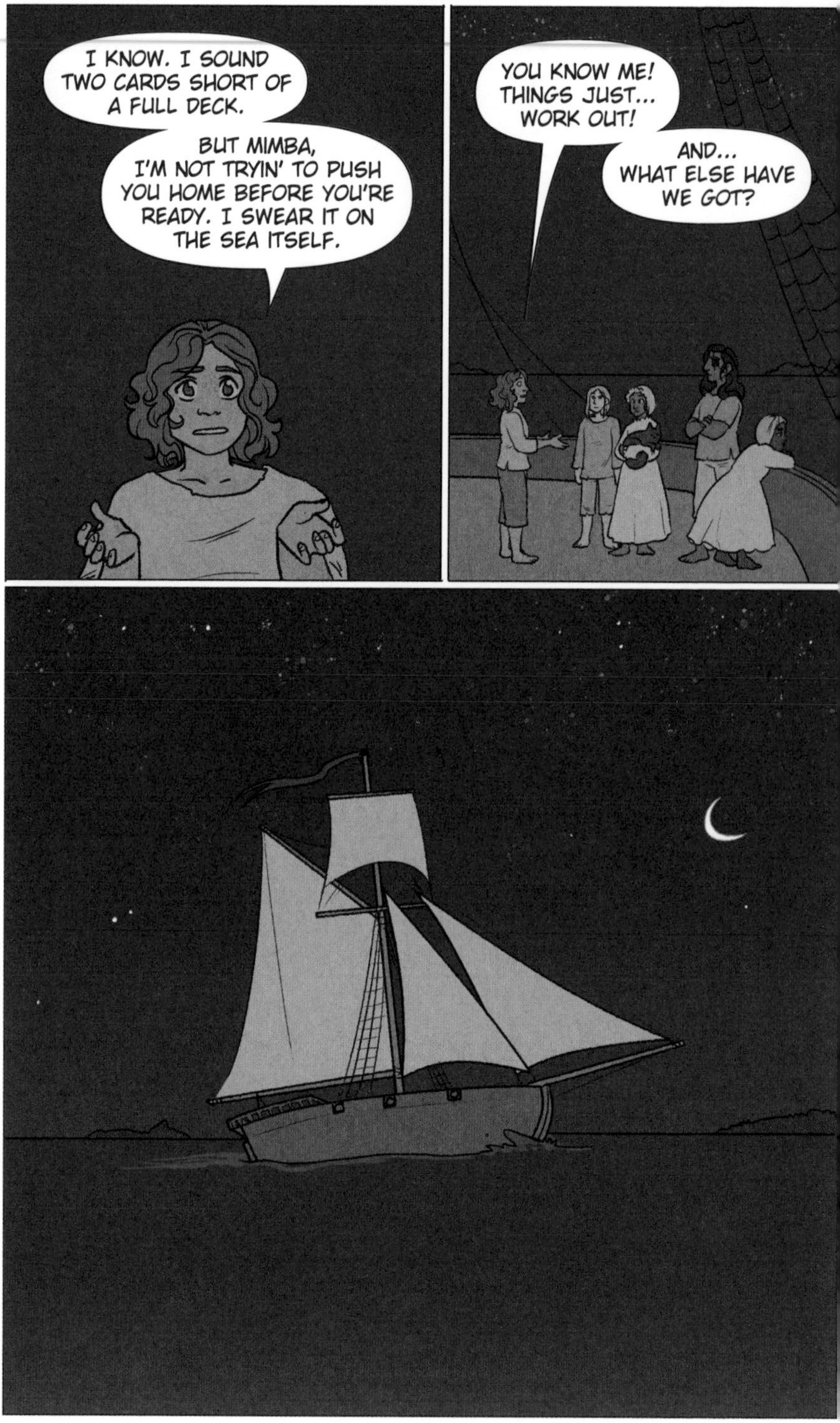
I KNOW. I SOUND TWO CARDS SHORT OF A FULL DECK.
BUT MIMBA, I'M NOT TRYIN' TO PUSH YOU HOME BEFORE YOU'RE READY. I SWEAR IT ON THE SEA ITSELF.
YOU KNOW ME! THINGS JUST... WORK OUT!
AND... WHAT ELSE HAVE WE GOT?

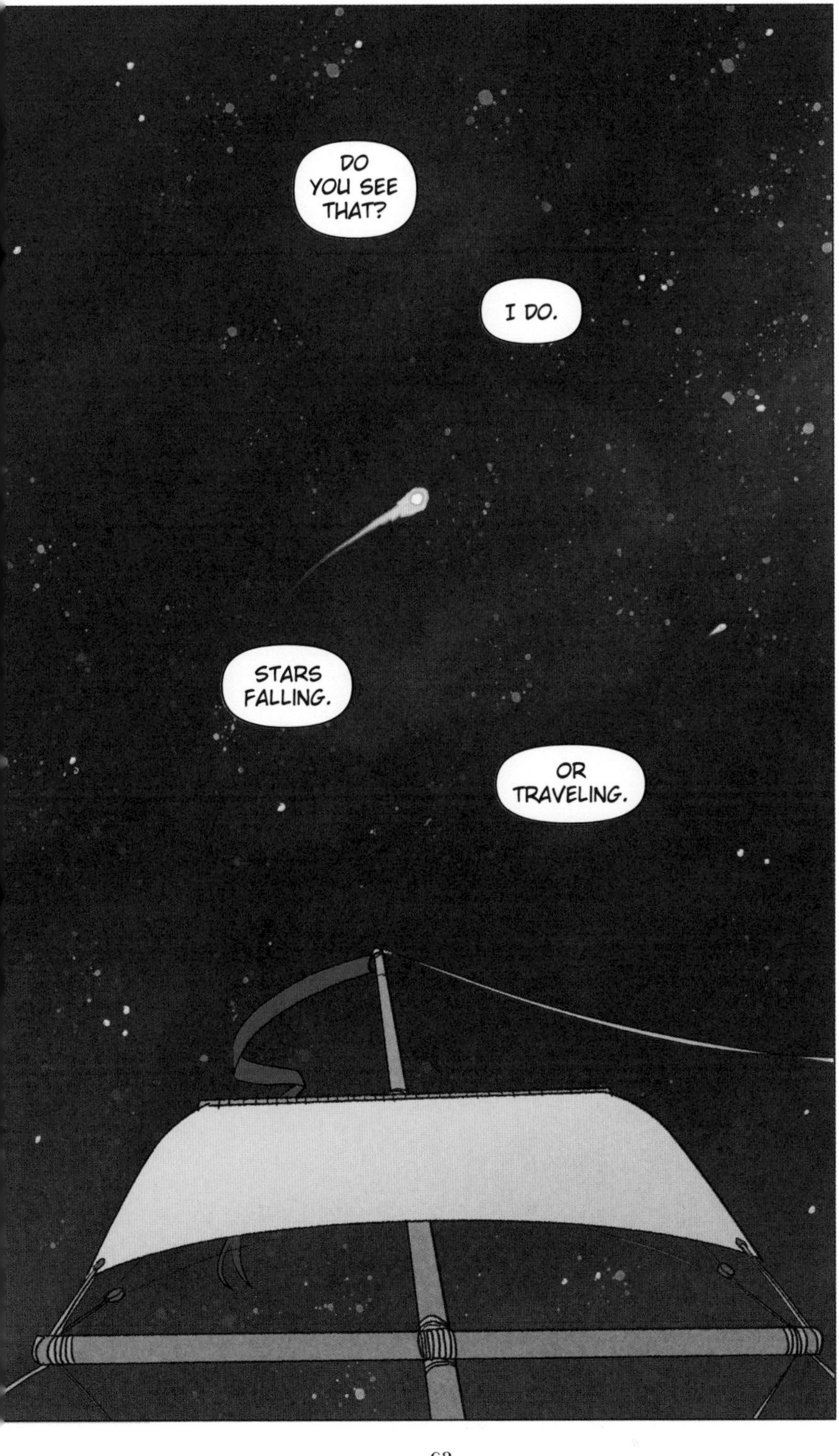
DO YOU SEE THAT?
I DO.
STARS FALLING.
OR TRAVELING.

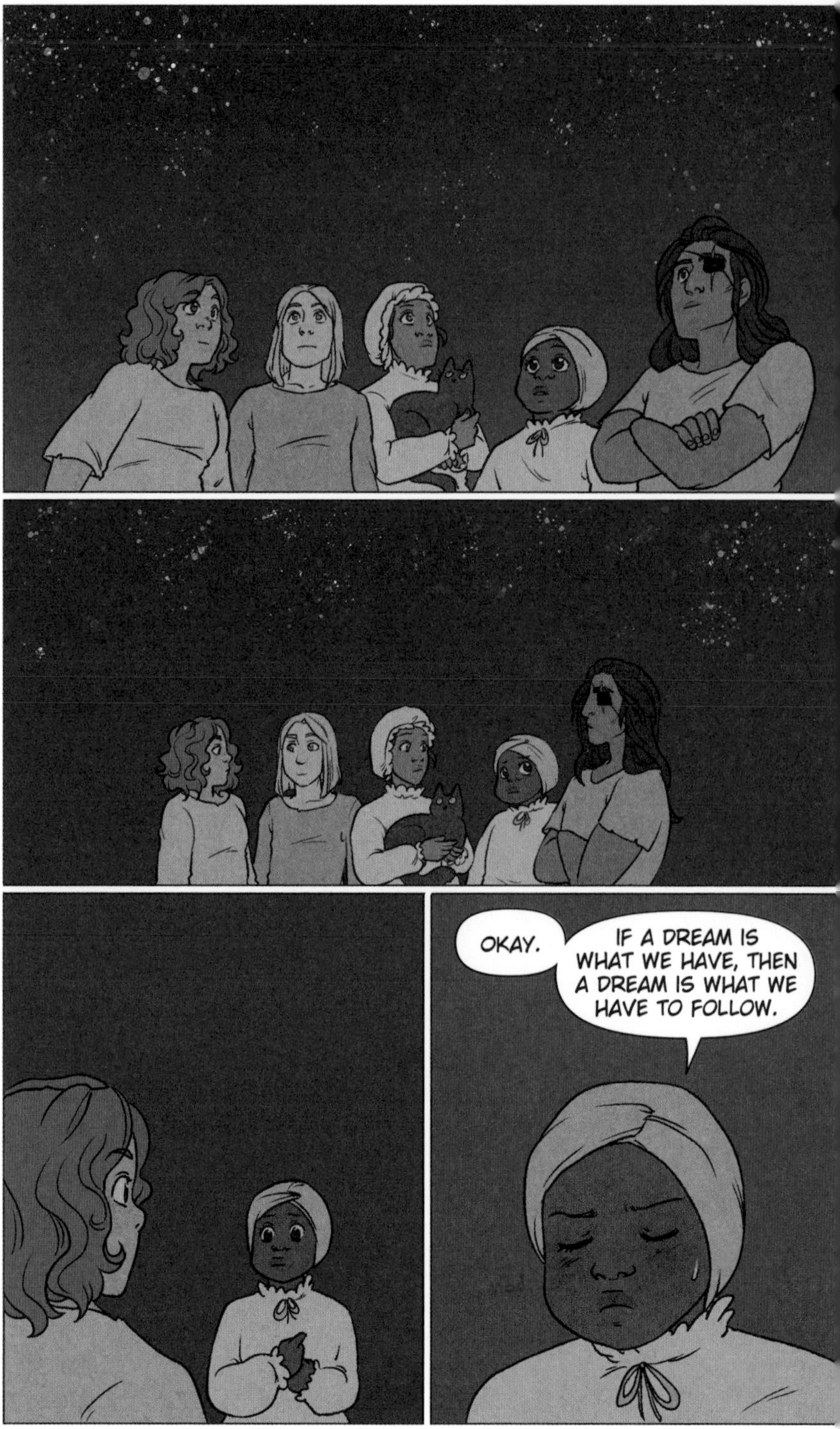
OKAY.
IF A DREAM IS WHAT WE HAVE, THEN A DREAM IS WHAT WE HAVE TO FOLLOW.

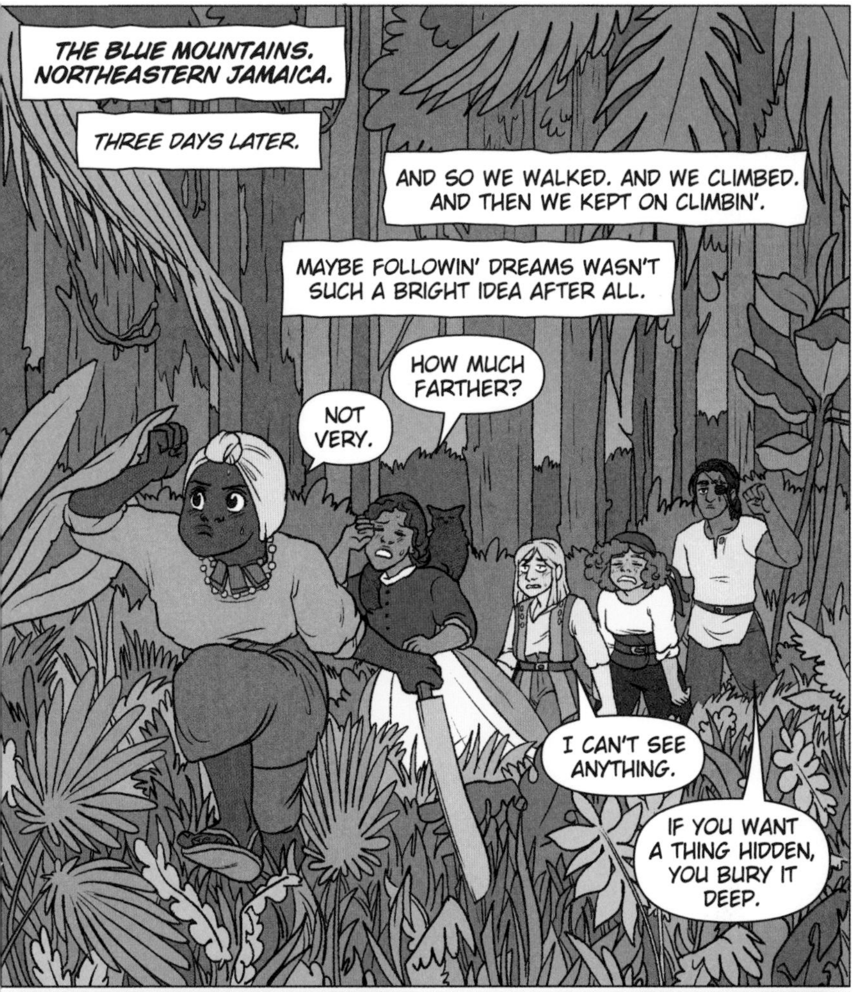
THE BLUE MOUNTAINS. NORTHEASTERN JAMAICA.
THREE DAYS LATER.
AND SO WE WALKED. AND WE CLIMBED. AND THEN WE KEPT ON CLIMBIN'.
MAYBE FOLLOWIN' DREAMS WASN'T SUCH A BRIGHT IDEA AFTER ALL.
HOW MUCH FARTHER?
NOT VERY.
I CAN'T SEE ANYTHING.
IF YOU WANT A THING HIDDEN, YOU BURY IT DEEP.

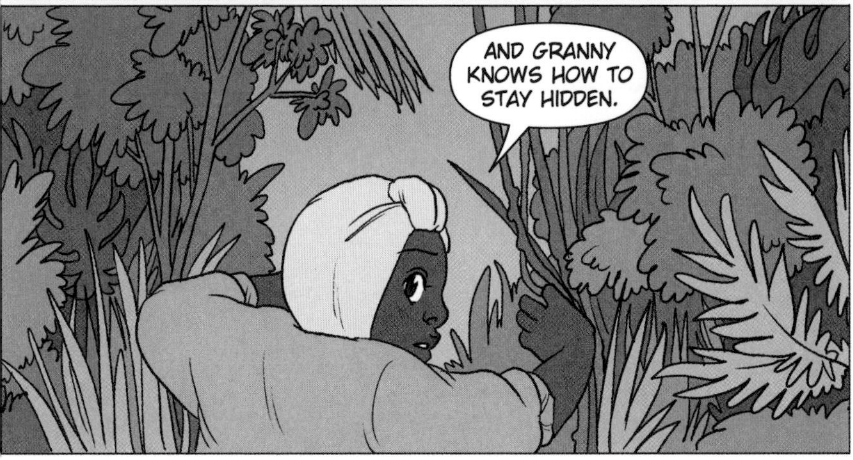
AND GRANNY KNOWS HOW TO STAY HIDDEN.

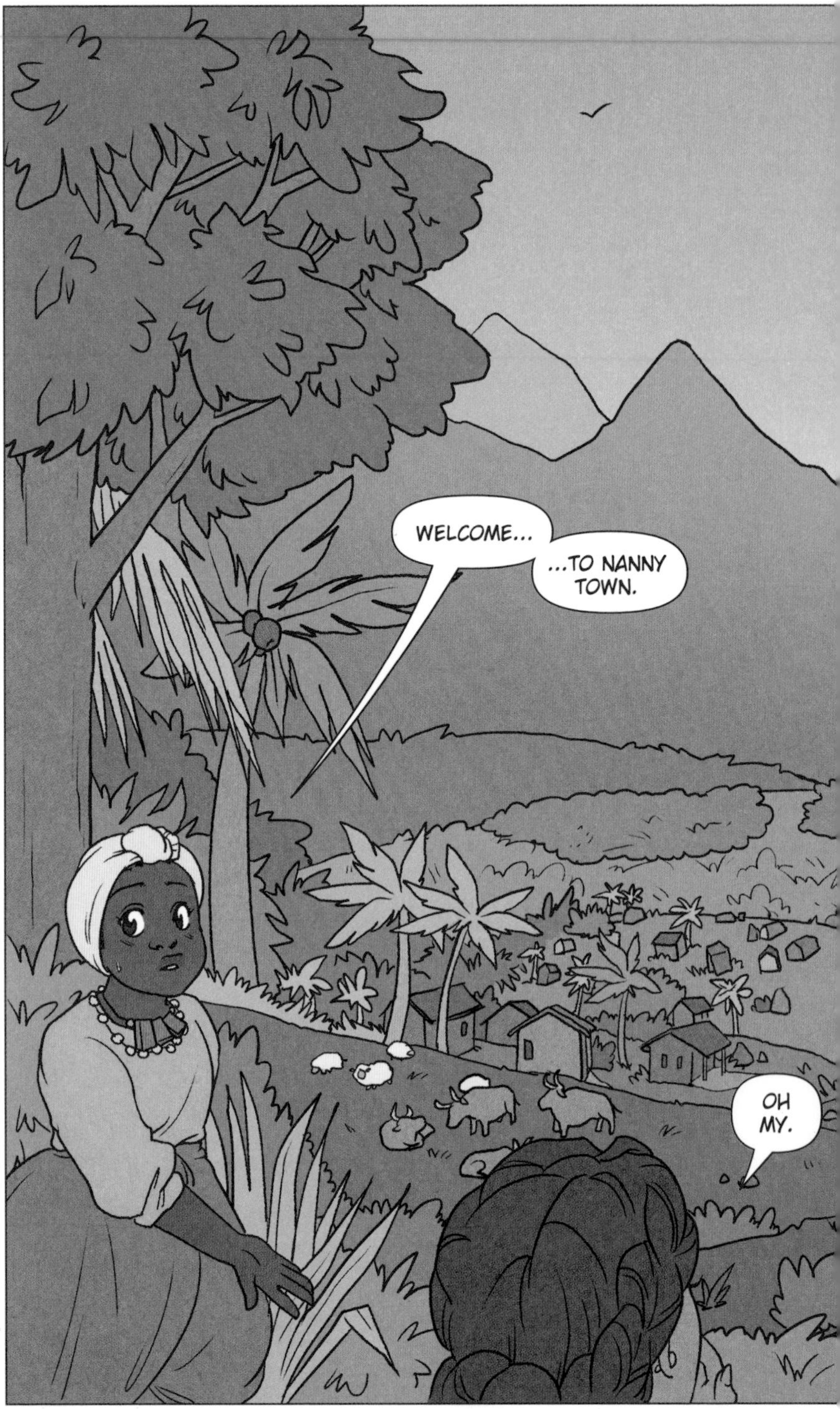
WELCOME...
...TO NANNY TOWN.
OH MY.

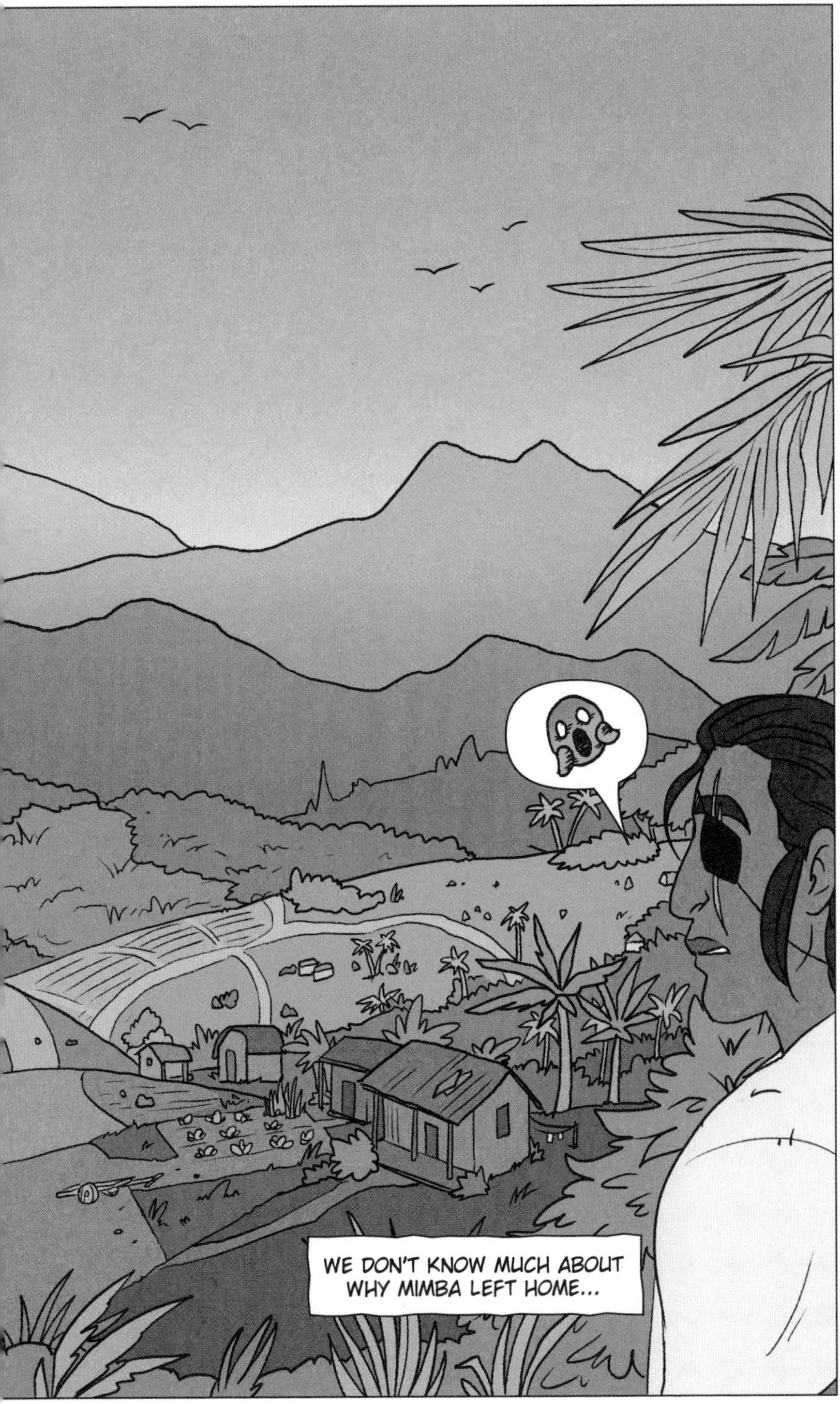
WE DON'T KNOW MUCH ABOUT WHY MIMBA LEFT HOME...

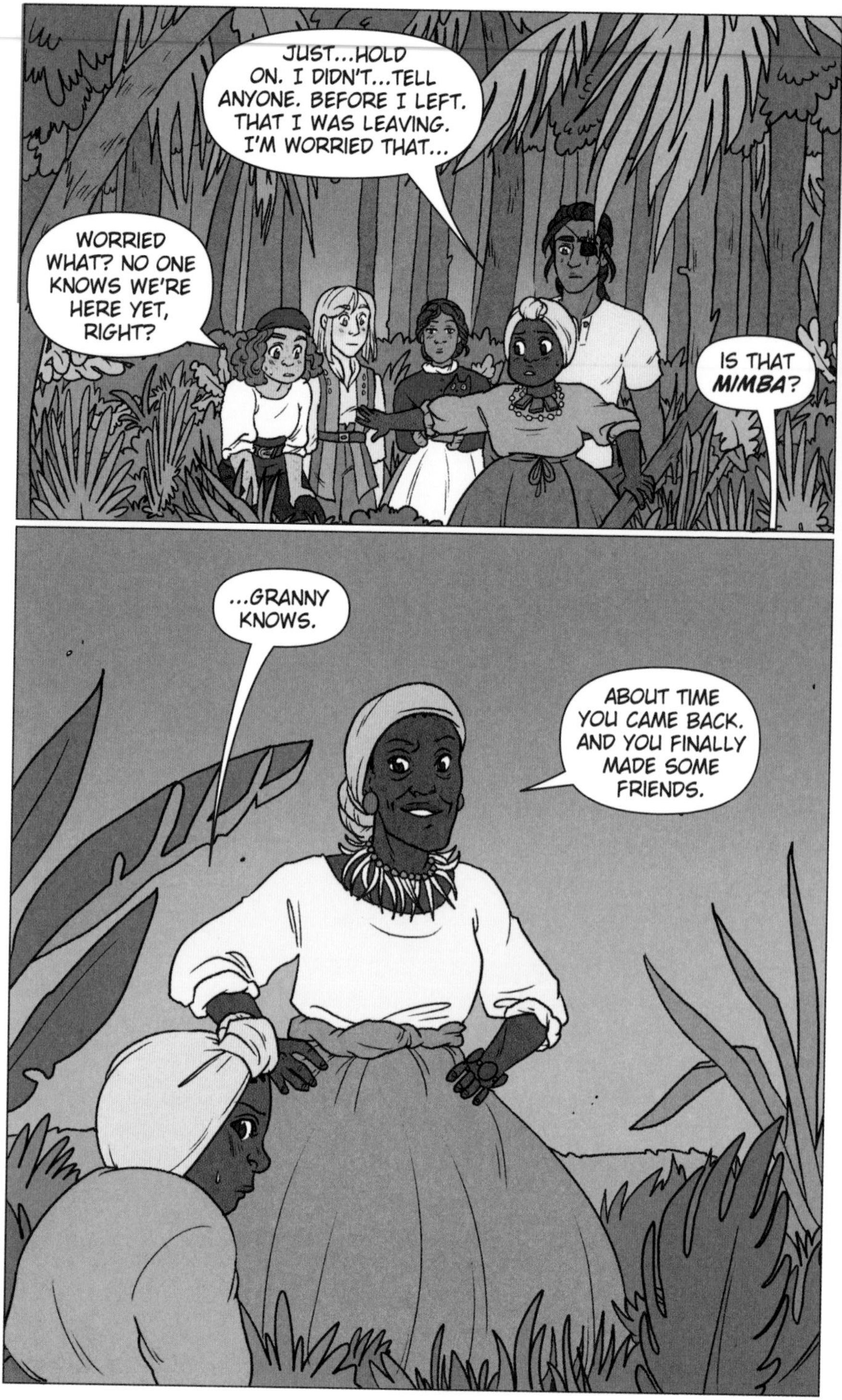
JUST...HOLD ON. I DIDN'T...TELL ANYONE. BEFORE I LEFT. THAT I WAS LEAVING. I'M WORRIED THAT...
WORRIED WHAT? NO ONE KNOWS WE'RE HERE YET, RIGHT?
IS THAT *MIMBA*?
...GRANNY KNOWS.
ABOUT TIME YOU CAME BACK. AND YOU FINALLY MADE SOME FRIENDS.

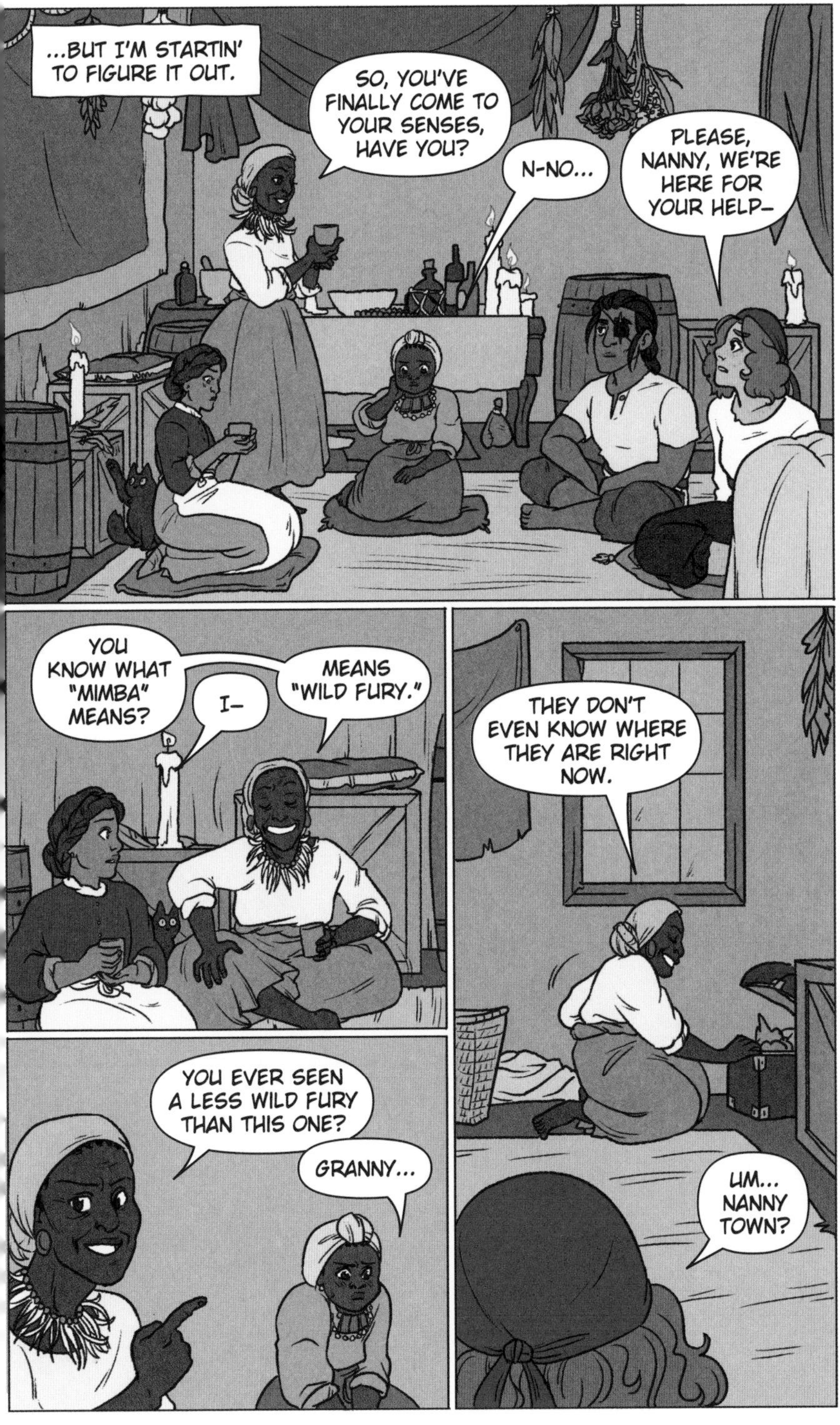
...BUT I'M STARTIN' TO FIGURE IT OUT.
SO, YOU'VE FINALLY COME TO YOUR SENSES, HAVE YOU?
N-NO...
PLEASE, NANNY, WE'RE HERE FOR YOUR HELP–
YOU KNOW WHAT "MIMBA" MEANS?
I–
MEANS "WILD FURY."
YOU EVER SEEN A LESS WILD FURY THAN THIS ONE?
GRANNY...
THEY DON'T EVEN KNOW WHERE THEY ARE RIGHT NOW.
UM... NANNY TOWN?

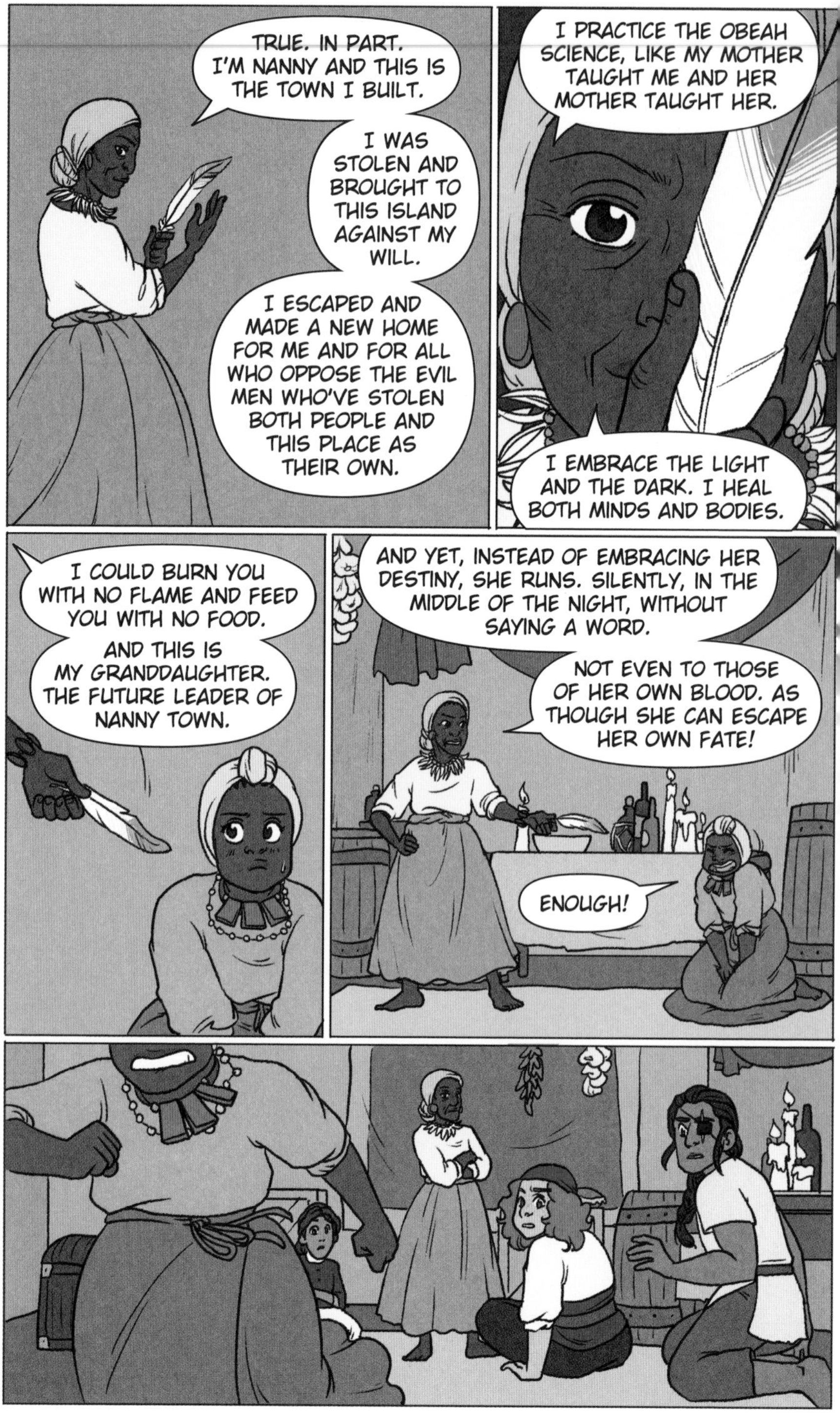
TRUE. IN PART. I'M NANNY AND THIS IS THE TOWN I BUILT.
I WAS STOLEN AND BROUGHT TO THIS ISLAND AGAINST MY WILL.
I ESCAPED AND MADE A NEW HOME FOR ME AND FOR ALL WHO OPPOSE THE EVIL MEN WHO'VE STOLEN BOTH PEOPLE AND THIS PLACE AS THEIR OWN.
I PRACTICE THE OBEAH SCIENCE, LIKE MY MOTHER TAUGHT ME AND HER MOTHER TAUGHT HER.
I EMBRACE THE LIGHT AND THE DARK. I HEAL BOTH MINDS AND BODIES.
I COULD BURN YOU WITH NO FLAME AND FEED YOU WITH NO FOOD.
AND THIS IS MY GRANDDAUGHTER. THE FUTURE LEADER OF NANNY TOWN.
AND YET, INSTEAD OF EMBRACING HER DESTINY, SHE RUNS. SILENTLY, IN THE MIDDLE OF THE NIGHT, WITHOUT SAYING A WORD.
NOT EVEN TO THOSE OF HER OWN BLOOD. AS THOUGH SHE CAN ESCAPE HER OWN FATE!
ENOUGH!

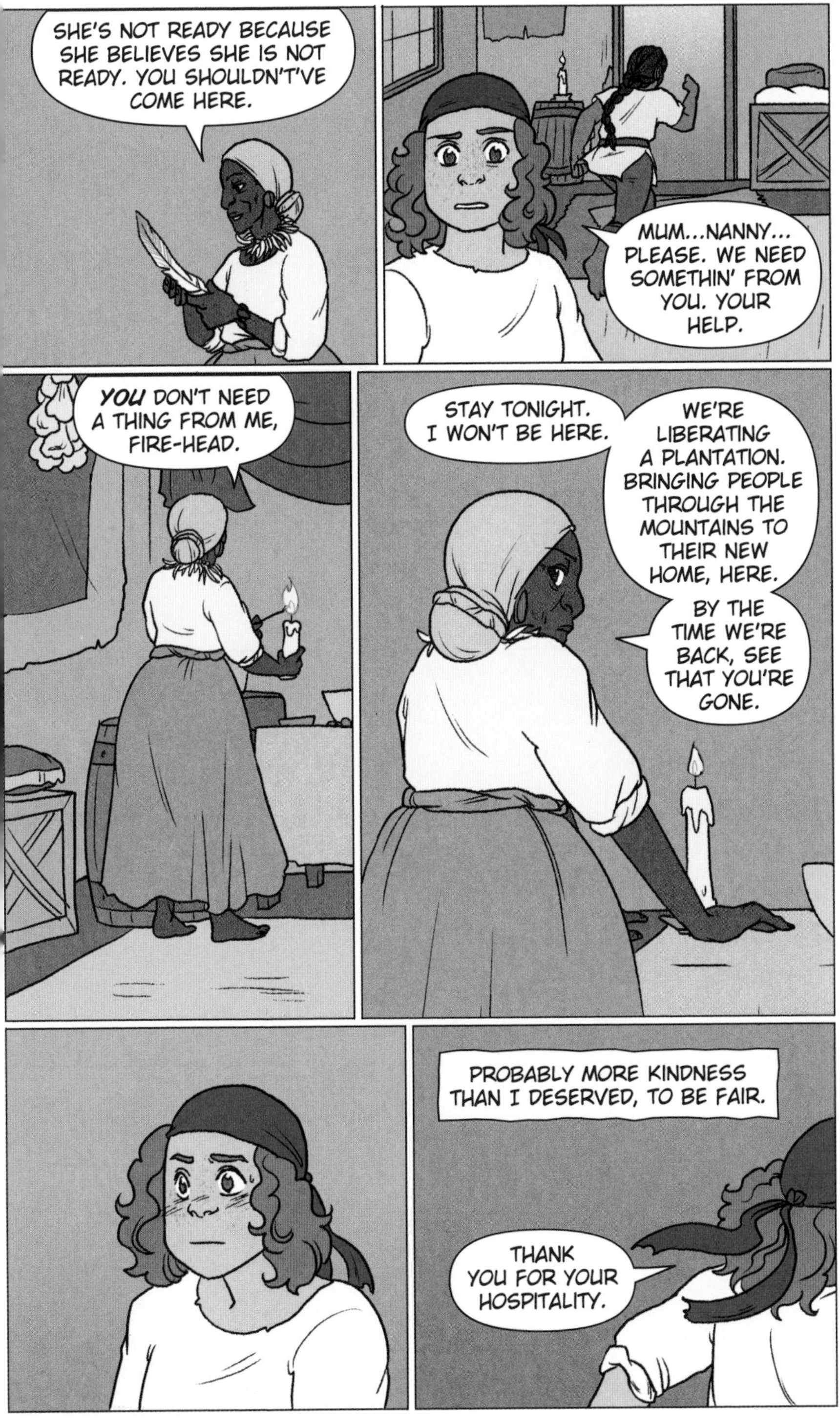
SHE'S NOT READY BECAUSE SHE BELIEVES SHE IS NOT READY. YOU SHOULDN'T'VE COME HERE.
MUM...NANNY... PLEASE. WE NEED SOMETHIN' FROM YOU. YOUR HELP.
YOU DON'T NEED A THING FROM ME, FIRE-HEAD.
STAY TONIGHT. I WON'T BE HERE.
WE'RE LIBERATING A PLANTATION. BRINGING PEOPLE THROUGH THE MOUNTAINS TO THEIR NEW HOME, HERE.
BY THE TIME WE'RE BACK, SEE THAT YOU'RE GONE.
PROBABLY MORE KINDNESS THAN I DESERVED, TO BE FAIR.
THANK YOU FOR YOUR HOSPITALITY.

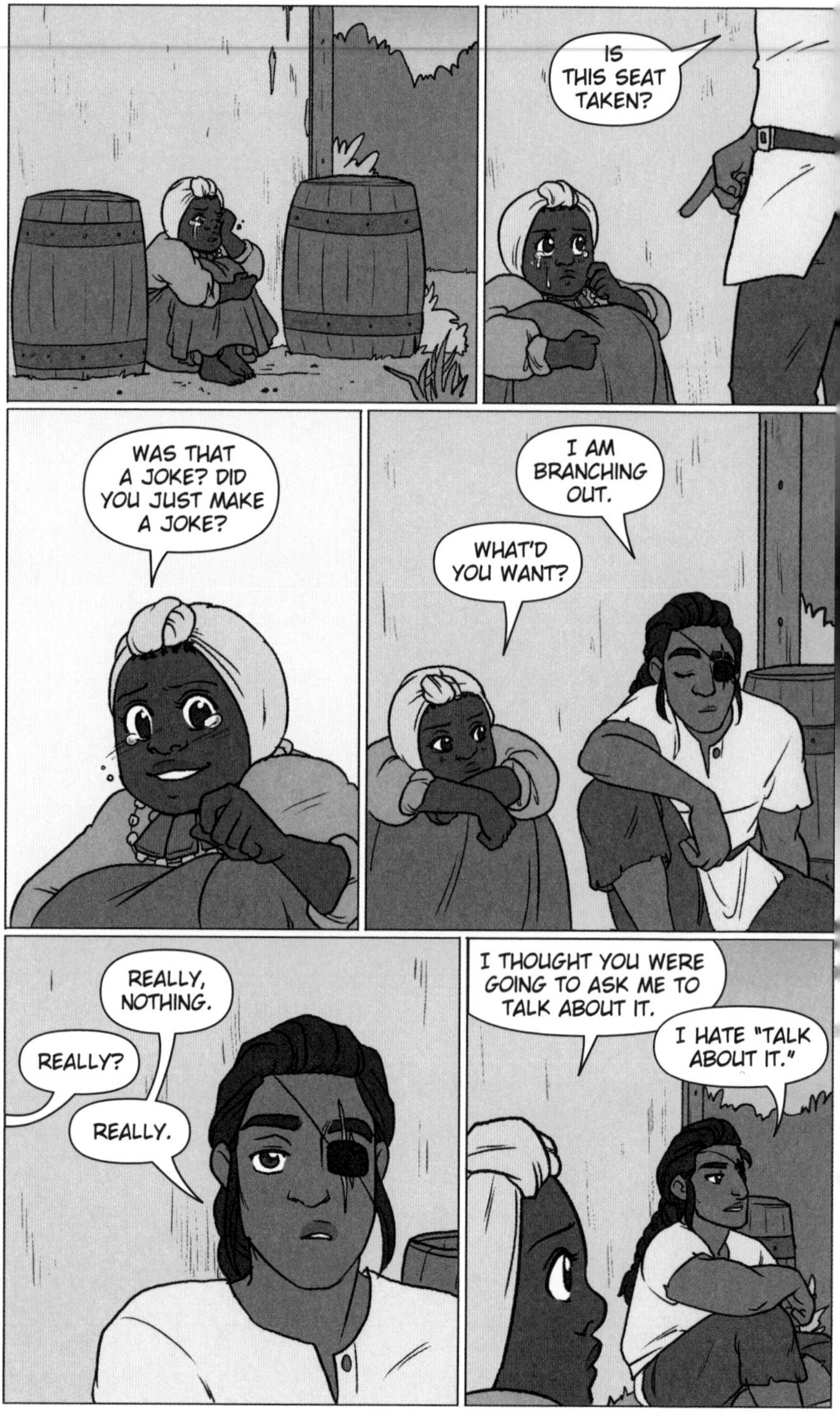
IS THIS SEAT TAKEN?
WAS THAT A JOKE? DID YOU JUST MAKE A JOKE?
I AM BRANCHING OUT.
WHAT'D YOU WANT?
REALLY, NOTHING.
REALLY?
REALLY.
I THOUGHT YOU WERE GOING TO ASK ME TO TALK ABOUT IT.
I HATE "TALK ABOUT IT."

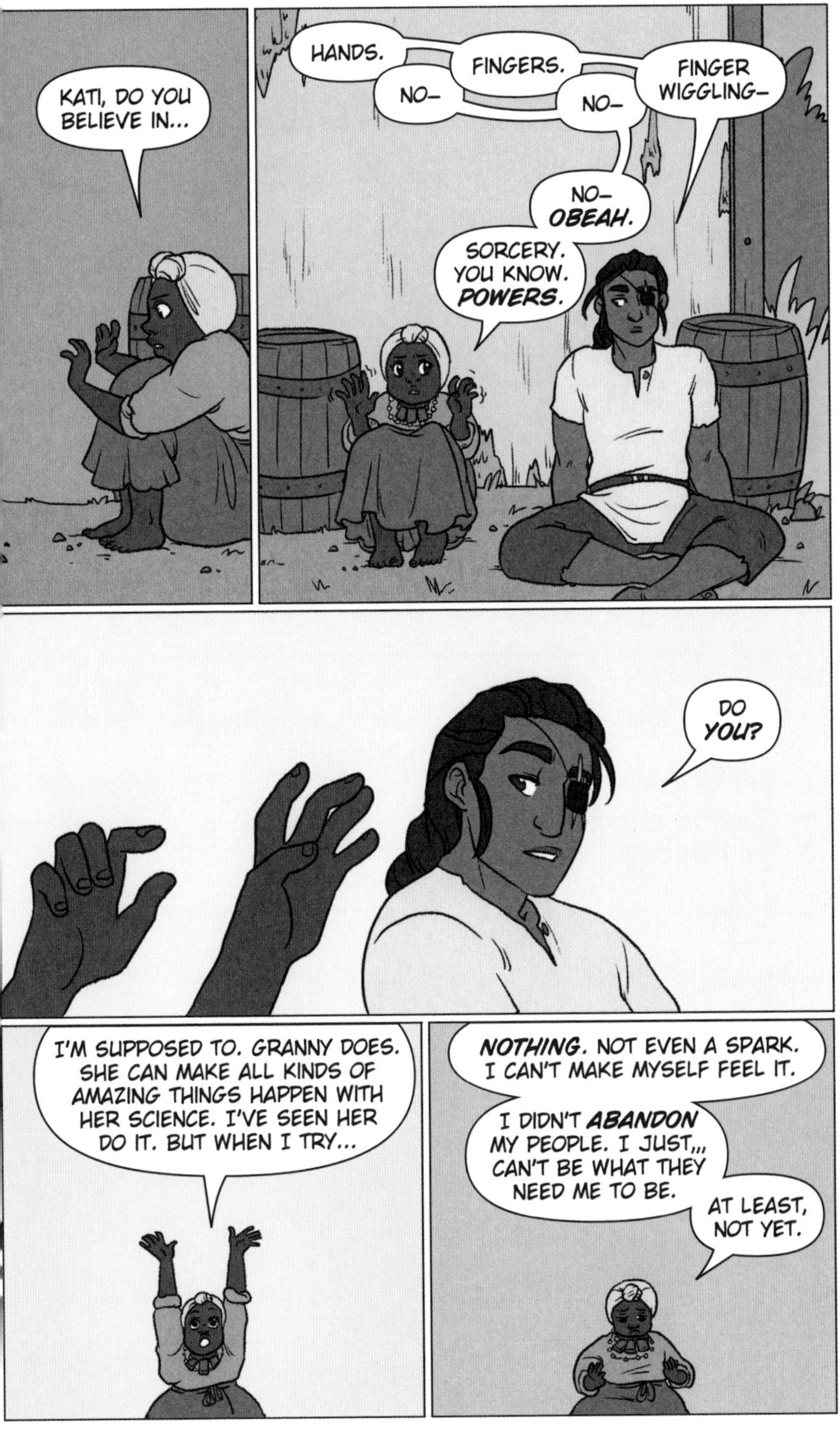
KATI, DO YOU BELIEVE IN...
HANDS.
NO-
FINGERS.
NO-
FINGER WIGGLING-
NO-
OBEAH.
SORCERY. YOU KNOW. POWERS.
DO YOU?
I'M SUPPOSED TO. GRANNY DOES. SHE CAN MAKE ALL KINDS OF AMAZING THINGS HAPPEN WITH HER SCIENCE. I'VE SEEN HER DO IT. BUT WHEN I TRY...
NOTHING. NOT EVEN A SPARK. I CAN'T MAKE MYSELF FEEL IT.
I DIDN'T ABANDON MY PEOPLE. I JUST,,, CAN'T BE WHAT THEY NEED ME TO BE.
AT LEAST, NOT YET.

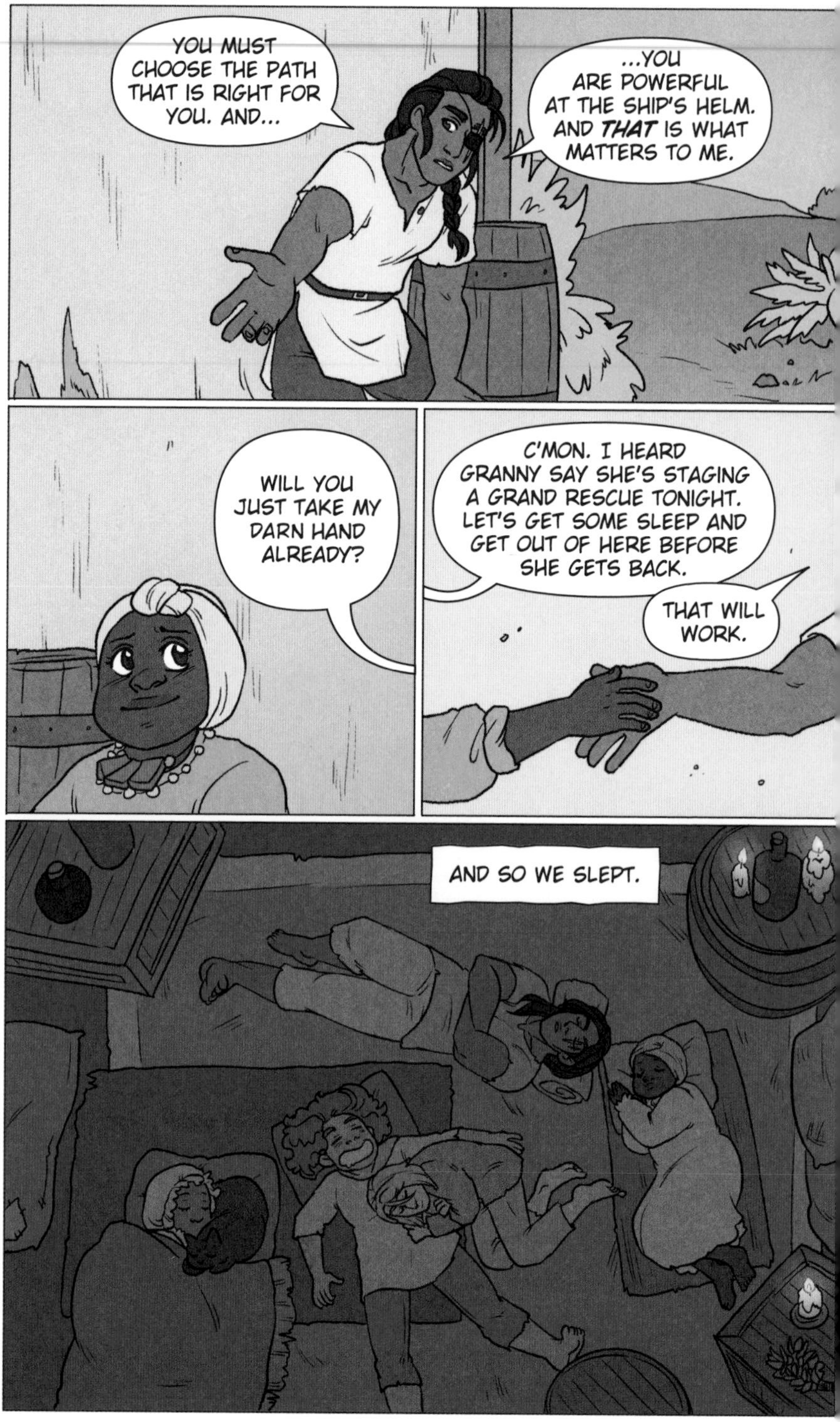
YOU MUST CHOOSE THE PATH THAT IS RIGHT FOR YOU. AND...
...YOU ARE POWERFUL AT THE SHIP'S HELM. AND *THAT* IS WHAT MATTERS TO ME.
WILL YOU JUST TAKE MY DARN HAND ALREADY?
C'MON. I HEARD GRANNY SAY SHE'S STAGING A GRAND RESCUE TONIGHT. LET'S GET SOME SLEEP AND GET OUT OF HERE BEFORE SHE GETS BACK.
THAT WILL WORK.
AND SO WE SLEPT.

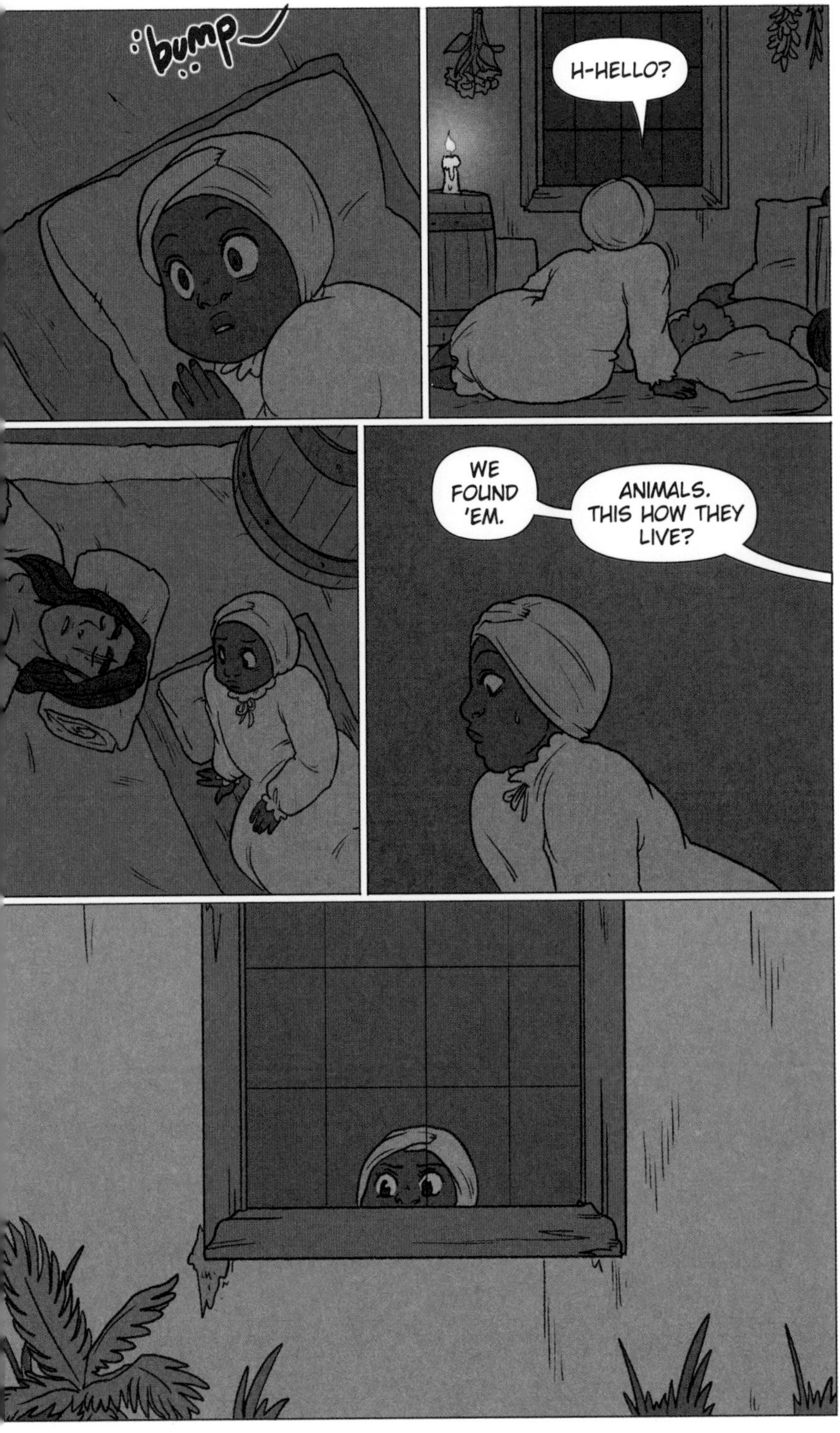
bump
H-HELLO?
WE FOUND 'EM.
ANIMALS. THIS HOW THEY LIVE?

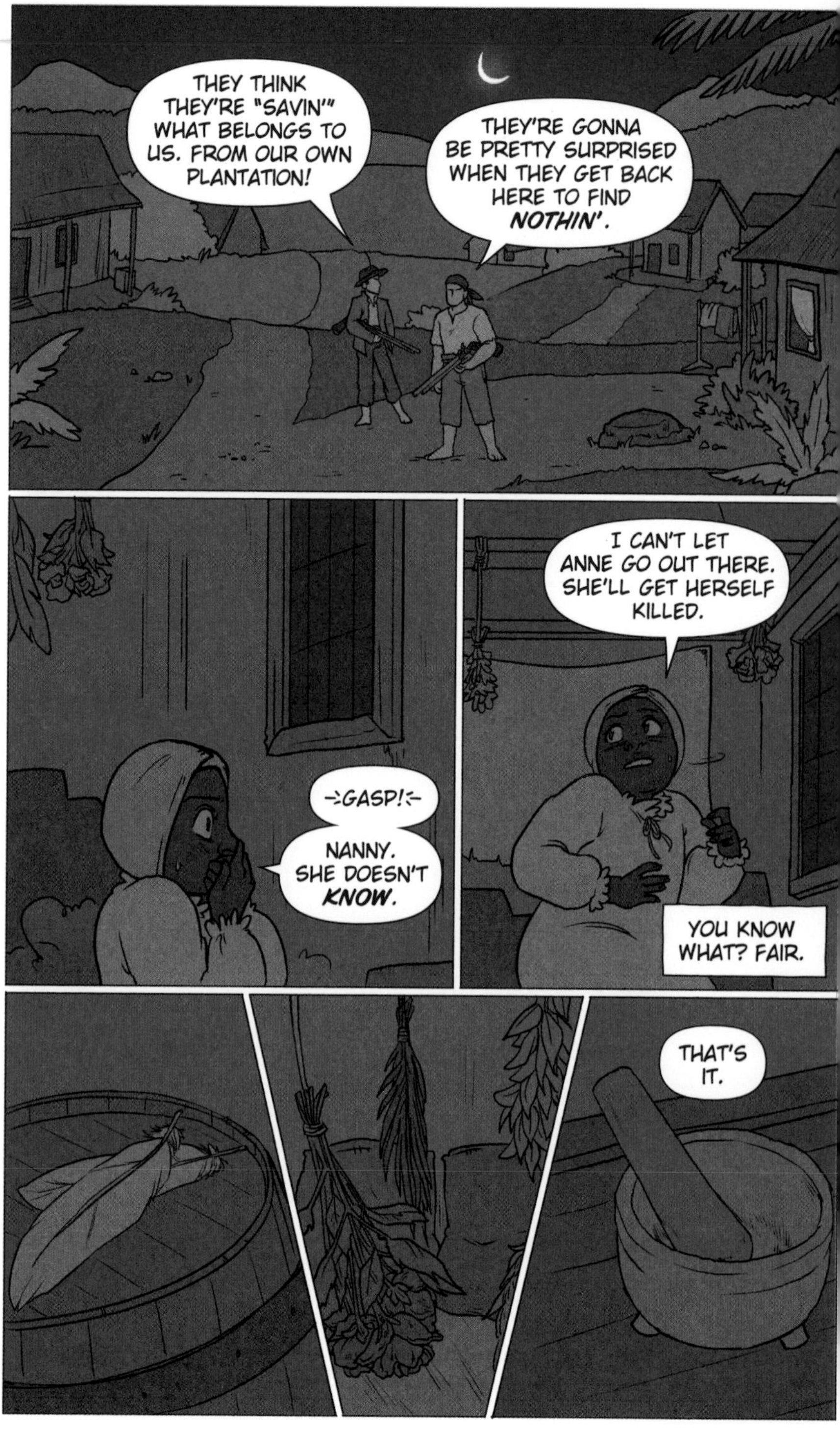
THEY THINK THEY'RE "SAVIN'" WHAT BELONGS TO US. FROM OUR OWN PLANTATION!
THEY'RE GONNA BE PRETTY SURPRISED WHEN THEY GET BACK HERE TO FIND NOTHIN'.
GASP!
NANNY. SHE DOESN'T KNOW.
I CAN'T LET ANNE GO OUT THERE. SHE'LL GET HERSELF KILLED.
YOU KNOW WHAT? FAIR.
THAT'S IT.

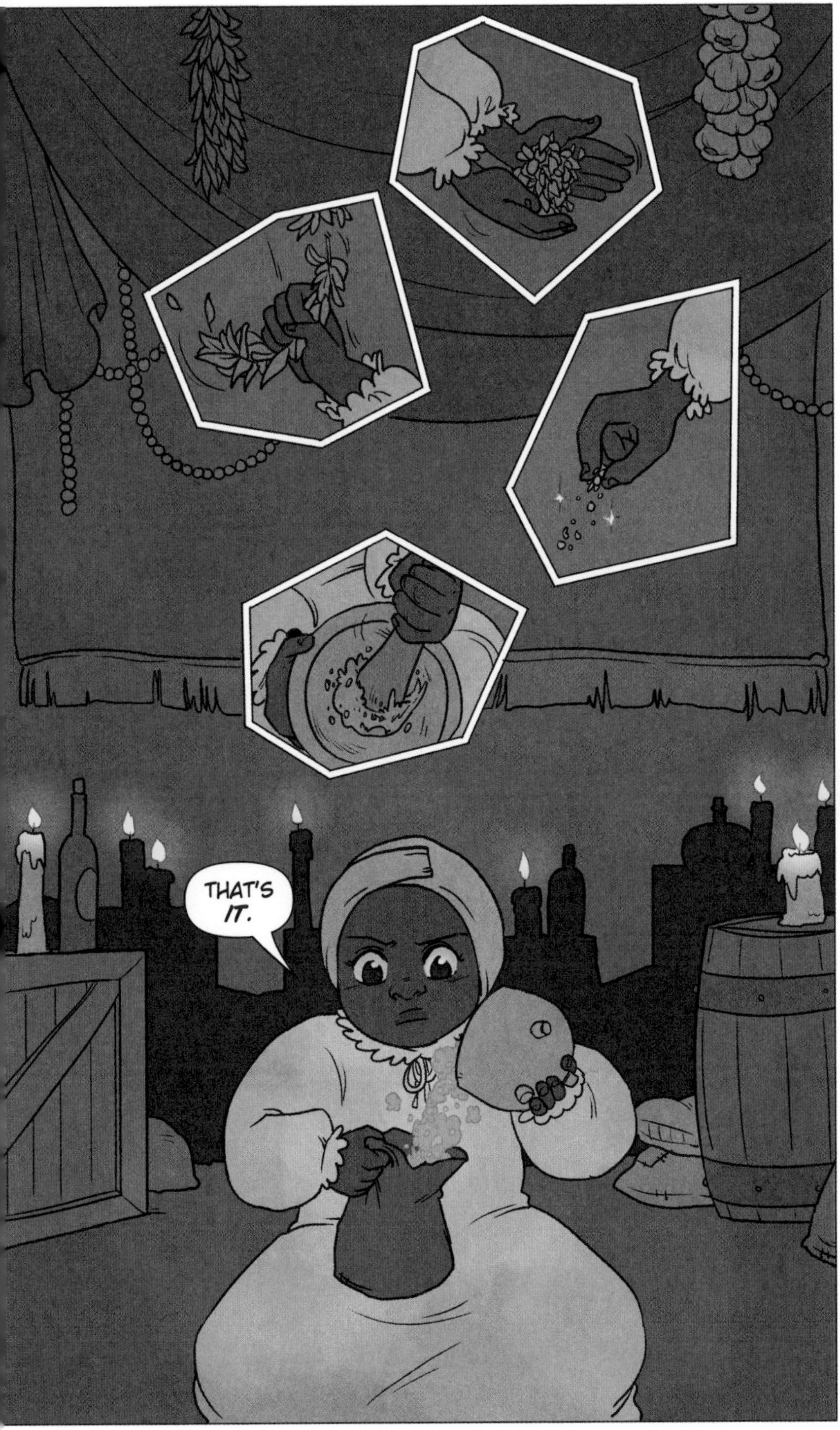
THAT'S IT.

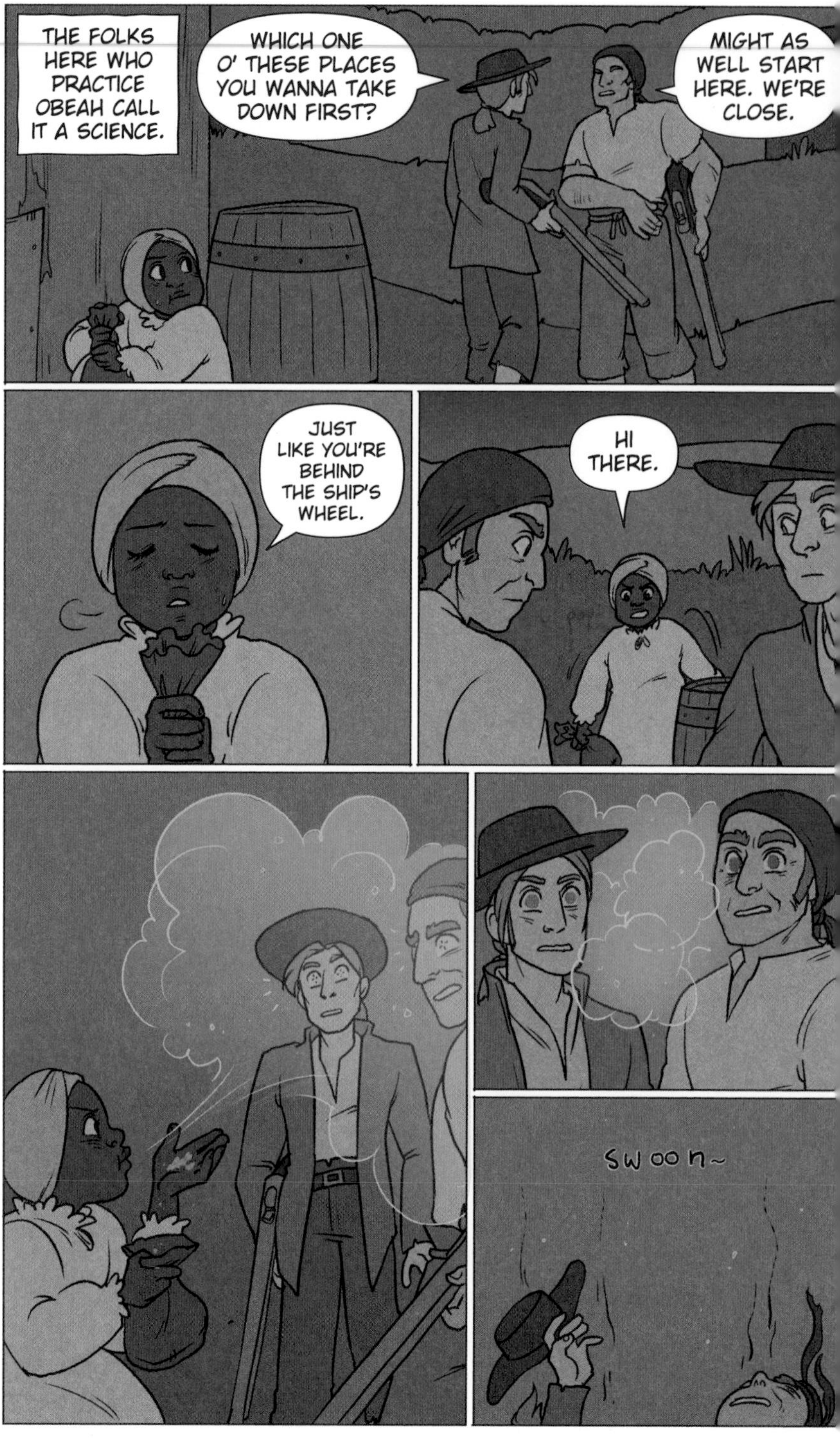
THE FOLKS HERE WHO PRACTICE OBEAH CALL IT A SCIENCE.
WHICH ONE O' THESE PLACES YOU WANNA TAKE DOWN FIRST?
MIGHT AS WELL START HERE. WE'RE CLOSE.
JUST LIKE YOU'RE BEHIND THE SHIP'S WHEEL.
HI THERE.
swoon~

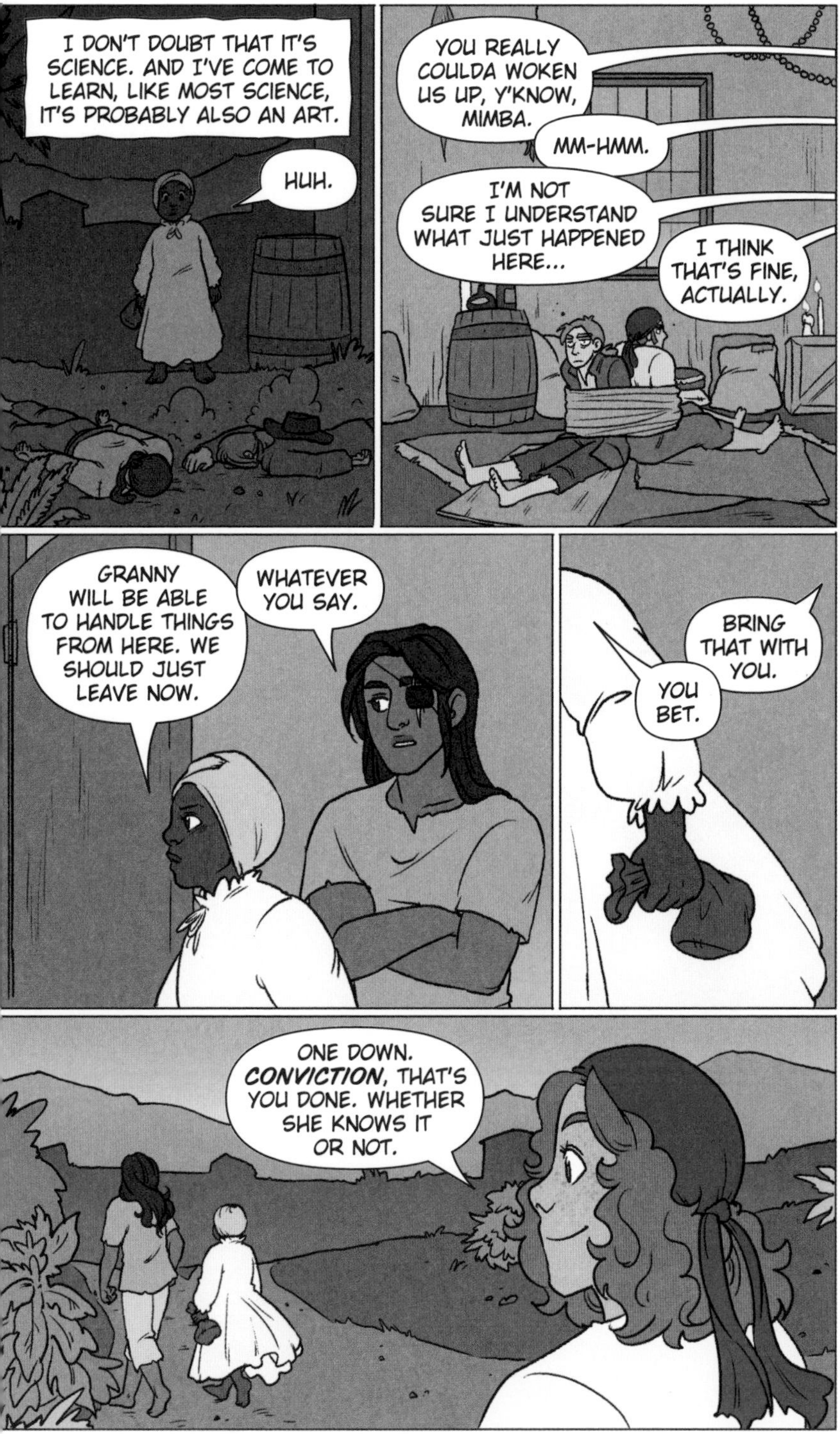
I DON'T DOUBT THAT IT'S SCIENCE. AND I'VE COME TO LEARN, LIKE MOST SCIENCE, IT'S PROBABLY ALSO AN ART.
HUH.
YOU REALLY COULDA WOKEN US UP, Y'KNOW, MIMBA.
MM-HMM.
I'M NOT SURE I UNDERSTAND WHAT JUST HAPPENED HERE...
I THINK THAT'S FINE, ACTUALLY.
GRANNY WILL BE ABLE TO HANDLE THINGS FROM HERE. WE SHOULD JUST LEAVE NOW.
WHATEVER YOU SAY.
BRING THAT WITH YOU.
YOU BET.
ONE DOWN. ***CONVICTION***, THAT'S YOU DONE. WHETHER SHE KNOWS IT OR NOT.

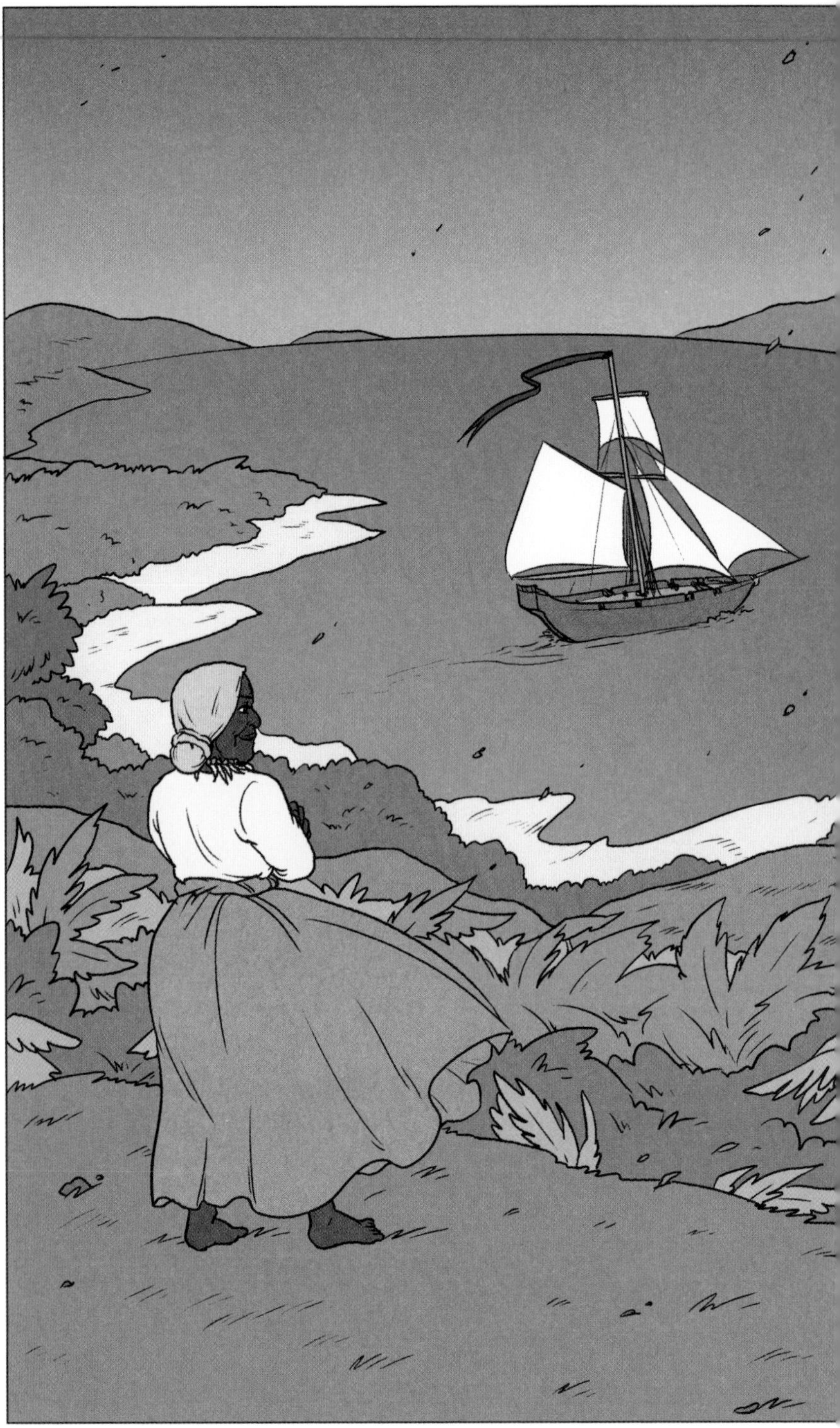

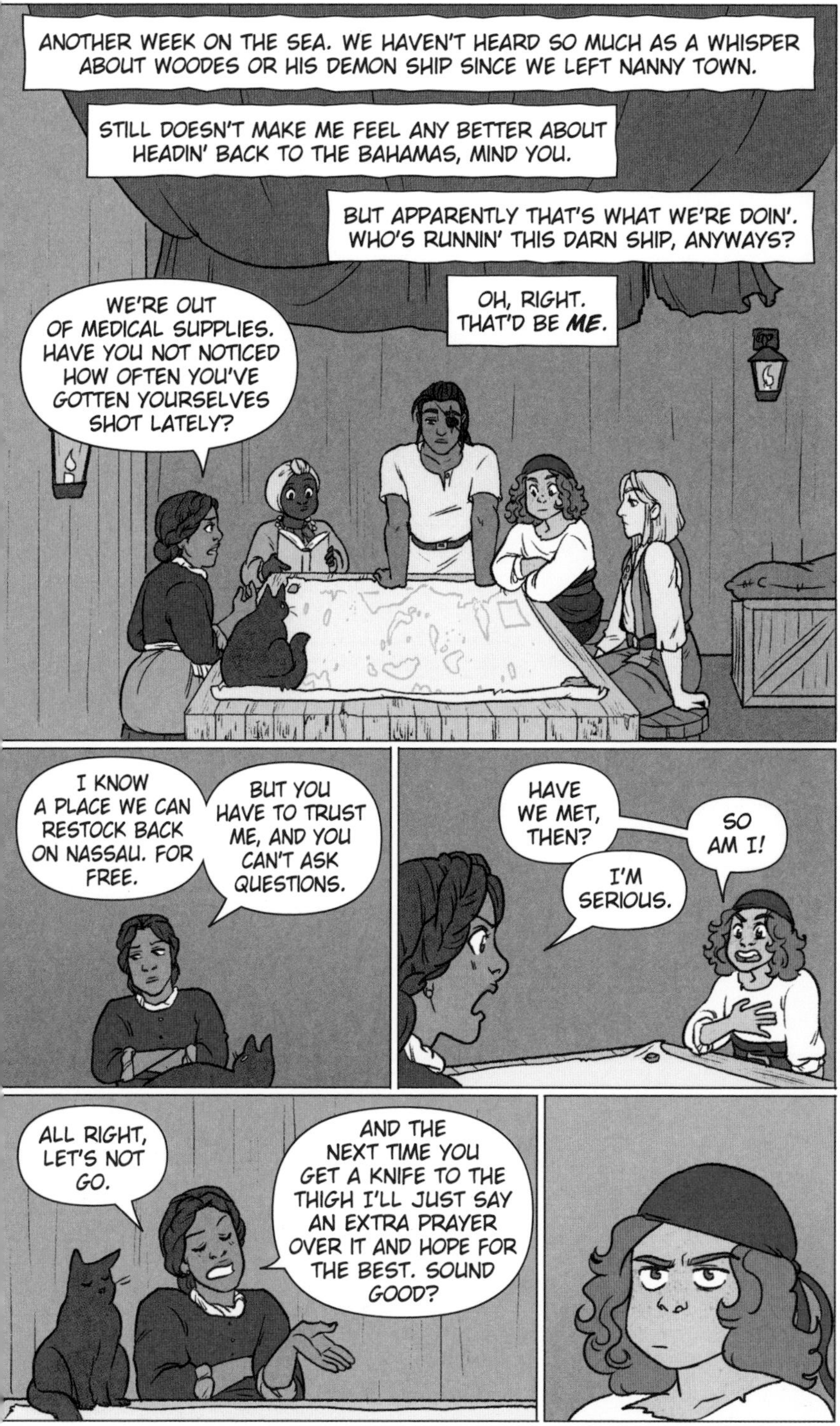
ANOTHER WEEK ON THE SEA. WE HAVEN'T HEARD SO MUCH AS A WHISPER ABOUT WOODES OR HIS DEMON SHIP SINCE WE LEFT NANNY TOWN.
STILL DOESN'T MAKE ME FEEL ANY BETTER ABOUT HEADIN' BACK TO THE BAHAMAS, MIND YOU.
BUT APPARENTLY THAT'S WHAT WE'RE DOIN'. WHO'S RUNNIN' THIS DARN SHIP, ANYWAYS?
OH, RIGHT. THAT'D BE *ME*.
WE'RE OUT OF MEDICAL SUPPLIES. HAVE YOU NOT NOTICED HOW OFTEN YOU'VE GOTTEN YOURSELVES SHOT LATELY?
I KNOW A PLACE WE CAN RESTOCK BACK ON NASSAU. FOR FREE.
BUT YOU HAVE TO TRUST ME, AND YOU CAN'T ASK QUESTIONS.
HAVE WE MET, THEN?
I'M SERIOUS.
SO AM I!
ALL RIGHT, LET'S NOT GO.
AND THE NEXT TIME YOU GET A KNIFE TO THE THIGH I'LL JUST SAY AN EXTRA PRAYER OVER IT AND HOPE FOR THE BEST. SOUND GOOD?

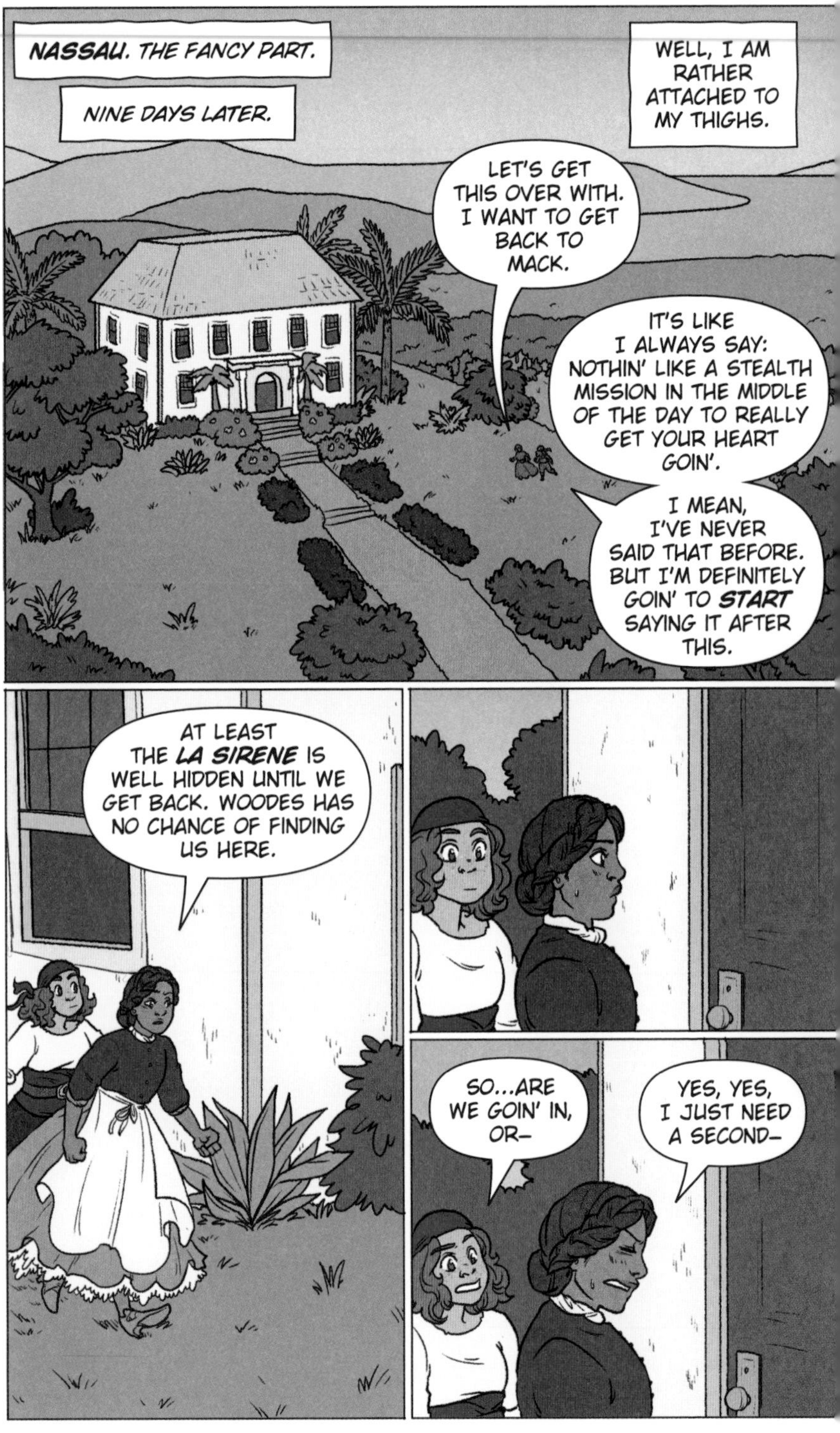
NASSAU. THE FANCY PART.
NINE DAYS LATER.
WELL, I AM RATHER ATTACHED TO MY THIGHS.
LET'S GET THIS OVER WITH. I WANT TO GET BACK TO MACK.
IT'S LIKE I ALWAYS SAY: NOTHIN' LIKE A STEALTH MISSION IN THE MIDDLE OF THE DAY TO REALLY GET YOUR HEART GOIN'.
I MEAN, I'VE NEVER SAID THAT BEFORE. BUT I'M DEFINITELY GOIN' TO START SAYING IT AFTER THIS.
AT LEAST THE LA SIRENE IS WELL HIDDEN UNTIL WE GET BACK. WOODES HAS NO CHANCE OF FINDING US HERE.
SO...ARE WE GOIN' IN, OR–
YES, YES, I JUST NEED A SECOND–

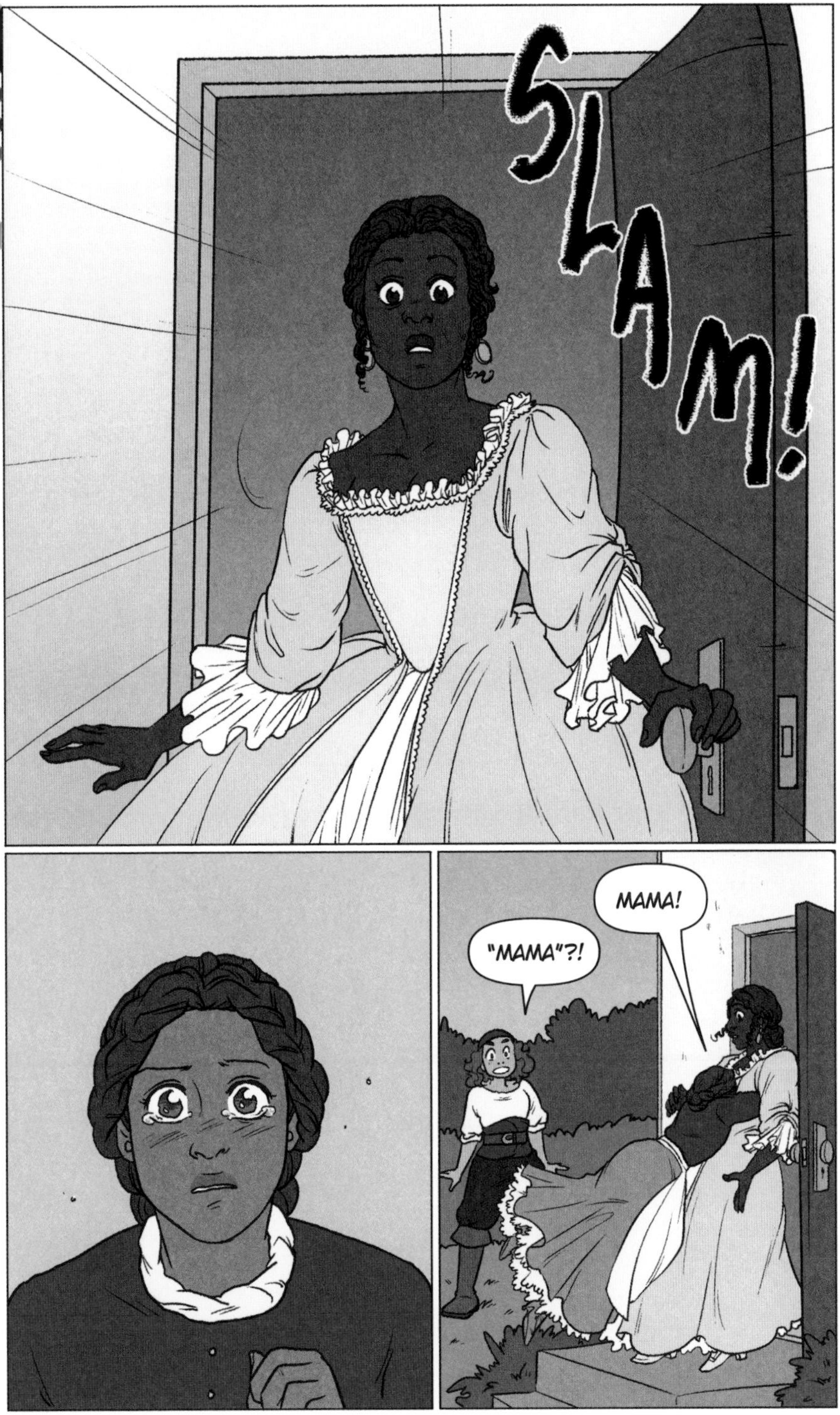
SLAM!
MAMA!
"MAMA"?!

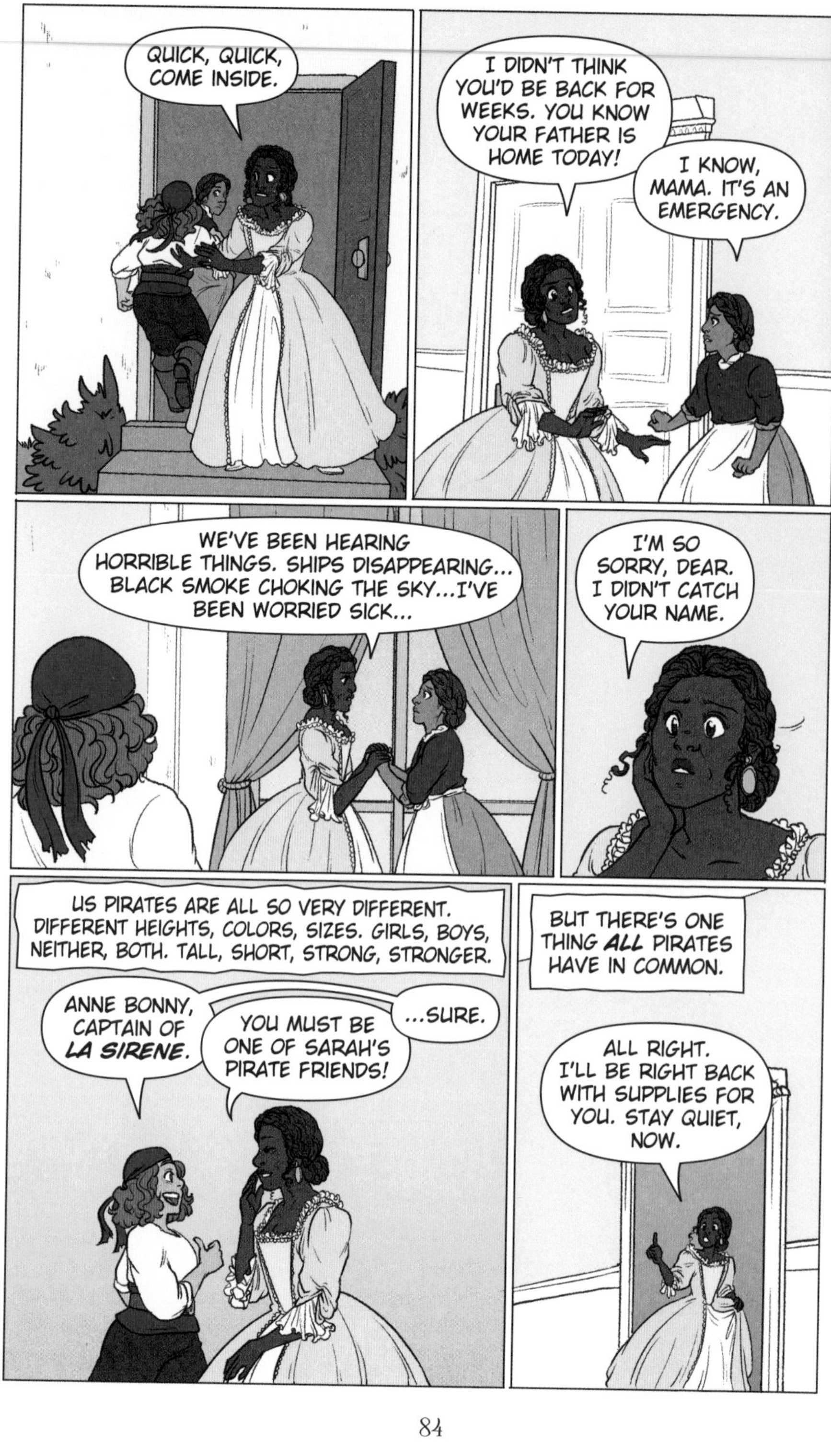

QUICK, QUICK, COME INSIDE.
I DIDN'T THINK YOU'D BE BACK FOR WEEKS. YOU KNOW YOUR FATHER IS HOME TODAY!
I KNOW, MAMA. IT'S AN EMERGENCY.
WE'VE BEEN HEARING HORRIBLE THINGS. SHIPS DISAPPEARING... BLACK SMOKE CHOKING THE SKY...I'VE BEEN WORRIED SICK...
I'M SO SORRY, DEAR. I DIDN'T CATCH YOUR NAME.
US PIRATES ARE ALL SO VERY DIFFERENT. DIFFERENT HEIGHTS, COLORS, SIZES. GIRLS, BOYS, NEITHER, BOTH. TALL, SHORT, STRONG, STRONGER.
ANNE BONNY, CAPTAIN OF ***LA SIRENE***.
YOU MUST BE ONE OF SARAH'S PIRATE FRIENDS!
...SURE.
BUT THERE'S ONE THING ***ALL*** PIRATES HAVE IN COMMON.
ALL RIGHT. I'LL BE RIGHT BACK WITH SUPPLIES FOR YOU. STAY QUIET, NOW.

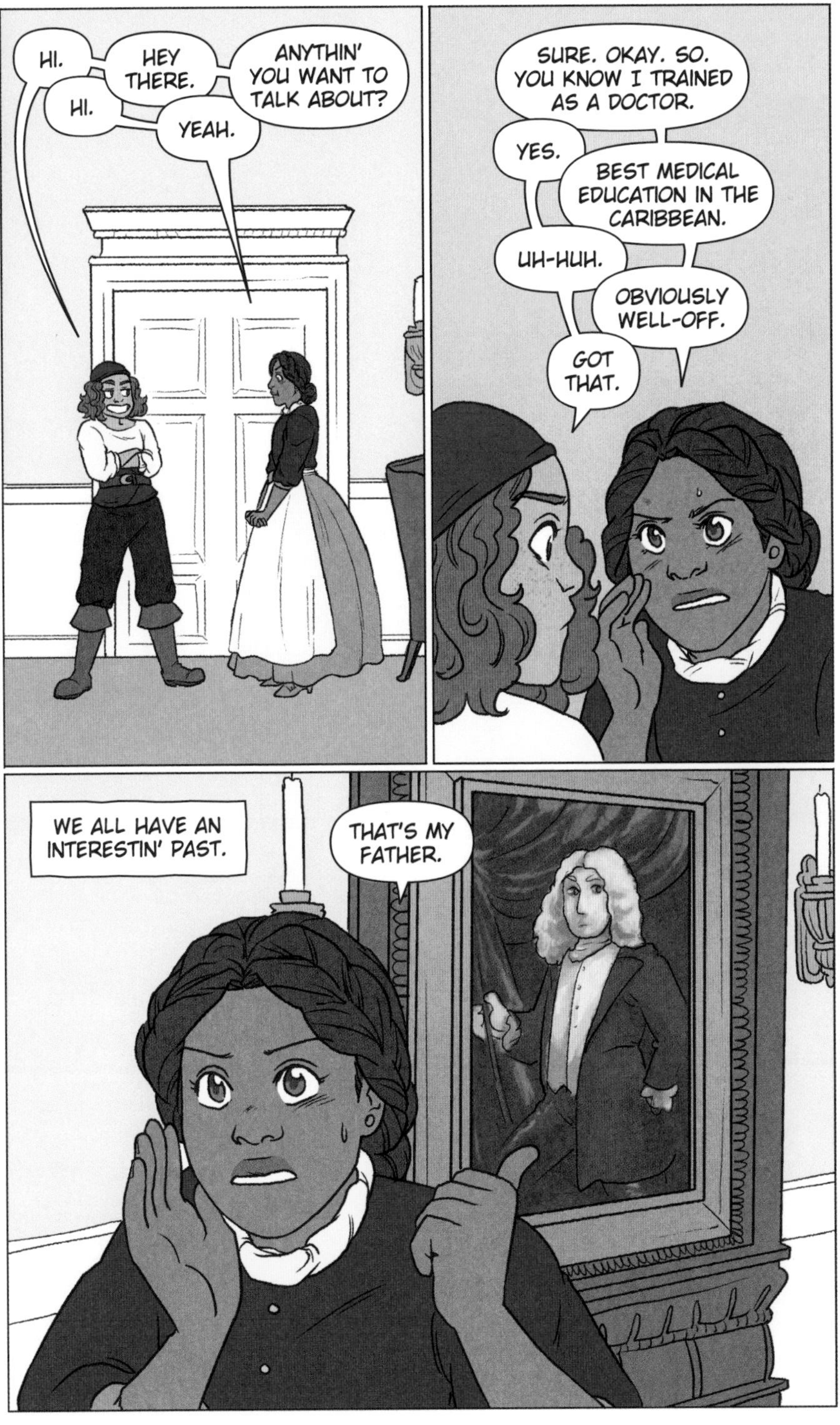
HI.
HEY THERE.
HI.
ANYTHIN' YOU WANT TO TALK ABOUT?
YEAH.
SURE. OKAY. SO. YOU KNOW I TRAINED AS A DOCTOR.
YES.
BEST MEDICAL EDUCATION IN THE CARIBBEAN.
UH-HUH.
OBVIOUSLY WELL-OFF.
GOT THAT.
WE ALL HAVE AN INTERESTIN' PAST.
THAT'S MY FATHER.

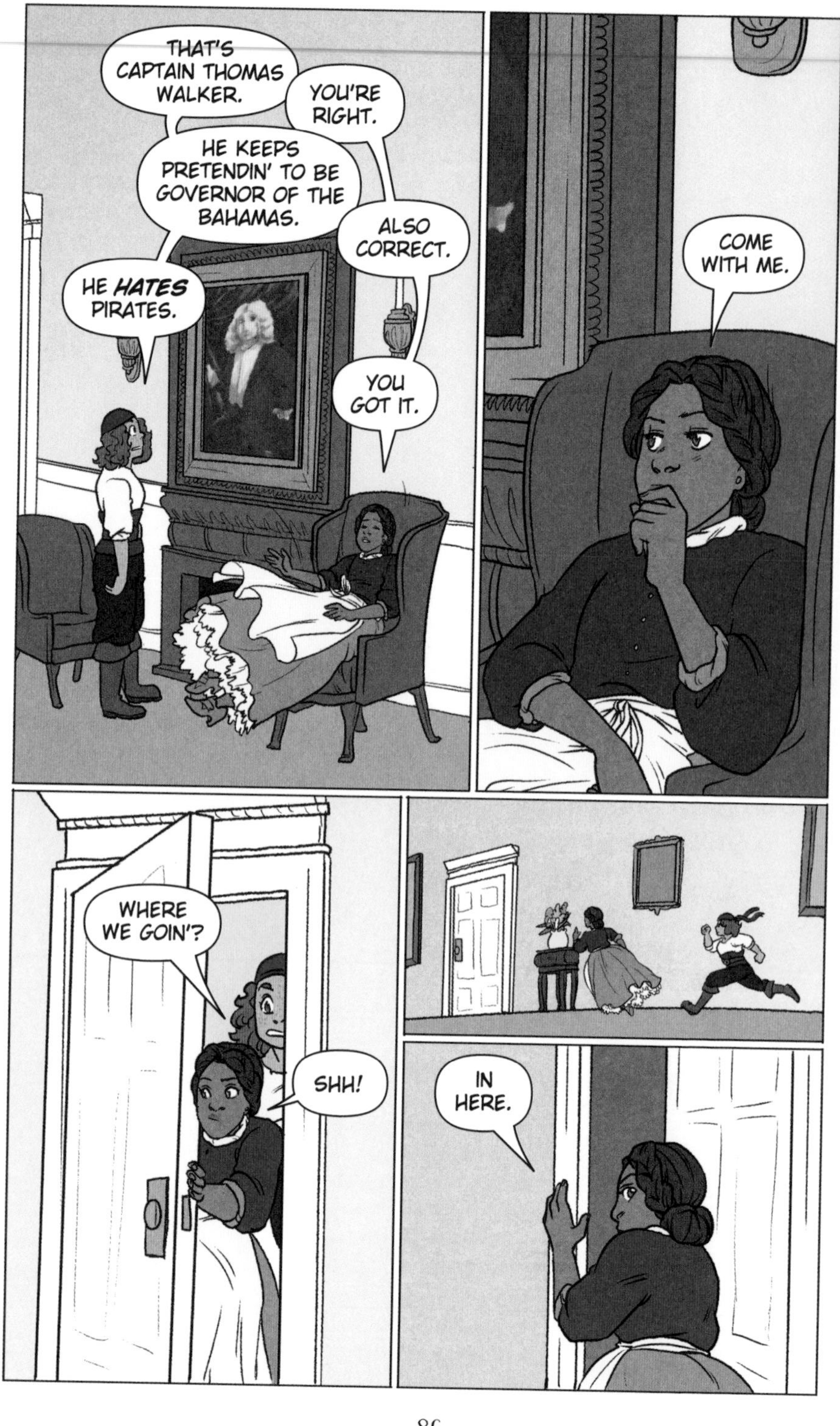
THAT'S CAPTAIN THOMAS WALKER.
YOU'RE RIGHT.
HE KEEPS PRETENDIN' TO BE GOVERNOR OF THE BAHAMAS.
ALSO CORRECT.
HE *HATES* PIRATES.
YOU GOT IT.
COME WITH ME.
WHERE WE GOIN'?
SHH!
IN HERE.

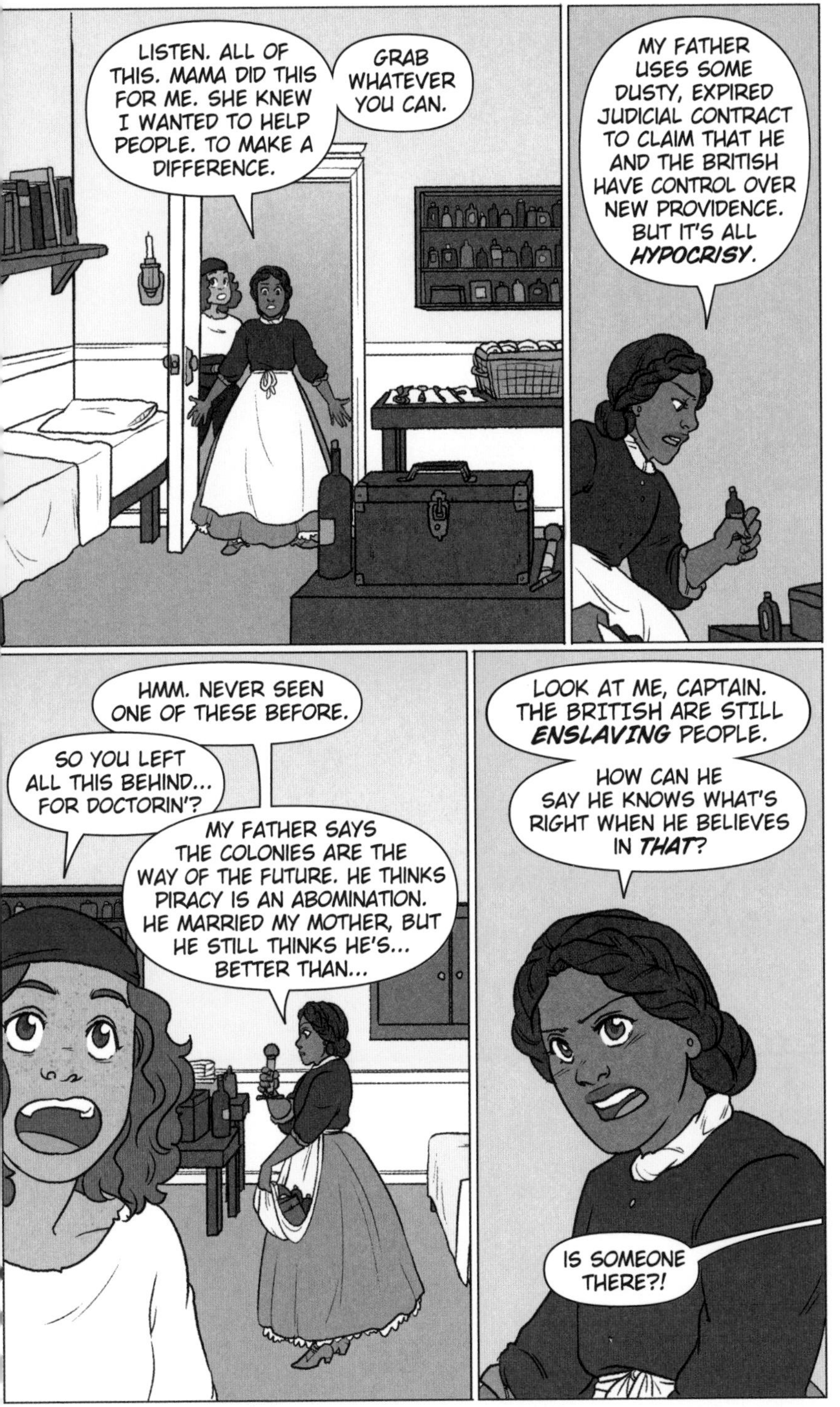
LISTEN. ALL OF THIS. MAMA DID THIS FOR ME. SHE KNEW I WANTED TO HELP PEOPLE. TO MAKE A DIFFERENCE.
GRAB WHATEVER YOU CAN.
MY FATHER USES SOME DUSTY, EXPIRED JUDICIAL CONTRACT TO CLAIM THAT HE AND THE BRITISH HAVE CONTROL OVER NEW PROVIDENCE. BUT IT'S ALL *HYPOCRISY*.
HMM. NEVER SEEN ONE OF THESE BEFORE.
SO YOU LEFT ALL THIS BEHIND... FOR DOCTORIN'?
MY FATHER SAYS THE COLONIES ARE THE WAY OF THE FUTURE. HE THINKS PIRACY IS AN ABOMINATION. HE MARRIED MY MOTHER, BUT HE STILL THINKS HE'S... BETTER THAN...
LOOK AT ME, CAPTAIN. THE BRITISH ARE STILL *ENSLAVING* PEOPLE.
HOW CAN HE SAY HE KNOWS WHAT'S RIGHT WHEN HE BELIEVES IN *THAT*?
IS SOMEONE THERE?!

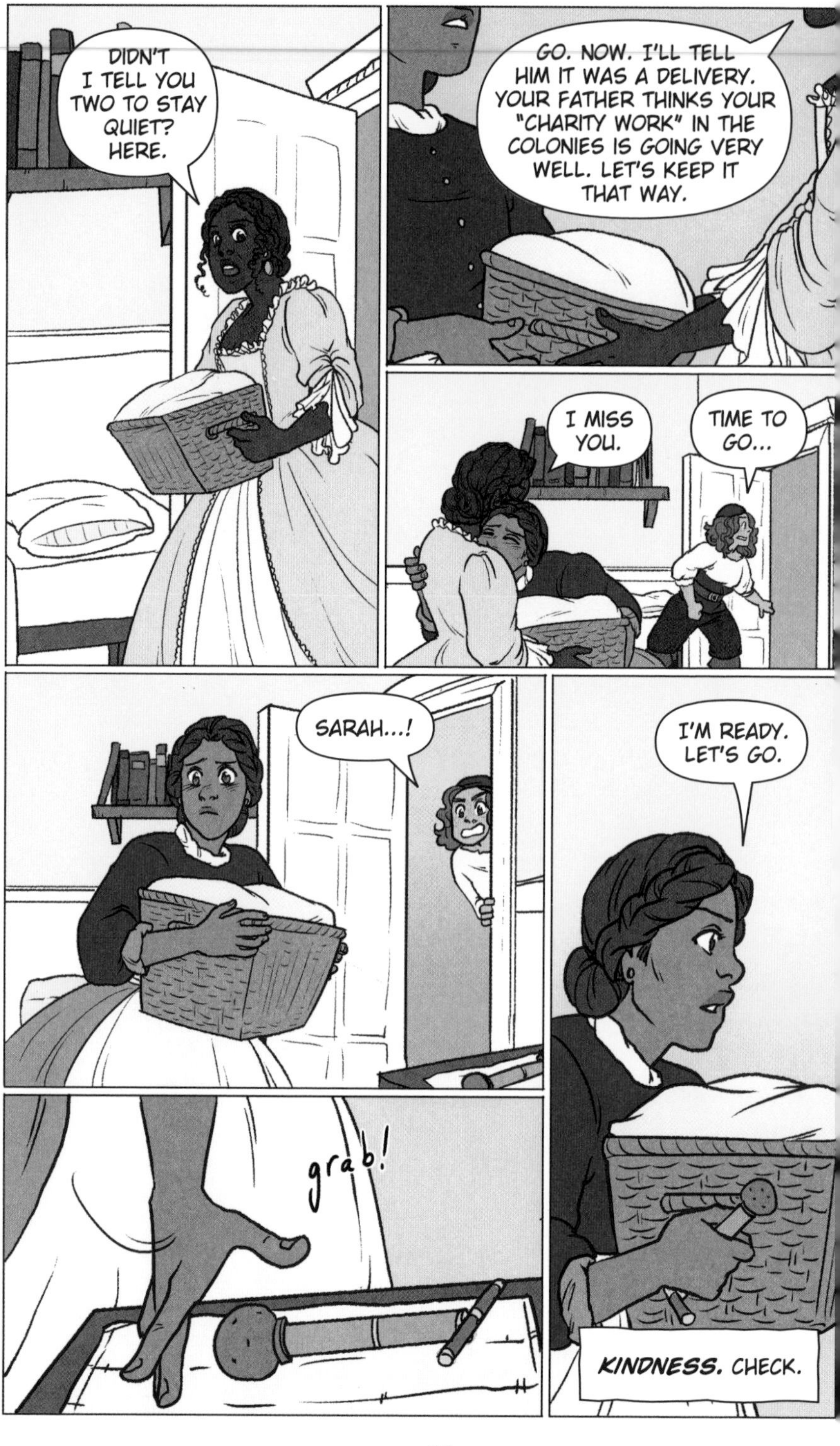

DIDN'T I TELL YOU TWO TO STAY QUIET? HERE.
GO. NOW. I'LL TELL HIM IT WAS A DELIVERY. YOUR FATHER THINKS YOUR "CHARITY WORK" IN THE COLONIES IS GOING VERY WELL. LET'S KEEP IT THAT WAY.
I MISS YOU.
TIME TO GO...
SARAH...!
I'M READY. LET'S GO.
grab!
KINDNESS. CHECK.

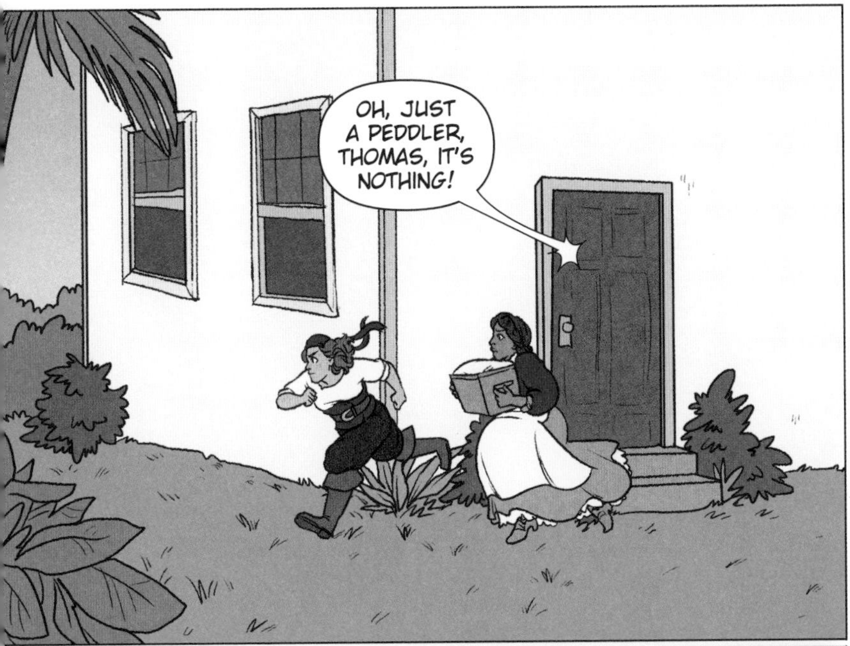
OH, JUST A PEDDLER, THOMAS, IT'S NOTHING!

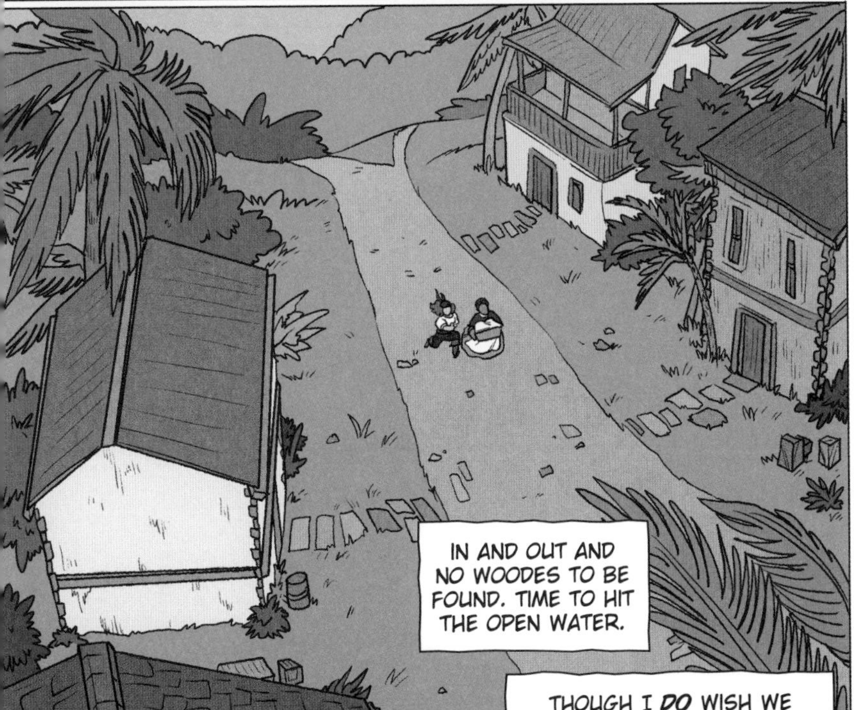
IN AND OUT AND NO WOODES TO BE FOUND. TIME TO HIT THE OPEN WATER.
THOUGH I ***DO*** WISH WE HAD TIME FOR A QUICK STOP AT THE CRIMSON TURTLE.

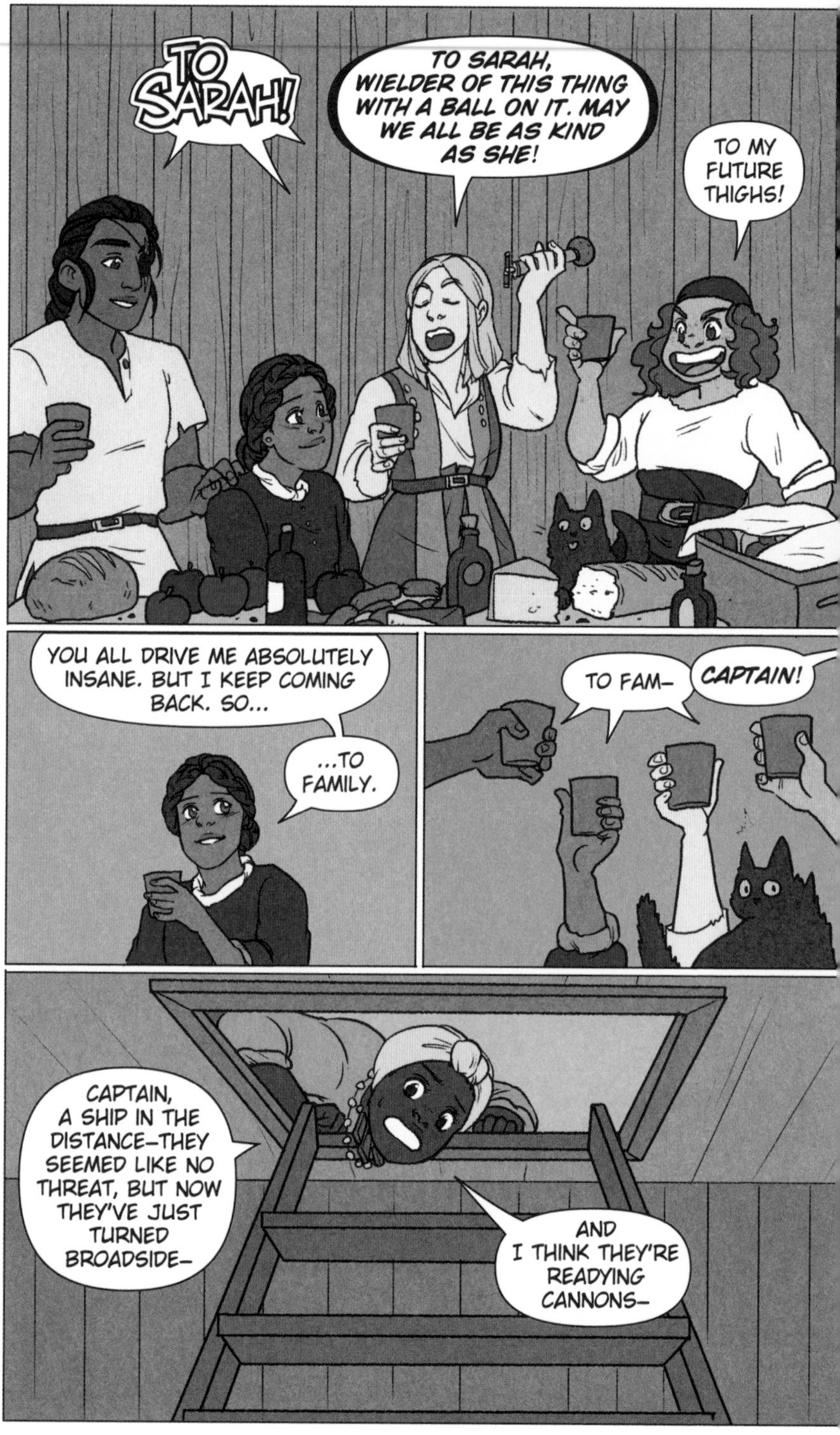
TO SARAH!
TO SARAH, WIELDER OF THIS THING WITH A BALL ON IT. MAY WE ALL BE AS KIND AS SHE!
TO MY FUTURE THIGHS!
YOU ALL DRIVE ME ABSOLUTELY INSANE. BUT I KEEP COMING BACK. SO...
...TO FAMILY.
TO FAM–
CAPTAIN!
CAPTAIN, A SHIP IN THE DISTANCE–THEY SEEMED LIKE NO THREAT, BUT NOW THEY'VE JUST TURNED BROADSIDE–
AND I THINK THEY'RE READYING CANNONS–

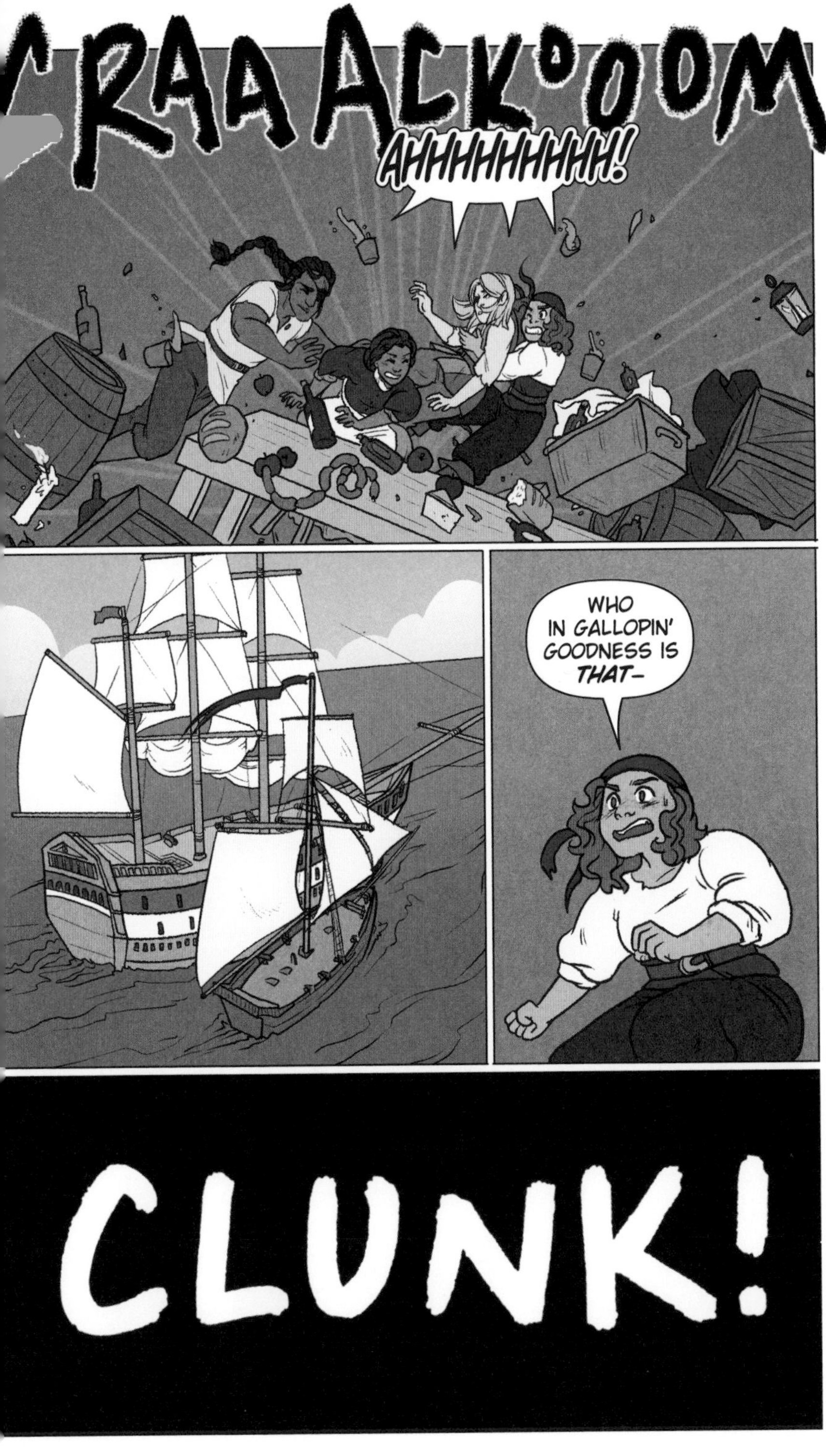
CRAAACKOOOM
AHHHHHHHHH!
WHO IN GALLOPIN' GOODNESS IS *THAT*–
CLUNK!

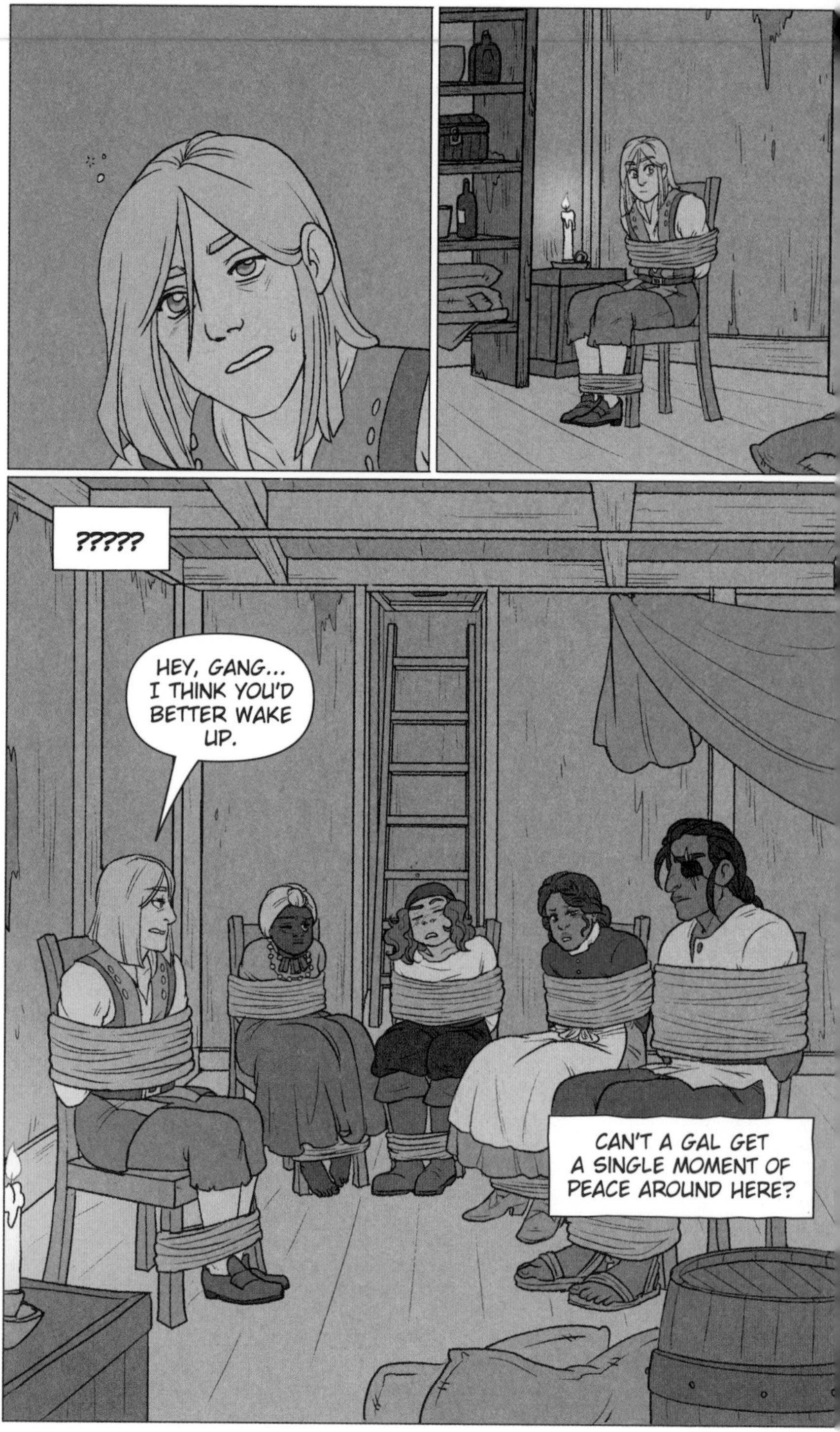
?????
HEY, GANG... I THINK YOU'D BETTER WAKE UP.
CAN'T A GAL GET A SINGLE MOMENT OF PEACE AROUND HERE?

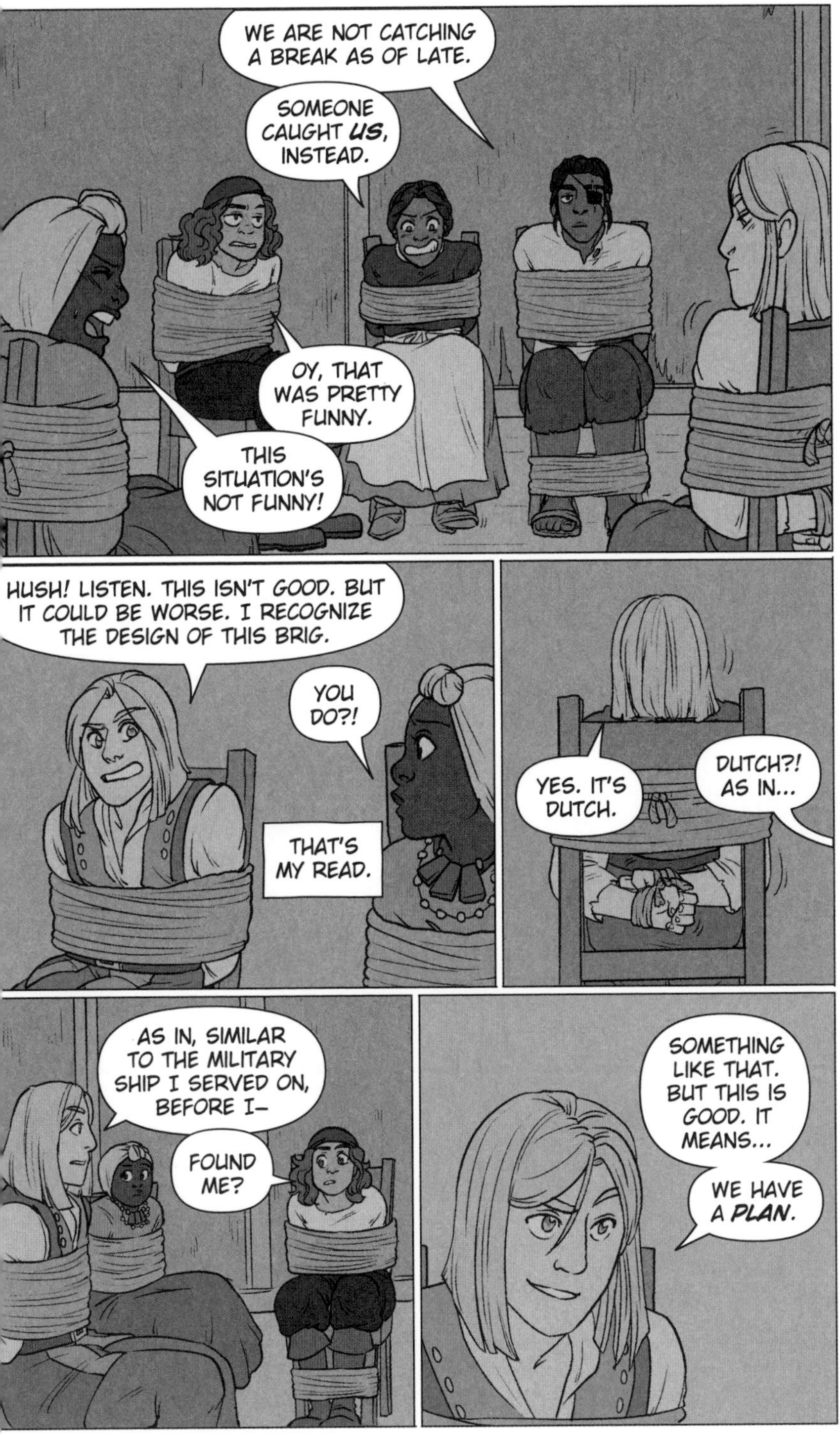
WE ARE NOT CATCHING A BREAK AS OF LATE.
SOMEONE CAUGHT *US*, INSTEAD.
OY, THAT WAS PRETTY FUNNY.
THIS SITUATION'S NOT FUNNY!
HUSH! LISTEN. THIS ISN'T GOOD. BUT IT COULD BE WORSE. I RECOGNIZE THE DESIGN OF THIS BRIG.
YOU DO?!
THAT'S MY READ.
YES. IT'S DUTCH.
DUTCH?! AS IN...
AS IN, SIMILAR TO THE MILITARY SHIP I SERVED ON, BEFORE I–
FOUND ME?
SOMETHING LIKE THAT. BUT THIS IS GOOD. IT MEANS...
WE HAVE A *PLAN*.

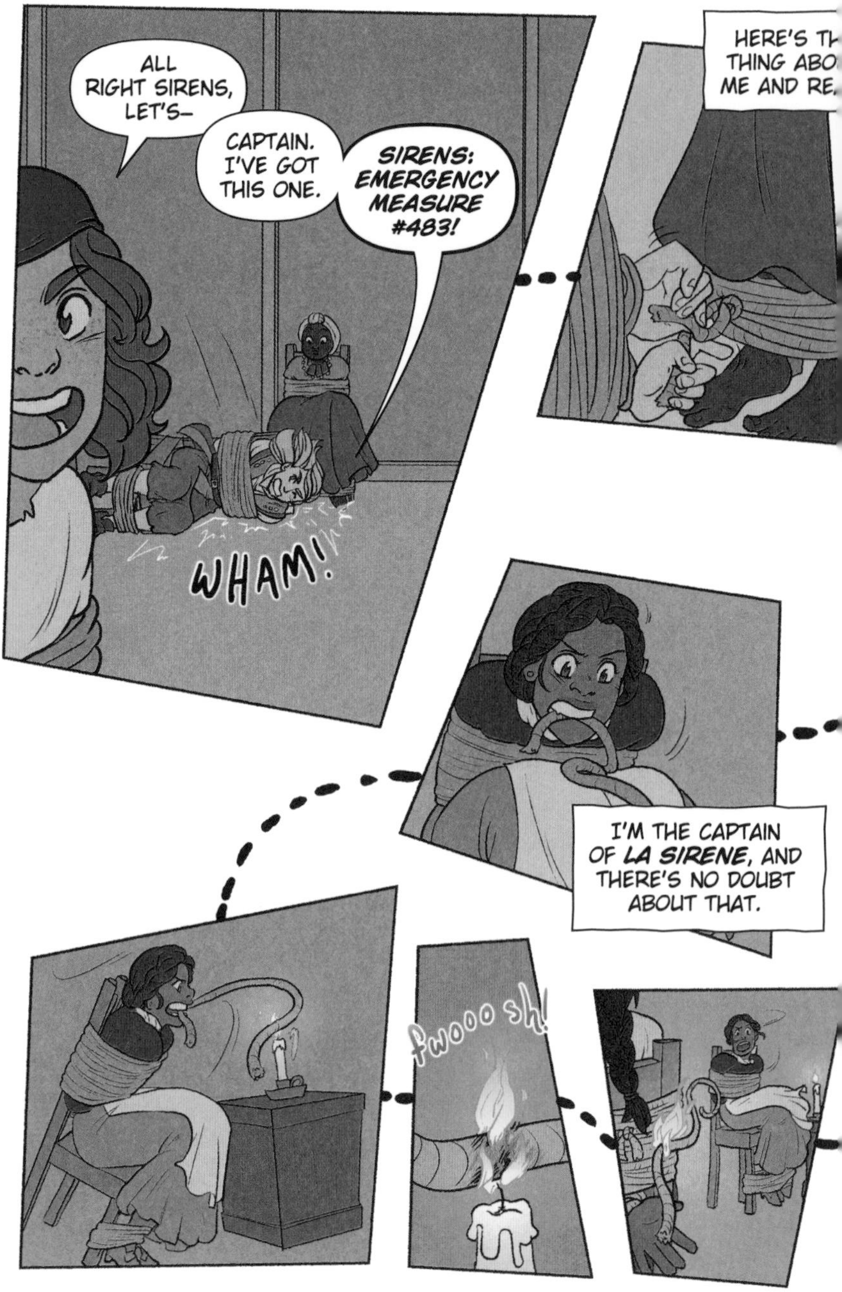
ALL RIGHT SIRENS, LET'S–
CAPTAIN. I'VE GOT THIS ONE.
SIRENS: EMERGENCY MEASURE #483!
WHAM!
HERE'S TH THING ABO ME AND RE
I'M THE CAPTAIN OF LA SIRENE, AND THERE'S NO DOUBT ABOUT THAT.
fwooo sh!

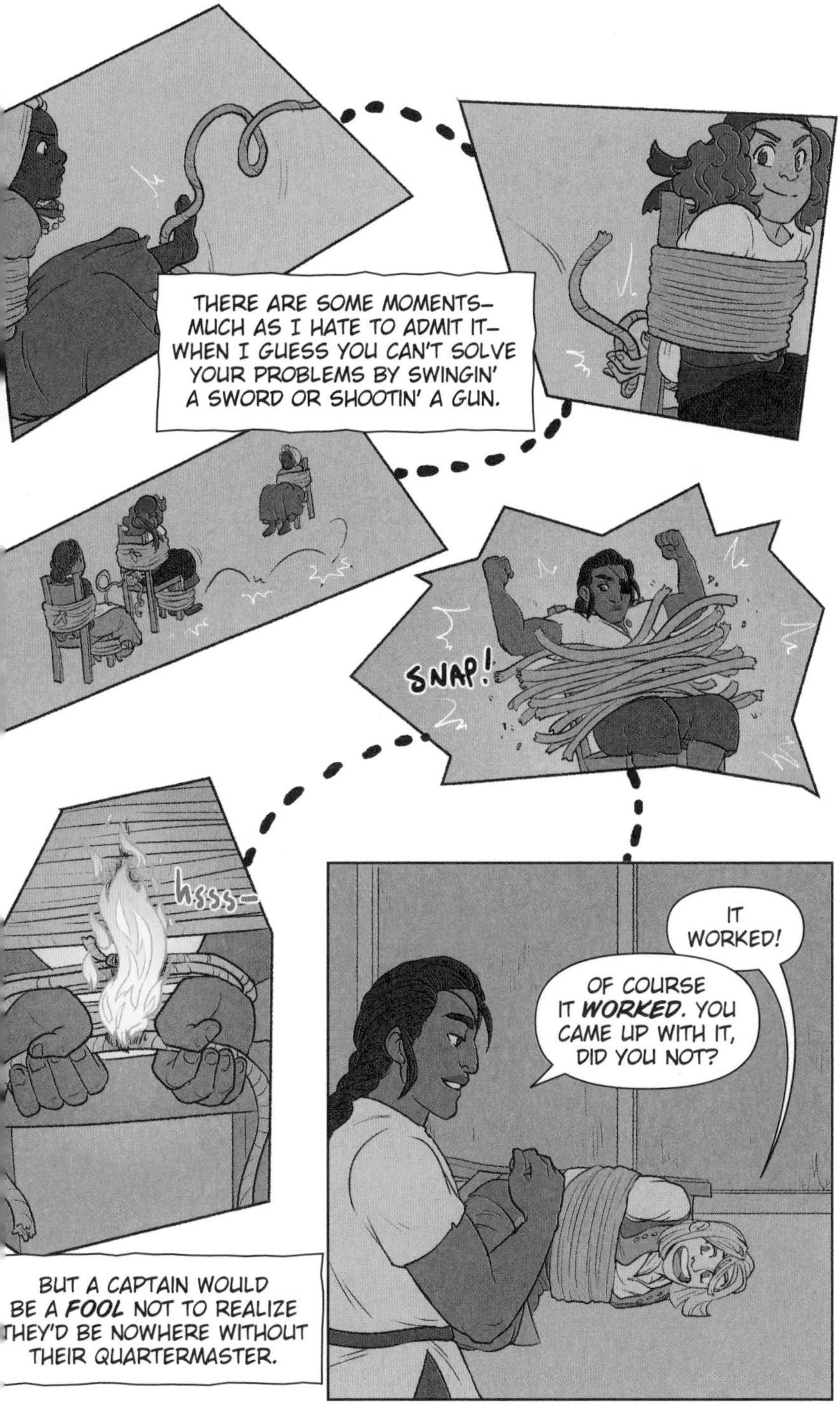
THERE ARE SOME MOMENTS– MUCH AS I HATE TO ADMIT IT– WHEN I GUESS YOU CAN'T SOLVE YOUR PROBLEMS BY SWINGIN' A SWORD OR SHOOTIN' A GUN.
SNAP!
hsss–
BUT A CAPTAIN WOULD BE A ***FOOL*** NOT TO REALIZE THEY'D BE NOWHERE WITHOUT THEIR QUARTERMASTER.
IT WORKED!
OF COURSE IT ***WORKED***. YOU CAME UP WITH IT, DID YOU NOT?

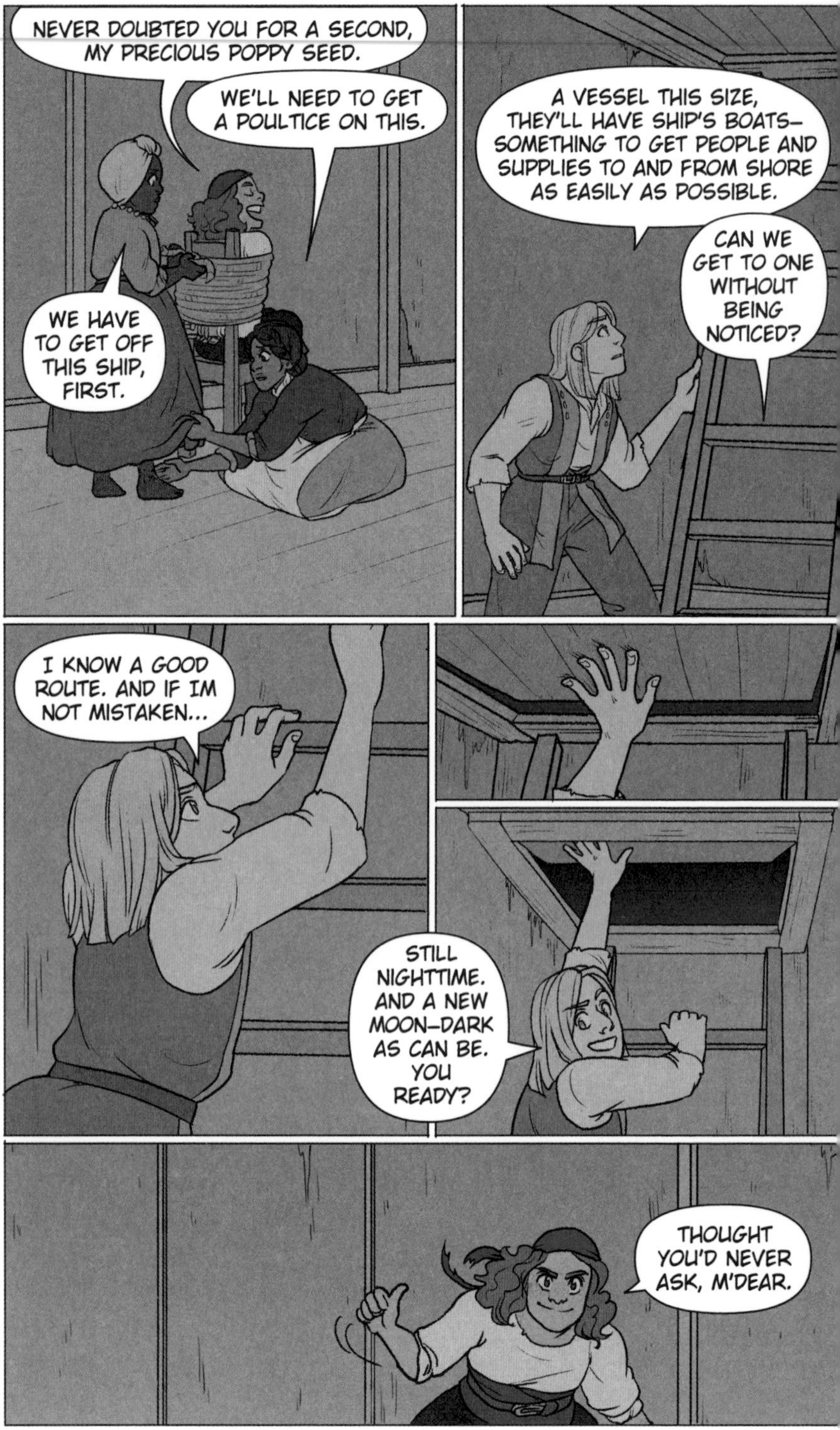
NEVER DOUBTED YOU FOR A SECOND, MY PRECIOUS POPPY SEED.
WE'LL NEED TO GET A POULTICE ON THIS.
WE HAVE TO GET OFF THIS SHIP, FIRST.
A VESSEL THIS SIZE, THEY'LL HAVE SHIP'S BOATS— SOMETHING TO GET PEOPLE AND SUPPLIES TO AND FROM SHORE AS EASILY AS POSSIBLE.
CAN WE GET TO ONE WITHOUT BEING NOTICED?
I KNOW A GOOD ROUTE. AND IF IM NOT MISTAKEN...
STILL NIGHTTIME. AND A NEW MOON—DARK AS CAN BE. YOU READY?
THOUGHT YOU'D NEVER ASK, M'DEAR.

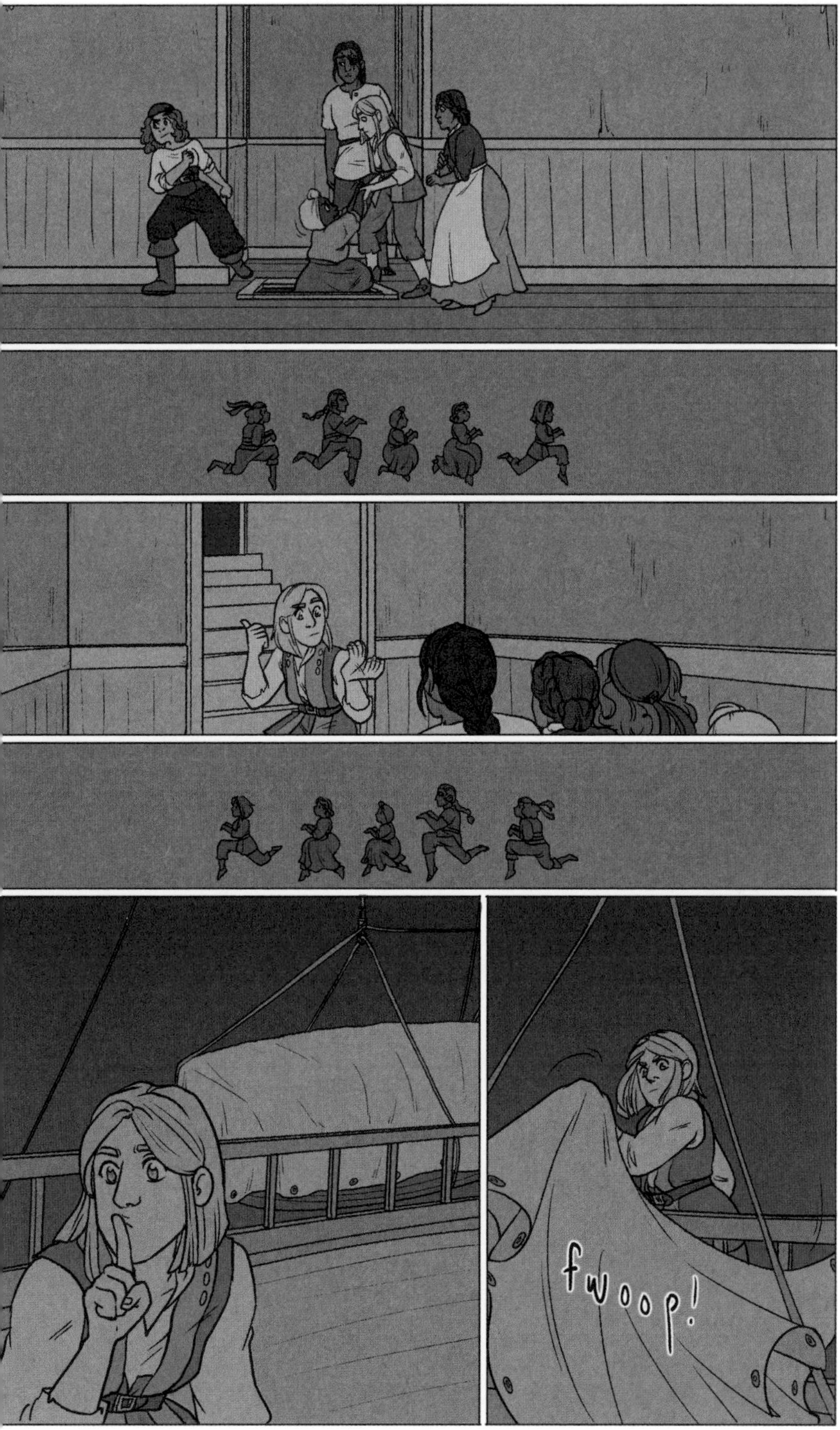
fwoop!

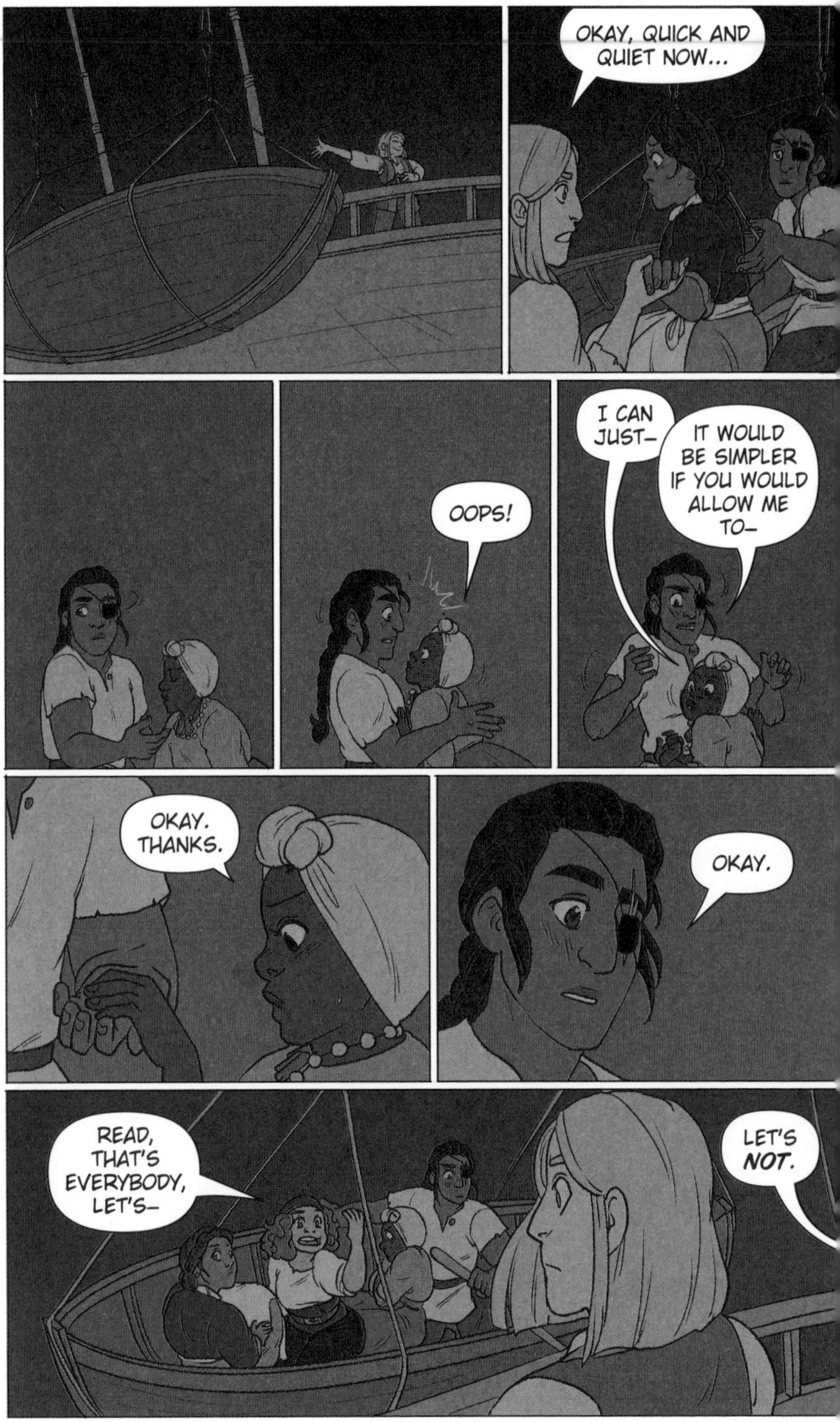
OKAY, QUICK AND QUIET NOW...
OOPS!
I CAN JUST–
IT WOULD BE SIMPLER IF YOU WOULD ALLOW ME TO–
OKAY. THANKS.
OKAY.
READ, THAT'S EVERYBODY, LET'S–
LET'S *NOT*.

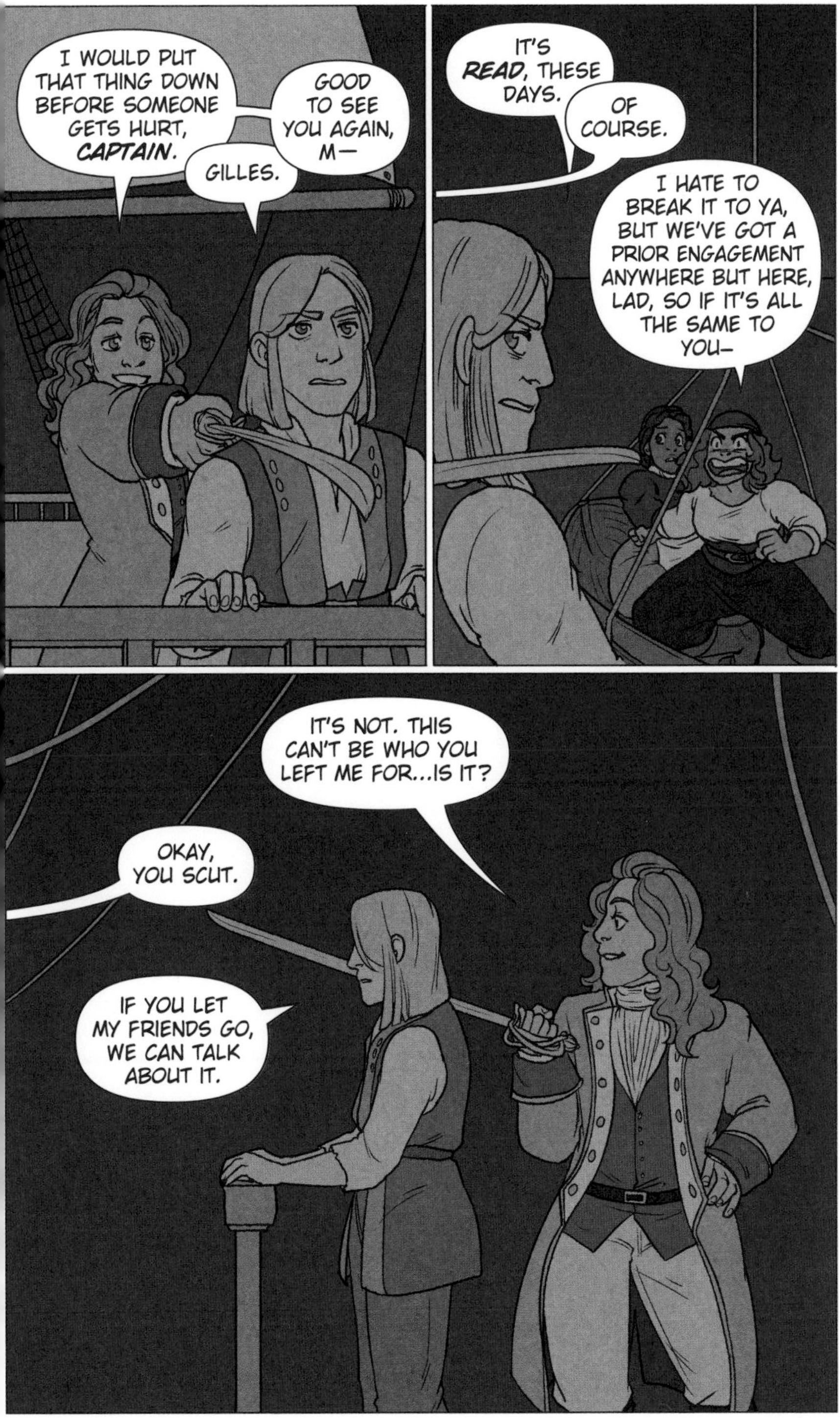
I WOULD PUT THAT THING DOWN BEFORE SOMEONE GETS HURT, *CAPTAIN*.
GOOD TO SEE YOU AGAIN, M—
GILLES.
IT'S *READ*, THESE DAYS.
OF COURSE.
I HATE TO BREAK IT TO YA, BUT WE'VE GOT A PRIOR ENGAGEMENT ANYWHERE BUT HERE, LAD, SO IF IT'S ALL THE SAME TO YOU—
IT'S NOT. THIS CAN'T BE WHO YOU LEFT ME FOR...IS IT?
OKAY, YOU SCUT.
IF YOU LET MY FRIENDS GO, WE CAN TALK ABOUT IT.

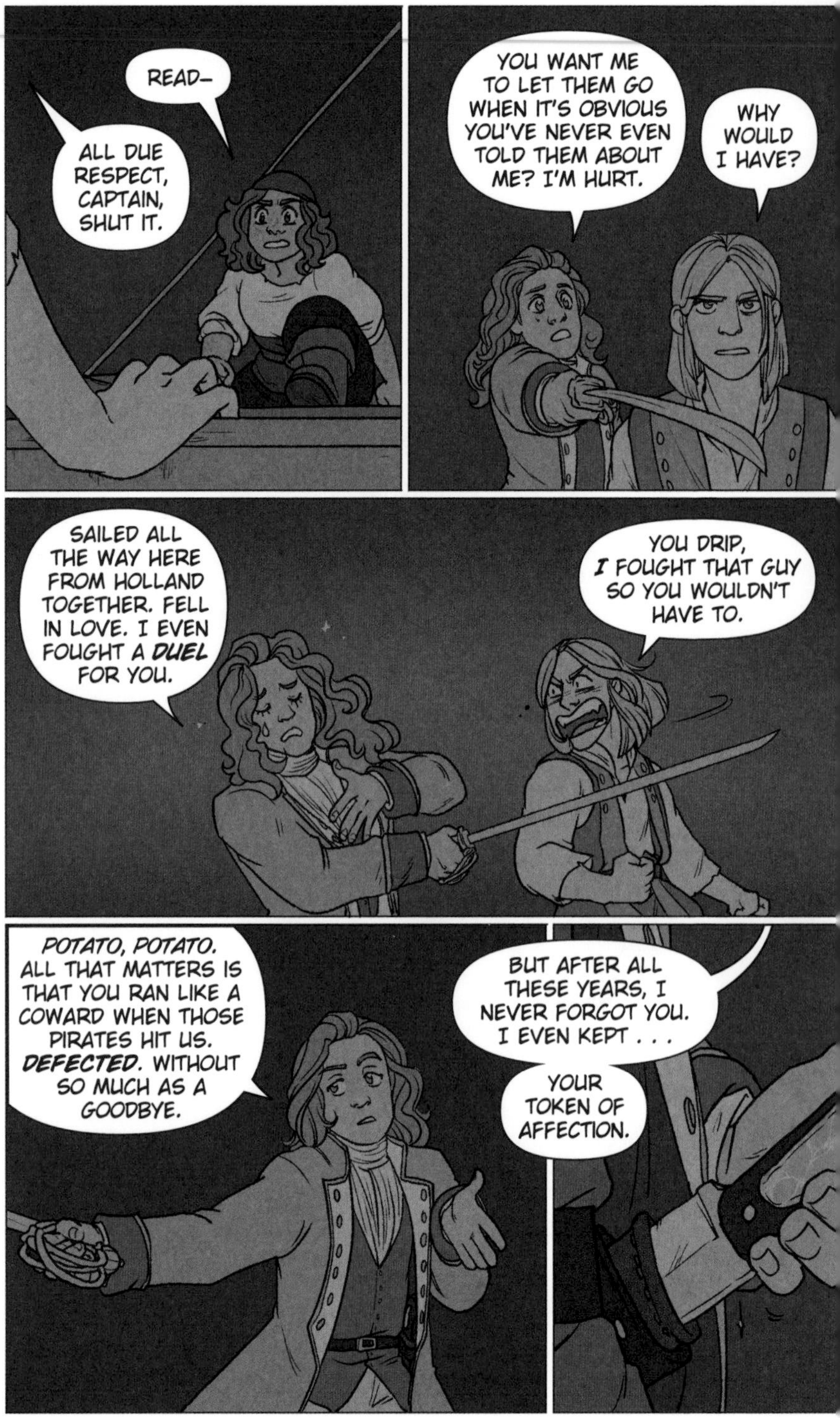
READ–
ALL DUE RESPECT, CAPTAIN, SHUT IT.
YOU WANT ME TO LET THEM GO WHEN IT'S OBVIOUS YOU'VE NEVER EVEN TOLD THEM ABOUT ME? I'M HURT.
WHY WOULD I HAVE?
SAILED ALL THE WAY HERE FROM HOLLAND TOGETHER. FELL IN LOVE. I EVEN FOUGHT A *DUEL* FOR YOU.
YOU DRIP, *I* FOUGHT THAT GUY SO YOU WOULDN'T HAVE TO.
POTATO, POTATO. ALL THAT MATTERS IS THAT YOU RAN LIKE A COWARD WHEN THOSE PIRATES HIT US. ***DEFECTED.*** WITHOUT SO MUCH AS A GOODBYE.
BUT AFTER ALL THESE YEARS, I NEVER FORGOT YOU. I EVEN KEPT . . .
YOUR TOKEN OF AFFECTION.

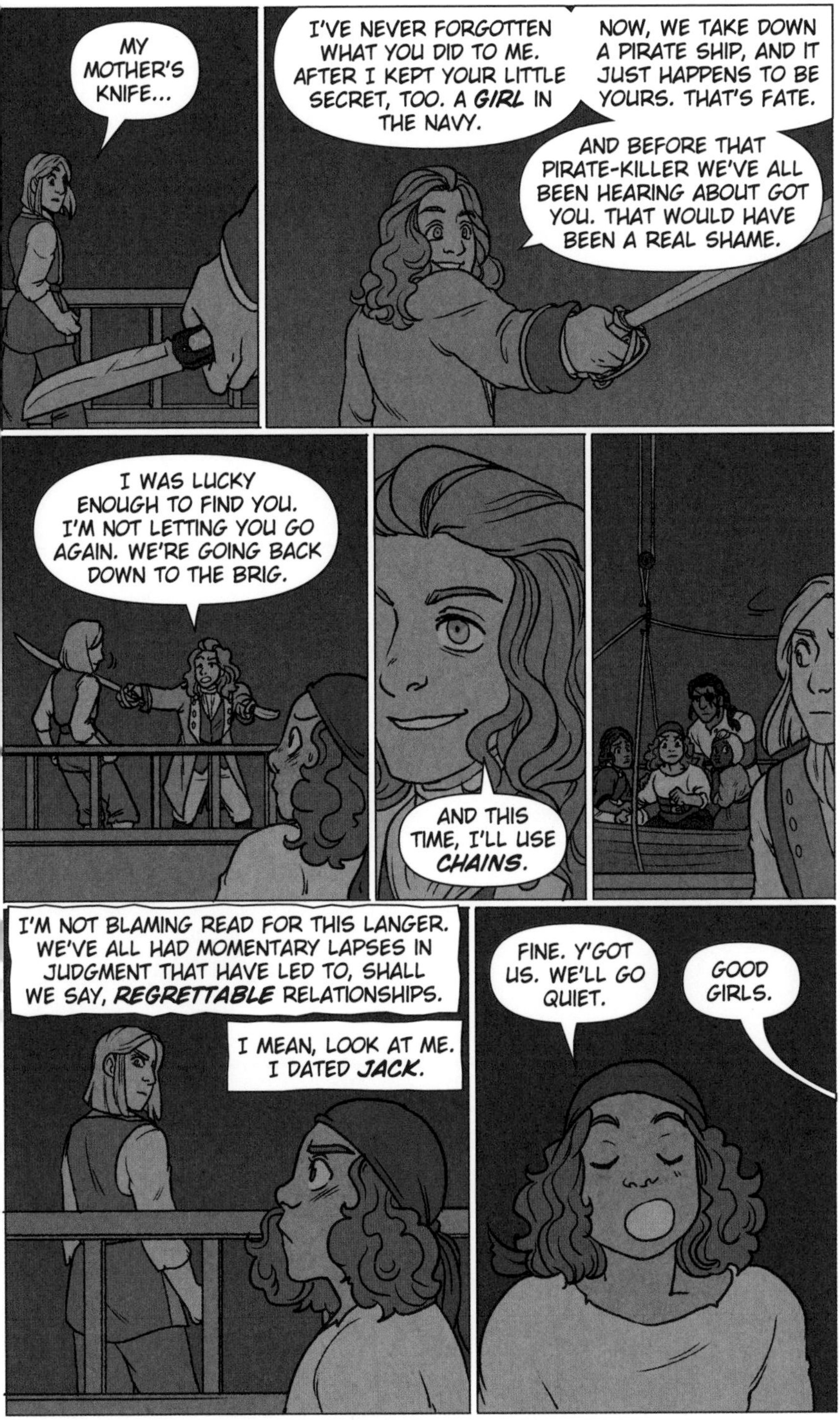
MY MOTHER'S KNIFE...
I'VE NEVER FORGOTTEN WHAT YOU DID TO ME. AFTER I KEPT YOUR LITTLE SECRET, TOO. A GIRL IN THE NAVY.
NOW, WE TAKE DOWN A PIRATE SHIP, AND IT JUST HAPPENS TO BE YOURS. THAT'S FATE.
AND BEFORE THAT PIRATE-KILLER WE'VE ALL BEEN HEARING ABOUT GOT YOU. THAT WOULD HAVE BEEN A REAL SHAME.
I WAS LUCKY ENOUGH TO FIND YOU. I'M NOT LETTING YOU GO AGAIN. WE'RE GOING BACK DOWN TO THE BRIG.
AND THIS TIME, I'LL USE CHAINS.
I'M NOT BLAMING READ FOR THIS LANGER. WE'VE ALL HAD MOMENTARY LAPSES IN JUDGMENT THAT HAVE LED TO, SHALL WE SAY, REGRETTABLE RELATIONSHIPS.
I MEAN, LOOK AT ME. I DATED JACK.
FINE. Y'GOT US. WE'LL GO QUIET.
GOOD GIRLS.

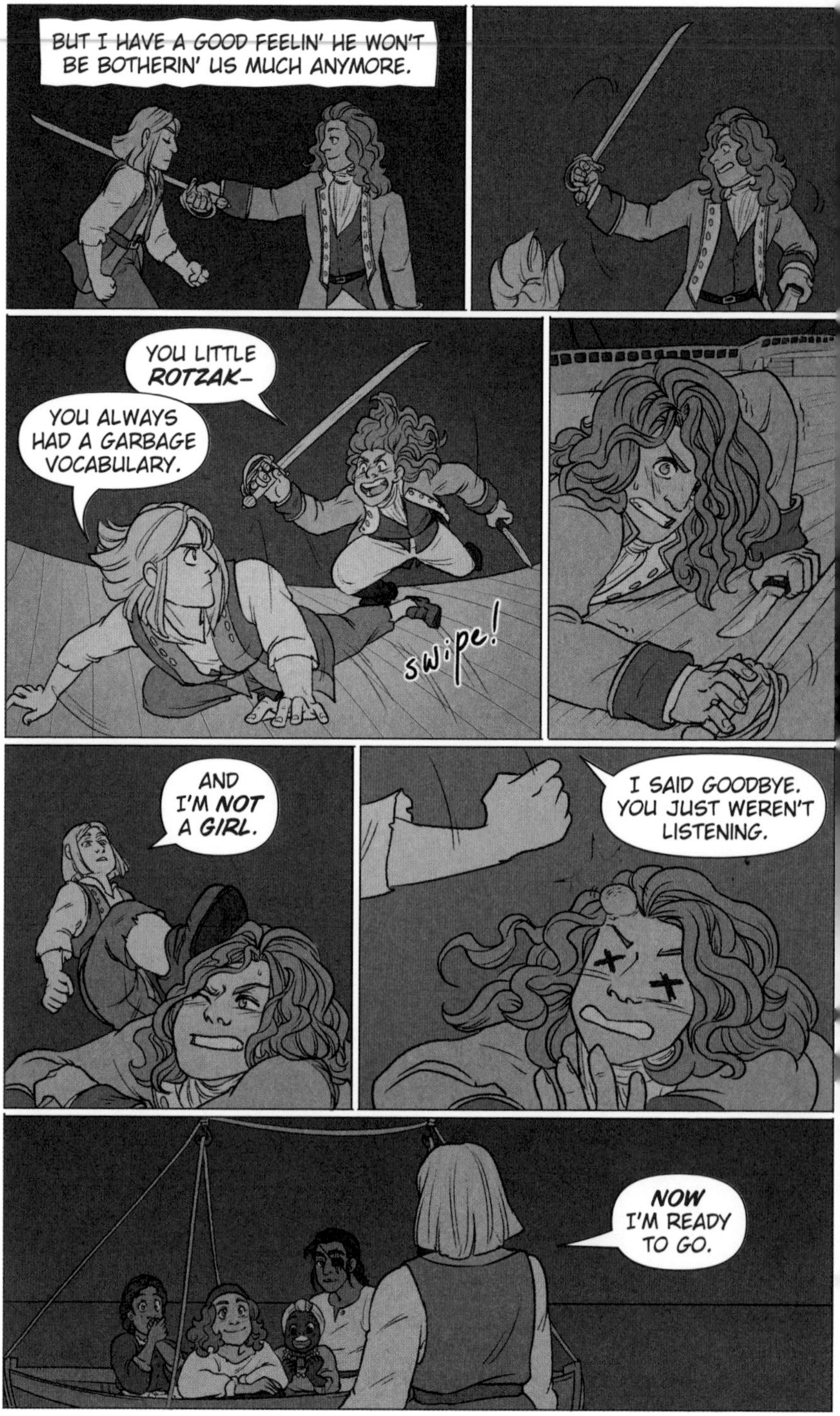
BUT I HAVE A GOOD FEELIN' HE WON'T BE BOTHERIN' US MUCH ANYMORE.
YOU LITTLE ROTZAK–
YOU ALWAYS HAD A GARBAGE VOCABULARY.
swipe!
AND I'M NOT A GIRL.
I SAID GOODBYE. YOU JUST WEREN'T LISTENING.
NOW I'M READY TO GO.

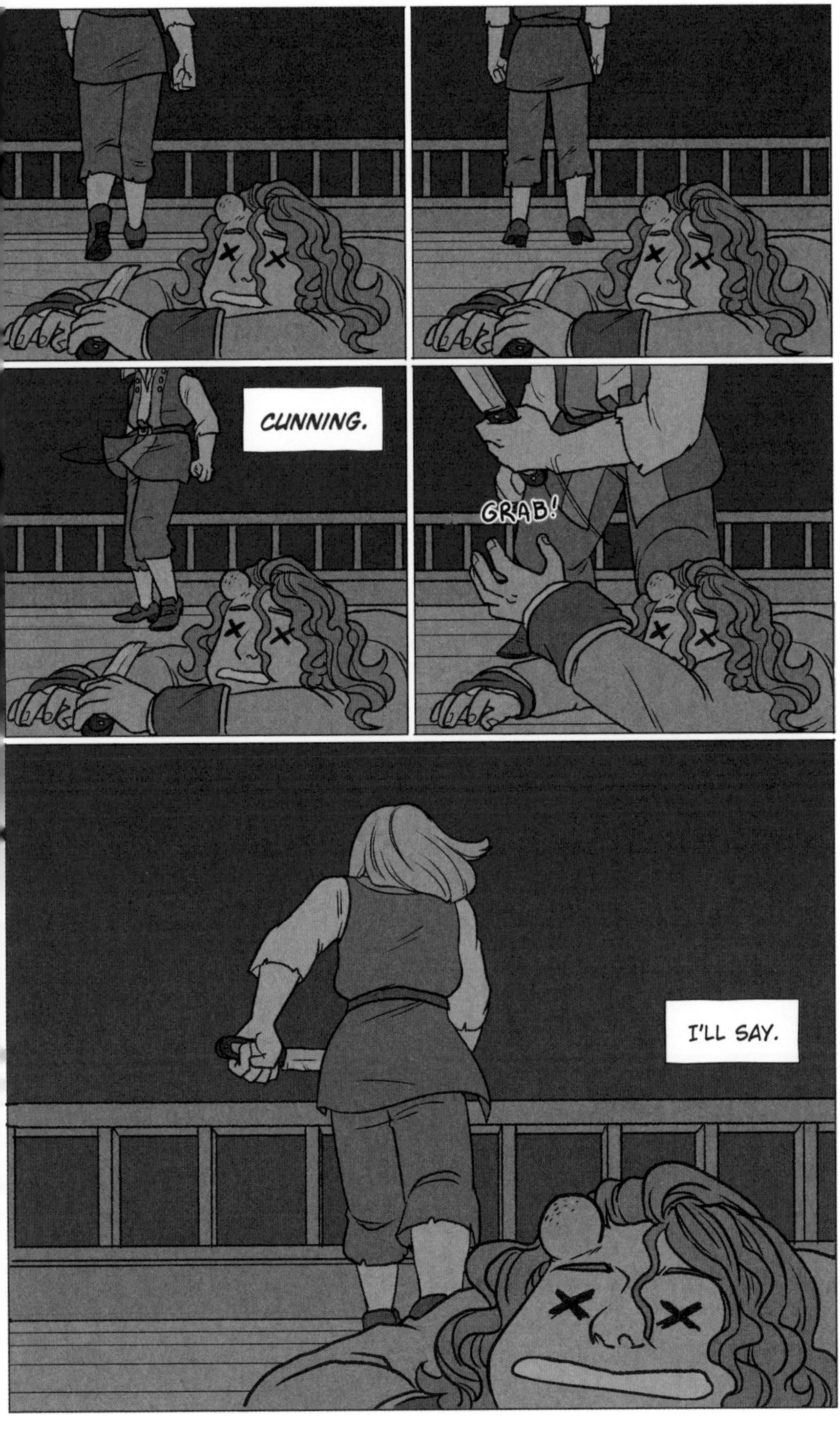
CUNNING.
GRAB!
I'LL SAY.

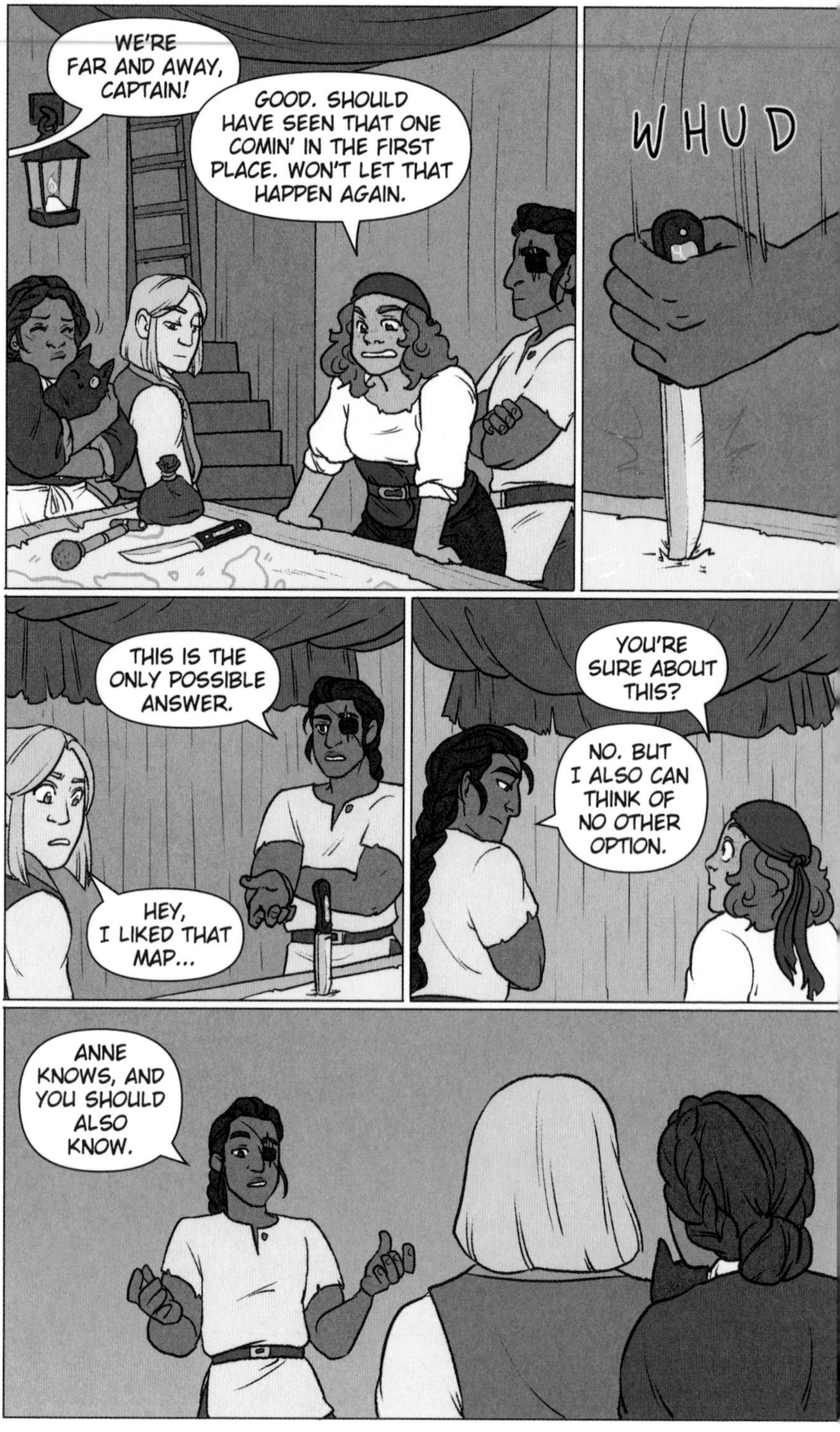
WE'RE FAR AND AWAY, CAPTAIN!
GOOD. SHOULD HAVE SEEN THAT ONE COMIN' IN THE FIRST PLACE. WON'T LET THAT HAPPEN AGAIN.
WHUD
THIS IS THE ONLY POSSIBLE ANSWER.
HEY, I LIKED THAT MAP...
YOU'RE SURE ABOUT THIS?
NO. BUT I ALSO CAN THINK OF NO OTHER OPTION.
ANNE KNOWS, AND YOU SHOULD ALSO KNOW.

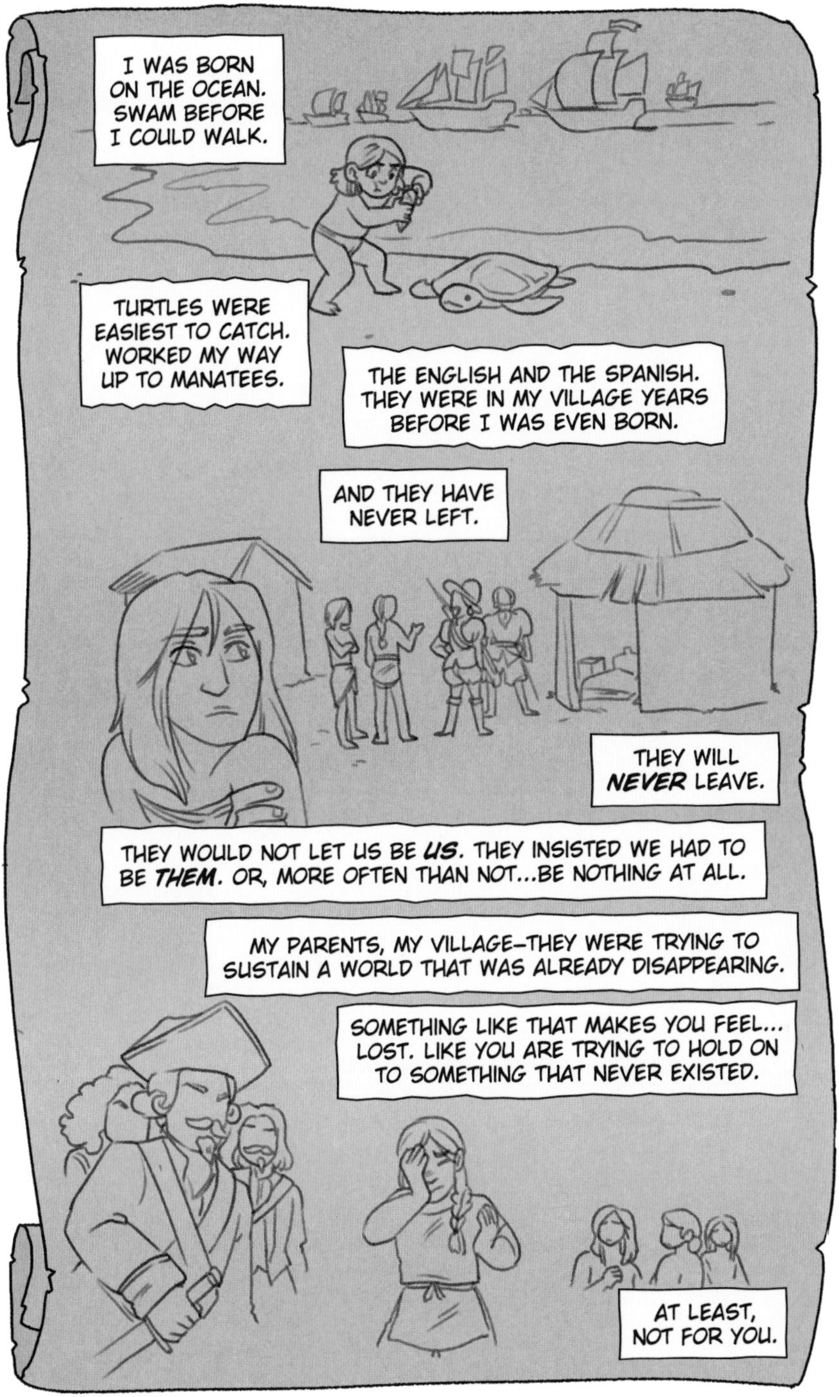
I WAS BORN ON THE OCEAN. SWAM BEFORE I COULD WALK.
TURTLES WERE EASIEST TO CATCH. WORKED MY WAY UP TO MANATEES.
THE ENGLISH AND THE SPANISH. THEY WERE IN MY VILLAGE YEARS BEFORE I WAS EVEN BORN.
AND THEY HAVE NEVER LEFT.
THEY WILL NEVER LEAVE.
THEY WOULD NOT LET US BE US. THEY INSISTED WE HAD TO BE THEM. OR, MORE OFTEN THAN NOT...BE NOTHING AT ALL.
MY PARENTS, MY VILLAGE—THEY WERE TRYING TO SUSTAIN A WORLD THAT WAS ALREADY DISAPPEARING.
SOMETHING LIKE THAT MAKES YOU FEEL... LOST. LIKE YOU ARE TRYING TO HOLD ON TO SOMETHING THAT NEVER EXISTED.
AT LEAST, NOT FOR YOU.

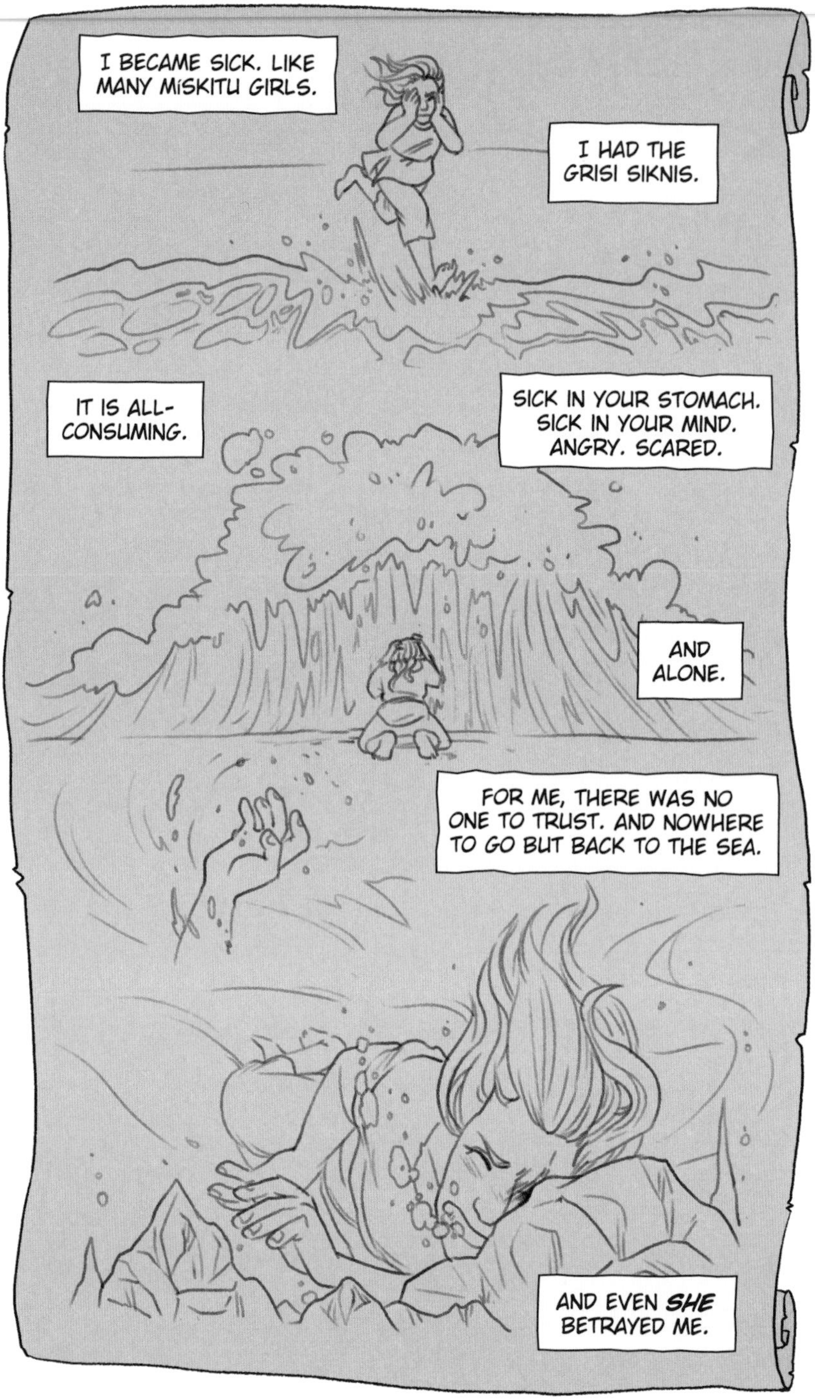
I BECAME SICK. LIKE MANY MISKITU GIRLS.
I HAD THE GRISI SIKNIS.
IT IS ALL-CONSUMING.
SICK IN YOUR STOMACH. SICK IN YOUR MIND. ANGRY. SCARED.
AND ALONE.
FOR ME, THERE WAS NO ONE TO TRUST. AND NOWHERE TO GO BUT BACK TO THE SEA.
AND EVEN ***SHE*** BETRAYED ME.

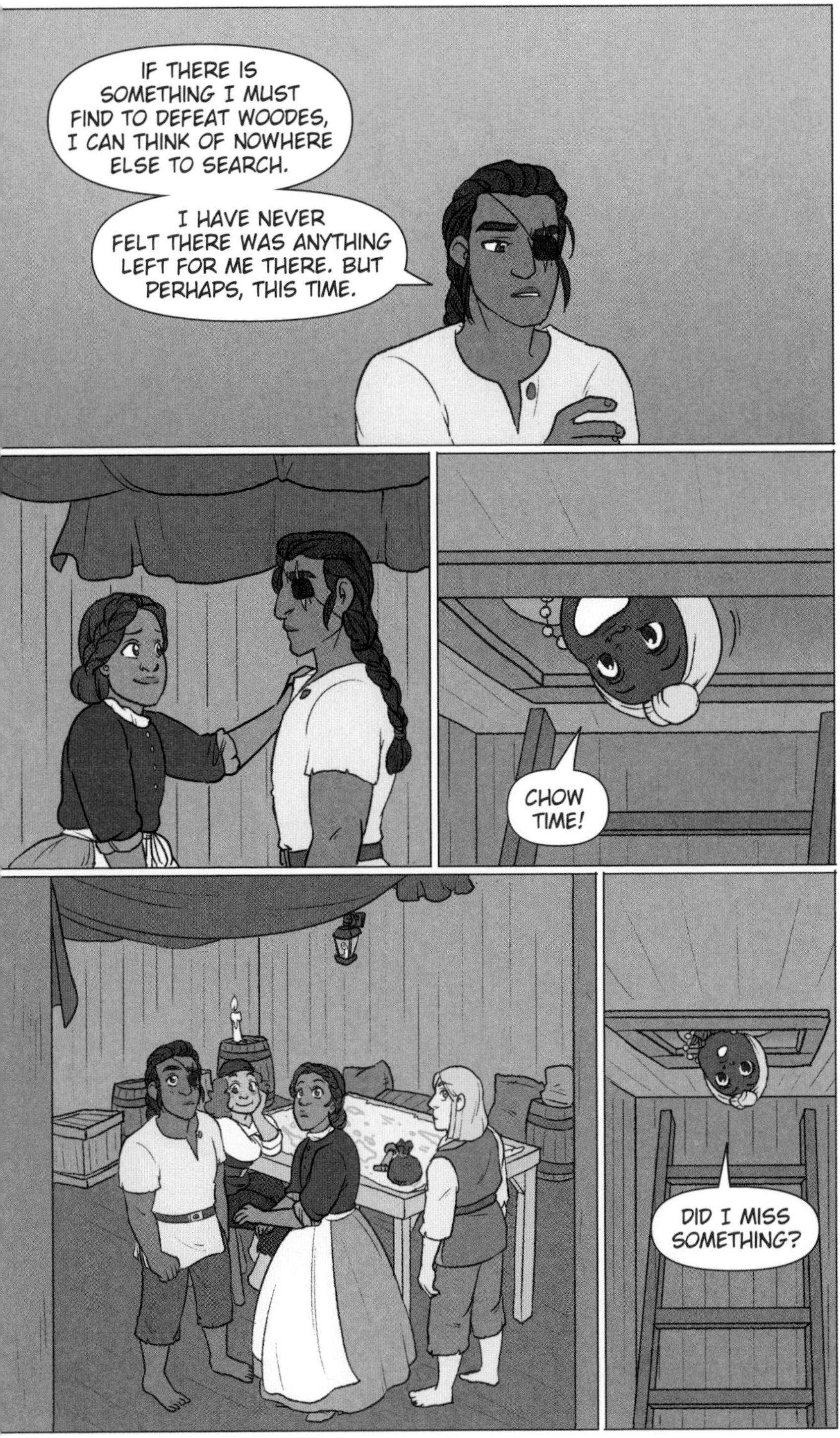
IF THERE IS SOMETHING I MUST FIND TO DEFEAT WOODES, I CAN THINK OF NOWHERE ELSE TO SEARCH.
I HAVE NEVER FELT THERE WAS ANYTHING LEFT FOR ME THERE. BUT PERHAPS, THIS TIME.
CHOW TIME!
DID I MISS SOMETHING?

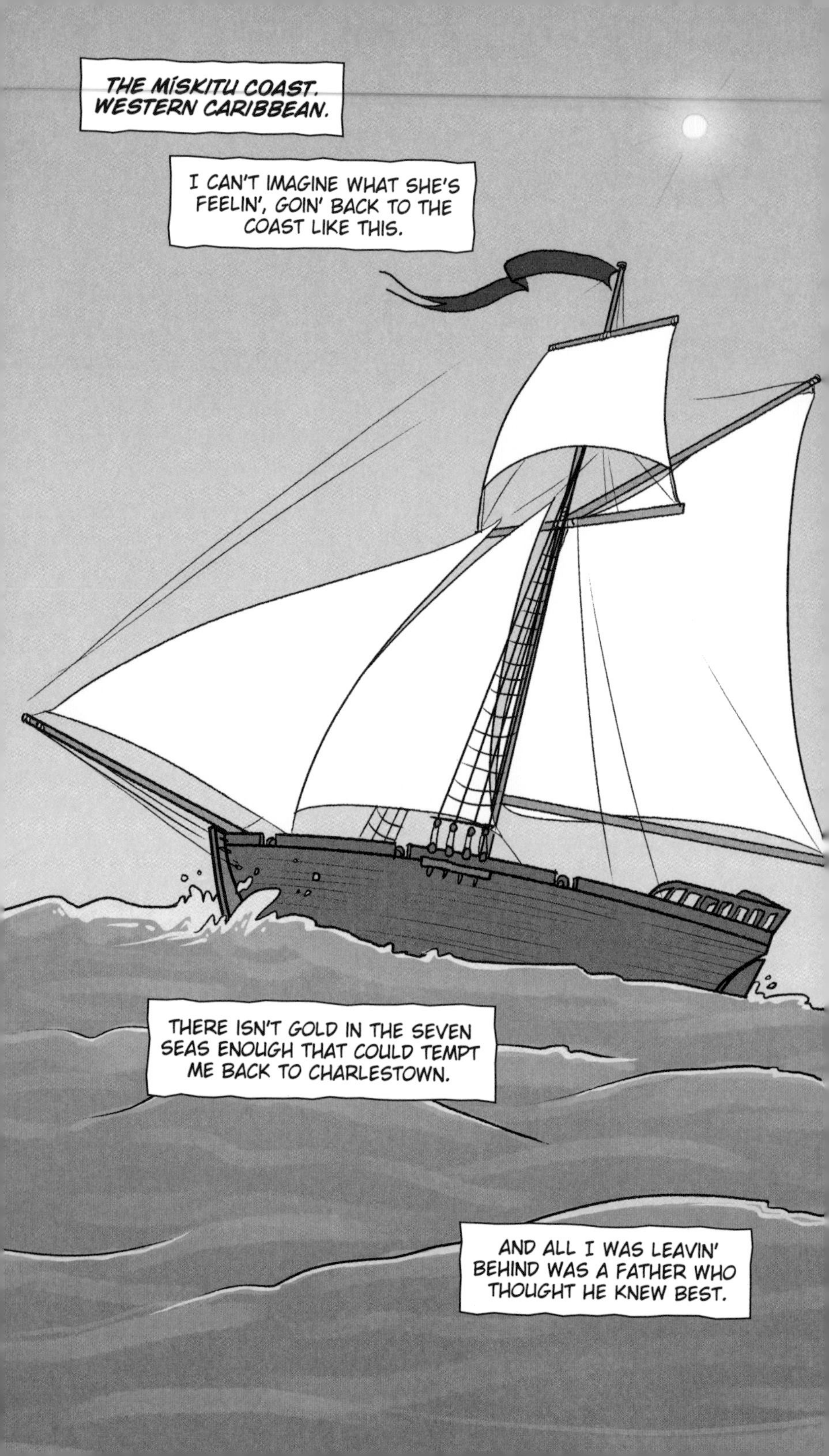
THE MISKITU COAST. WESTERN CARIBBEAN.
I CAN'T IMAGINE WHAT SHE'S FEELIN', GOIN' BACK TO THE COAST LIKE THIS.
THERE ISN'T GOLD IN THE SEVEN SEAS ENOUGH THAT COULD TEMPT ME BACK TO CHARLESTOWN.
AND ALL I WAS LEAVIN' BEHIND WAS A FATHER WHO THOUGHT HE KNEW BEST.

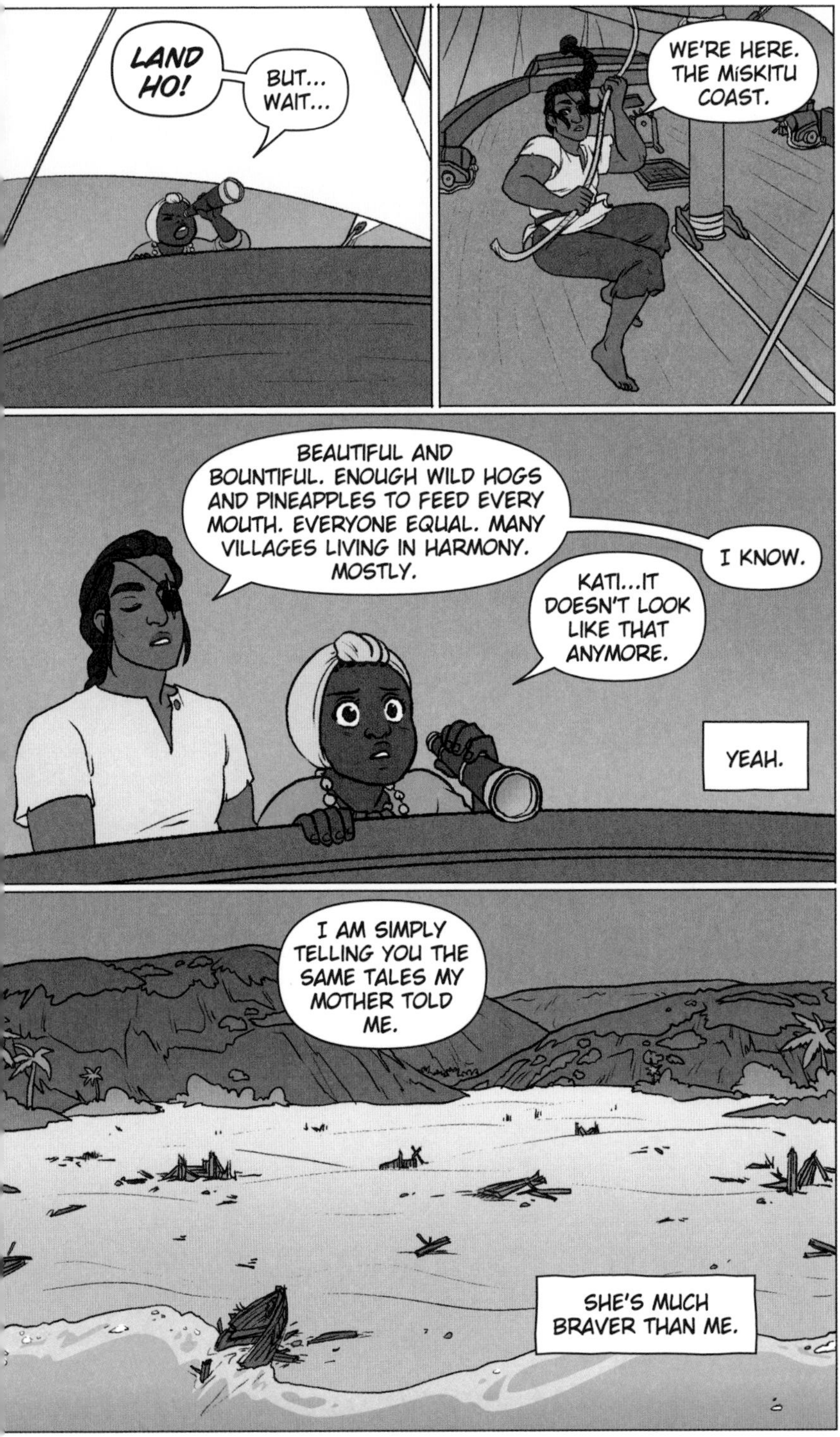
LAND HO!
BUT... WAIT...
WE'RE HERE. THE MiSKITU COAST.
BEAUTIFUL AND BOUNTIFUL. ENOUGH WILD HOGS AND PINEAPPLES TO FEED EVERY MOUTH. EVERYONE EQUAL. MANY VILLAGES LIVING IN HARMONY. MOSTLY.
I KNOW.
KATI...IT DOESN'T LOOK LIKE THAT ANYMORE.
YEAH.
I AM SIMPLY TELLING YOU THE SAME TALES MY MOTHER TOLD ME.
SHE'S MUCH BRAVER THAN ME.

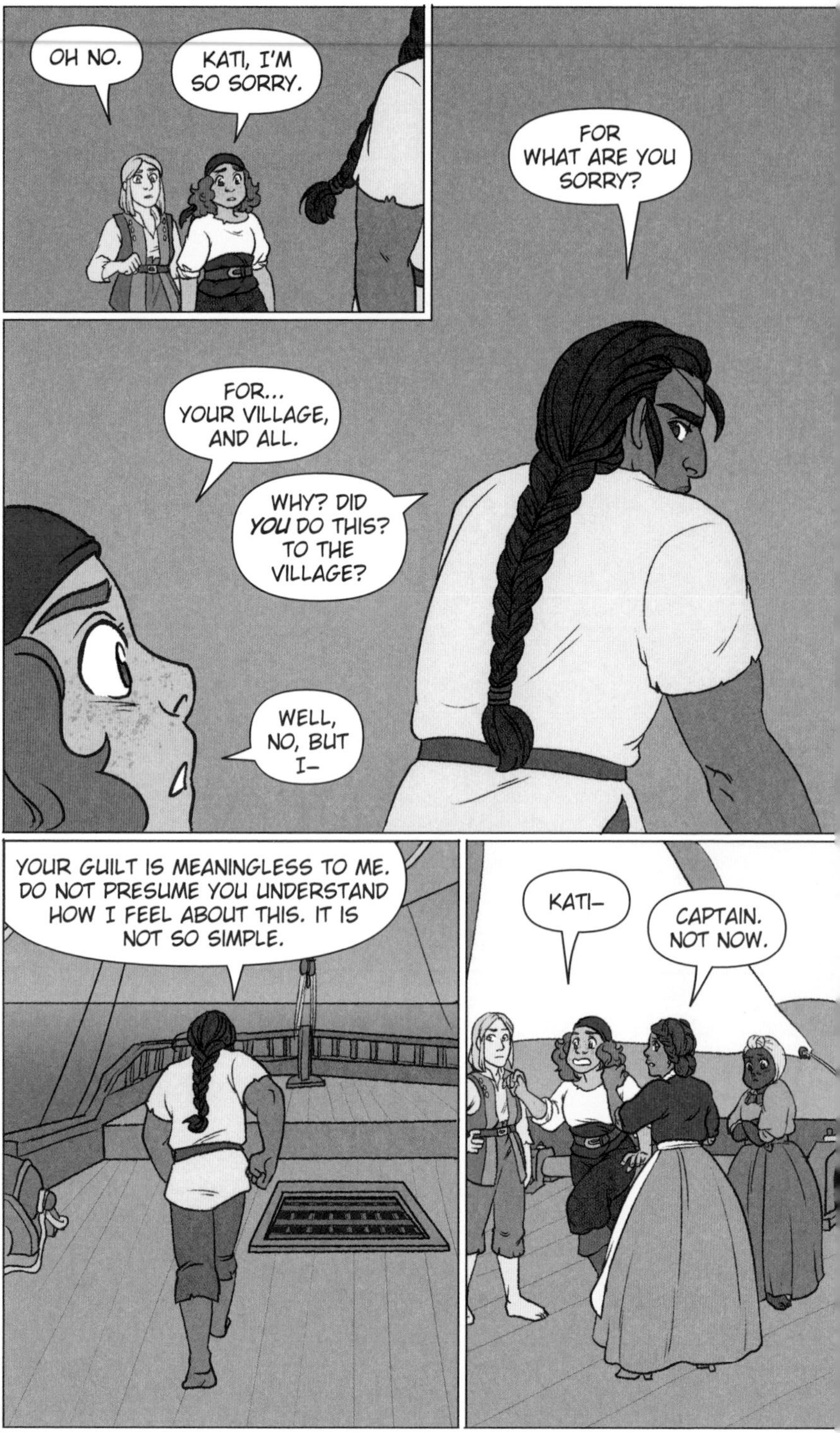
OH NO.
KATI, I'M SO SORRY.
FOR WHAT ARE YOU SORRY?
FOR... YOUR VILLAGE, AND ALL.
WHY? DID *YOU* DO THIS? TO THE VILLAGE?
WELL, NO, BUT I–
YOUR GUILT IS MEANINGLESS TO ME. DO NOT PRESUME YOU UNDERSTAND HOW I FEEL ABOUT THIS. IT IS NOT SO SIMPLE.
KATI–
CAPTAIN. NOT NOW.

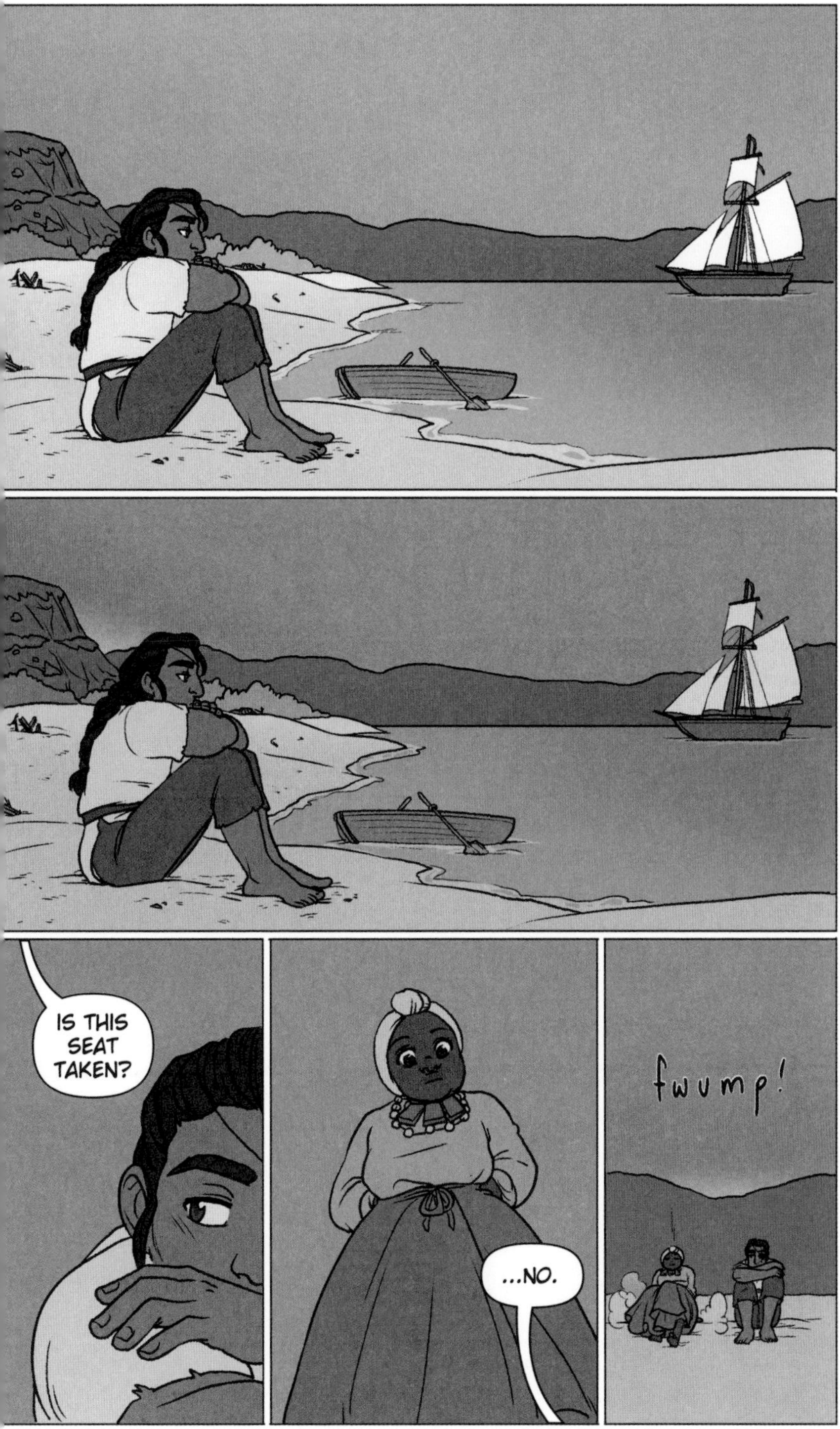
IS THIS SEAT TAKEN?
...NO.
fwump!

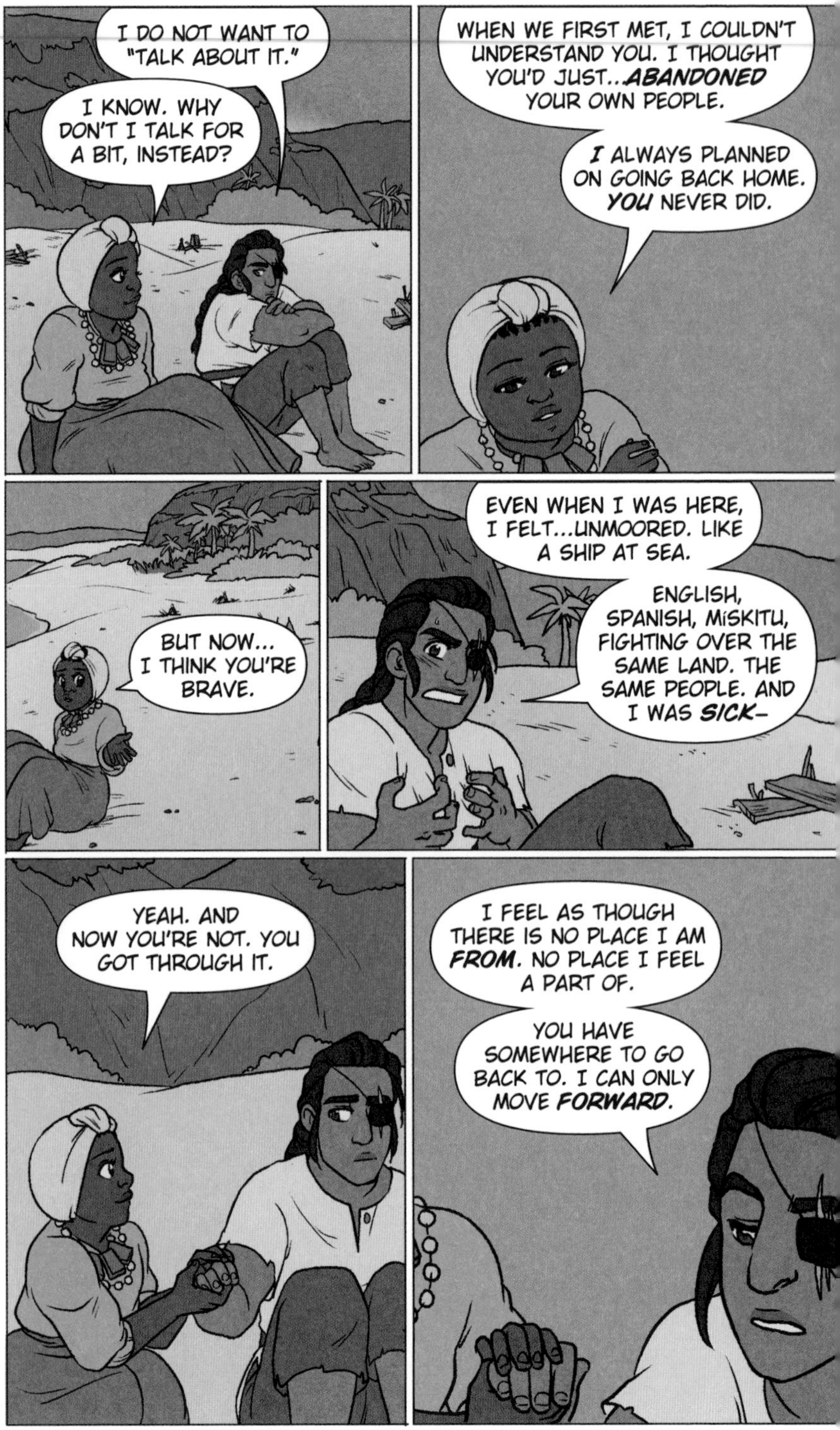
I DO NOT WANT TO "TALK ABOUT IT."
I KNOW. WHY DON'T I TALK FOR A BIT, INSTEAD?
WHEN WE FIRST MET, I COULDN'T UNDERSTAND YOU. I THOUGHT YOU'D JUST...**ABANDONED** YOUR OWN PEOPLE.
I ALWAYS PLANNED ON GOING BACK HOME. ***YOU*** NEVER DID.
BUT NOW... I THINK YOU'RE BRAVE.
EVEN WHEN I WAS HERE, I FELT...UNMOORED. LIKE A SHIP AT SEA.
ENGLISH, SPANISH, MiSKITU, FIGHTING OVER THE SAME LAND. THE SAME PEOPLE. AND I WAS ***SICK***–
YEAH. AND NOW YOU'RE NOT. YOU GOT THROUGH IT.
I FEEL AS THOUGH THERE IS NO PLACE I AM ***FROM***. NO PLACE I FEEL A PART OF.
YOU HAVE SOMEWHERE TO GO BACK TO. I CAN ONLY MOVE ***FORWARD***.

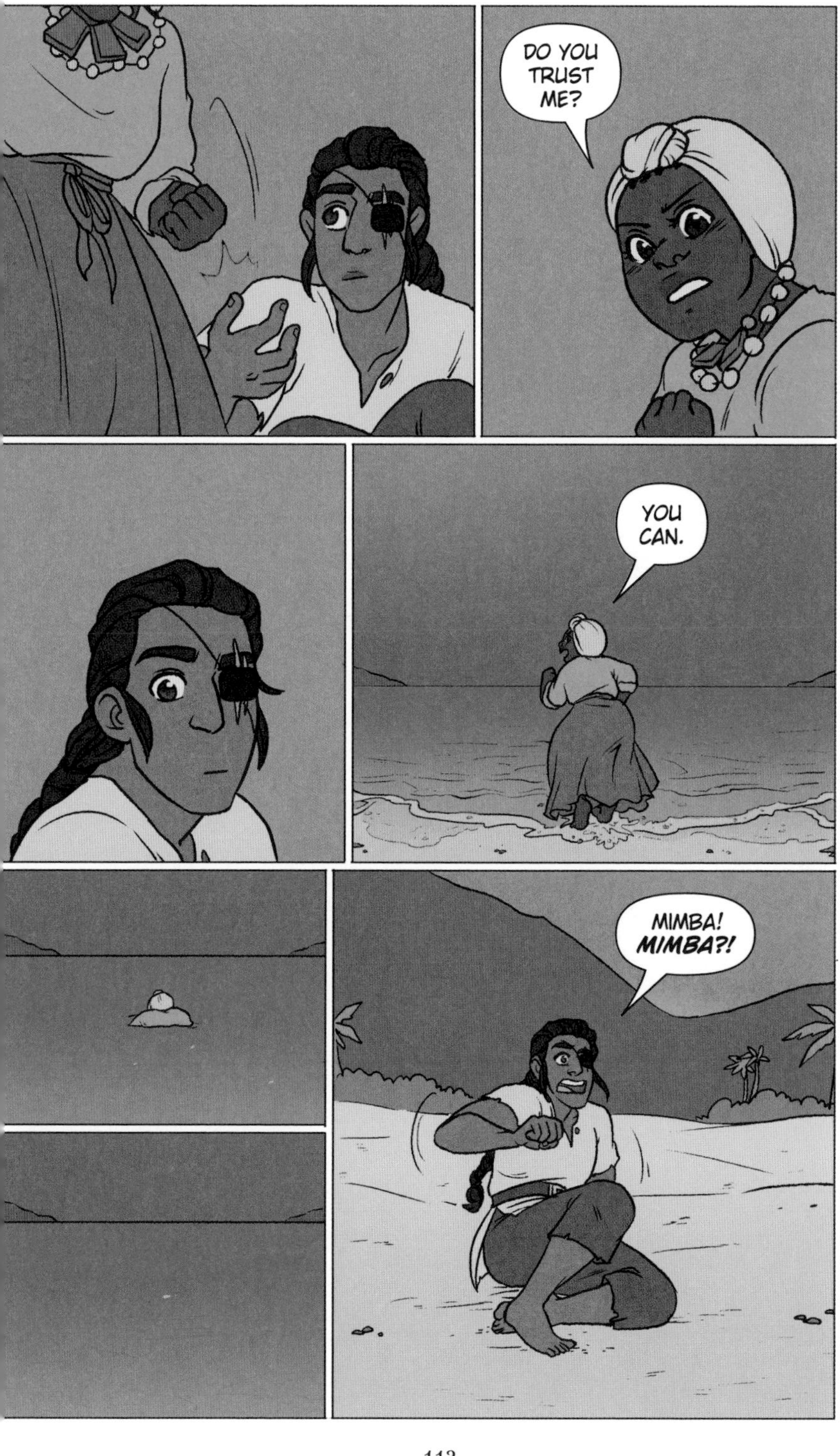
DO YOU TRUST ME?
YOU CAN.
MIMBA! MIMBA?!

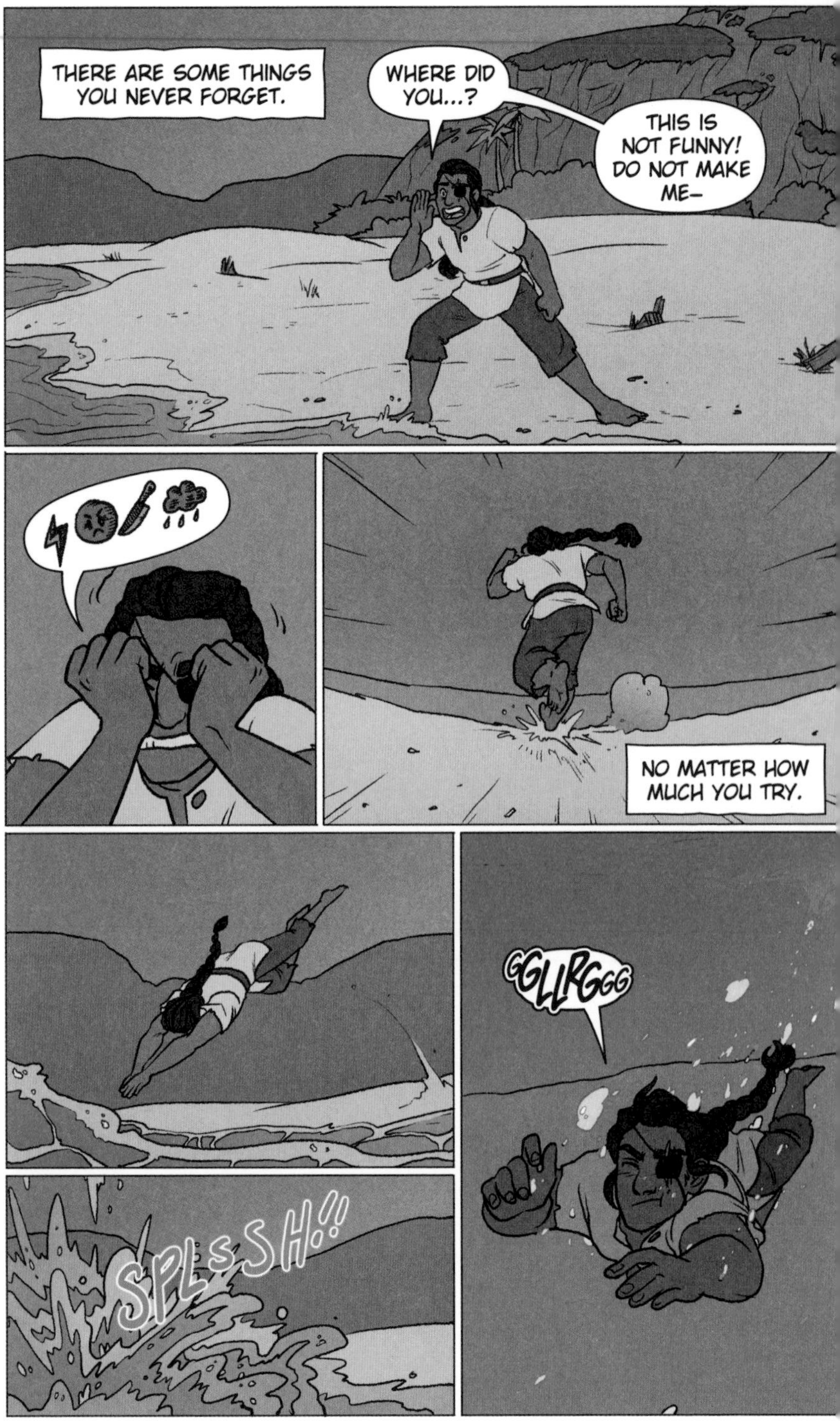
THERE ARE SOME THINGS YOU NEVER FORGET.
WHERE DID YOU...?
THIS IS NOT FUNNY! DO NOT MAKE ME–
NO MATTER HOW MUCH YOU TRY.
SPLSSH!!
GGLLRGGG

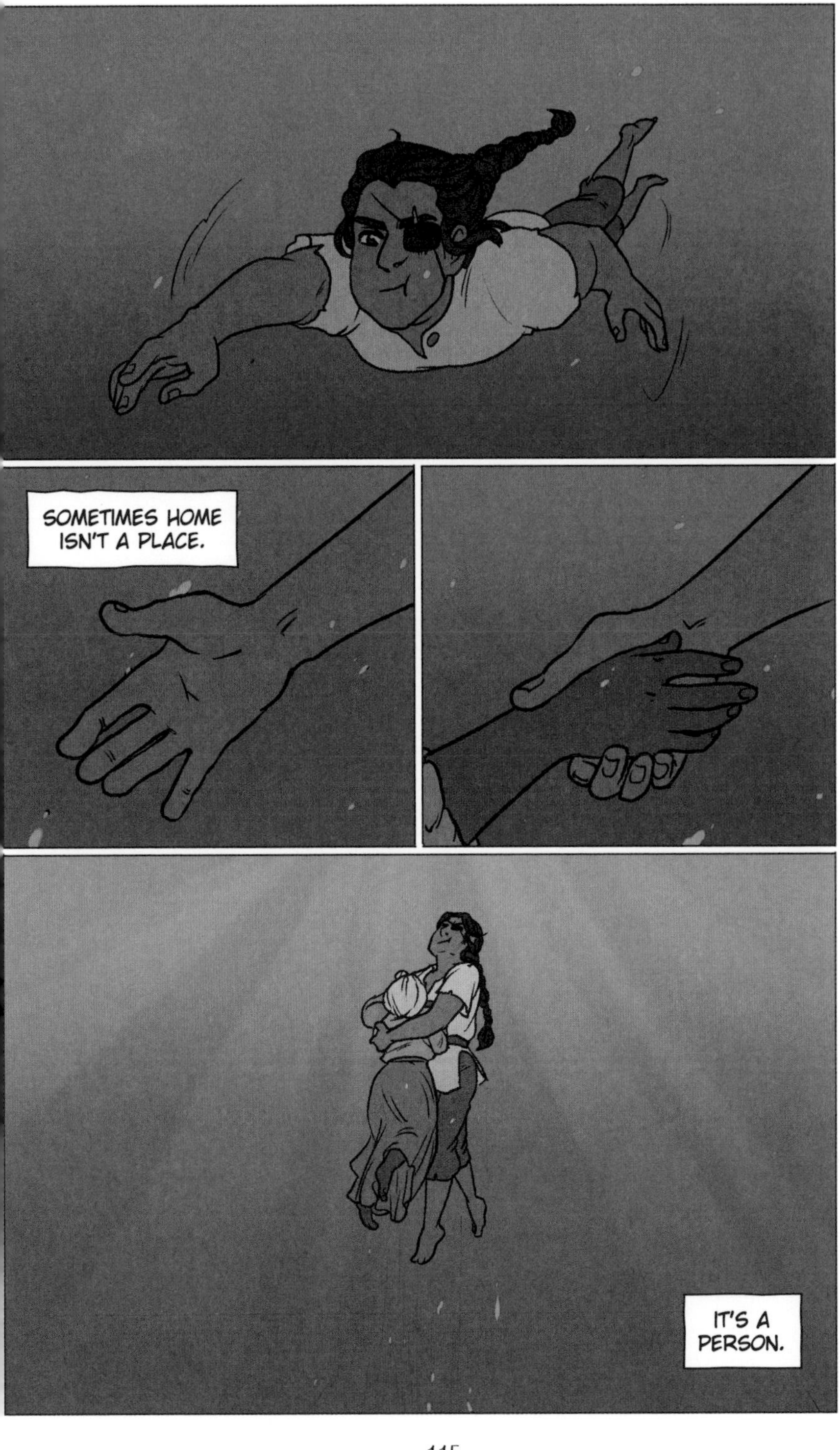
SOMETIMES HOME
ISN'T A PLACE.
IT'S A
PERSON.

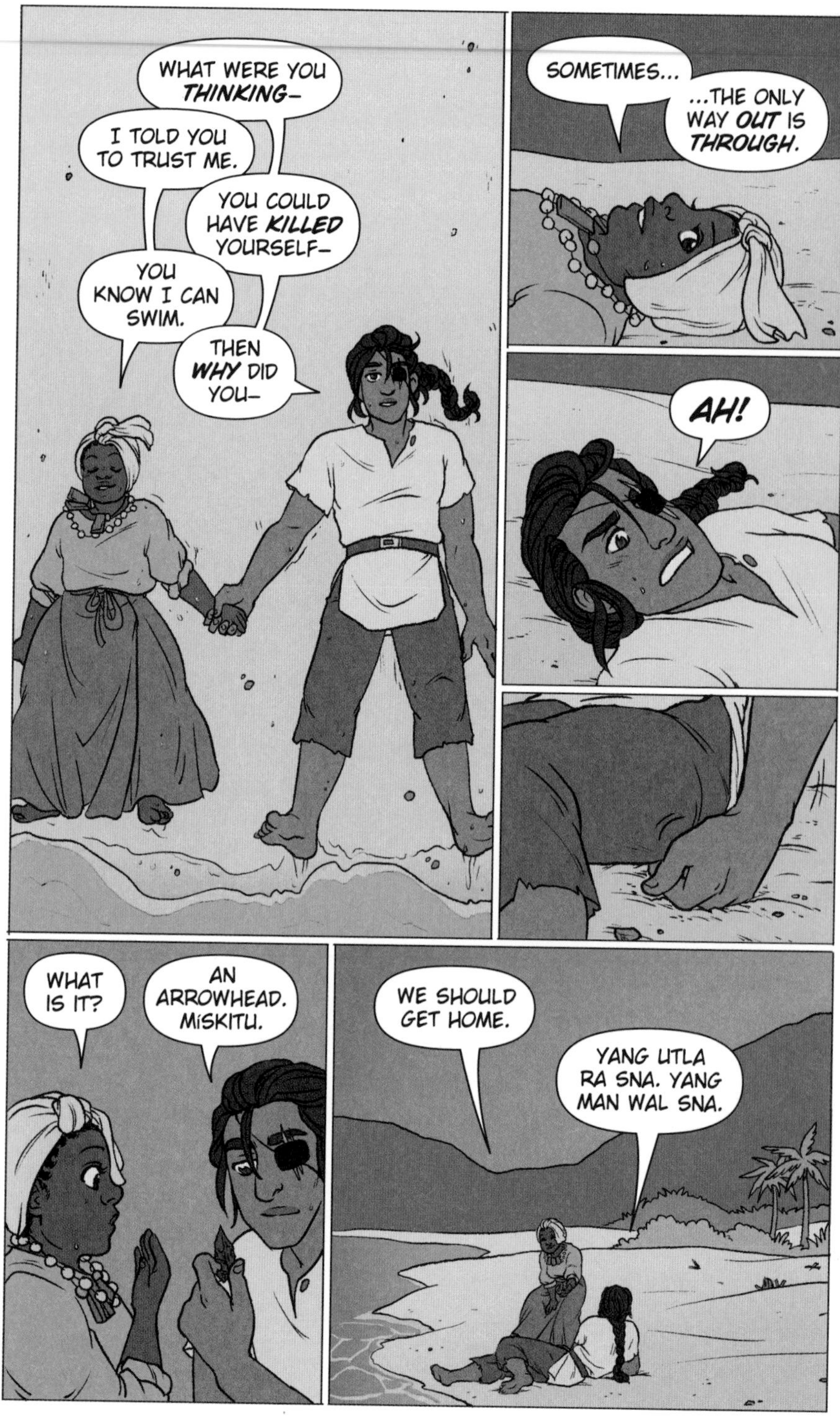
WHAT WERE YOU THINKING–
I TOLD YOU TO TRUST ME.
YOU COULD HAVE KILLED YOURSELF–
YOU KNOW I CAN SWIM.
THEN WHY DID YOU–
SOMETIMES...
...THE ONLY WAY OUT IS THROUGH.
AH!
WHAT IS IT?
AN ARROWHEAD. MISKITU.
WE SHOULD GET HOME.
YANG UTLA RA SNA. YANG MAN WAL SNA.

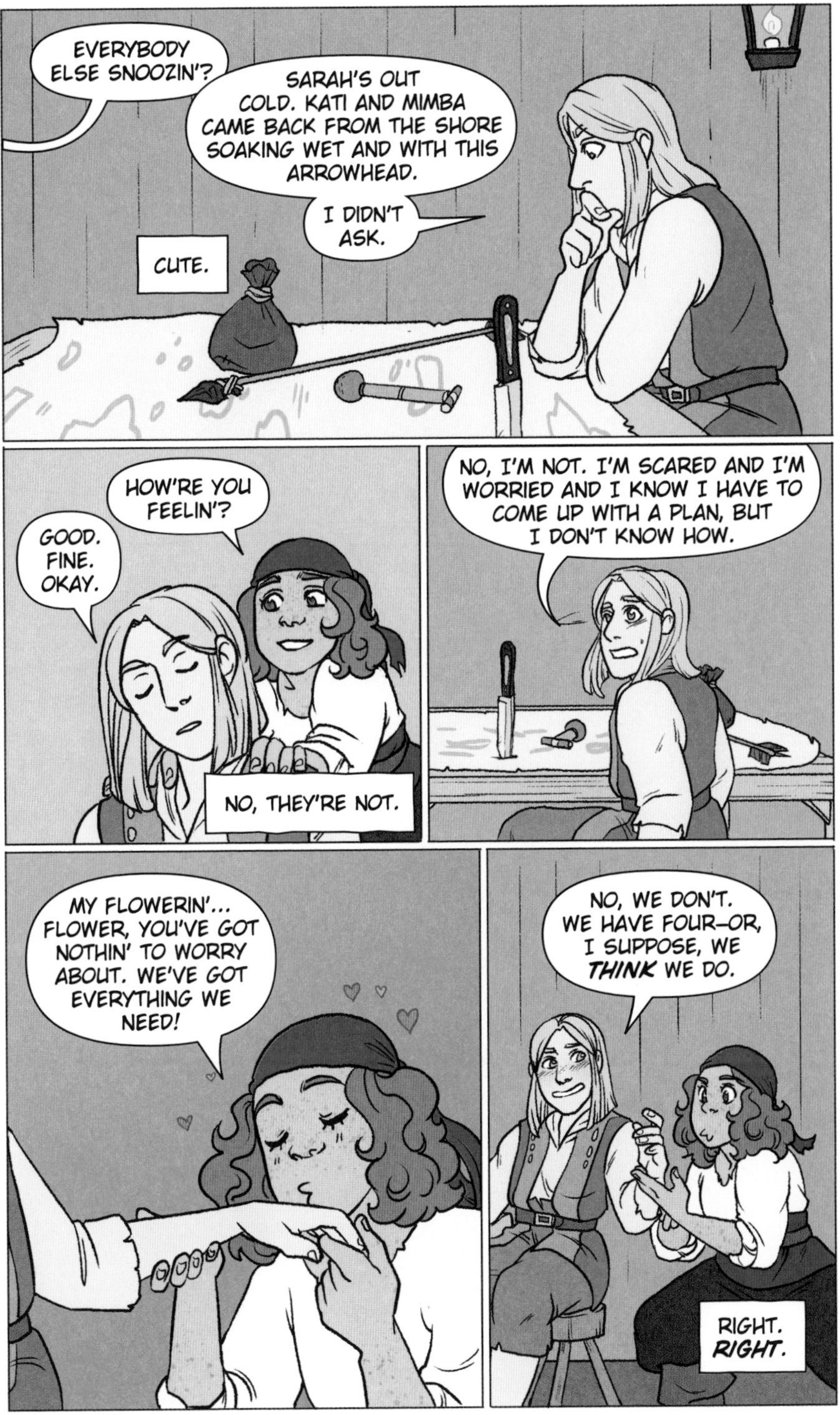
EVERYBODY ELSE SNOOZIN'?
SARAH'S OUT COLD. KATI AND MIMBA CAME BACK FROM THE SHORE SOAKING WET AND WITH THIS ARROWHEAD.
I DIDN'T ASK.
CUTE.
HOW'RE YOU FEELIN'?
GOOD. FINE. OKAY.
NO, THEY'RE NOT.
NO, I'M NOT. I'M SCARED AND I'M WORRIED AND I KNOW I HAVE TO COME UP WITH A PLAN, BUT I DON'T KNOW HOW.
MY FLOWERIN'... FLOWER, YOU'VE GOT NOTHIN' TO WORRY ABOUT. WE'VE GOT EVERYTHING WE NEED!
NO, WE DON'T. WE HAVE FOUR—OR, I SUPPOSE, WE *THINK* WE DO.
RIGHT. *RIGHT*.

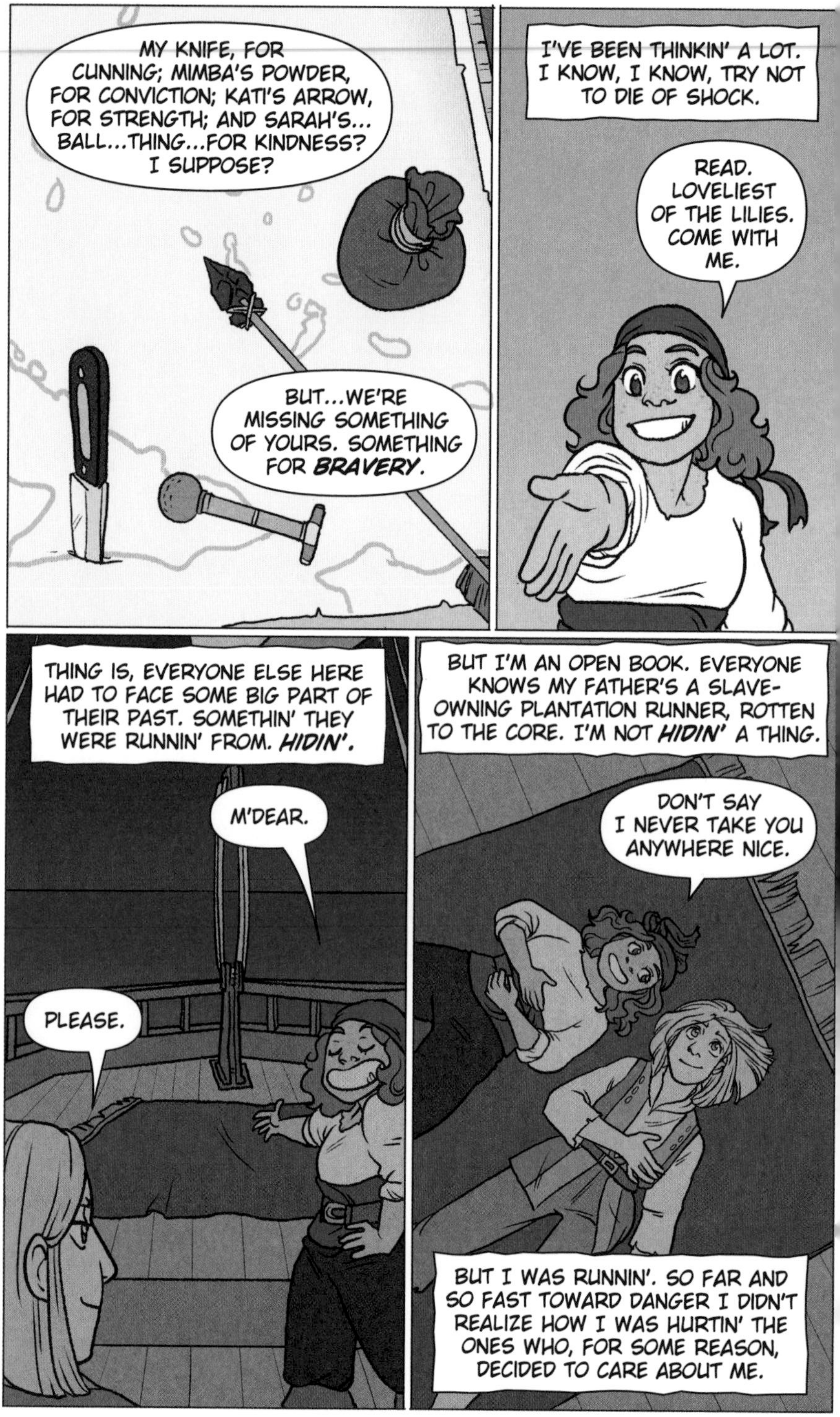
MY KNIFE, FOR CUNNING; MIMBA'S POWDER, FOR CONVICTION; KATI'S ARROW, FOR STRENGTH; AND SARAH'S... BALL...THING...FOR KINDNESS? I SUPPOSE?
BUT...WE'RE MISSING SOMETHING OF YOURS. SOMETHING FOR BRAVERY.
I'VE BEEN THINKIN' A LOT. I KNOW, I KNOW, TRY NOT TO DIE OF SHOCK.
READ. LOVELIEST OF THE LILIES. COME WITH ME.
THING IS, EVERYONE ELSE HERE HAD TO FACE SOME BIG PART OF THEIR PAST. SOMETHIN' THEY WERE RUNNIN' FROM. HIDIN'.
M'DEAR.
PLEASE.
BUT I'M AN OPEN BOOK. EVERYONE KNOWS MY FATHER'S A SLAVE-OWNING PLANTATION RUNNER, ROTTEN TO THE CORE. I'M NOT HIDIN' A THING.
DON'T SAY I NEVER TAKE YOU ANYWHERE NICE.
BUT I WAS RUNNIN'. SO FAR AND SO FAST TOWARD DANGER I DIDN'T REALIZE HOW I WAS HURTIN' THE ONES WHO, FOR SOME REASON, DECIDED TO CARE ABOUT ME.

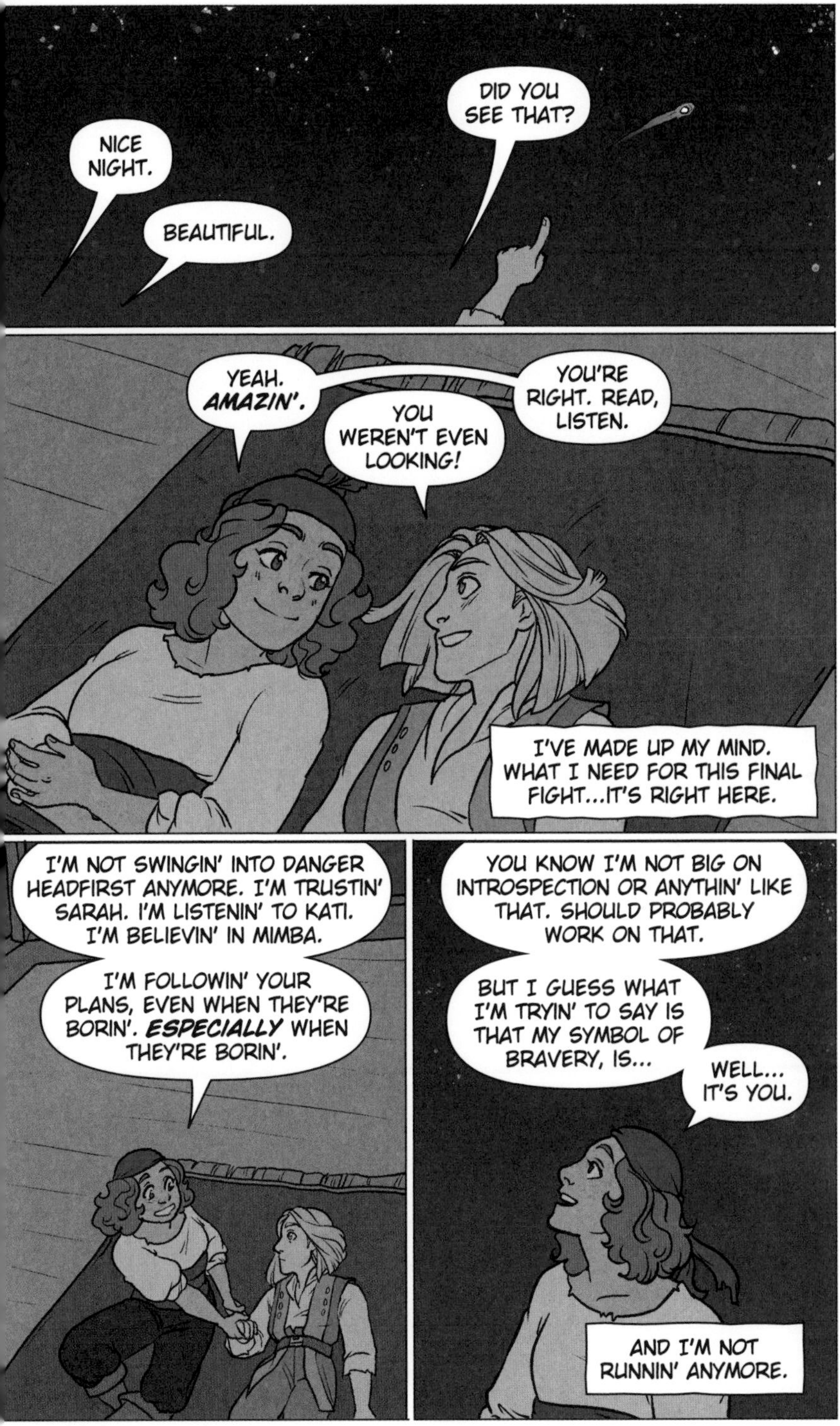
NICE NIGHT.
BEAUTIFUL.
DID YOU SEE THAT?
YEAH. AMAZIN'.
YOU WEREN'T EVEN LOOKING!
YOU'RE RIGHT. READ, LISTEN.
I'VE MADE UP MY MIND. WHAT I NEED FOR THIS FINAL FIGHT...IT'S RIGHT HERE.
I'M NOT SWINGIN' INTO DANGER HEADFIRST ANYMORE. I'M TRUSTIN' SARAH. I'M LISTENIN' TO KATI. I'M BELIEVIN' IN MIMBA.
I'M FOLLOWIN' YOUR PLANS, EVEN WHEN THEY'RE BORIN'. ESPECIALLY WHEN THEY'RE BORIN'.
YOU KNOW I'M NOT BIG ON INTROSPECTION OR ANYTHIN' LIKE THAT. SHOULD PROBABLY WORK ON THAT.
BUT I GUESS WHAT I'M TRYIN' TO SAY IS THAT MY SYMBOL OF BRAVERY, IS...
WELL... IT'S YOU.
AND I'M NOT RUNNIN' ANYMORE.

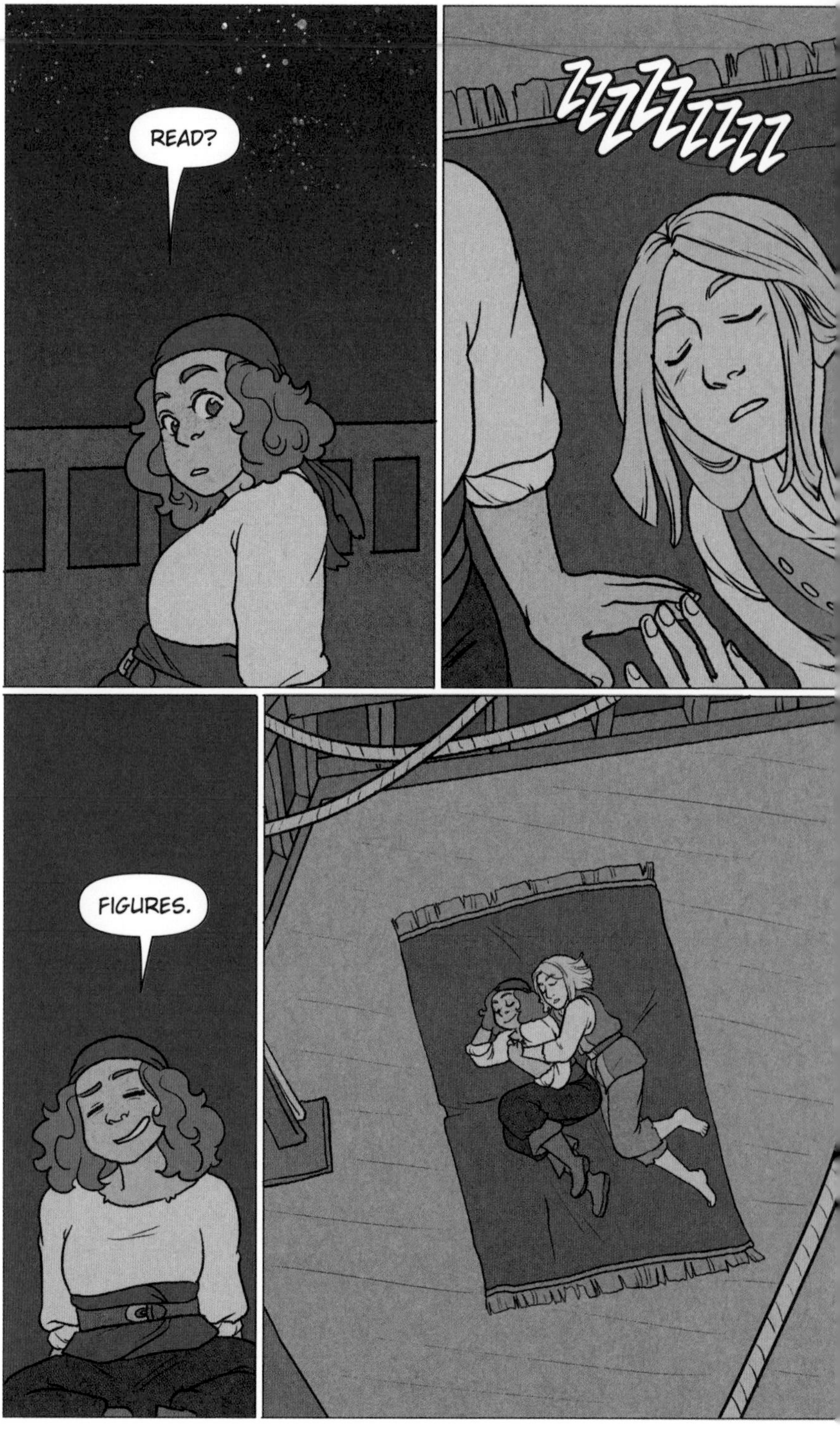
READ?
ZZZZZZZZZ
FIGURES.

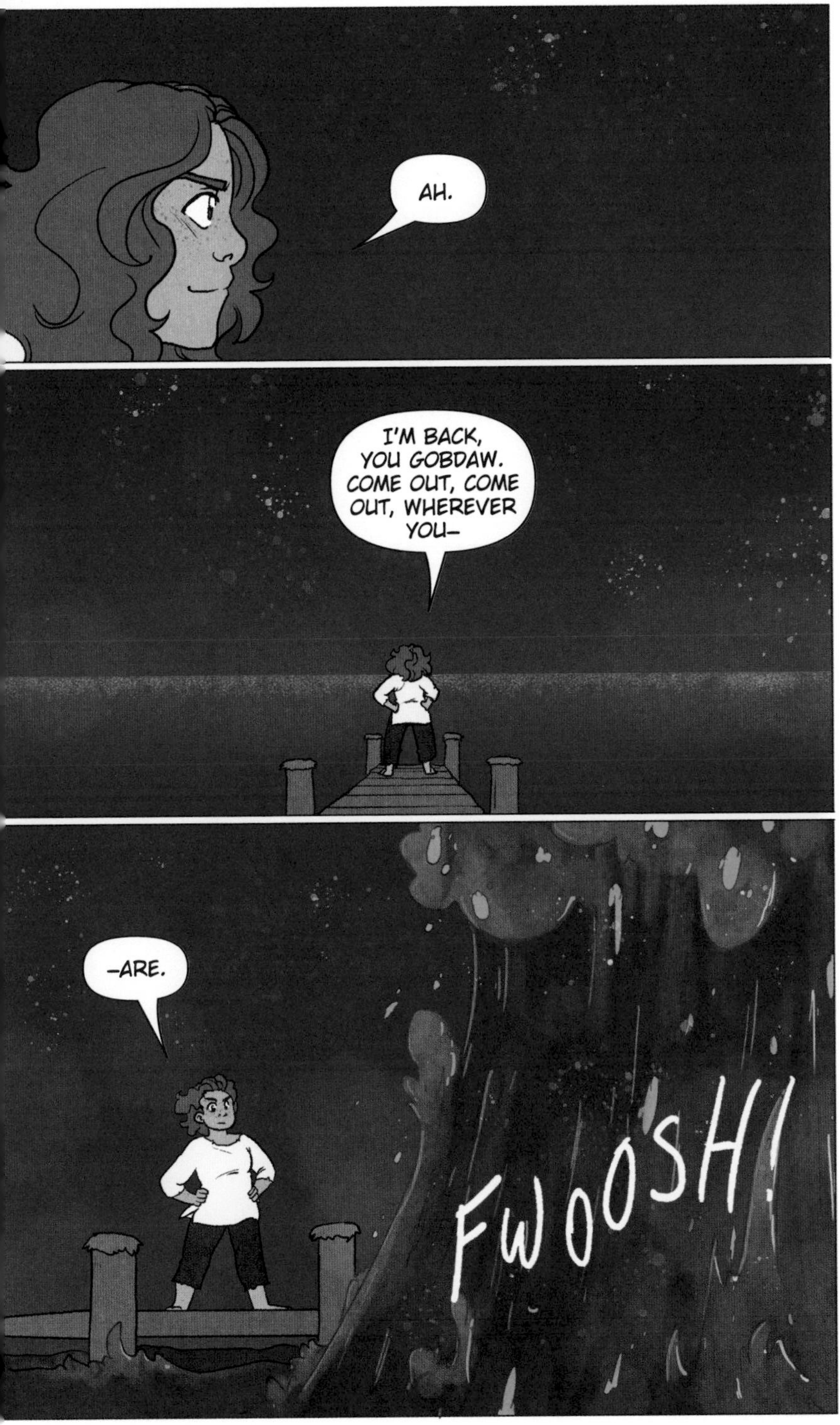
AH.
I'M BACK, YOU GOBDAW. COME OUT, COME OUT, WHEREVER YOU–
–ARE.
FWOOSH!

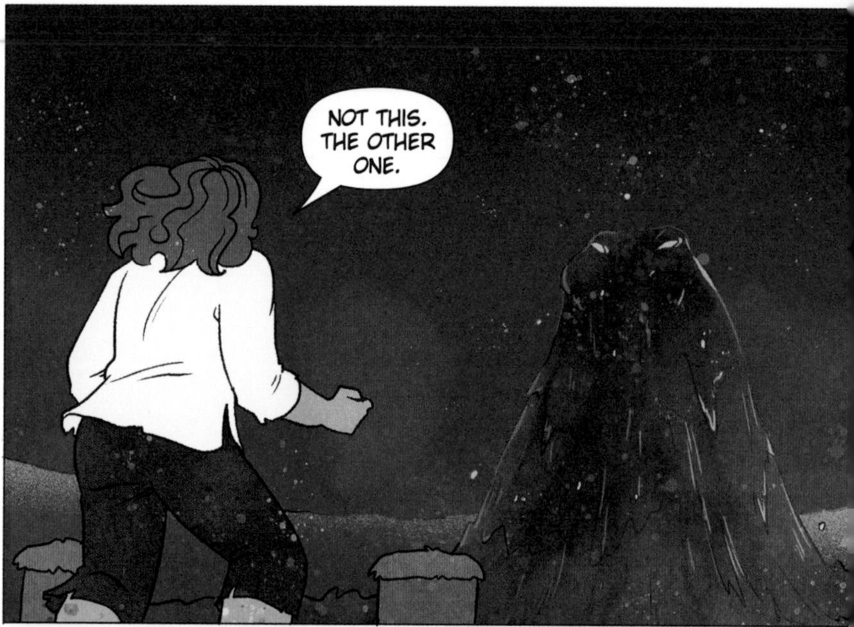
NOT THIS. THE OTHER ONE.

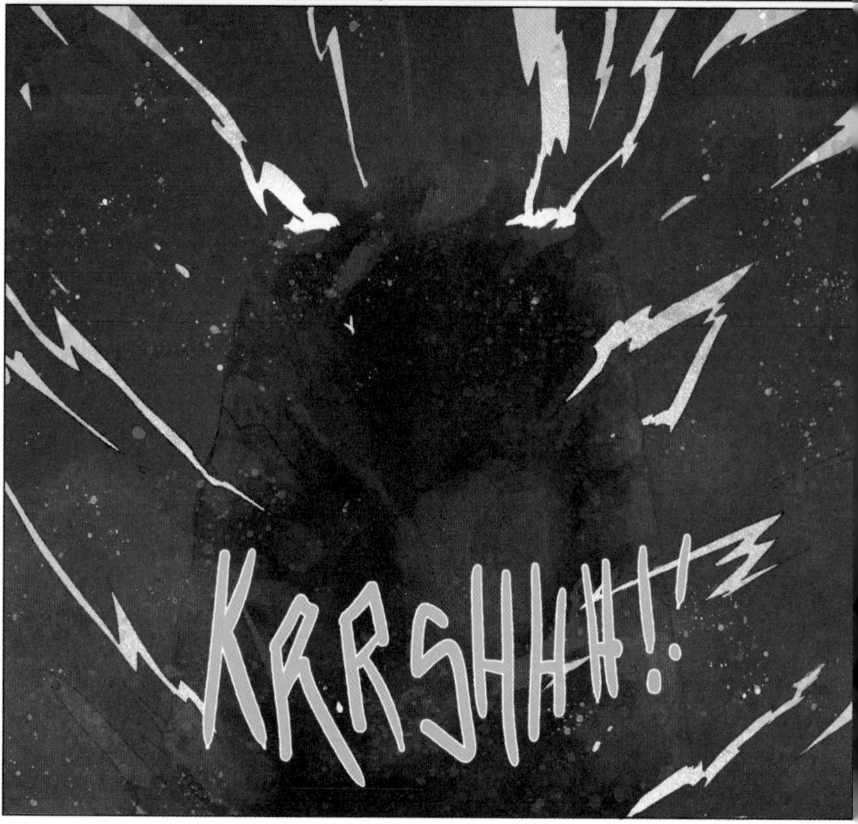
KRRSHHH!

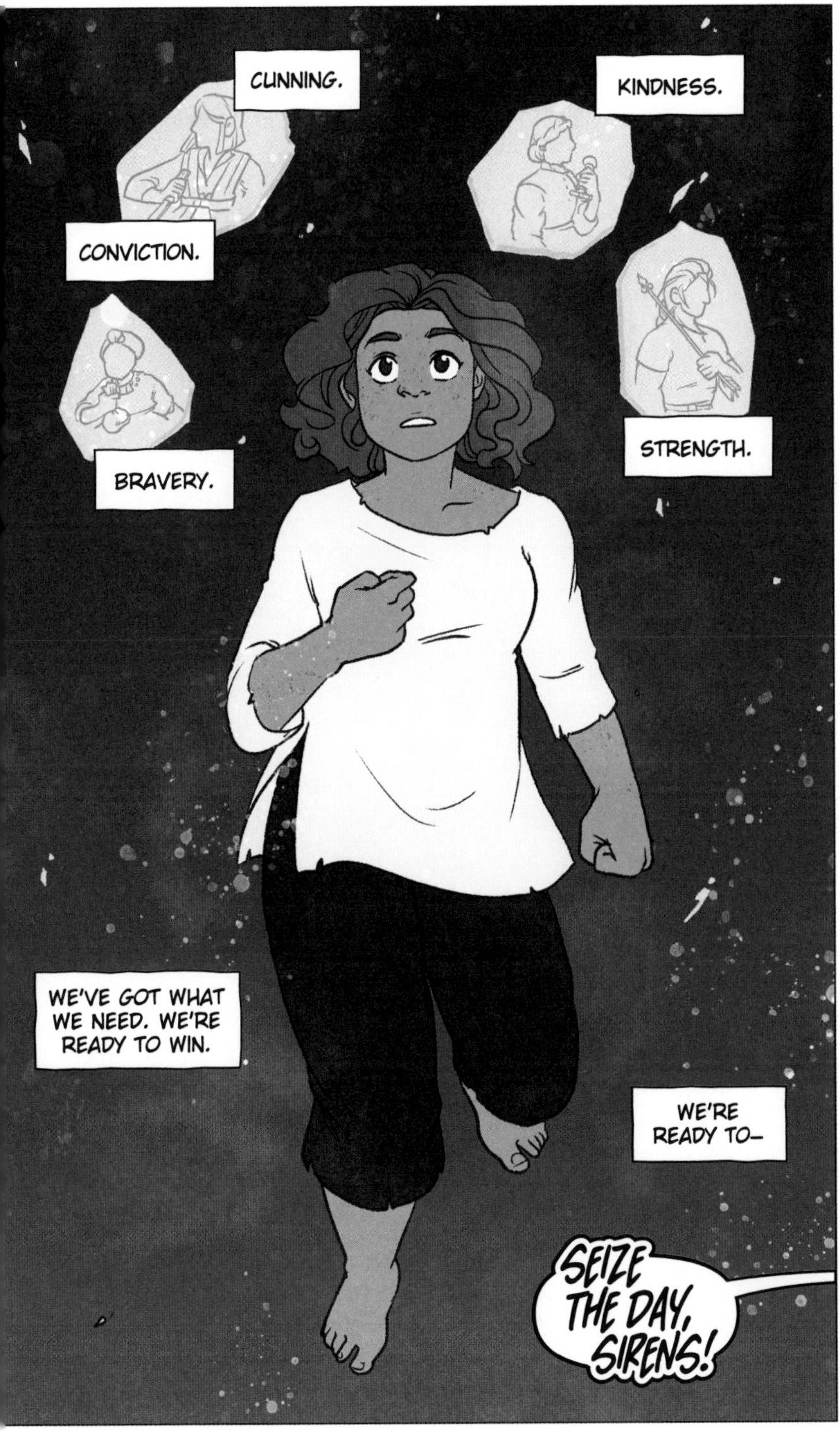
CUNNING.
KINDNESS.
CONVICTION.
BRAVERY.
STRENGTH.
WE'VE GOT WHAT WE NEED. WE'RE READY TO WIN.
WE'RE READY TO—
SEIZE THE DAY, SIRENS!

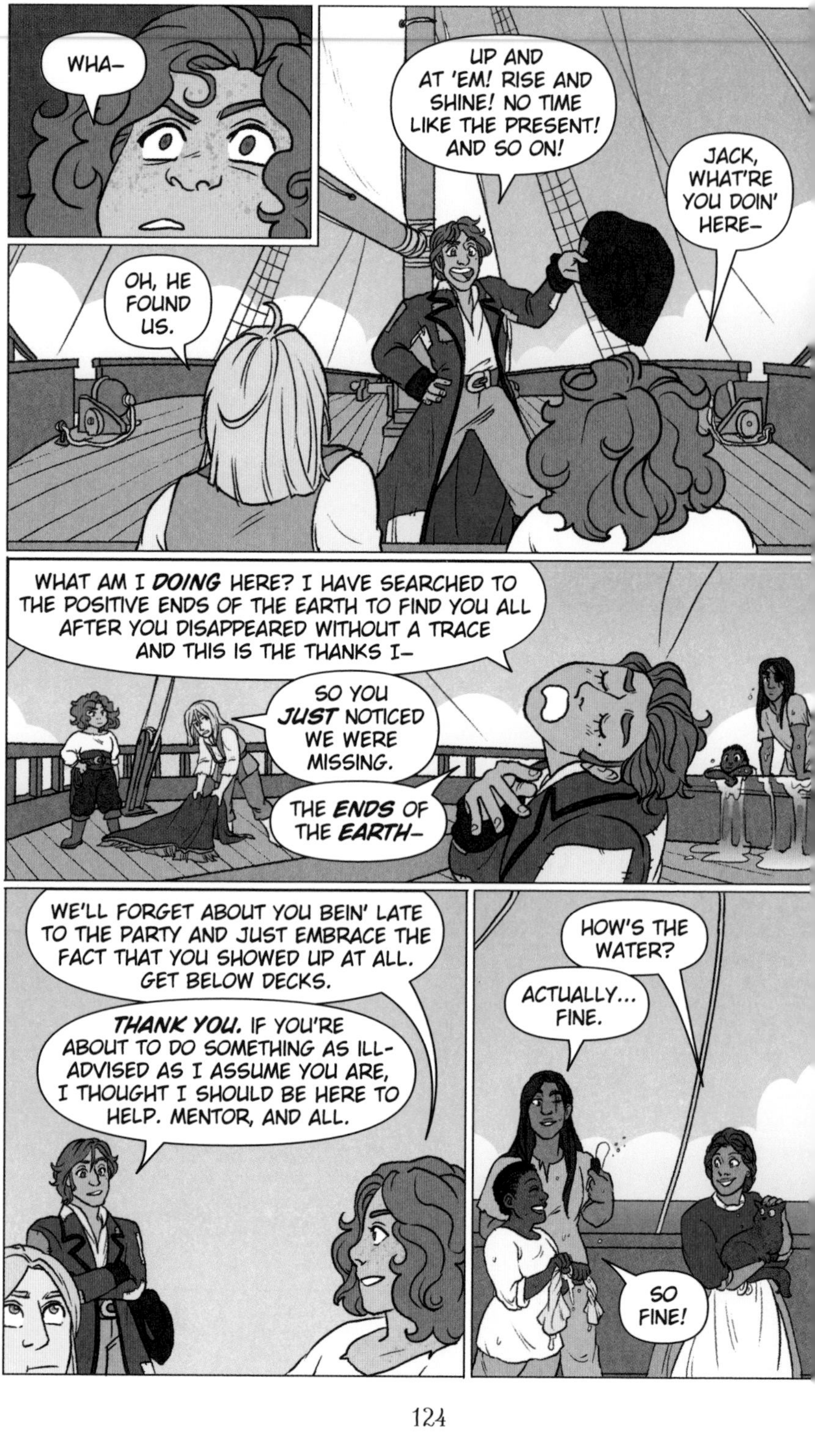
WHA-
UP AND AT 'EM! RISE AND SHINE! NO TIME LIKE THE PRESENT! AND SO ON!
JACK, WHAT'RE YOU DOIN' HERE-
OH, HE FOUND US.
WHAT AM I DOING HERE? I HAVE SEARCHED TO THE POSITIVE ENDS OF THE EARTH TO FIND YOU ALL AFTER YOU DISAPPEARED WITHOUT A TRACE AND THIS IS THE THANKS I-
SO YOU JUST NOTICED WE WERE MISSING.
THE ENDS OF THE EARTH-
WE'LL FORGET ABOUT YOU BEIN' LATE TO THE PARTY AND JUST EMBRACE THE FACT THAT YOU SHOWED UP AT ALL. GET BELOW DECKS.
THANK YOU. IF YOU'RE ABOUT TO DO SOMETHING AS ILL-ADVISED AS I ASSUME YOU ARE, I THOUGHT I SHOULD BE HERE TO HELP. MENTOR, AND ALL.
HOW'S THE WATER?
ACTUALLY... FINE.
SO FINE!

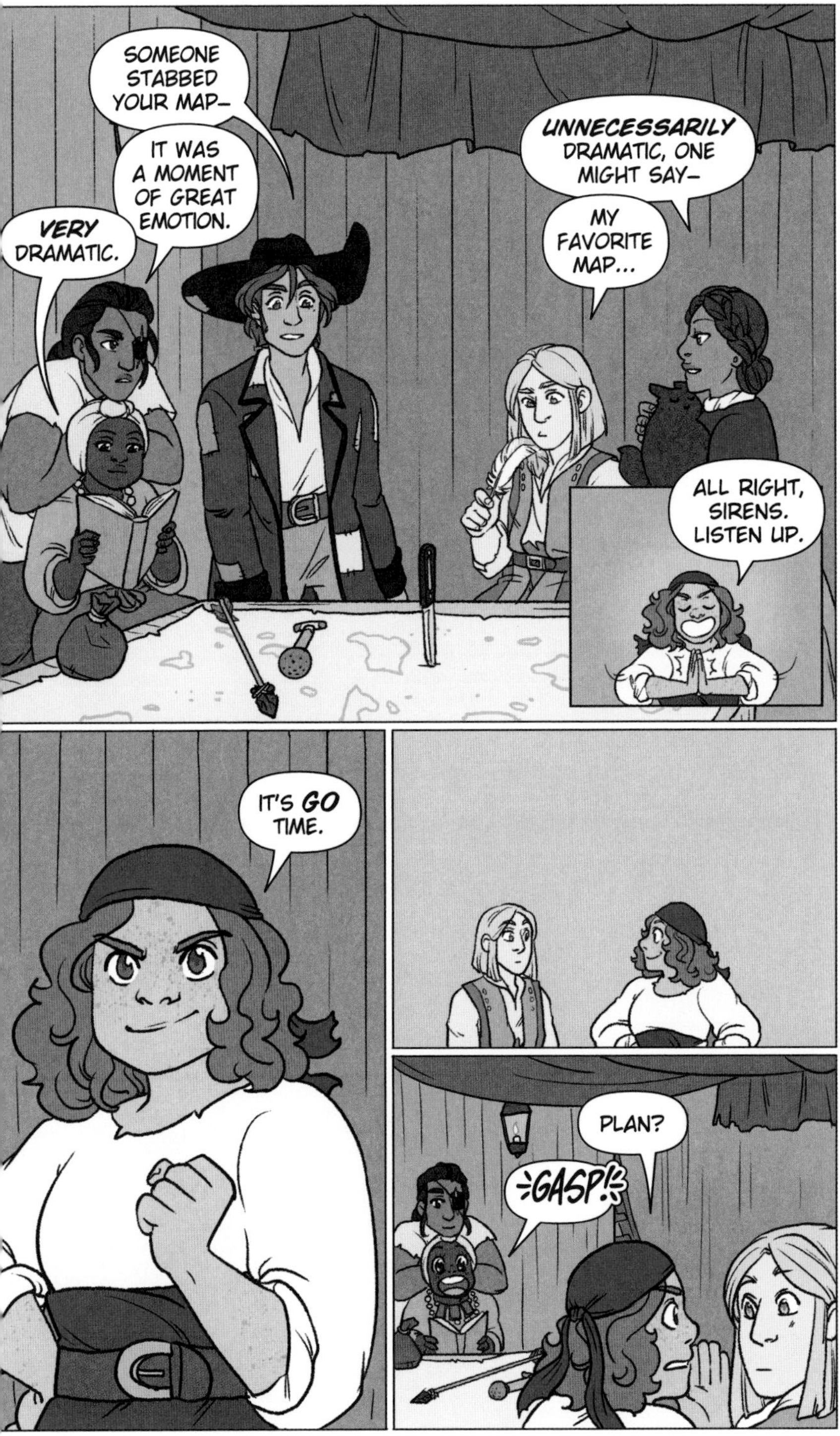
SOMEONE STABBED YOUR MAP—
IT WAS A MOMENT OF GREAT EMOTION.
VERY DRAMATIC.
UNNECESSARILY DRAMATIC, ONE MIGHT SAY—
MY FAVORITE MAP...
ALL RIGHT, SIRENS. LISTEN UP.
IT'S GO TIME.
PLAN?
GASP!

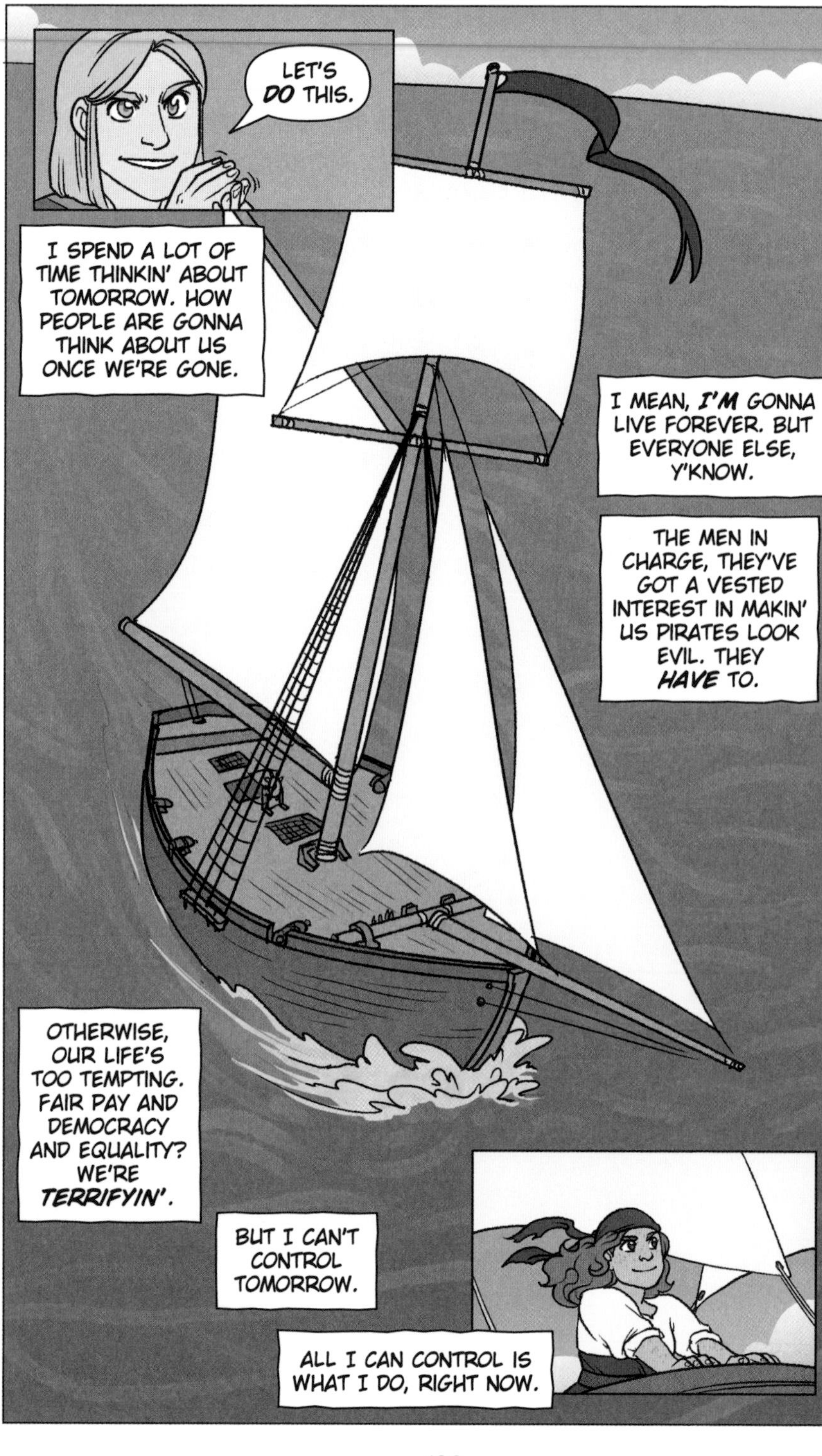
LET'S **DO** THIS.
I SPEND A LOT OF TIME THINKIN' ABOUT TOMORROW. HOW PEOPLE ARE GONNA THINK ABOUT US ONCE WE'RE GONE.
I MEAN, ***I'M*** GONNA LIVE FOREVER. BUT EVERYONE ELSE, Y'KNOW.
THE MEN IN CHARGE, THEY'VE GOT A VESTED INTEREST IN MAKIN' US PIRATES LOOK EVIL. THEY ***HAVE*** TO.
OTHERWISE, OUR LIFE'S TOO TEMPTING. FAIR PAY AND DEMOCRACY AND EQUALITY? WE'RE ***TERRIFYIN'***.
BUT I CAN'T CONTROL TOMORROW.
ALL I CAN CONTROL IS WHAT I DO, RIGHT NOW.

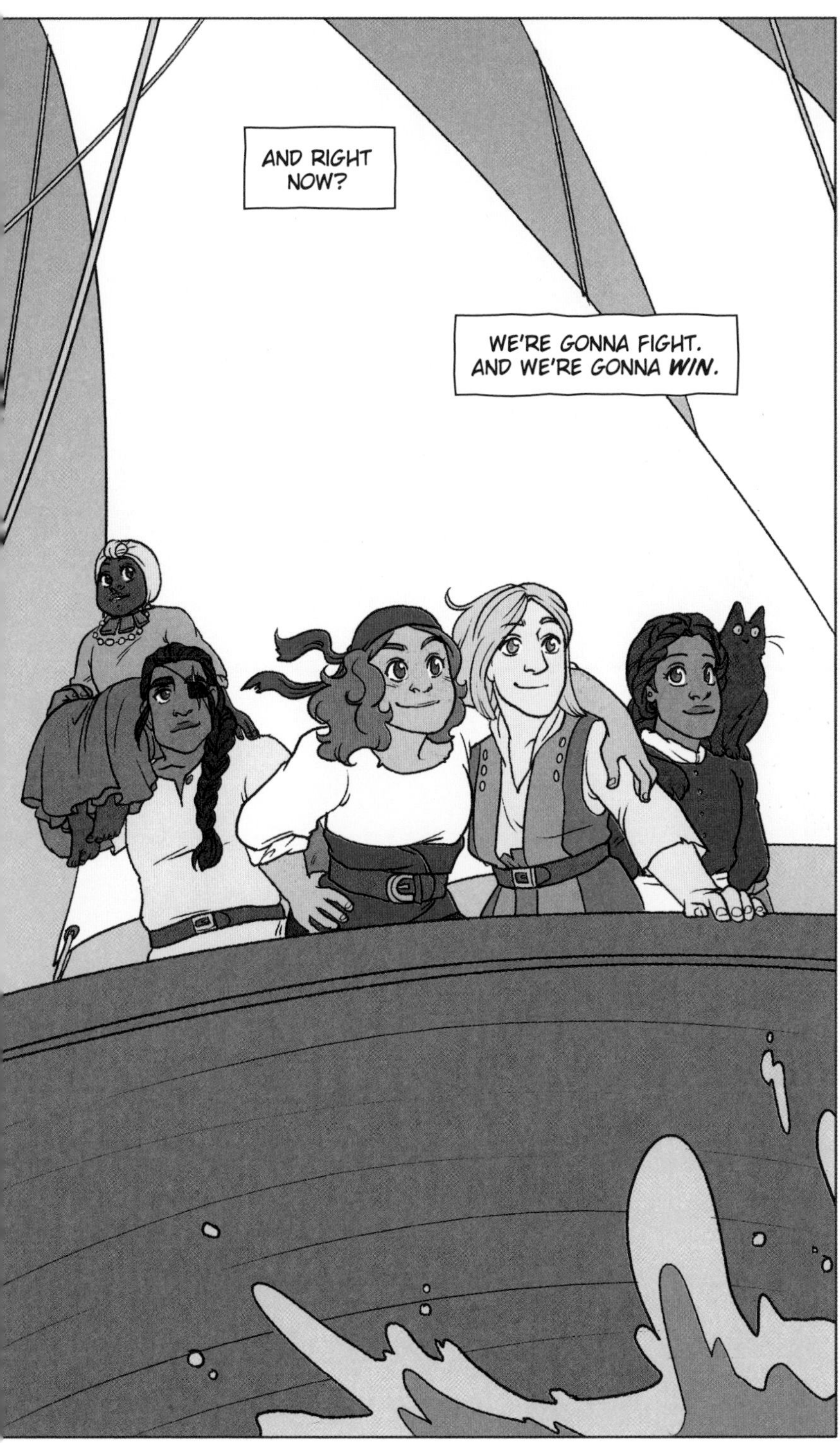
AND RIGHT NOW?
WE'RE GONNA FIGHT. AND WE'RE GONNA *WIN*.

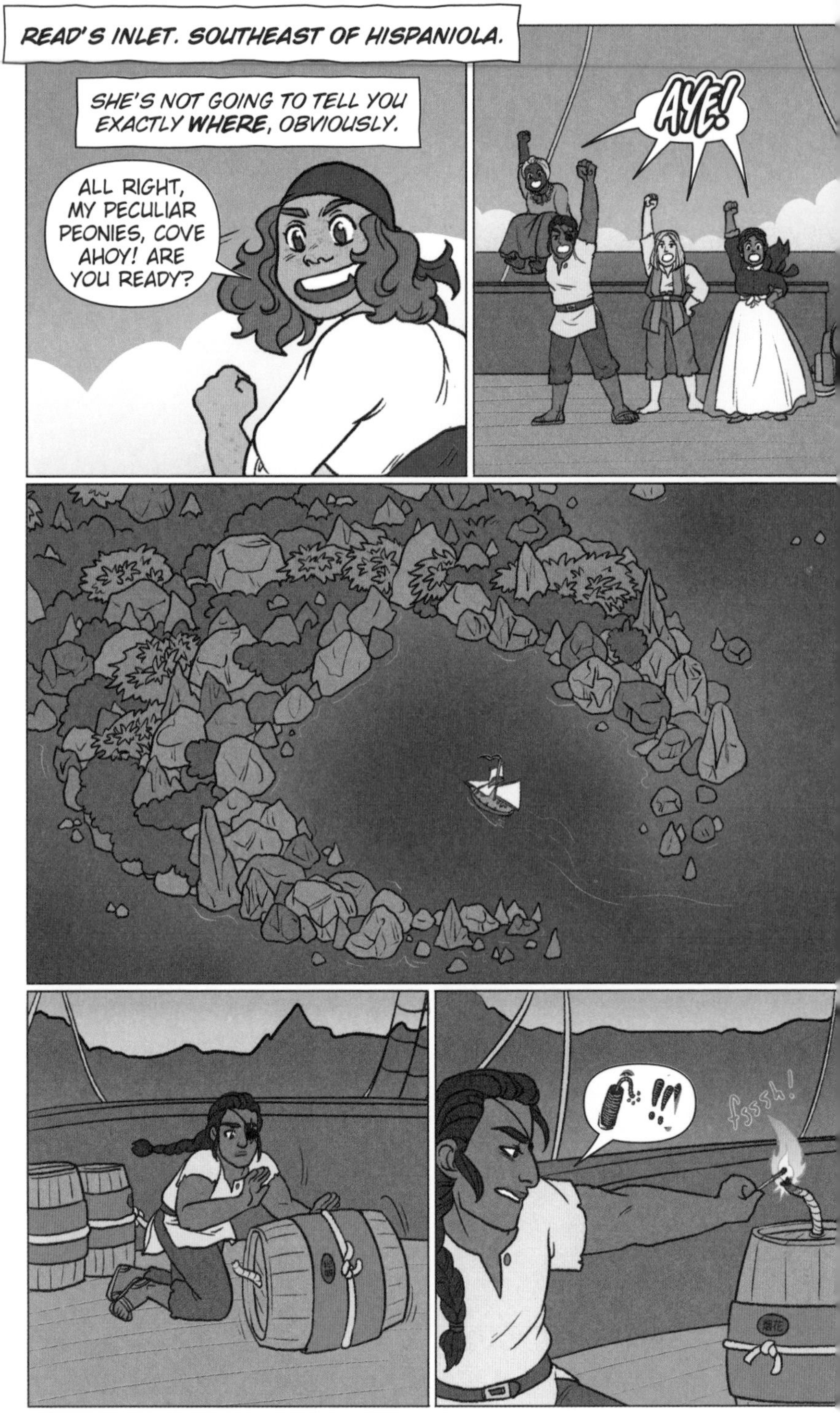
READ'S INLET. SOUTHEAST OF HISPANIOLA.
SHE'S NOT GOING TO TELL YOU EXACTLY WHERE, OBVIOUSLY.
ALL RIGHT, MY PECULIAR PEONIES, COVE AHOY! ARE YOU READY?
AYE!
!!!
fsssh!

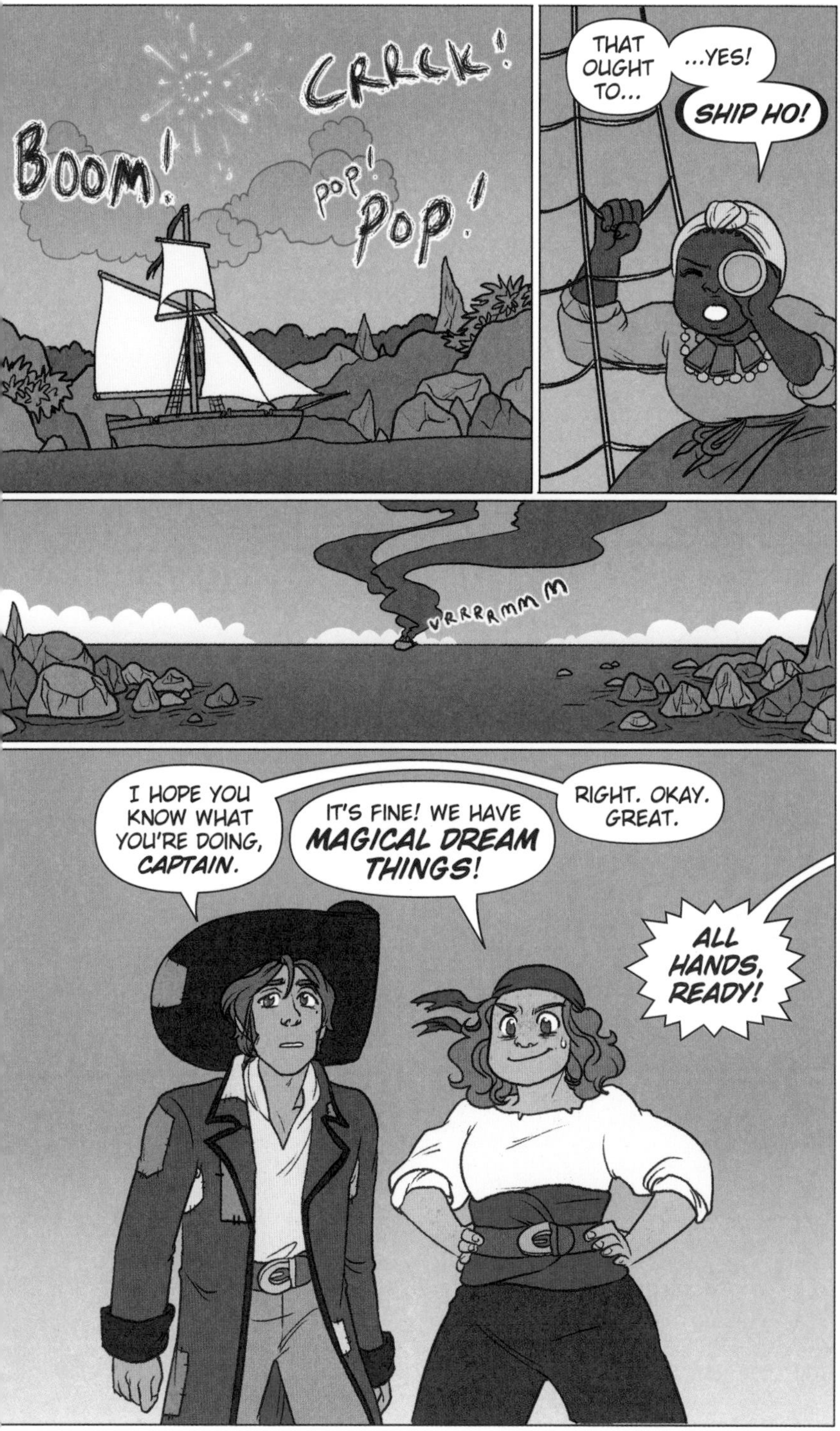
Boom!
CRRCK!
pop!
Pop!
THAT OUGHT TO...
...YES!
SHIP HO!
VRRRAMMM
I HOPE YOU KNOW WHAT YOU'RE DOING, CAPTAIN.
IT'S FINE! WE HAVE MAGICAL DREAM THINGS!
RIGHT. OKAY. GREAT.
ALL HANDS, READY!

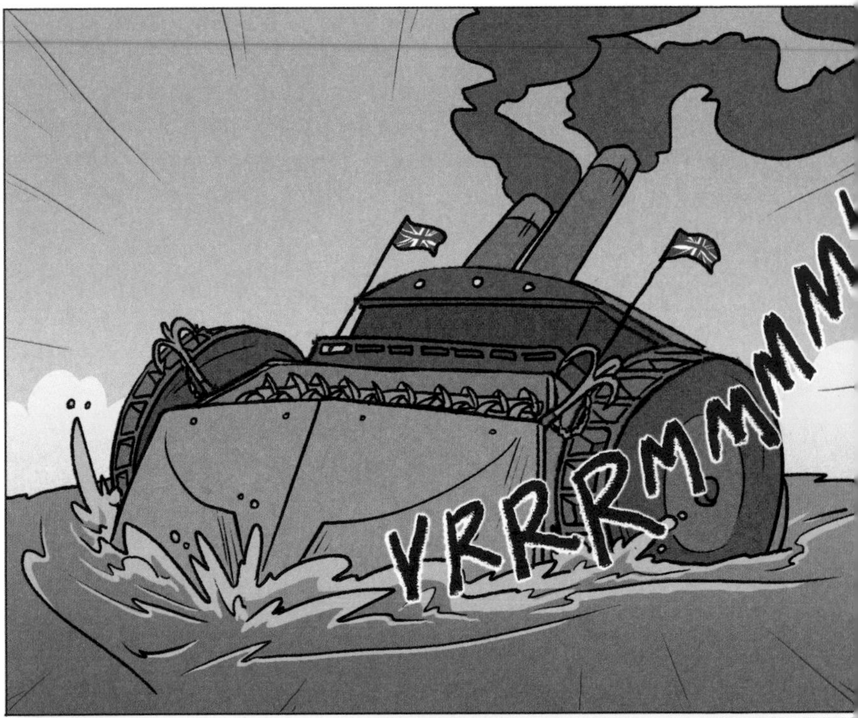
VRRRMMMMM

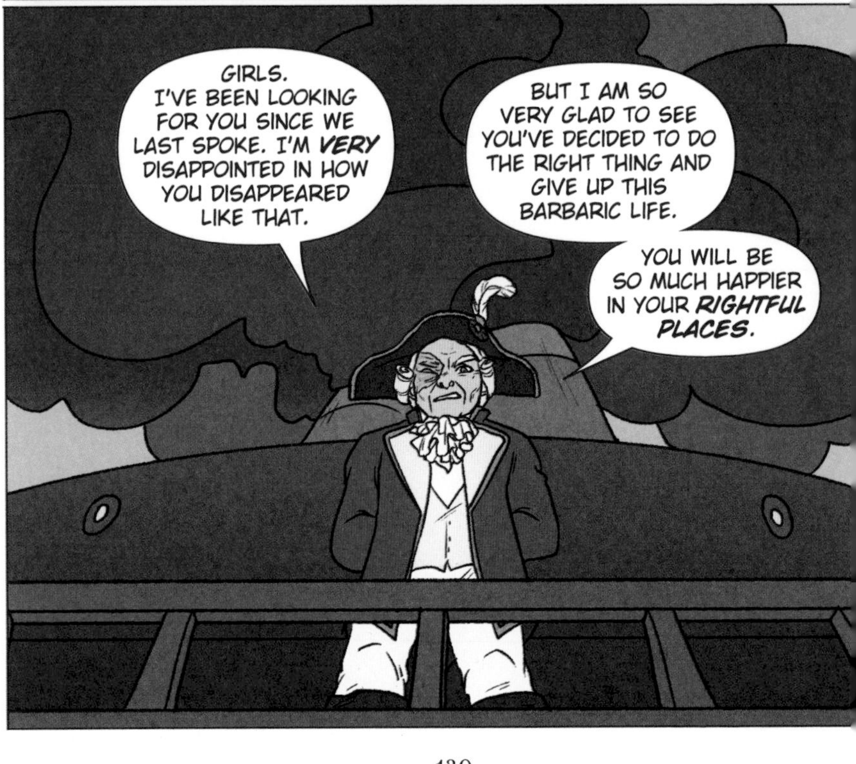
GIRLS.
I'VE BEEN LOOKING FOR YOU SINCE WE LAST SPOKE. I'M ***VERY*** DISAPPOINTED IN HOW YOU DISAPPEARED LIKE THAT.
BUT I AM SO VERY GLAD TO SEE YOU'VE DECIDED TO DO THE RIGHT THING AND GIVE UP THIS BARBARIC LIFE.
YOU WILL BE SO MUCH HAPPIER IN YOUR ***RIGHTFUL PLACES***.

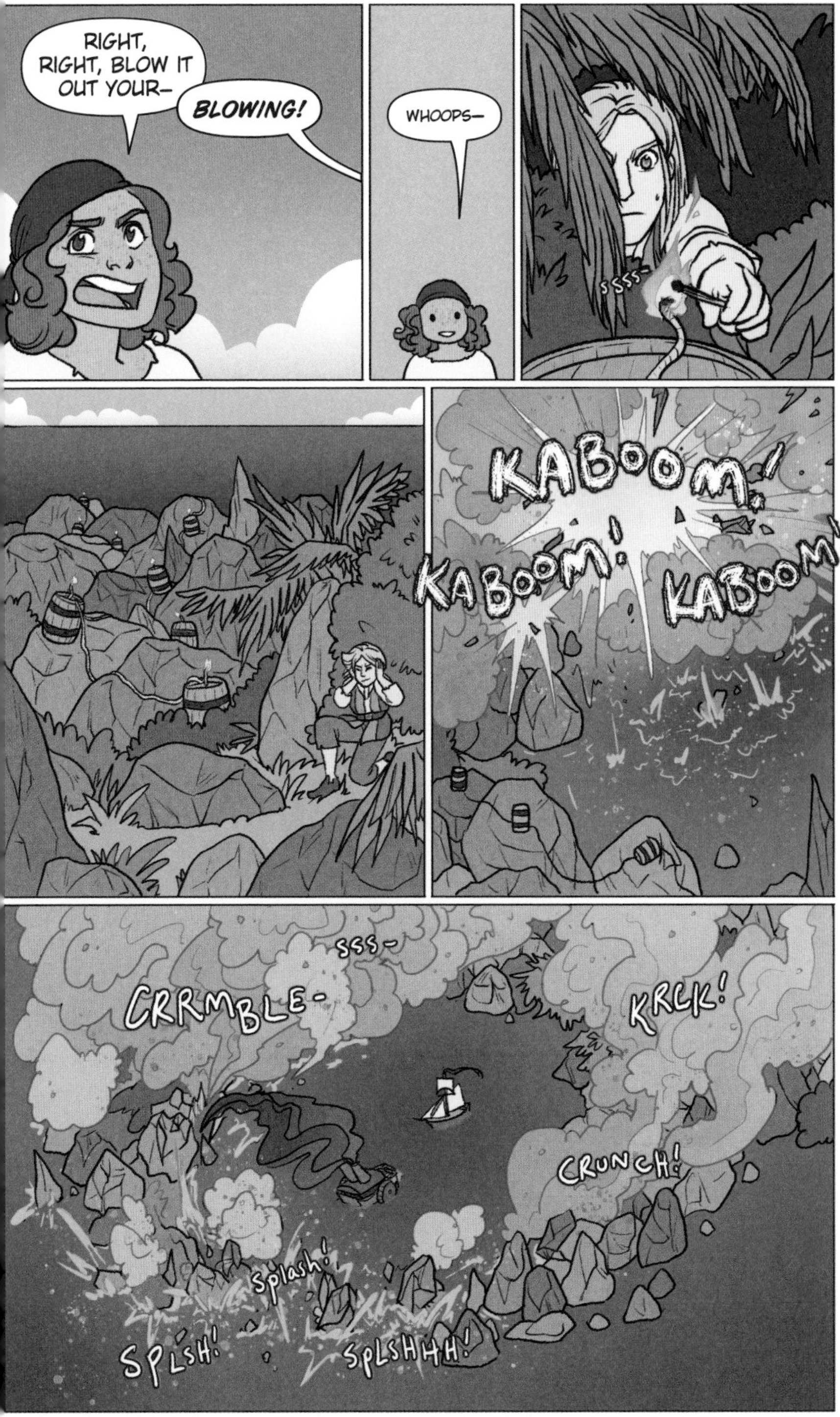
RIGHT, RIGHT, BLOW IT OUT YOUR—
BLOWING!
WHOOPS—
SSSS-
KABOOM!
KABOOM!
KABOOM!
SSS-
CRRMBLE-
KRCK!
CRUNCH!
Splash!
SPLSH!
SPLSHHH!

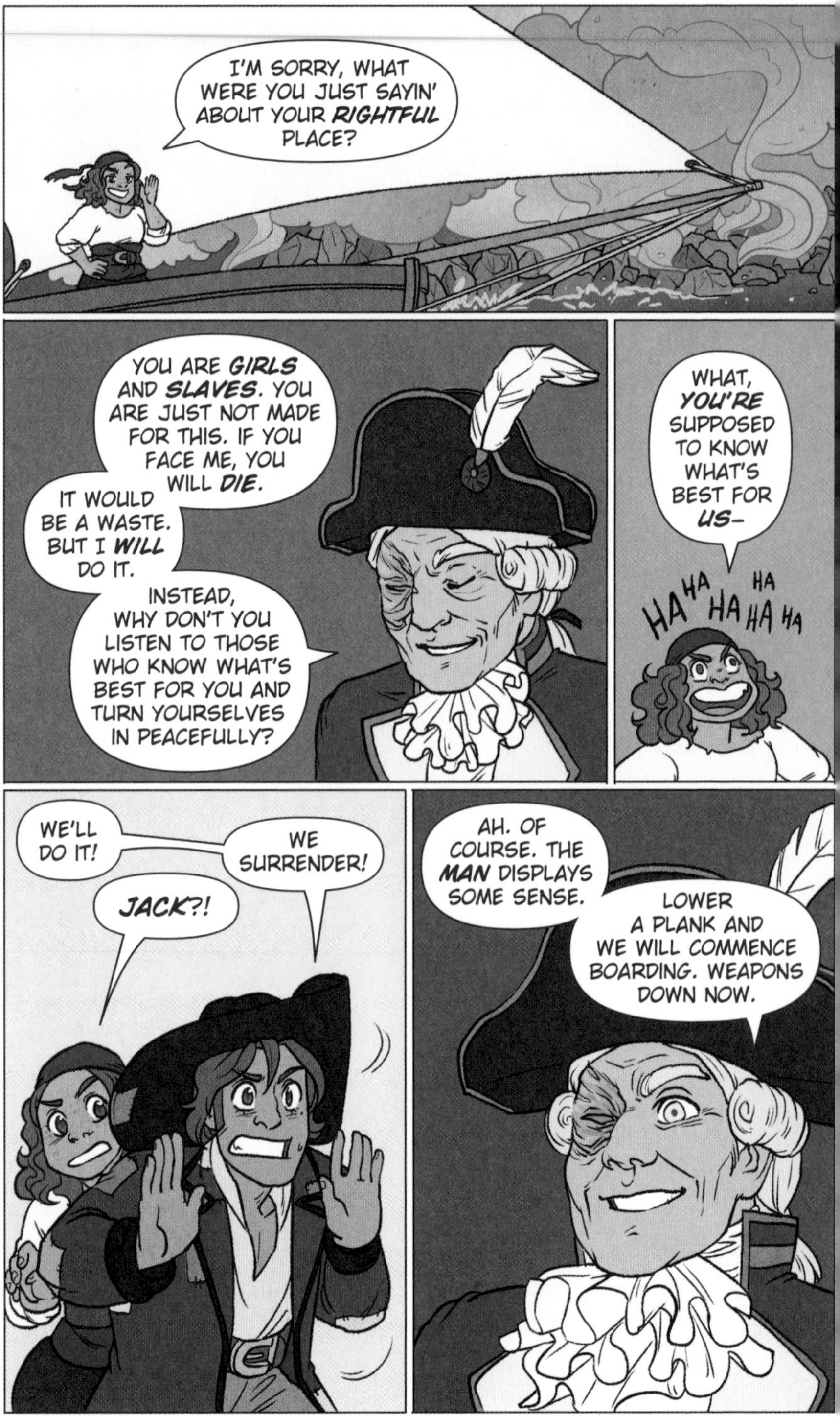
I'M SORRY, WHAT WERE YOU JUST SAYIN' ABOUT YOUR RIGHTFUL PLACE?
YOU ARE GIRLS AND SLAVES. YOU ARE JUST NOT MADE FOR THIS. IF YOU FACE ME, YOU WILL DIE.
IT WOULD BE A WASTE. BUT I WILL DO IT.
INSTEAD, WHY DON'T YOU LISTEN TO THOSE WHO KNOW WHAT'S BEST FOR YOU AND TURN YOURSELVES IN PEACEFULLY?
WHAT, YOU'RE SUPPOSED TO KNOW WHAT'S BEST FOR US–
HA HA HA HA HA HA HA
WE'LL DO IT!
WE SURRENDER!
JACK?!
AH. OF COURSE. THE MAN DISPLAYS SOME SENSE.
LOWER A PLANK AND WE WILL COMMENCE BOARDING. WEAPONS DOWN NOW.

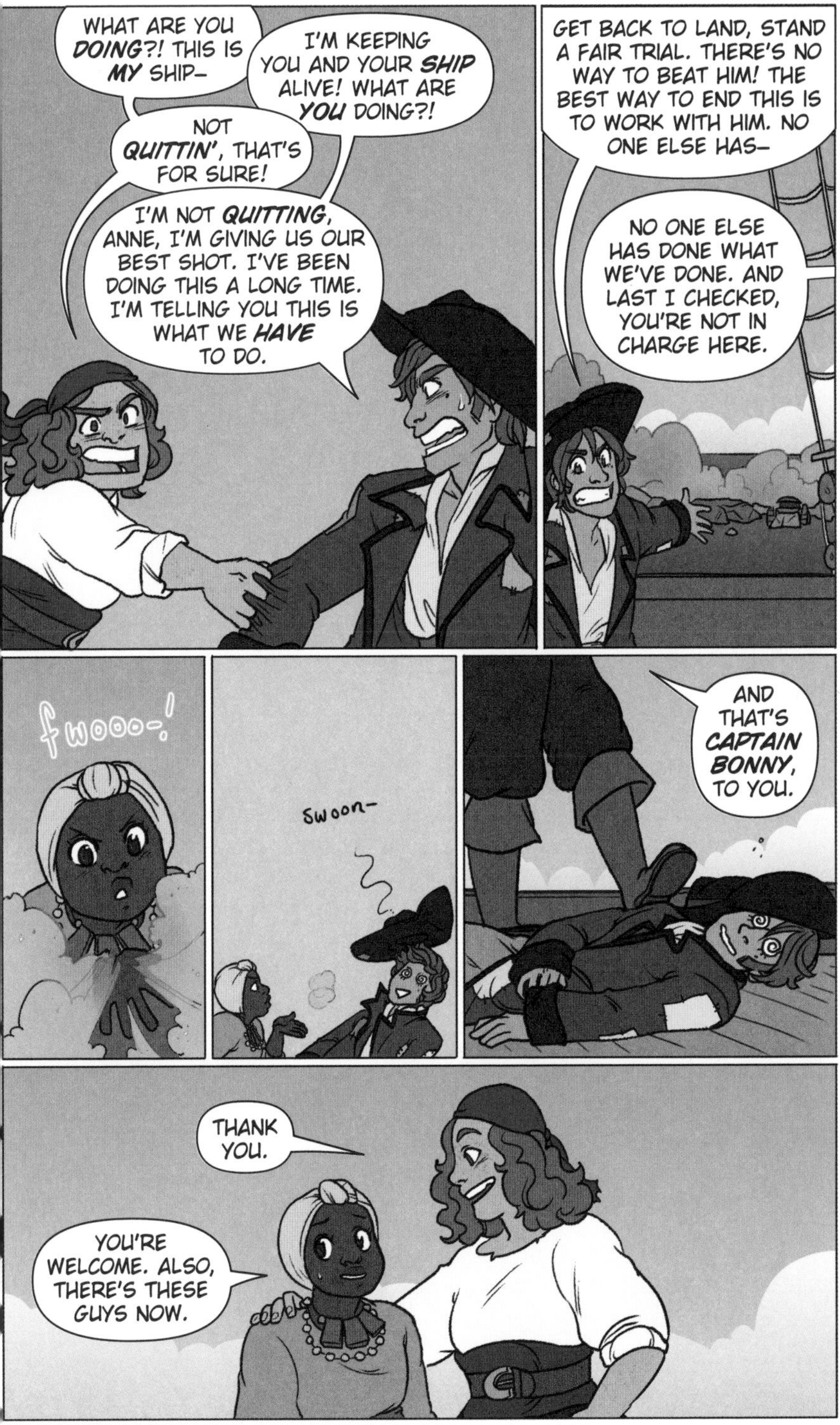
WHAT ARE YOU DOING?! THIS IS MY SHIP–
I'M KEEPING YOU AND YOUR SHIP ALIVE! WHAT ARE YOU DOING?!
NOT QUITTIN', THAT'S FOR SURE!
I'M NOT QUITTING, ANNE, I'M GIVING US OUR BEST SHOT. I'VE BEEN DOING THIS A LONG TIME. I'M TELLING YOU THIS IS WHAT WE HAVE TO DO.
GET BACK TO LAND, STAND A FAIR TRIAL. THERE'S NO WAY TO BEAT HIM! THE BEST WAY TO END THIS IS TO WORK WITH HIM. NO ONE ELSE HAS–
NO ONE ELSE HAS DONE WHAT WE'VE DONE. AND LAST I CHECKED, YOU'RE NOT IN CHARGE HERE.
fwooo-!
swoon-
AND THAT'S CAPTAIN BONNY, TO YOU.
THANK YOU.
YOU'RE WELCOME. ALSO, THERE'S THESE GUYS NOW.

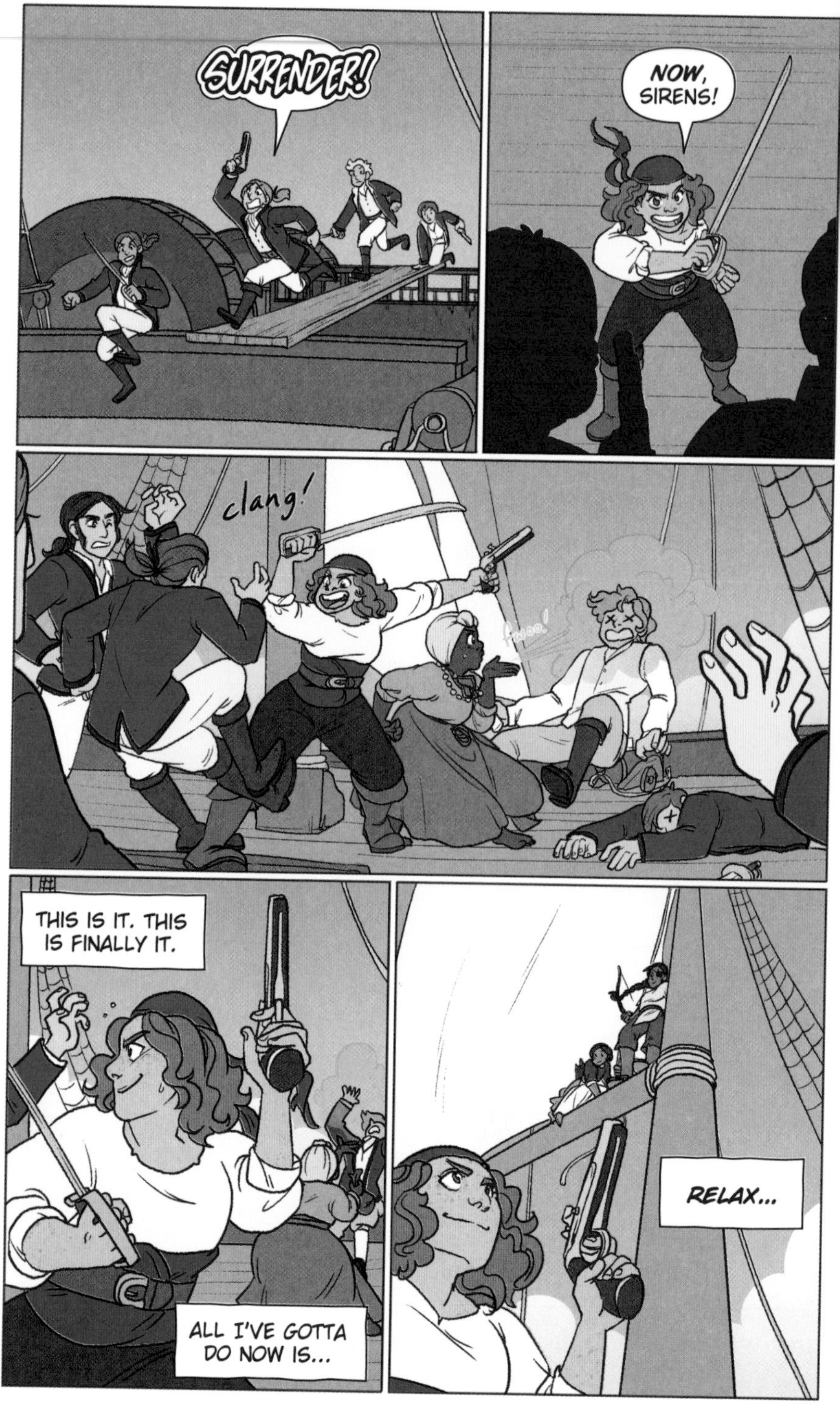
SURRENDER!
NOW, SIRENS!
clang!
THIS IS IT. THIS IS FINALLY IT.
ALL I'VE GOTTA DO NOW IS...
RELAX...

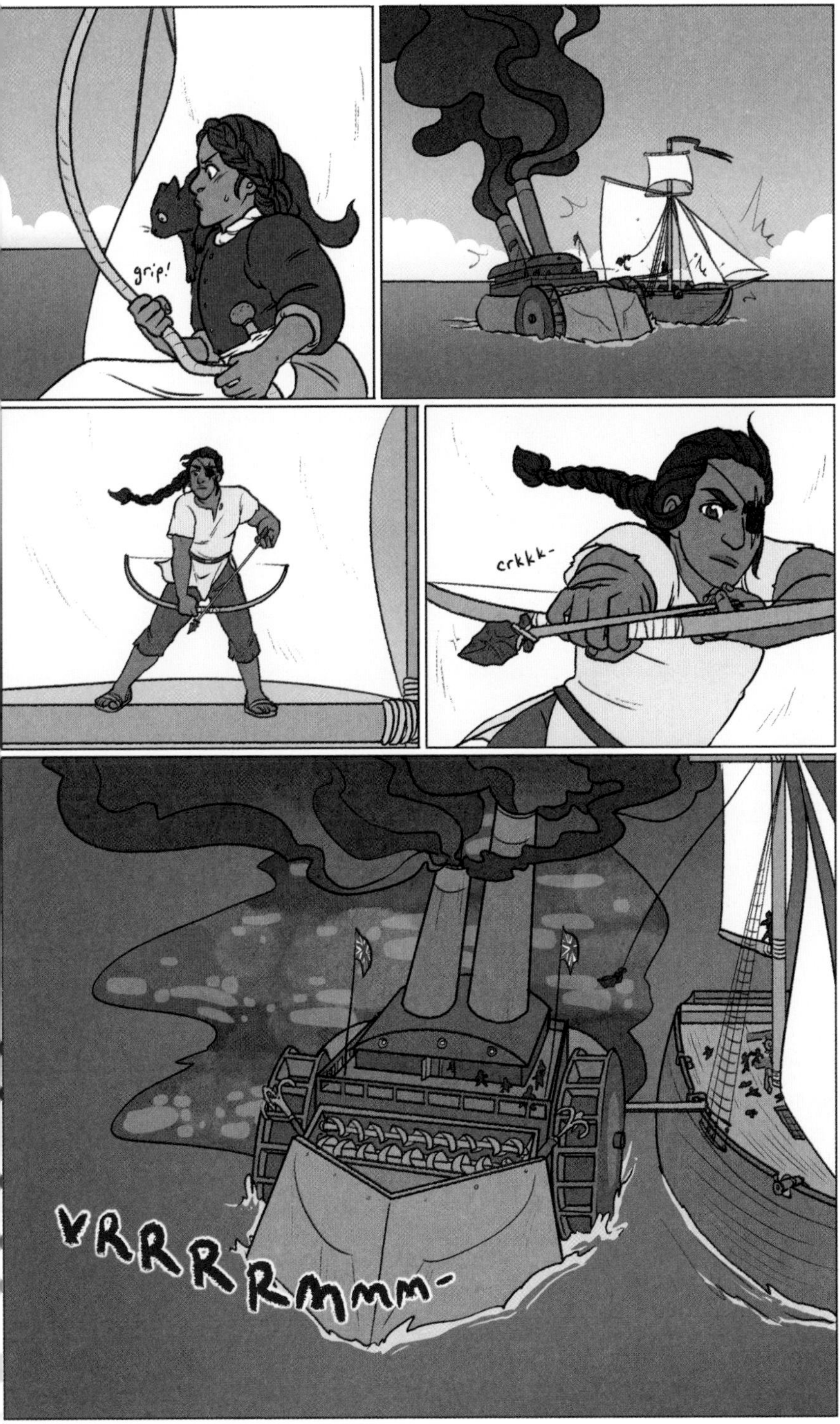
grip!
crkkk-
VRRRRMMMM-

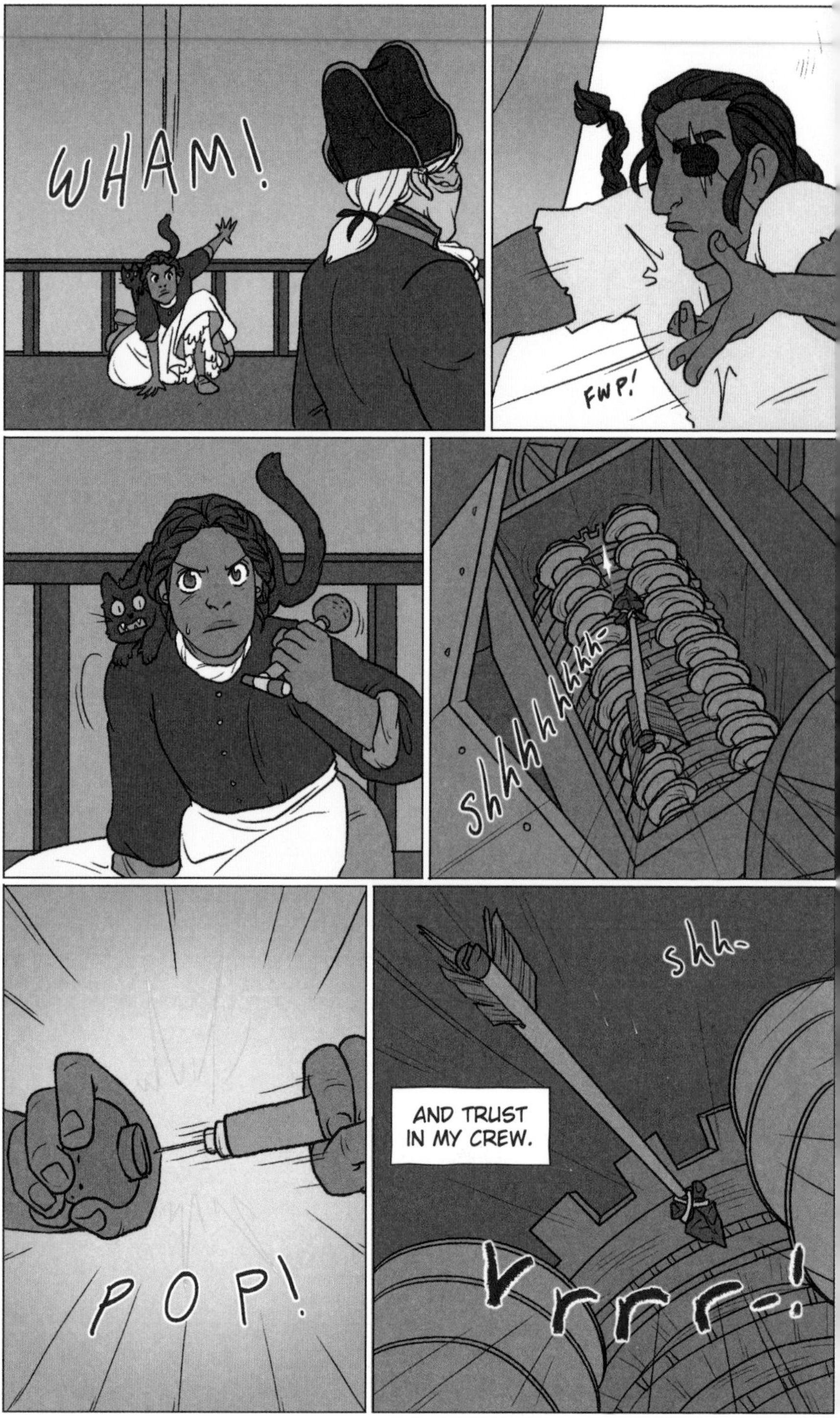
WHAM!
FWP!
shhhhhhhh-
POP!
shh-
AND TRUST IN MY CREW.
Vrrr-!

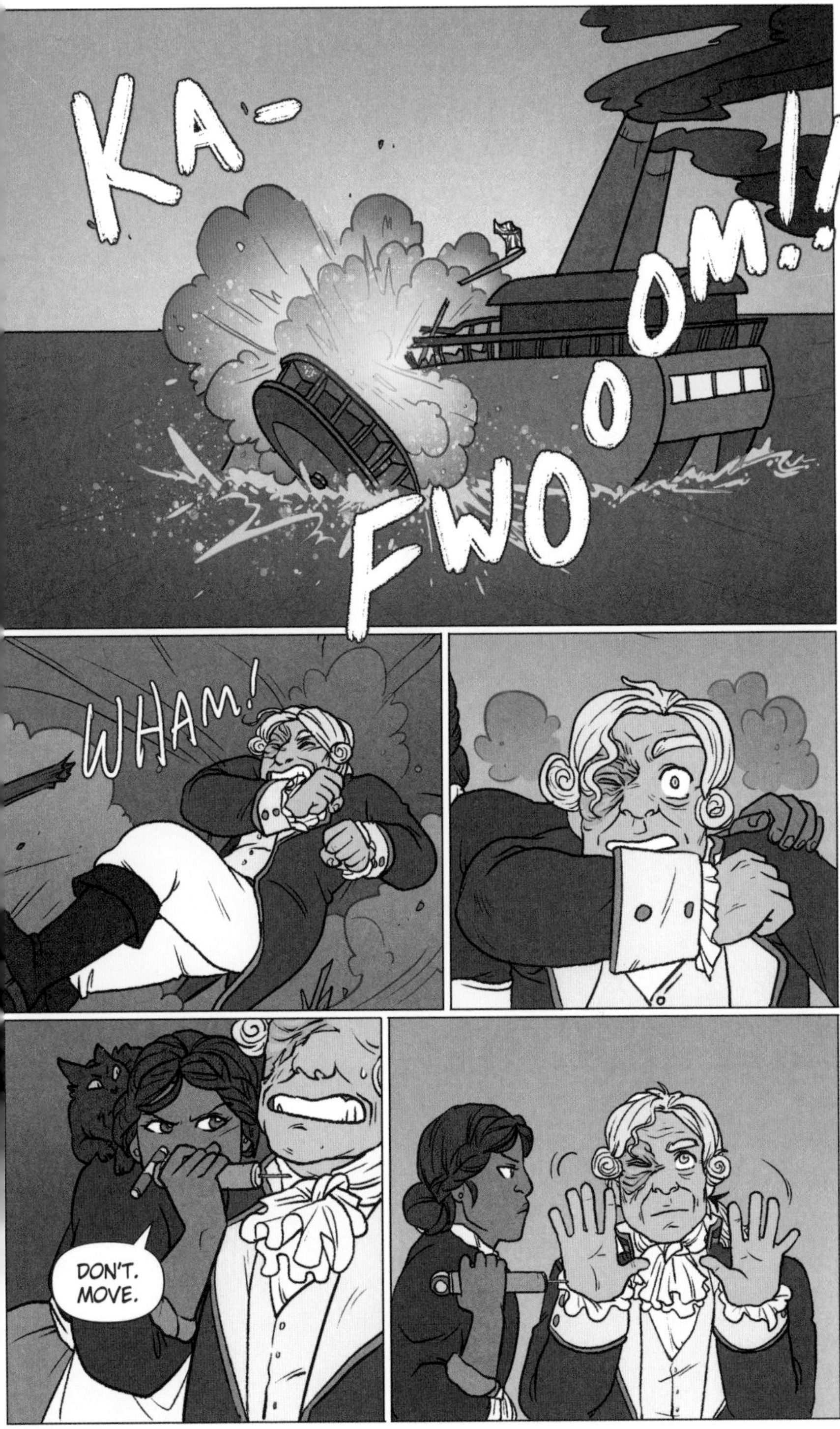
KA-
FWOOOM!!
WHAM!
DON'T. MOVE.

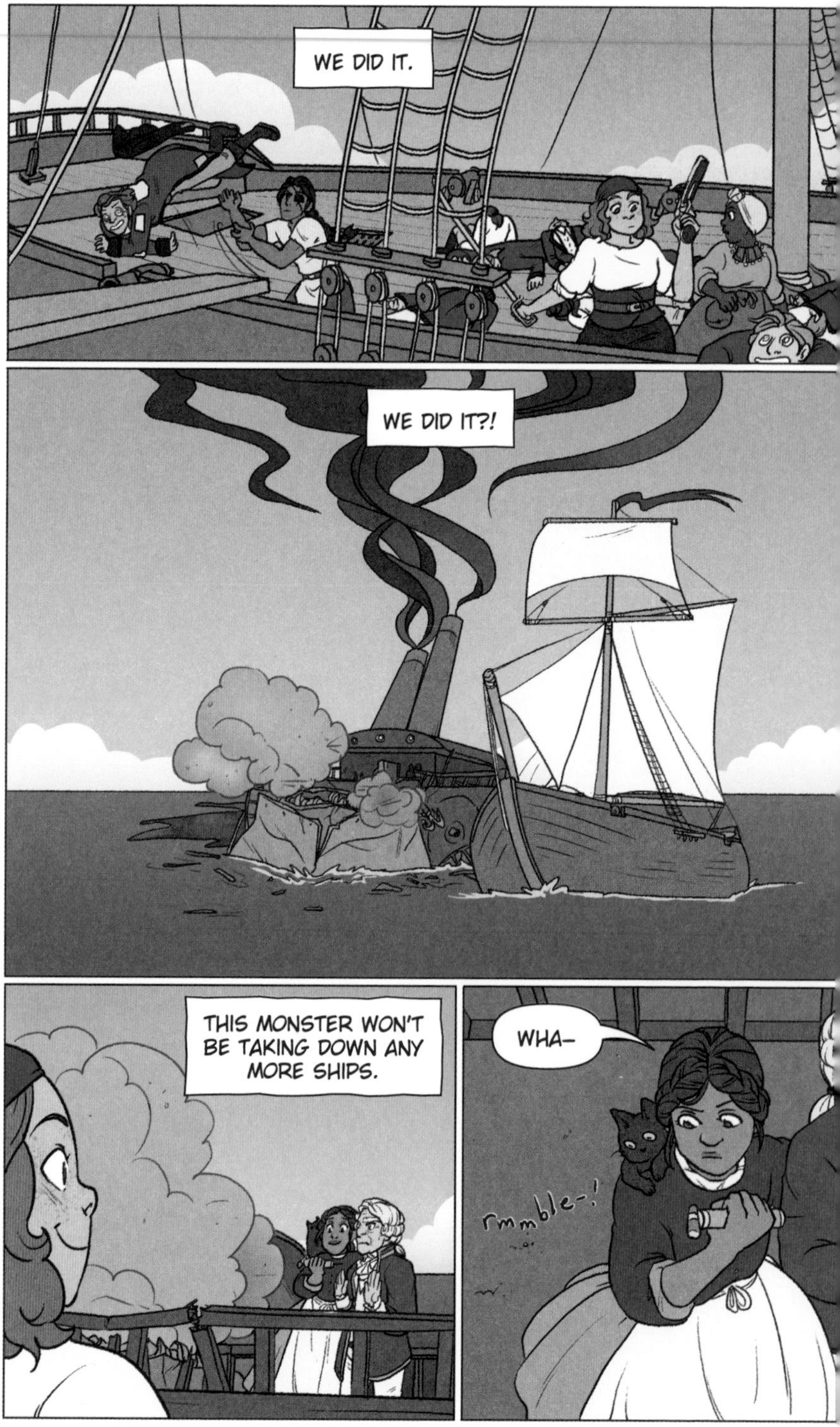
WE DID IT.
WE DID IT?!
THIS MONSTER WON'T BE TAKING DOWN ANY MORE SHIPS.
WHA–
rmmble–!

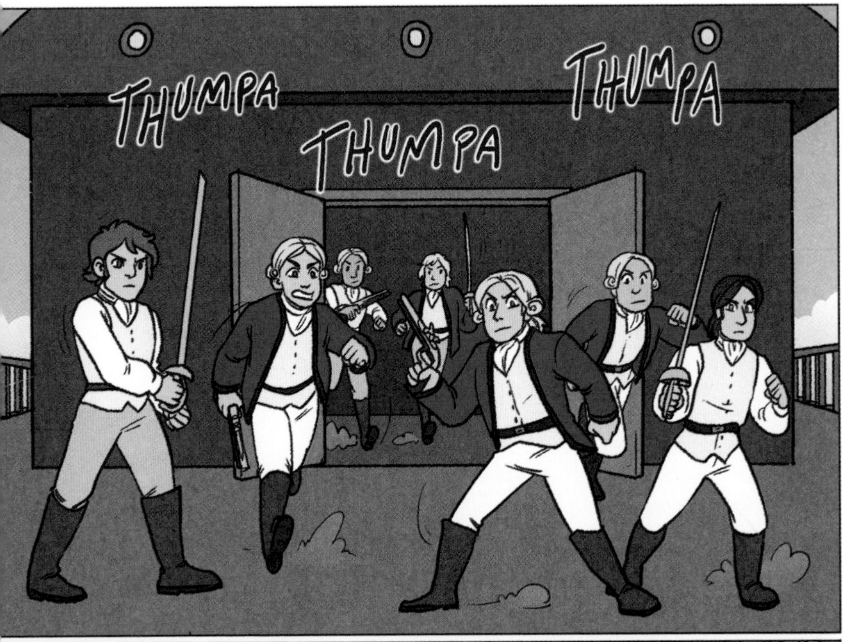
THUMPA
THUMPA
THUMPA

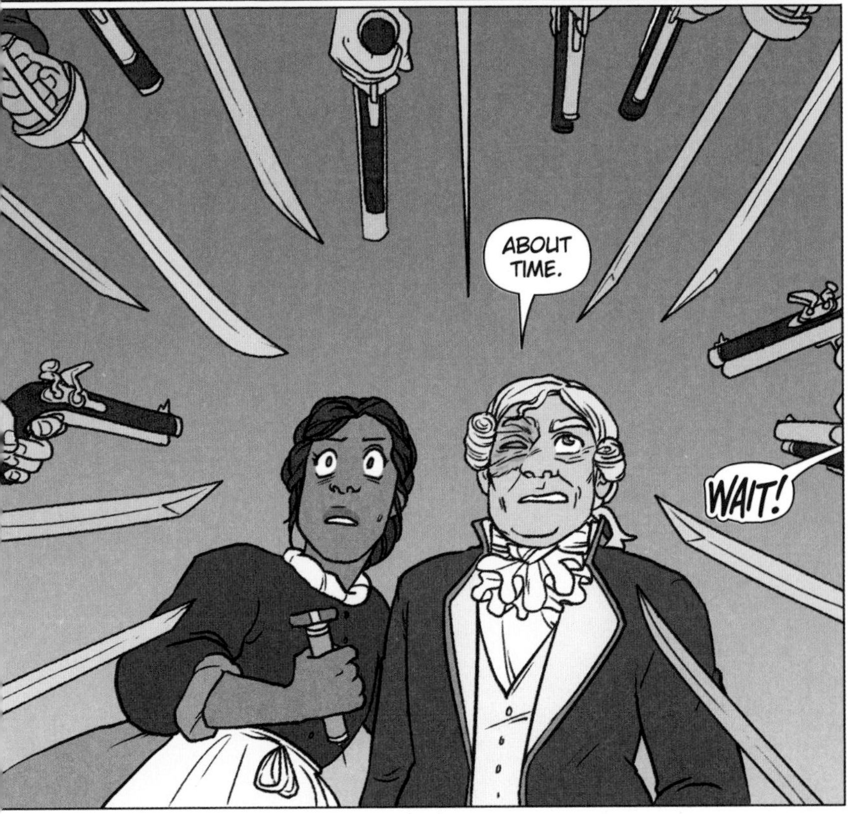
ABOUT TIME.
WAIT!

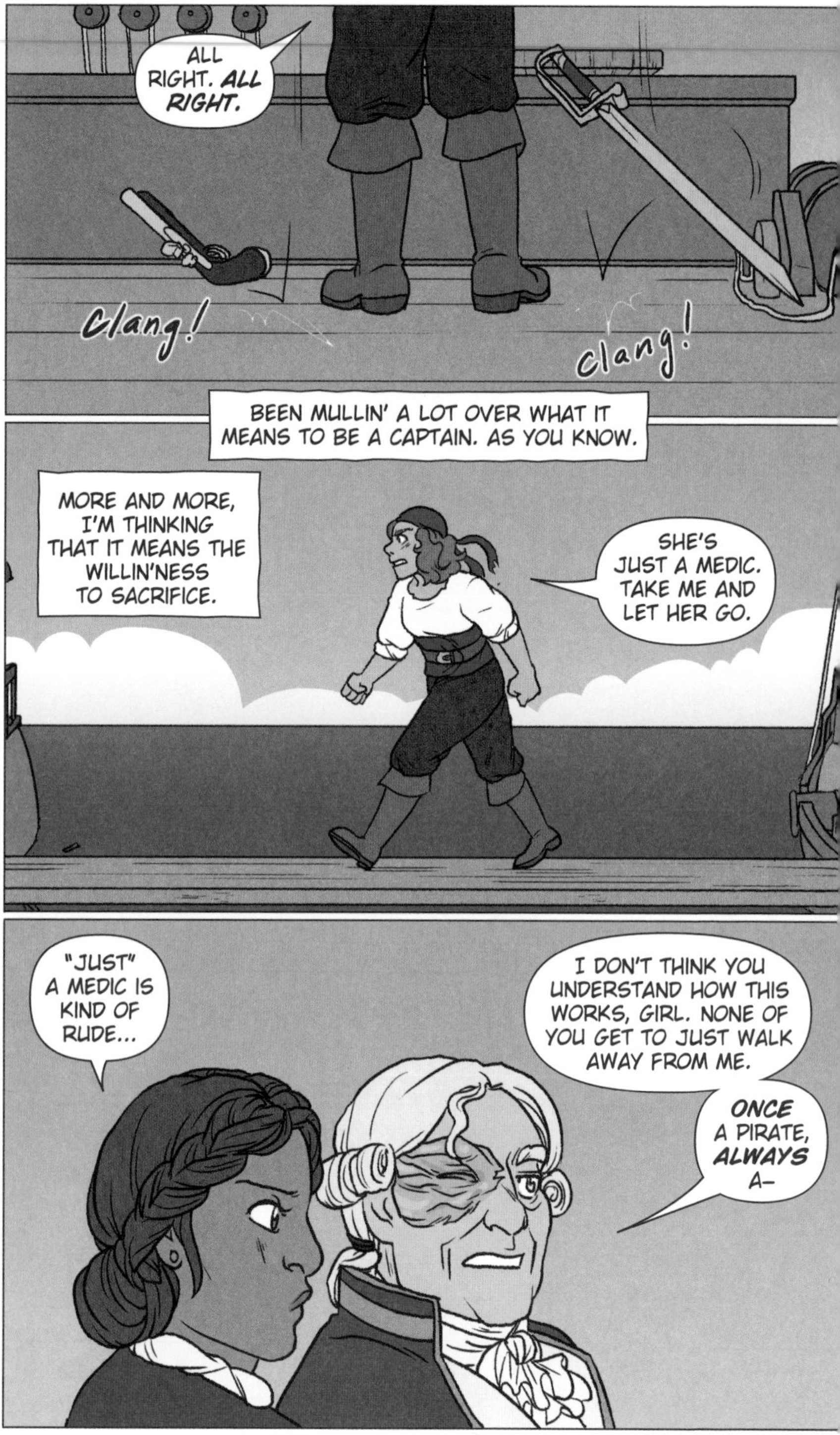
ALL RIGHT. **ALL RIGHT.**
Clang!
Clang!
BEEN MULLIN' A LOT OVER WHAT IT MEANS TO BE A CAPTAIN. AS YOU KNOW.
MORE AND MORE, I'M THINKING THAT IT MEANS THE WILLIN'NESS TO SACRIFICE.
SHE'S JUST A MEDIC. TAKE ME AND LET HER GO.
"JUST" A MEDIC IS KIND OF RUDE...
I DON'T THINK YOU UNDERSTAND HOW THIS WORKS, GIRL. NONE OF YOU GET TO JUST WALK AWAY FROM ME.
ONCE A PIRATE, **ALWAYS** A–

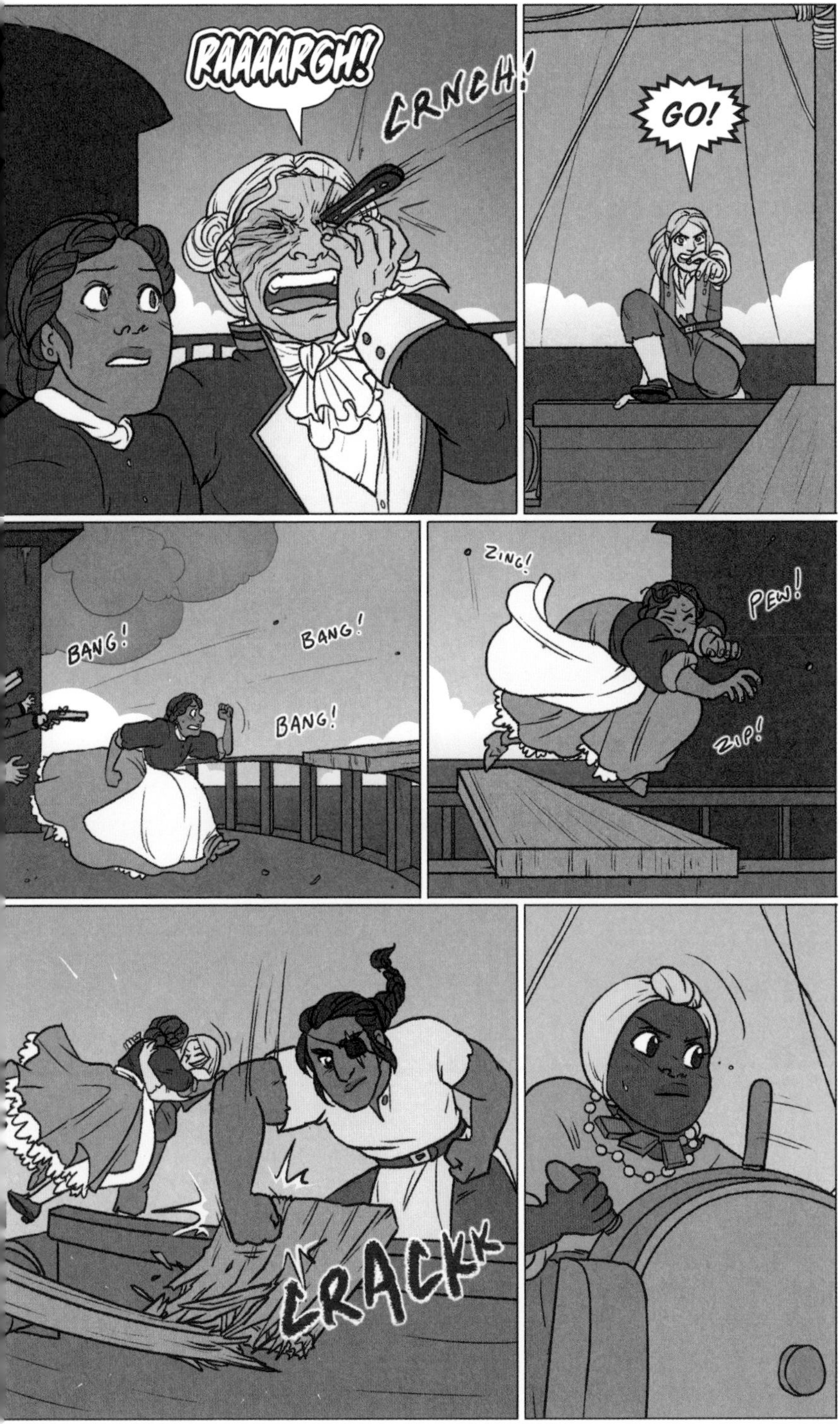
RAAAARGH!
CRNCH!
GO!
BANG!
BANG!
BANG!
ZING!
PEW!
ZIP!
CRACKK

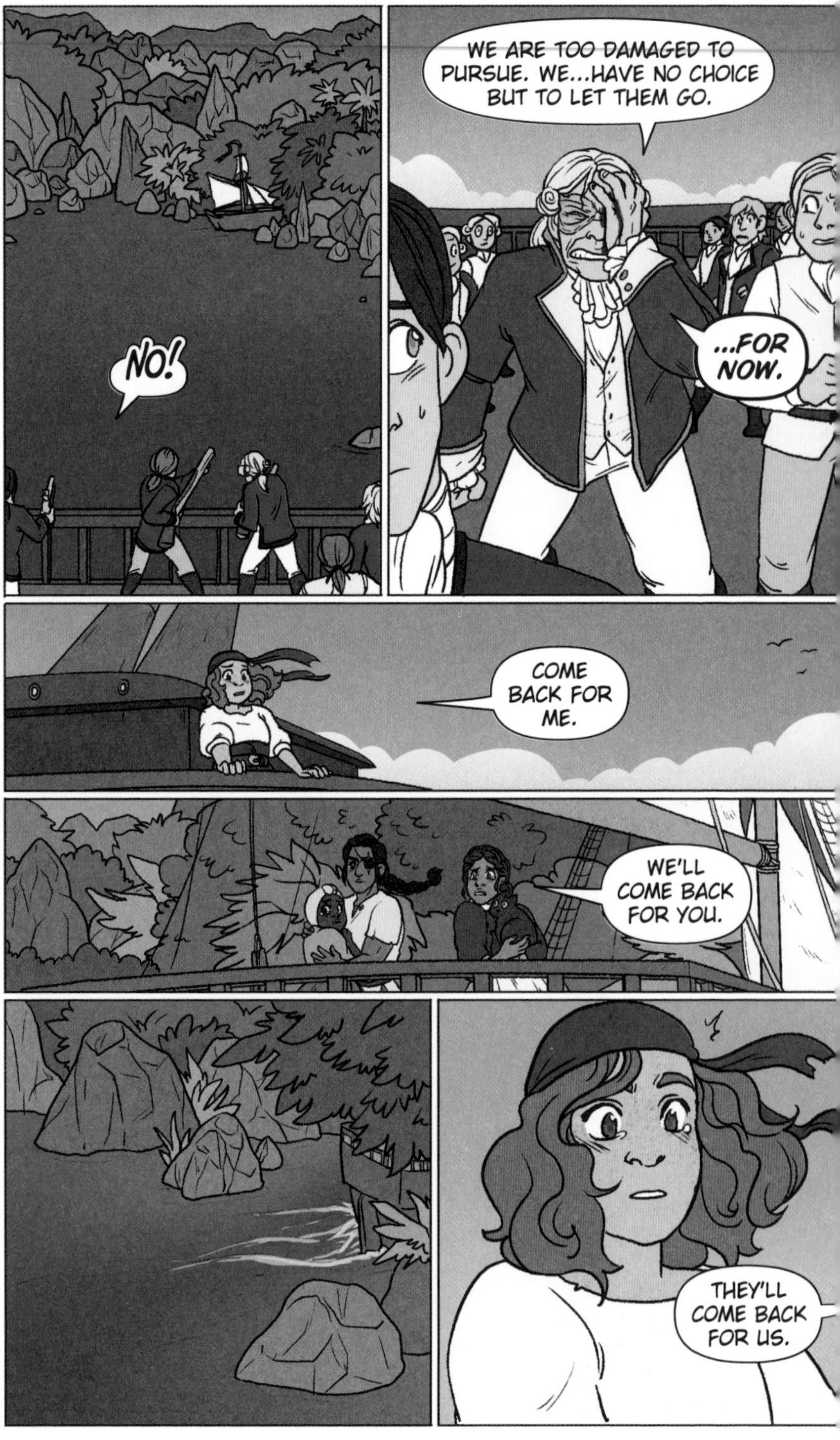
NO!
WE ARE TOO DAMAGED TO PURSUE. WE...HAVE NO CHOICE BUT TO LET THEM GO.
...FOR NOW.
COME BACK FOR ME.
WE'LL COME BACK FOR YOU.
THEY'LL COME BACK FOR US.

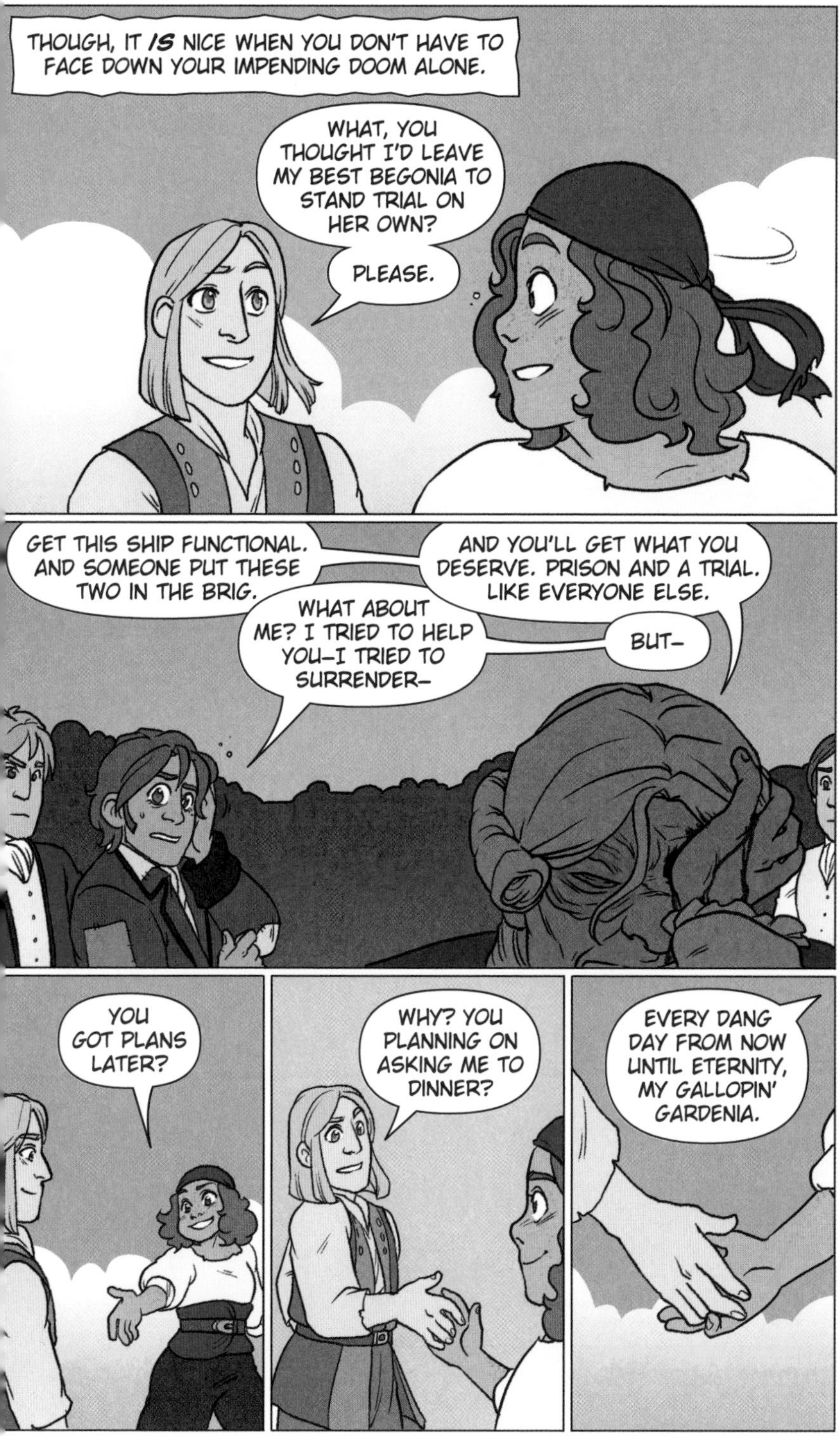
THOUGH, IT *IS* NICE WHEN YOU DON'T HAVE TO FACE DOWN YOUR IMPENDING DOOM ALONE.
WHAT, YOU THOUGHT I'D LEAVE MY BEST BEGONIA TO STAND TRIAL ON HER OWN?
PLEASE.
GET THIS SHIP FUNCTIONAL. AND SOMEONE PUT THESE TWO IN THE BRIG.
WHAT ABOUT ME? I TRIED TO HELP YOU–I TRIED TO SURRENDER–
AND YOU'LL GET WHAT YOU DESERVE. PRISON AND A TRIAL. LIKE EVERYONE ELSE.
BUT–
YOU GOT PLANS LATER?
WHY? YOU PLANNING ON ASKING ME TO DINNER?
EVERY DANG DAY FROM NOW UNTIL ETERNITY, MY GALLOPIN' GARDENIA.

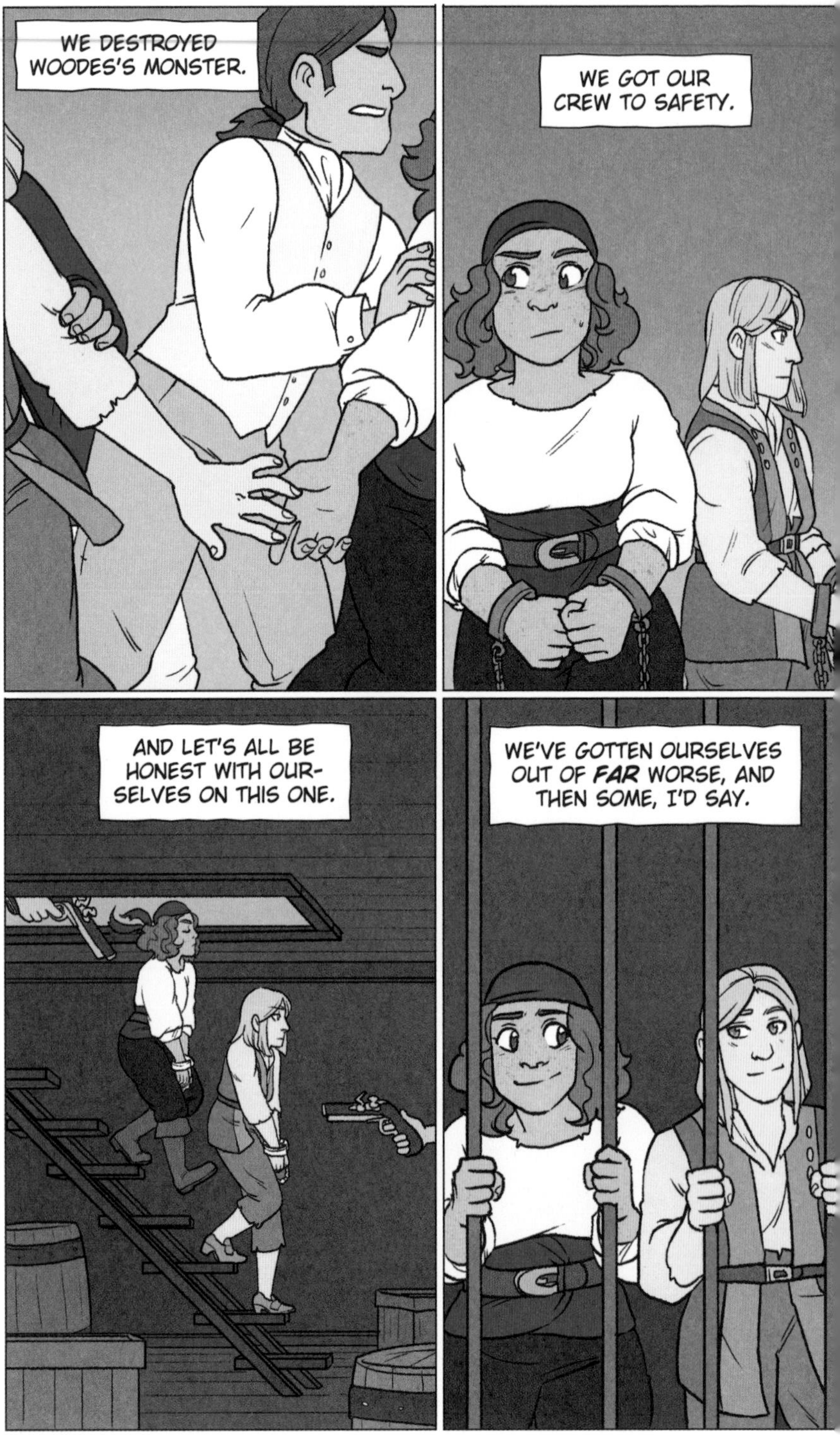
WE DESTROYED WOODES'S MONSTER.
WE GOT OUR CREW TO SAFETY.
AND LET'S ALL BE HONEST WITH OURSELVES ON THIS ONE.
WE'VE GOTTEN OURSELVES OUT OF **FAR** WORSE, AND THEN SOME, I'D SAY.

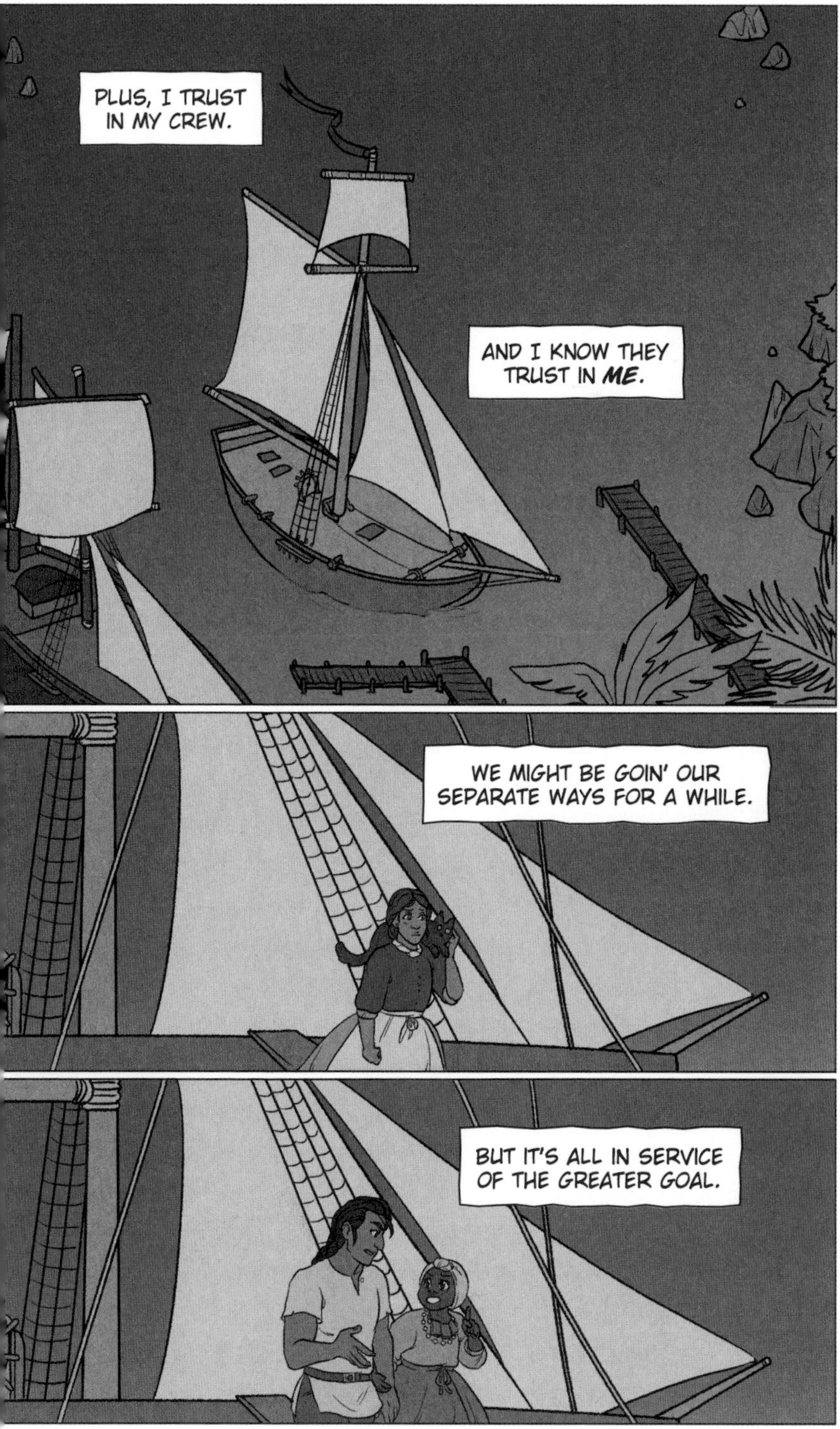
PLUS, I TRUST IN MY CREW.
AND I KNOW THEY TRUST IN ***ME***.
WE MIGHT BE GOIN' OUR SEPARATE WAYS FOR A WHILE.
BUT IT'S ALL IN SERVICE OF THE GREATER GOAL.

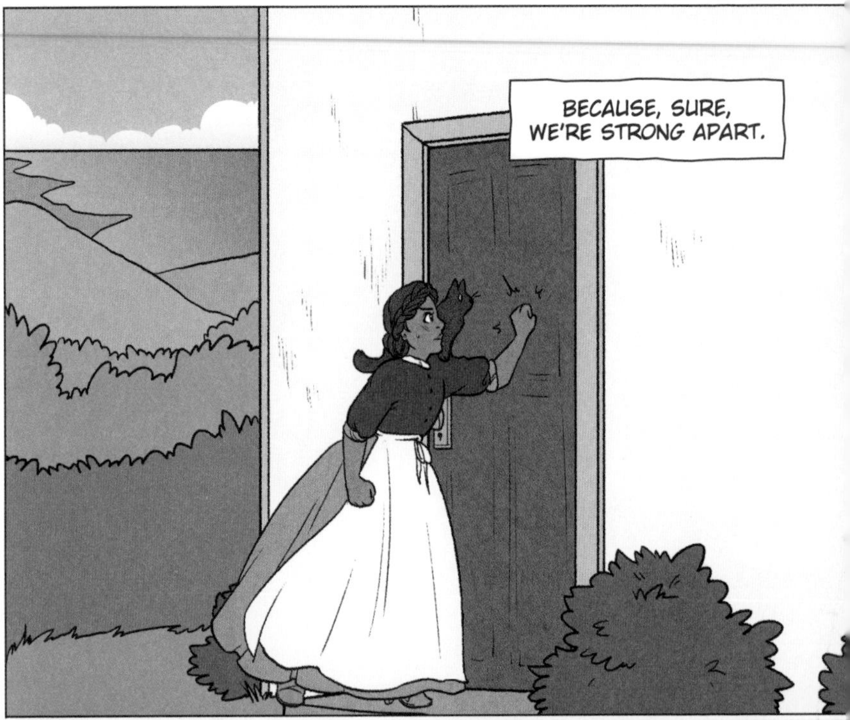
BECAUSE, SURE, WE'RE STRONG APART.

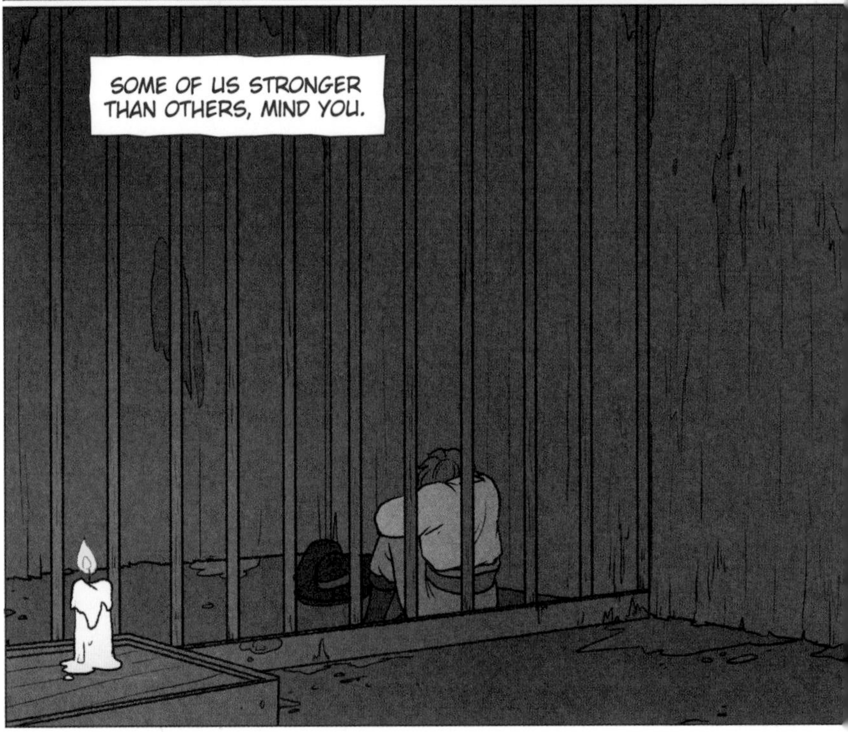
SOME OF US STRONGER THAN OTHERS, MIND YOU.

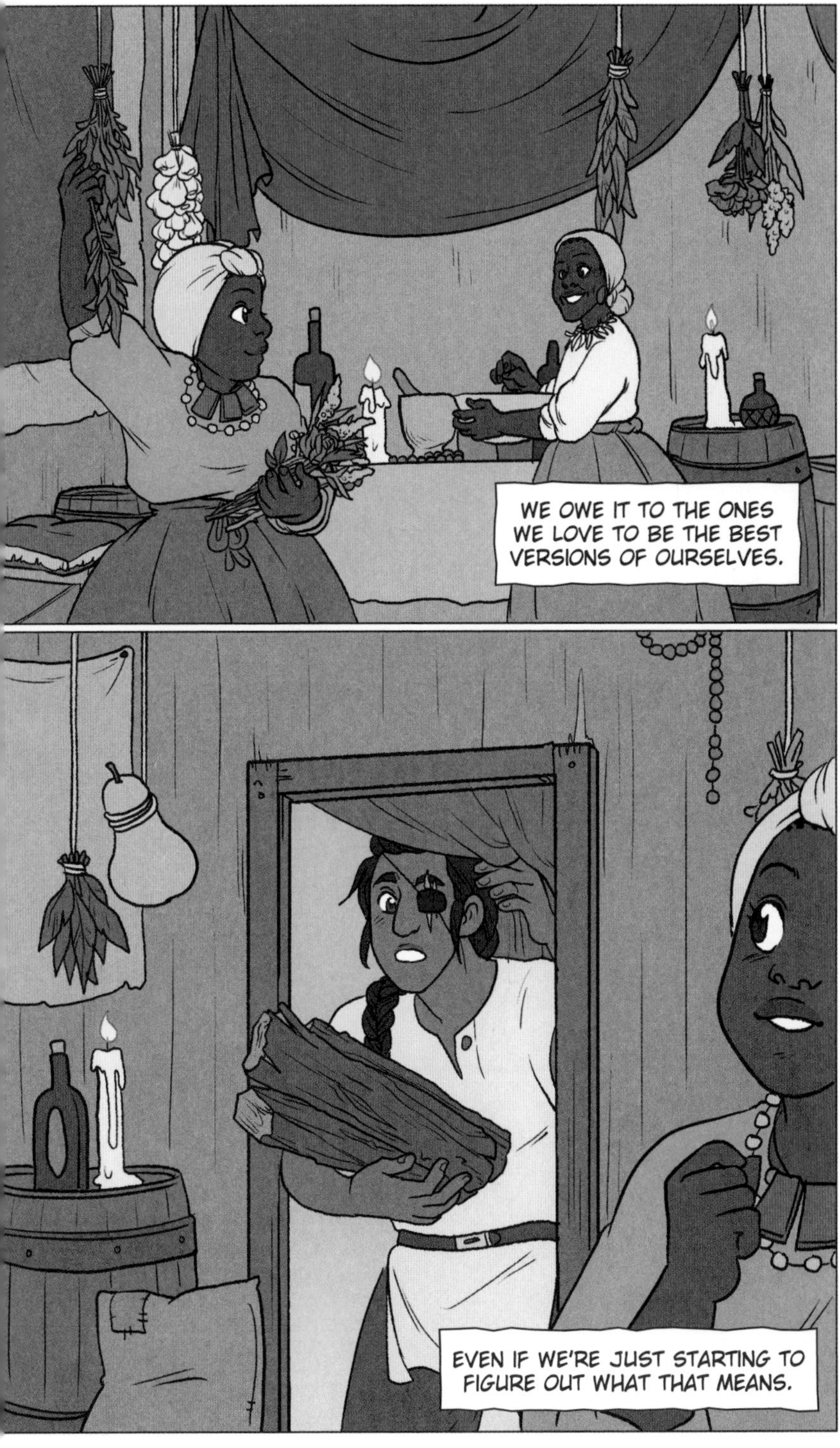
WE OWE IT TO THE ONES WE LOVE TO BE THE BEST VERSIONS OF OURSELVES.
EVEN IF WE'RE JUST STARTING TO FIGURE OUT WHAT THAT MEANS.

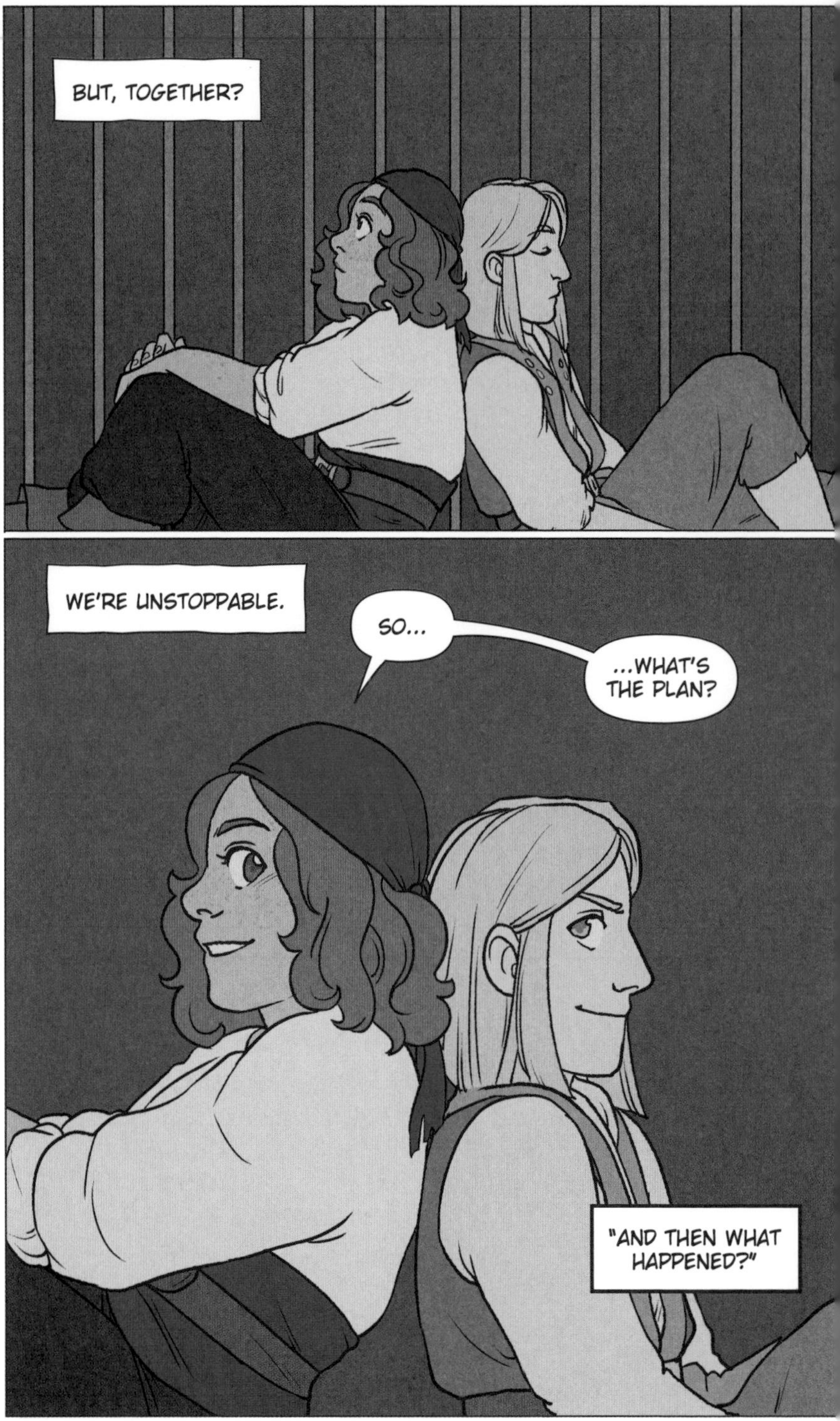
BUT, TOGETHER?
WE'RE UNSTOPPABLE.
SO...
...WHAT'S THE PLAN?
"AND THEN WHAT HAPPENED?"

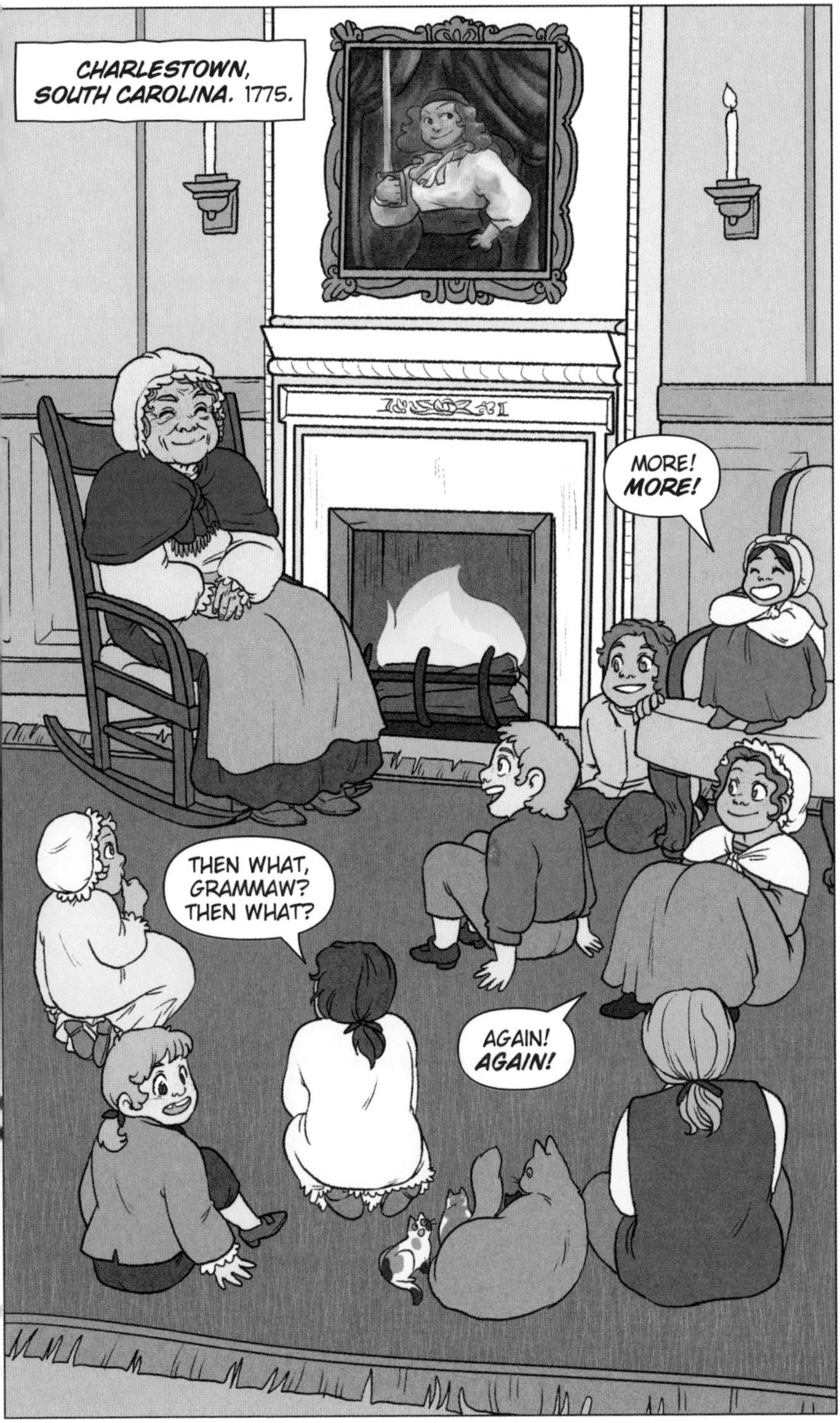
CHARLESTOWN, SOUTH CAROLINA. 1775.
MORE! MORE!
THEN WHAT, GRAMMAW? THEN WHAT?
AGAIN! AGAIN!

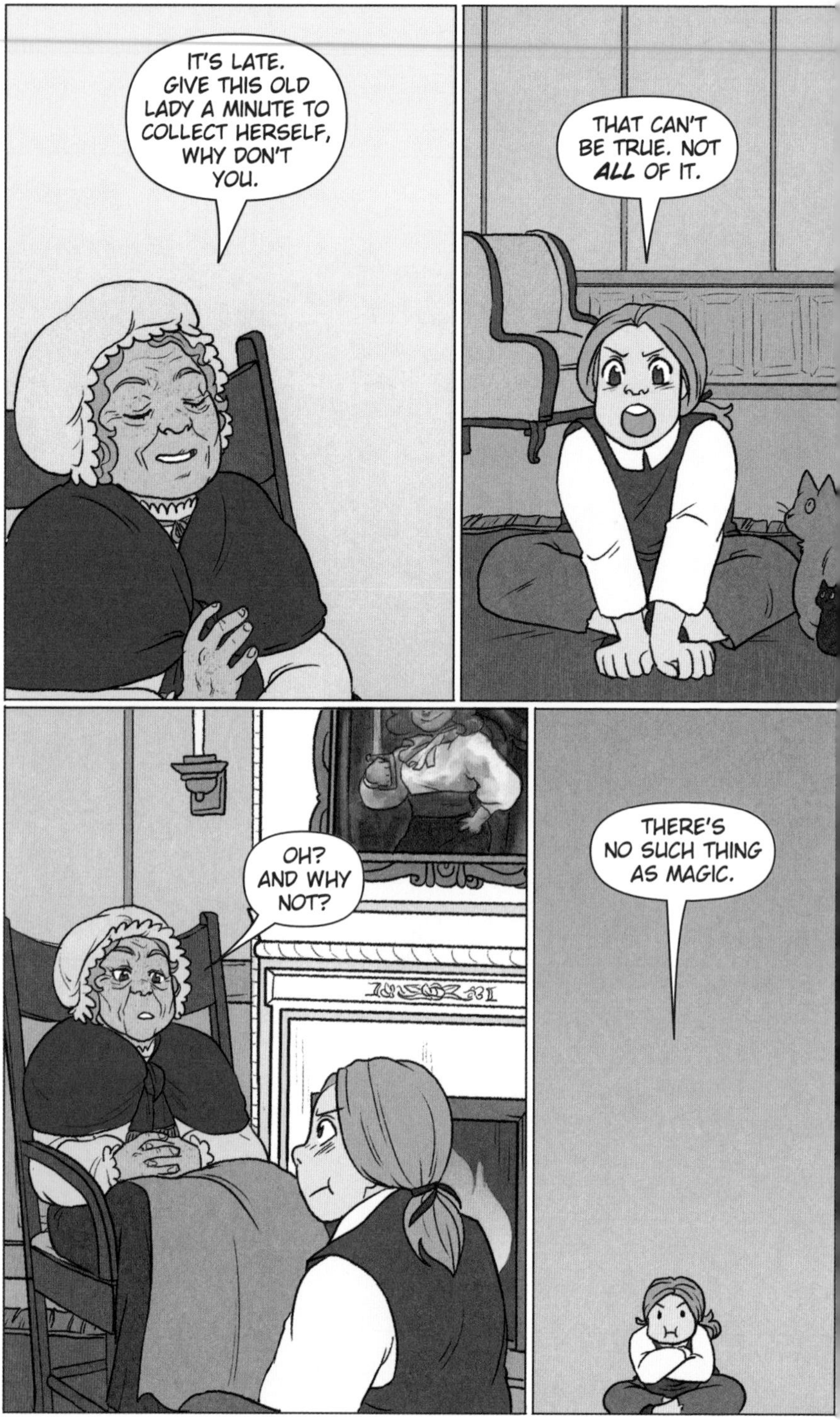
IT'S LATE. GIVE THIS OLD LADY A MINUTE TO COLLECT HERSELF, WHY DON'T YOU.
THAT CAN'T BE TRUE. NOT **ALL** OF IT.
OH? AND WHY NOT?
THERE'S NO SUCH THING AS MAGIC.

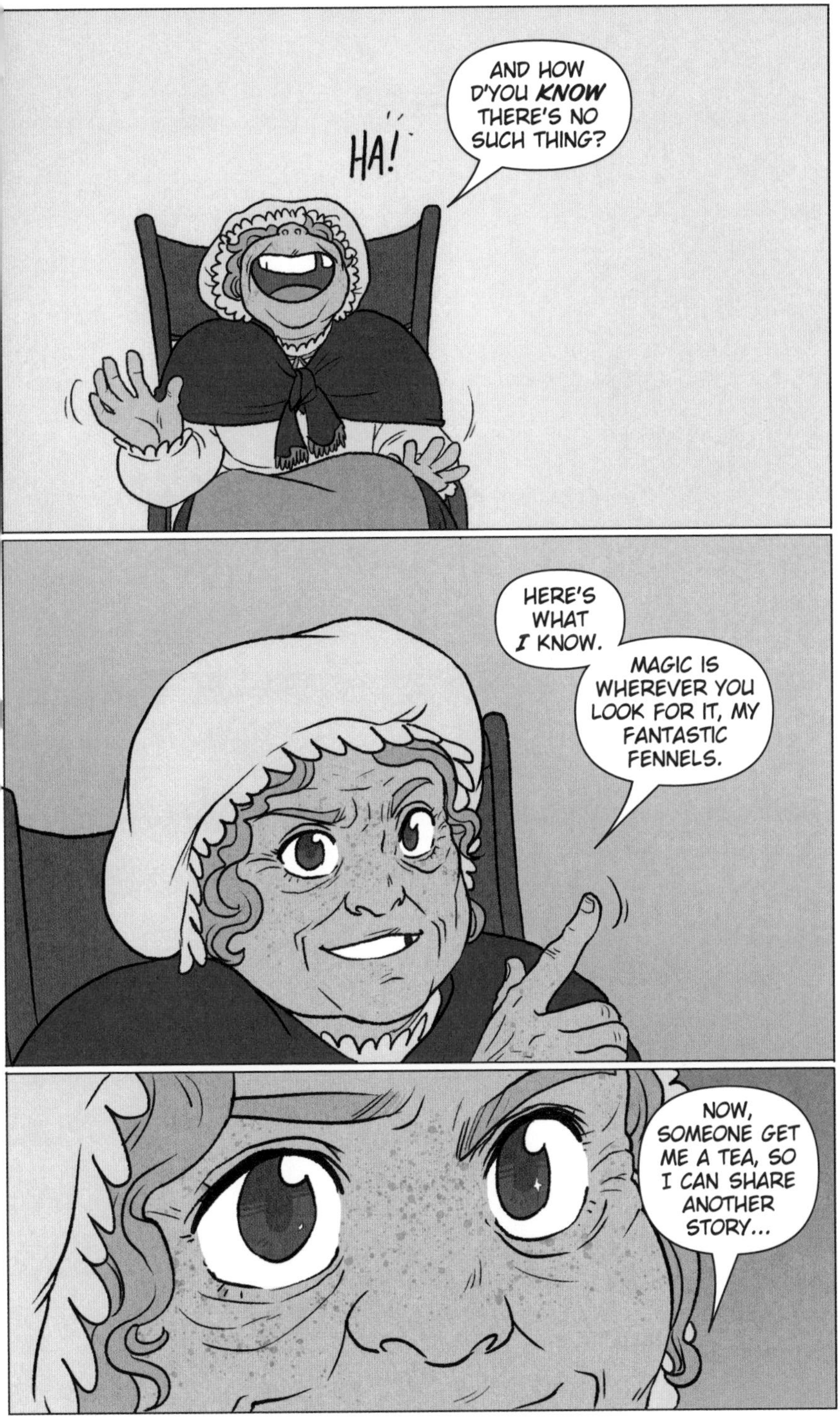
HA!
AND HOW D'YOU **KNOW** THERE'S NO SUCH THING?
HERE'S WHAT *I* KNOW.
MAGIC IS WHEREVER YOU LOOK FOR IT, MY FANTASTIC FENNELS.
NOW, SOMEONE GET ME A TEA, SO I CAN SHARE ANOTHER STORY...

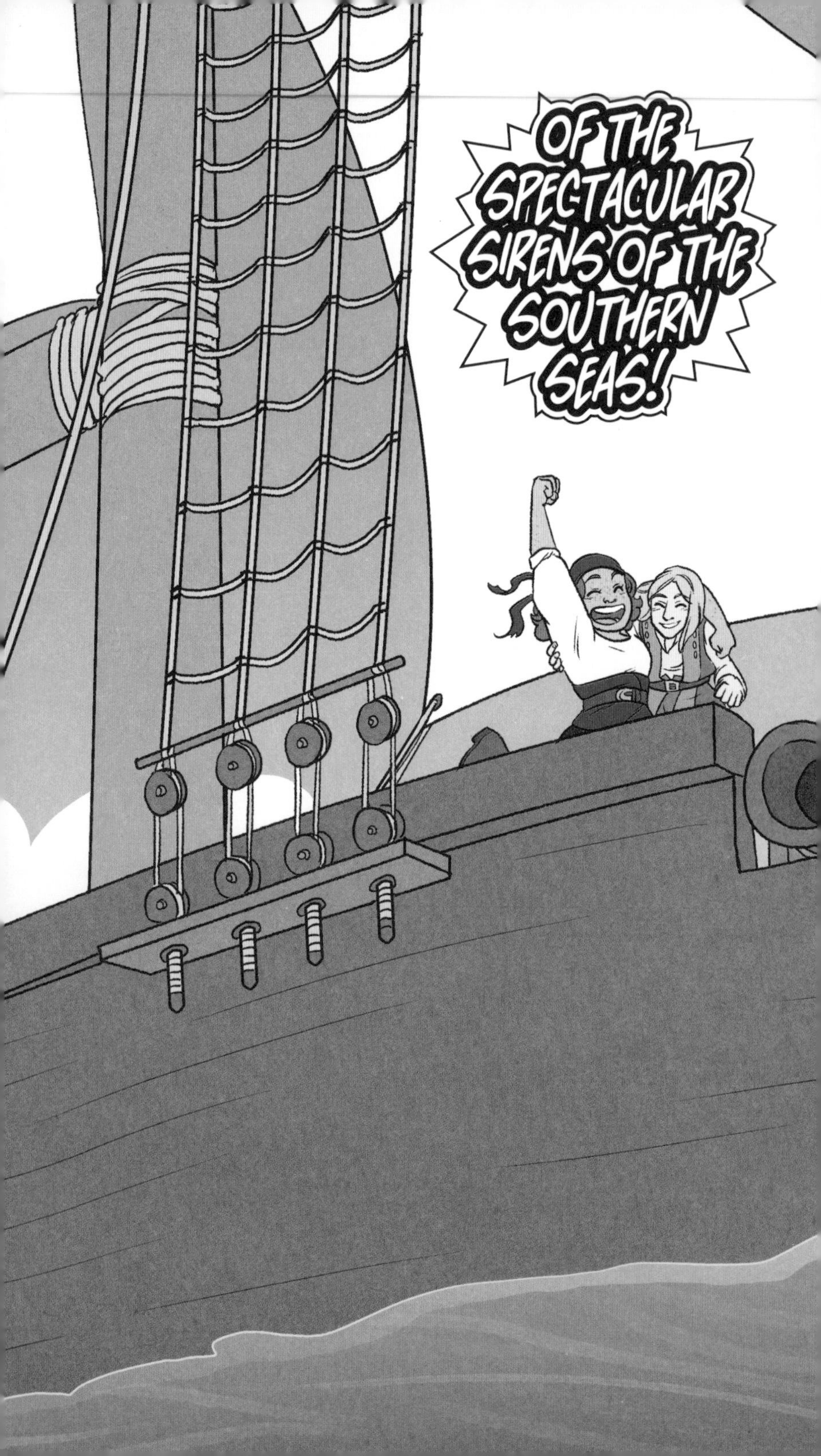
OF THE SPECTACULAR SIRENS OF THE SOUTHERN SEAS!

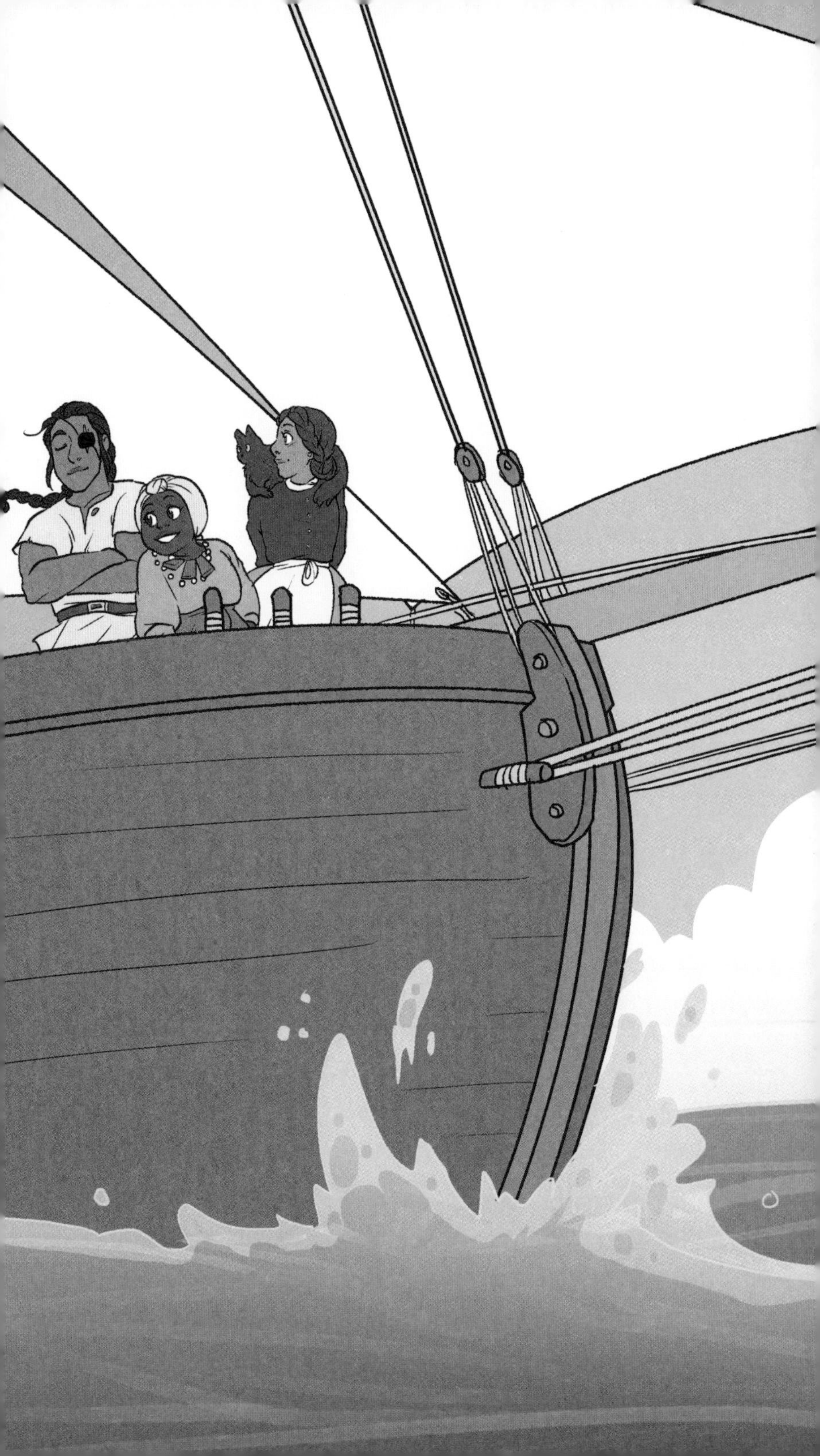

TELL NO TALES: OKAY . . . TELL ONE TALE

Here's the truth: The pirates we're all familiar with from pop culture didn't exist for very long. They only sailed the seas for about a decade, during what we now call the Golden Age of Piracy: 1715 to 1725. And these pirates have a bad reputation today mostly because of what amounted to a large and effective PR campaign against them. Piracy was an exciting alternative for people who were used to being underpaid and mistreated in government navies, an alternative so appealing that it scared the establishment. Those same navies only allowed white men to work aboard their ships, doing difficult, backbreaking labor with little to no benefits. They would leave the navy with life-altering injuries—if they left at all.

Pirate ships, on the other hand, offered much, much more to people in the eighteenth century. These independent vessels prized freedom and teamwork above all. Pirate ships were run like a democracy, where all crewmembers voted for their captain and on difficult decisions, splitting all their bounties equally. They would help out other ships in need and provided disability benefits to injured crew. They admitted women and people of color to their ranks, often people escaping servitude or poverty. They attacked ships carrying enslaved Africans and offered these newly liberated people a life of freedom on the high seas—in fact, formerly enslaved workers made up about a quarter of many pirate crews. Their thing really was stealing from the rich (colonizers and enslavers) and giving to the poor (themselves!). These pirates were viewed as heroes of the common people—and that's what made them so threatening to the establishments of the time. Thus, the coordinated campaign to make people think pirates were bad when, actually, that couldn't have been further from the truth.

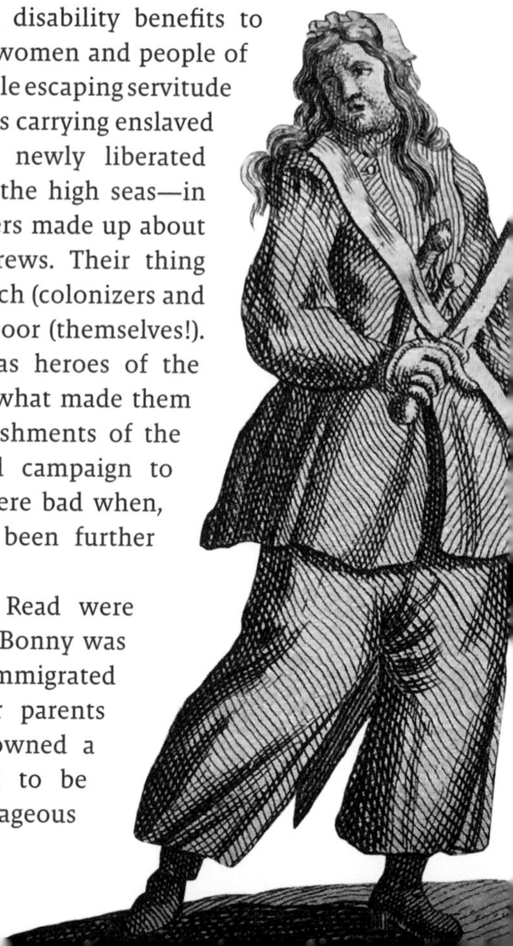

Anne Bonny and Mary Read were two of these real-life pirates. Bonny was born in Ireland in 1698 and immigrated to South Carolina with her parents as a little girl. Her father owned a plantation, but Bonny—said to be "robust" with a "fierce and courageous temper"—ran away from home at twenty, landing in New Providence, an island in the Bahamas. There, she met Captain Jack Rackham, also known as "Calico Jack" for his bright patterned clothes. He told Bonny about his wild adventures as a pirate, and Bonny joined up right away. Pants on and sword buckled, it was on this ship that Bonny ran into another pants-wearing pirate: Mary Read. Read had been born in London, England, in 1695, and grew up mostly pretending to be a boy to earn money for an impoverished single mother. Read was "bold and strong" and at thirteen signed up to be a sailor, first for the British navy and then for a Dutch merchant's ship. That Dutch ship was attacked by pirates—and Read quickly decided to switch sides in the hopes of a better life.

Bonny "took a particular liking to" Read immediately, at first assuming that Read was a boy. When the two revealed to each other the truth about themselves, they developed an instant "intimacy." Together with Captain Jack, Bonny and Read sailed the Caribbean, stealing from fishing and merchant ships around Cuba, Haiti, Bermuda, and Jamaica. It was well-known that Bonny and Read were the boldest members of Jack's crew, "both very profligate, cursing, and swearing much, and ready and willing to do any thing on board." Though they often wore dresses, Bonny and Read also ". . . wore men's jackets, and long trousers, and handkerchiefs tied about their heads, and each of them had a machete and pistol in their hands." They sailed the southern seas, and they defied class and gender norms in the process.

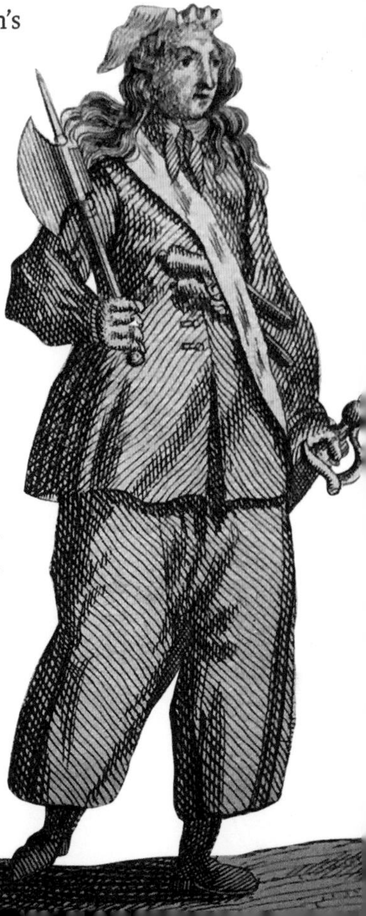

The rest of Anne's crew was inspired by people and places in and around the Golden Age of Piracy. Sarah Walker was a real person; her father, Captain Thomas Walker, made himself "the de facto governor of New Providence" in the Bahamas using an expired contract. But New Providence was a pirate haven, and Captain Walker had no real authority. Historical accounts describe Sarah as biracial; her mother may have been a formerly enslaved worker or a freeborn woman of color. We don't know much about her personality, and she probably wasn't a medical student, but that's where the magic of fiction comes in!

Kati wasn't inspired by any particular person, but rather by a people: the Miskitu, a Central American society formed by the local indigenous population and formerly enslaved Africans along the Caribbean coastline of what is now Honduras and Nicaragua. This once-fertile region for hunting and agriculture remains home to the Miskitu people, though their lands and way of life are under threat. We've messed with historical timelines a bit for the sake of our book, here—the Miskitu maintained independence until 1894 but did face many battles with Spanish colonizers throughout the eighteenth century. The *grisi siknis* Kati experiences is a real affliction, mostly found in teenaged Miskitu girls and is still studied by doctors and researchers today.

Mimba, too, is an invention—but Nanny and her Maroons are not. Enslaved Africans in Jamaica escaped their British captors and fled into the mountains, forming their own, independent community with other free people of color and indigenous people. They were called the Windward Maroons, probably from the Spanish word for fugitive. We adjusted timelines here again, a little, but the Maroons were led by Queen Nanny, a title of respect, from 1728 to 1740. This middle-aged woman held many roles: She was a warrior, general, and military strategist who executed many raids against the British and successfully defended her community from attack, freeing more than a thousand enslaved workers despite being vastly outnumbered. She was responsible for maintaining her peoples' traditional culture, music, and legends from Africa. And she was a spiritual priestess with supernatural powers, an Obeah woman who gained her power from her ancestors. After years of fighting (including Nanny Town's destruction), Nanny secured a treaty that guaranteed the Maroons' freedom.

And Woodes Rogers was real, too: a failed English captain with a chip on his shoulder against pirates. He was generally the worst at being a captain. His crews mutinied and got scurvy; they sued him for not paying wages, and he was forced into bankruptcy; he took a musketball to the face . . . But Rogers's stories did contribute to the best history book we have about pirates, the book from which we get most of our pirate tales, *A*

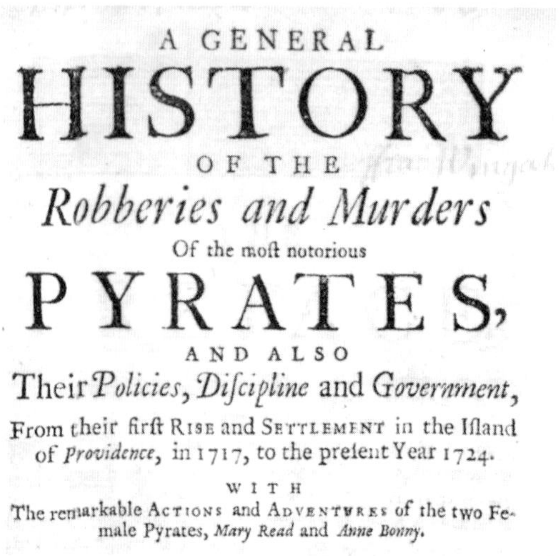
A GENERAL
HISTORY
OF THE
Robberies and Murders
Of the moſt notorious
PYRATES,
AND ALSO
Their *Policies*, *Diſcipline* and *Government*,
From their firſt Rise and Settlement in the Iſland of *Providence*, in 1717, to the preſent Year 1724.
WITH
The remarkable Actions and Adventures of the two Female Pyrates, *Mary Read* and *Anne Bonny*.

General History of the Robberies and Murders of the Most Notorious Pyrates by someone writing under the pseudonym Captain Charles Johnson in 1724. And it's from Johnson's book that we get one of our records of Bonny and Read's time on the seas, including the only known illustration we have of them, standing on a beach, surrounded by palm trees, swords out. They look happy, they're together, and they look free. And that's Bonny and Read, to me.

Even though we know so much about Anne Bonny, Mary Read, and the people they may have interacted with during their time at sea, I always felt like we didn't know *enough*. I wanted to know what it would be like if Bonny had broken off from Rackham and gotten her own ship, if she and Read really had been a couple, if they'd picked up any other awesome folks while out plundering on the water. I've always been fascinated by their true story . . . but what if there was just a little *more*? That's the question Kendra and I asked ourselves when we sat down to come up with the plot and characters of *Tell No Tales*. So much of history is written by the victors—and, usually, the victors have mostly looked the same (straight, white, dudes, etc.). Kendra and I decided we wanted to reclaim some of our lost history—the history of women and non-binary and queer folks that *must* have existed, but has been hidden or kept quiet for so long that it may never be recovered. So instead of waiting . . . we decided to create our own.

We hope you enjoyed our interpretation of Bonny and Read and their crew on the southern seas, and we hope you'll come back for more. We all tell our own tales. What's yours?

NOTES

154 "robust": Johnson, Charles. *A General History of the Pyrates, from Their First Rise and Settlement in the Island of Providence, to the Present Time,* 171.

154–155 "fierce and courageous temper": Johnson, Charles, 171.

155 "bold and strong": Johnson, Charles, 158.

155 "took a particular liking to", "intimacy": Johnson, Charles, 162.

155 "both very profligate . . . willing to do any thing on board" and "wore men's jackets . . . each of them had a machete and pistol in their hands": *The Tryals of Captain John Rackam and other Pirates,* 18.

155 "the de facto governor of New Providence": Bartlinksi, Jim. "A Brief Account of Sarah Walker Fairfax, the Mother of Sarah Fairfax Carlyle," 2.

SELECTED BIBLIOGRAPHY

Appleby, John C. "Women and Piracy in Ireland: From Gráinne O'Malley to Anne Bonny." In *Bandits at Sea: A Pirates Reader*, edited by C. R. Pennell, 283–298. New York: New York University Press, 2001.

Bartlinski, Jim. "A Brief Account of Sarah Walker Fairfax, the Mother of Sarah Fairfax Carlyle." *Carlyle House Docent Dispatch*, June 2009.

Bethell, A. Talbot. *Early Settlers of the Bahamas and Colonists of North America*. Phoenix, AZ: Heritage, 2008.

Brathwaite, Edward Kamau. *Nanny, Sam Sharpe, and the Struggle for People's Liberation*. Kingston, Jamaica: Agency for Public Information, 1977.

"By his Excellency Woodes Rogers, Esq; Governour of New-Providence, &c. A Proclamation." *Boston Gazette*, 10-17 October 1720.

Campbell, Mavis Christine. *The Maroons of Jamaica, 1655–1796: A History of Resistance, Collaboration & Betrayal*. Granby, MA: Bergin & Garvey, 1988.

Canfield, Rob. "Something's Mizzen: Anne Bonny, Mary Read, 'Polly,' and Female Counter-Roles on the Imperialist Stage." *South Atlantic Review* 66, no. 2 (Spring 2001): 45–63.

Carey, Bev. *The Maroon Story: The Authentic and Original History of the Maroons in the History of Jamaica, 1490–1880*. St. Andrew, Jamaica: Agouti Press, 1997.

Cary, Wilson Miles. *Sally Cary: A Long Hidden Romance of Washington's Life*. New York: The De Vinne Press, 1916.

Cordingly, David. "Bonny, Anne (1698–1782)." In *Oxford Dictionary of National Biography*, edited by Sir David Cannadine. Oxford: Oxford University Press, 2008.

———. *Life Among the Pirates: The Romance and the Reality*. Abacus, 1996.

———. "Read, Mary (c. 1695–1721)." In *Oxford Dictionary of National Biography*, edited by Sir David Cannadine. Oxford: Oxford University Press, 2008.

———. *Under the Black Flag: The Romance and the Reality of Life Among the Pirates*. New York: Random House, 2006.

Cueto, Gail A. "Nanny of the Maroons." In *Notable Caribbeans and Caribbean Americans: A Biographical Dictionary*, edited by Serafín Méndez-Méndez and Gail A. Cueto, 324–26. Westport, CT: Greenwood Press, 2003.

Cwik, Christian. "The Africanization of Amerindians in the Greater Caribbean: The Wayuu and Miskito, Fifteenth to Eighteenth Centuries." *Dimensions of African and Other Diasporas*, edited by Franklin W. Knight and Ruth Iyob, 83–104. Kingston, Jamaica: University Press of the West Indies, 2014.

Duncombe, Laura Sook. *Pirate Women: The Princesses, Prostitutes, and Privateers Who Ruled the Seven Seas*. Chicago: Chicago Review Press, 2017.

Fallon, Joseph E. "Miskitu History." *Miskitu Nation Foundation*. savemnf.org/miskitu-history/

Frankel, Estelle Valerie. *Women in Game of Thrones: Power, Conformity, and Resistance*. Jefferson, NC: MacFarland, 2014.

Goldsmith, Oliver. "Essay X: Female Warriors." *The Miscellaneous Works of Oliver Goldsmith, with an Account of his Life and Writings*, Volume 4, edited by Washington Irvine, Esq, 314–19. Paris: Baudry's European Library, 1837.

Gottlieb, Karla. *The Mother of Us All: A History of Queen Nanny, Leader of the Windward Jamaican Maroons*. Trenton, NJ: Africa World Press, 2000.

Herlihy, Laura Hobson. "Matrifocality and Women's Power on the Miskito Coast." *Ethnology* 46, no. 2 (Spring 2007): 133–149.

———. *The Mermaid and the Lobster Diver: Gender, Sexuality, and Money on the Miskito Coast*. Albuqueque: University of New Mexico Press, 2012.

Johnson, Charles. *A General History of the Pyrates*. London: T. Warner, 1724.

Little, Benerson. *The Golden Age of Piracy: The Truth Behind Pirate Myths*. New York: Skyhorse, 2016.

Meyer, W. R., revised by Randolph Cock. "Rackam, John [nicknamed Calico Jack] (d. 1720)." In *Oxford Dictionary of National Biography*, edited by Sir David Cannadine. Oxford: Oxford University Press, 2008.

Munson, James Donald. *Col. John Carlyle, Gent., 1720–1780: A true and just account of the man and his house*. Alexandria: Northern Virginia Regional Park Authority, 1986.

Noveck, Daniel. "Class, Culture, and the Miskito Indians: A Historical Perspective." *Dialectical Anthropology* 13 (March 1988): 17–29.

O'Driscoll, Sally. "The Pirate's Breasts: Criminal Women and the Meanings of the Body." *The Eighteenth Century* 53, no. 3 (September 2012): 357–79.

Rediker, Marcus. "Liberty beneath the Jolly Roger: The Lives of Anne Bonny and Mary Read, Pirates." In *Iron Men, Wooden Women: Gender and Seafaring in the Atlantic World, 1700–1920*, edited by Margaret S. Creighton and Lisa Norling, 1–33. Baltimore, MD: Johns Hopkins University Press, 1996.

Riley, Sandra. *Homeward Bound: A History of the Bahama Islands to 1850 with a Definitive Study of Abaco in the American Loyalist Plantation Period*. Miami, FL: Riley Hall, 2000.

Salmonson, Jessica Amanda. *The Encyclopedia of Amazons: Women Warriors from Antiquity to the Modern Era*. New York: Paragon House, 1991.

Sharp, Anne Wallace. *Daring Pirate Women*. Minneapolis, MN: Lerner Publications Company, 2002.

Sharpe, Jenny. *Ghosts of Slavery A Literary Archaeology of Black Women's Lives*. Minneapolis, MN: University of Minnesota Press, 2002.

Sivapragasam, Michael. "After the Treaties: A Social, Economic and Demographic History of Maroon Society in Jamaica, 1739–1842." PhD dissertation, University of Southampton, 2018.

Sjoholm, Barbara. *The Pirate Queen: In Search of Grace O'Malley and Other Legendary Women of the Sea*. Berkeley, CA: Seal Press, 2004.

Thornton, John K. "The Zambos and the Transformation of the Miskitu Kingdom, 1636–1740." *Hispanic American Historical Review* 97, no. 1 (February 2017): 1–28.

Tryals of Captain John Rackam and other Pirates, The. Pamphlet, printed by Robert Baldwin, 1721.

Twaska, Josephenie Hendy Hebbert. *Yapti Tasbia: The Miskitu Motherland*. Self-published, Lulu, 2014.

Vasquez, Dr. Jorge J. *Miskitos: A Brief Profile of an Indomitable Nation*. Converse, TX: Instituto de Formación de Líderes Espirituales, 2019.

Wedel, Johan. "Involuntary mass spirit possession among the Miskitu." *Anthropology & Medicine* 19, no .3 (July 2012): 303–14.

"Preface." In *Calendar of State Papers Colonial, America and West Indies: Volume 28, 1714–1715*, edited by Cecil Headlam, v–xlvi. London: His Majesty's Stationery Office, 1928. *British History Online*. british-history .ac.uk/cal-state-papers/colonial/america-west-indies /vol28/v-xlvi.

Williams, Caroline A. "Living Between Empires: Diplomacy and Politics in the Late Eighteenth-Century Mosquitia." *The Americas* 70, no. 2 (October 2013): 237–68.

Woodward, Colin. *The Republic of Pirates: Being the True and Surprising Story of the Caribbean Pirates and the Man Who Brought Them Down*. Orlando, FL: Harcourt, 2007.

Yolen, Jane. *Sea Queens: Women Pirates Around the World*. Watertown, MA: Charlesbridge, 2008.